THE FASTER REDDER ROAD

THE FASTER REDDER ROAD

The Best UnAmerican Stories of
Stephen Graham Jones

Edited by Theodore C. Van Alst Jr.

UNIVERSITY OF NEW MEXICO PRESS | ALBUQUERQUE

Library of Congress Cataloging-in-Publication Data
Jones, Stephen Graham, 1972– author.
  [Short stories. Selections]
  The faster redder road : the best unamerican stories of Stephen Graham Jones /
  edited by Theodore C. Van Alst Jr.
     pages cm
  ISBN 978-0-8263-5583-6 (pbk. : alk. paper) — ISBN 978-0-8263-5584-3 (electronic)
  I. Van Alst, Theodore C., 1965– editor. II. Title.
  PS3560.O5395A6 2015
  813'.6—dc23
                          2014026273

COVER PHOTOGRAPH © Corbis and Fotosearch
DESIGNED BY Felicia Cedillos
COMPOSED IN Minion Pro 10.25/14
DISPLAY FONTS are Dirty Ego and Myriad Pro

For Amie, Emily, and Max

CONTENTS

ACKNOWLEDGMENTS

The people who have been inspiring and supportive in my life and in getting this out in the world are many, and precious. To my wife, Amie, your Jobian patience is a true marvel and precious gift, much like yourself. Emily and Max, the bestest kids ever. Ever. #Ever. To my dad, Theodore Sr.; Uncle Theo; Grandma; Grandpa (and the Greats); Aunts Janet, Jackie, Mary Jo; Uncles Mike, Bob, Jim, Jerry; and all of my ancestors—I hope I'm being a good ancestor too. My family and brothers and sisters and nieces and nephews at the lodge. My kola, my brother from another mother Aaron Athey. Mitcheline, Jacoby, and Maki Athey; Steve and Heather Bernier; Ruben and Kristen Perez; Jim Blauvelt; Saucier; Andy; and everyone else who comes through— that includes you, Junebug Kills Back. Chris Brooks. Wanagi Oyate. Hehaka Oyate. Tuzayas Royce Freeman and Angela Semple (sorry, Junior Garcia and Simon Moya-Smith, can't get that new orthography quite right yet). Chad Uran and Carol Warrior. The Native American Literature Symposium Clan Mothers and Brothers, for your invaluable support, especially Gwen Westerman; thank you for my introduction to you and this world, LeAnne Howe, Patrice Hollrah, P. Jane Hafen, Jill Doerfler, Gordon Henry, and Niigaan! Niigaanwewidam Sinclair (I love and miss you, brother), my big little brother, Steve Sexton, and everyone else at NALS (Brian Twenter and Scott Andrews—that's you too. Heya's to Brian Burkhart!), incl. the inimitable Jesse Peters, as well as Angel Lawson (and Clint Carroll) and Danika Medak-Saltzman, my very first panel mates way back when, and Denise Cummings, my fellow Film Wrangler. Jodi Byrd . . . NALS! To the always-inspiring Native American and Indigenous Studies Association—your support is amazing and you are legion. Howdies to the Council and the Membership! Rob Innes! Brendan Hokowhitu for all the inspiring conversations, along with Glenn Coulthard and Vaughan Bidois, for the reengagement with the two Fs—Fanon & Foucault, to the person who introduced me to them, Raymond Rice, and the people who really made sure I understood why: Norma Bouchard, Robert Tilton, Jacqueline Loss, and Lucy McNeece. Martin Billheimer, *DBH*. The Adelphi, State Lake, Woods, Chicago, Oriental, McVickers, Clark, 400, Nortown, and Devon theaters in Chicago. North Side. Used bookstores. Used record stores. And that last NAISA panel with you, Billy Stratton, and John Gamber and Fantasia Painter? Yeah. Kate Shanley and David L. Moore. Luana Ross and Dan Hart. Laura Davulis at Yale University Press. Michael Jacobs at Abrams. Bob Weil at Norton. Jim Antony. Pat Rogers. Laura Adams Weaver.

And because he should have his own line or two, Jace Weaver. Thank you ever so much, sir, for your tireless support. It means so much to me.

Adrian Louis.

My students and colleagues at the University of Connecticut (Jeffrey Ogbar, many thanks!) and at Yale. Ito Romo. Elise McHugh, editor extraordinaire. All at the University of New Mexico Press. You know what? I'm missing people, I know, but it's Friday, late. I'll get back to this tomorrow. If you see your name after this, don't read too much into it, because I probably already stuck it in the list up there ^ anyway.

And finally to Stephen Graham Jones. Your gifts and generosity are only matched by your coolness, man. Thank you.

INTRODUCTION

Theodore C. Van Alst Jr.

MAYBE IT'S BECAUSE my favorite house in town always turns out to be owned by the morticians. Maybe it's because I enjoy imagining the look on the face of someone who forgot they ate asparagus for dinner and goes to the bathroom; that cocked eye happens a lot when you read these stories. This then is to be a selection, a collection, a primer on the work of an author who's been doing twenty-first century since he started to write, since he first published back in the '90s, to be sure. He headed out quick on the Fast Red Road and hasn't looked back since.

I started reading the work of Stephen Graham Jones (according to the digital receipts) back in 2010. Probably late to the game for some, I nevertheless moved through the novels and shorts continuously fascinated. Not just fascinated with the inventiveness that I hadn't seen since early Clive Barker, but fascinated with the compelling fearlessness of a writer who's none too worried about *any* generation's reception of his work, never mind the contemporary reader. Over and over again, I felt that visceral shudder brought on by hearing, say, the creepy Dwight Yoakam version of "Wichita Lineman," the same song that was your accompaniment the time you ate a vending machine sausage biscuit in a bus station somewhere in Texas just south of the Red River while the rain sheeted down outside, feeding the humidity, and you felt the fuzziness on your face after a twenty-four-hour bus ride from Arizona. Like that. But better. Like this:

I followed him that day, and kept following, through all the shit, the rolled-over cars and beer bottles to the back of the head and fires we didn't know anything about and the walking back to town at four in the morning, the northern lights so hard and pink we even had watery shadows on the asphalt once. It made us feel like ghosts after about a quarter mile of it, and we started walking on the grass instead.

They were the same though, our shadows. And I remember thinking that they maybe weren't going to be. Because, the way the old people looked at Doby, it was like he was different, like he was a deer who'd just walked into the IGA, and didn't really know he was a deer yet, that none of this was for him. (*Ledfeather*, 22)

I've got to say here that when I read Stephen Graham Jones, one of the joys for me—I don't know how he's done this—is that finally, *finally*, when I read these stories, unless I'm told otherwise, all of the characters are Indian. But best of all, very best of all, they're incidentally Indian. It would be easy to say Jones points down the road to being Indian in the twenty-first century, but I suspect he's just pointing down the road to *being* in the twenty-first century. It would be even easier to posit a linkage from one Blackfeet (and Gros Ventre) writer to another (the late James Welch), someone with whom Jones shares an affinity for the experimental, the irruptional, the procedural, and the vital, as well as true winter in the blood (read the exterior scenes of *Demon Theory* for more on deep, relentless snow, greyest of grey skies, and the utter acoustic isolation of nothing but your own slow-moving fluids in your ears), but there's more here. From a writer who we're told in an *Los Angeles Review of Books* piece is "proud of his Blackfoot heritage, [but] has no desire to be classified as a Native American writer," we receive one of the most important contributions to contemporary Native literature* (whatever that category might be at this moment, just as whatever it was when Welch first began writing) we could hope for—the zero specificity of naturally Native characters. Of *course* they're Native (except most of the Final Girls. That's just something else, chalked up to the power of film. And maybe the Depeche Mode reference. At any rate, while it's a whole 'nother story, it's a story to which you'll nonetheless receive an introduction—*The Fast Red Road* excerpt, to be exact. *The Last Final Girl* is in a category [in addition to the UK online journal *This Is Horror*'s 2012 Novel of the Year] we'll call "Long-Form Works of Jones's I REALLY Hope You Will Read"). What else could they be to us, who else could they be to us, we who have literarily waited so long *for* . . . us.

Amazing.

Leah Larson's aforementioned *Los Angeles Review of Books* write-up on *Growing Up Dead in Texas* continues: "Stephen Graham Jones does for this area [West Texas] what Faulkner did for northwestern Mississippi," meaning, one supposes, that we had better take his writing seriously. That decision, though, is one best left, as it usually is, to the reader. Needless to say, even if you don't know a thing about West Texas right now, you'll be involuntarily wiping Odessan grit off your neck before you know it.

Jones will do that to you. You'll be reading along and you'll find yourself in the middle of a story, not really remembering how you got there. And what kind of story is it, you'd like to know. Well, Jones will do that to you as well. His ability to move across boundaries will forever keep you on edge. It's like some strange, truly independent cinema, where you're forever going, "ah f——, what next?" You'll see this for yourself in "Foreverafterword" (an incredibly rich offering that says far more in far better ways than I could), his sign-off for a project published by *mixer*, which had him write one issue in six different genres.

So as we do in this age, we add folks on Facebook. We connect via social media. We talk, and even write, somehow. My first note to SGJ goes, "I just started *It Came from Del Rio*. With apologies, as I am about to not articulate this very well, the noir sense is palpable. Dodd feels like a shady but honest younger player in *Touch of Evil*. And it moves so quickly. Of all your other work, I've only read *Demon Theory*. *Del Rio* has your voice, if you had a second voice. Fascinating. I am inarticulate. Told ya. At any rate—thanks!" Stephen Graham Jones replies, "hey, thanks for reading. hope it's decent. and, if I had to try to zero my one true voice it'd probably be *The Long Trial of Nolan Dugatti*. b/c I wrote it in 72hrs, I had no time to disguise." I hope I'm not giving anything away there, Prof. Jones, but yeah. I thought these fine folks might like to know.

Net of it, I meet this extraordinarily generous person online, and we correspond, as they would say in the old days. Suggestions and investigations lead me to read fifteen of his books—novels and short-story collections (and five more since then at the time of this writing)—along with dozens and dozens of uncollected short stories and countless book/film reviews and interviews. Well, when the writer you're working with is this generous, that's one thing, but when that writer is this prolific, well, that's another thing entirely. That will get you the old *yeah, oh, and by the way, here's a new collection with forty-nine stories that I put together while you were figuring out the table of contents.*

"Cette supér."

More reading. More head-slamming, heart-shaking reading. Nice. I'm not gonna lie. It can be a bit distracting, but that's a good, good thing.

Finally, sitting here, putting this collection together, I say, "OK. I'll put this one in right here." I look it up for its source, go to the directory, find the file, yup, scroll to the title, and

read

the whole thing.

Again.

Because you can't look away, get away, from these stories. So where do I stop? What sits this one out? What "stays in the picture?" Well, these do. The offerings for this volume are the smartest, bestest, illustrativest, revealingest ones I could actually settle on. I've worked to find stories of whole cloth that will leave you wanting more just as well as the excerpts do. Examining Jones's work in detail is exhausting and rewarding—here is an author who can wrench your gut with horror and humor, leave you wandering and wondering, and ultimately make you ask for more hours in the day. His raw tellings match your own while scouring your soul—you can manage to feel reborn and in need of a shower in one sitting. He is a writer's writer, and he is a worker's writer. The attention to detail in bars and restaurants, motels and truck stops, offices, city streets, and storage units all tell of someone who has been there. Effortless descriptions of the places inhabited by those who make them work lend an instant and indisputable authenticity. There is no doubt these stories carry the voices of the common women and men of city, country, and suburb, but they also carry other voices; voices that will continue to speak to you, probably during your next uncomfortable trip to a rest stop in the middle of nowhere, so there's that to look forward to. And in finding the voice of this collection, I had some suggestions and plenty of help from the author himself, so there's that too. What we can also concern ourselves with here is the depth and breadth of Jones's work. We have love stories, sci-fi, games and gaming, noir voice, and YA. There is work here that falls under the realm of experimental and work that makes the shelves for folks in Native Lit (no footnote this time; I think we've covered that a bit). There is horror for us and about us, there is humor of all types, from the tragi-comic to the hilarious, both black-black and light-hearted, infused with nostalgia, hope, and dread. In Jones's work we read our dreams, remember our night-mares, and imagine our futures. We can argue and discuss (because that's part of the fun, yes?) Jones as a Native writer, a Blackfeet writer, a genre writer, an academic, or whatever we might like, I suppose, but we should remember in the end what matters. When Jones writes, whether it's about working-class were-wolves (*Mongrels*) or drive-through bathroom attendants (*Flushboy*), or as in this volume, love affairs that start in cereal aisles or roadside ditches, he has this humanizing style that makes you remember we're all in this together, and that it *is* the details that matter—so you do that thing right along with his characters when he says, "I pulled my top lip in, tried to focus on her, relisten to what she was saying" (*It Came from Del Rio*, 12), or "And yes, I laughed then. That kind that's just through your nose . . ." (*The Long Trial of Nolan Dugatti*, 7). As for Jones and genre itself? He says, "I really only write in one genre. It's the same genre we all write in, I hope. It's called 'What I would like to read.'" [*] Short of it all, with the work so wide, these pieces are meant to start the reader on a journey to fill shelves. I'm pretty sure Jones has two more collections (at least) and "some" novels underway as I put this together.

What do we have to look forward to so far from a writer who said, "And stories have to be more, have to actually *do* something"? What's this collection about? What's this collection of his stories *doing*? It's a 12-gauge bird-shot bone mist of the splattergories that make up who we are. It's the scatter-gunned road sign you're squinting at through your cracked windshield, and it's the ashy, angled sun at dusk that makes your eyes water.

Trying to figure out where you're going (and sort of) forgetting where you've been? Yeah. America's headed along there with you, and Jones is gonna be your guide. And what might he want you to know? "If there's ever a thesis to what I do, I suspect that's it: everything matters. Especially the stuff you don't want to."

Now pull on those boots. Tie off that mask, and stretch on those gloves. Let's get started.

NOTES

[*] Let's talk a minute about "Native American Literature." I in no way believe "Native American Literature" is *any* sort of footnote (or endnote, for that matter, whatever the format we tell our stories in), but I'm using endnotes here as a way to illustrate how

Jones's writing has the ability to . . . infect . . . things. My own haunted, haunting reading of *Demon Theory* (a reading that I strongly urge you to undertake) has mutated my ardent love of the footnote/endnote, such that it oftentimes enters into my thinking process. This thinking in notes has led to writing in the same. I've posed this question of "What is Native literature?" in an earlier publication.[★]

The actual first line of the piece is a question and attempted answer:

> What is American Indian literature and who is it for? One of Native America's most prominent and important authors attempts to answer this question in part in an excerpt from Joelle Fraser's *Iowa Review* interview:
>
>> **Sherman Alexie**[♂]: If it's not tribal, if it's not accessible to Indians, then how can it be Native American literature? I think about it all the time. Tonight I'll look up from the reading and 95% of the people in the crowd will be white. There's something wrong with my not reaching Indians.
>> **Joelle Fraser**: But there's the ratio of whites to Indians.
>> **Sherman Alexie**: Yeah. But I factor that in and realize there still should be more Indians. I always think that. Generally speaking Indians don't read books. It's not a book culture. That's why I'm trying to make movies. Indians go to movies; Indians own VCRs.[♪]

Obviously Indians now own DVD players, too, and I think we know they read books as well. One of Sherman Alexie's own accounts remarks on this fact in a very powerful way. Hold on a minute. I've got to get this link I saw the other day. Here it is: http://www.youtube.com/watch?v=8JophviFfxM. Alexie (at 1:16 or so) is talking about meeting the young actors on the set of the film version of James Welch's *Winter in the Blood*. He mentions teasing them and wondering if they knew who he was. He says, "I said [to them], 'I made *Smoke Signals*,'[א] and he [the young actor Yancy Hawley] goes 'Yeah,' and then he said, 'Uh, you wrote *True Diary*,' and I said 'Yeah,' and he goes, 'My favorite book of all time,' and that just kills me. I get so, you know . . ." and the next bit is just emotion from Alexie. And from us as viewers, too, you know? Native people *do* read books, but I think it's likely that for many, if not all, the stakes have been raised. They want to read the books that respond to them, and that they respond to. Alexie's work has had a big hand in pulling the stories up. Jones's will bring Native readers (and everyone else) over that edge. Enjoy the ride, as they say.

Moreover, as regards the persistent and unanswered (and hopefully in the end, complicated and unanswerable) question of "What is Native American literature?" I recently found a partial answer in Ulster. Let's head to the Shankill Road (or "Auld Kirk Gate," if you prefer) in Belfast. The entire wall of one of the housing units on the Protestant side of things is adorned with a mural that reads, "Nothing about us without us is for us."

Hmm.

"Nothing about us without us is for us."

I think that's true. And I also think Jones has made it about us. With us. And for us. But especially he's made it for you. With you. About you.
Enjoy, you.

★ In "Sherman Shoots Alexie: Working with and without Reservation(s) in *The Business of Fancydancing*" in *Visualities: Perspectives on Contemporary American Indian Film and Art*, ed. Denise K. Cummings (Michigan State University Press, 2011).
ⵣ A question from a *Buffalo Almanack* (no. 3) interview (page 83) about a Sherman Alexie comment on Jones's work nets us one possible answer to "What is Native American Literature?":

> **BA**: Sherman Alexie has stated that he admires you for introducing a "whole new moral and aesthetic sense" to the Native American Literary canon. Though your status as a Blackfeet is prominent in novels such as *Ledfeather* and *The Bird is Gone*, it usually takes on a softer presence in your work. How do you manage to blend the seemingly opposing threads of personal identity and mainline pop culture citizenship with such success?
> **SGJ**: I just don't think about it. If I did, I'm afraid everything would blow up on the page. ☺ So, I just figure I'm Blackfeet, whatever I do's going to be Blackfeet, and then try hard to write exactly the book I'd most like to read."♦

☺ And in that line, "I'm afraid everything would blow up on the page," Jones condenses the issue we might encounter when trying to categorize "Native American Literature"—that is, where does one even begin? As an author, trying to tell the stories, all of the stories, the stories that live and breathe and leap from your hand want to be on the page in their messy and incisive and living ways—what do you do? Do you leave it to the critics to decide what is "Native American Literature"? See? Just more questions. But in the interests of getting your money's worth, I will give you a bit of advice in your reading of certain Jones works: Do not mistake the tenderness for the slasher as metaphor for the restoration of the "innocence" of Native America . . .
♦ http://issuu.com/buffaloalmanack/docs/issue3/82

℘ Joelle Fraser, "Sherman Alexie's *Iowa Review* Interview," *Modern American Poetry*, July 20, 2004, http://www.english.uiuc.edu/maps/poets/a_f/alexie/fraser.htm.
א 1998's *Smoke Signals* was a watershed moment in Native cinema, a Native-written (Alexie) and -directed (Chris Eyre) feature-length film that was a hopeful offering in the Hollywood system, whose success on a national level has yet to be repeated.
✖ http://www.thenervousbreakdown.com/tnbfiction/2014/05/stephen-graham-jones-the-tnb-self-interview/.

PROLOGUE

The Gospel According to Demon Theory*

Stephen Graham Jones

THE BEST PLACE to hide from an axe-wielding maniac is with your back pressed up against a wooden door you're pretty sure is both solid and impenetrable. This is because that maniac who's after you, his first strike with the axe will nearly always be from two to six inches from the left side of your face, thus allowing you both to know exactly where she or he is and thus escape into the next room, and getting the maniac's axe caught in the door long enough for you to make that escape. As for why these maniacs strike the door to the left of your head instead of your right, there's at least two theories.

The first is that these maniacs—"slashers," if you will—being singularly unimaginative enough to use the same weapon for murder after murder, must of course be left-brained: especially prone to the type of repetitive behavior that both sequels and franchises are built upon. And left-brained people (or, yes, zombies, or other assorted-but-driven shufflers), are of course right-handed. The immediate objection to this, of course, is that, even if we accept this, still—the maniac's hitting the left side of the door, not the right, right? Correct. Except, as this illustration demonstrates, proper axe-swinging form is to lead with the left side of the body, thus giving the axe a greater range of travel—more momentum, deeper impact. What this suggests is that, yes, a right-handed axe maniac, if he or she is using proper form (and their proficiency with said weapon would suggest they are), will tend to strike the left side of the door more often than not, simply because

---

* Originally published in January 2007: http://www.demontheory.net/the-gospel-according-to-demon-theory/

she or he will be swinging the axe not in a perfect, vertical arc, as if chopping stovewood, but one angled to his or her right a few degrees, to allow for the low ceilings of most homes. So of course the terminus of that arc, that swing, it'll be a few inches off-center, to the left. As for why the axe doesn't appear angled when it penetrates the door, this of course is an acceptable continuity error, as it allows for stronger shot composition: were the head of the axe tilted away from your face—your back is still pressed up against the door, remember—then, when you looked to the side as the director's already told you to, it would be unclear if you're to look at the "top," nearer portion of the blade, or the "bottom," lower portion, which has actually penetrated farther through the wood. To say nothing of how vertical lines accent the human face, as Madonna established in 1990, with her "Vogue" music video. And, yes, there are those who use this "reaction" shot (often excerpted for the trailers, as it suggests the "money" shot without actually giving it away already) to formulate a reverse-engineered sort of explanation for the axe appearing on the left instead of the right, but, as that explanation is dependent upon the audience having been conditioned by the Bangles' 1986 "Walk Like an Egyptian" video, wherein Susanna Hoffs famously ("alluringly") looks first left, then right, suggesting the "sinister possibilities" the night still holds for whoever she's looking away from, this argument is of course, as yet, still just that. As to whether human victims are genetically programmed to look left in fear rather than right, then, yes, these victims are of course right-brained and just as unimaginative as their slashers; any approach which suggests that the right brain is essentially "looking" to the left for help out of this dire situation might be credible, though it would depend on the director or his staff cueing into this tendency, either consciously or subconsciously. Which might prove hard to establish, as the director would probably become overly aware of his own eye movements at that time, and perhaps find a way of ending the interview. The second theory as to why axe-wielding maniacs tend to strike the door to the left of center—and of course this is where you stand: the center (see "shot composition," above)—is more pedestrian, but perhaps more difficult to object to as well: as stunt people (from John Wayne to Lee Majors's character in *The Fall Guy* to Kane Hodder) are, in spite of what you may have suspected, simply a subset of "humans," and humans are of course predominantly right-handed, and stunt people need to, as best they can, exhibit the same body language as the character they're portraying, who, also being a subset of "human," is probably right-handed him or herself, then of course, just for the safety of the stunt person (and this has to be paramount), who's in all likelihood not ambidextrous, a right-handed swing of the axe just makes sense. At which point, simply refer again to the illustration above.

A distant third theory—possibility, really—as to why axes tend to show up to the left of your head instead of the right is that these maniacs, being maniacs, and only "aware" in the dimmest of ways, probably retain at least enough understanding of rudimentary concepts like "doors" to still make an association between doorknobs and getting through a door, an association which would of course, were it verifiable, probably cause them to hit closer to the knob rather than farther from it. Just because their ultimate goal is to get through that door, and hack to pieces whoever's obviously hiding directly behind it. However, this "dim awareness," it's a slippery slope at best. While it may apply to certain incarnations, say, of Jason Voorhees, Michael Myers, on the other hand, has been able at times to drive a car. To say nothing of the ingenuity these slashers often display in the final reel—the knots and various apparatuses necessary to cantilever bloodied victims suddenly up against whoever's currently discovering them is very sophisticated. Granted, haunted house technicians can achieve this once a year, but that's with months of planning, and many hands, possibly even diagrams, to say nothing of no distractions. Slashers, on the other hand, they express this mastery of mechanics, this "inbuilt ability," in the most casual manner possible, as if doing that with victims, it's instinct rather than intelligence, the same way a spider, perhaps, just "knows" how to cocoon its victims in web. Which, if the slashers have this much instinct, then chances are they also understand the "mysteries" of the doorknob, but are just too proud to do something so obvious as to use it. Perhaps this is the statement their latest representative (in *The Hills Have Eyes* remake) was trying to make, Dog Soldier style, when, evidently insulted by the whole concept of "door," he simply crashed through the far thinner wall. Which, of course, was to the character's left . . .

The mother nodded. A cordless phone in her hand. William wondered how anybody ever strangled anybody anymore.

"Interstate Love Affair," *Three Miles Past* (2013)

Inside places like that, the refrigerator wouldn't even smell anymore. There'd be a mummified dog by the couch sometimes, maybe squirrels nesting in the closet, a hole chewed in the ceiling. And sometimes it would just be quiet. The delicate sound of photographs in kitchen drawers, losing their color. The slick paint on the doorframes peeling up, fluttering down in flakes if you pulled your hand across, like you'd stepped into a snowglobe. A good place to die, if you had to.

The Gospel of Z (2014)

FOREVERAFTERWORD[*]

Stephen Graham Jones

YOU NEVER HIT a story that's only one genre, do you? Westerns tend to have some element of romance, horror uses comedy as pressure-release valve, fantasy's nearly always got a few solid action sequences, science fiction and spy thrillers trade schematics all the time, and they *all* walk through erotica's steamy bedrooms, and erotica, it dresses up like each of them, doesn't it? And mystery, sometimes I think that's the backbone of everything. Why else turn the page than because you want to get to the solution, the big reveal, that disinhibiting symbol or gesture or image at the end that both releases and compounds the narrative tension?

Where does that leave "literary," though, I know. Hopefully where it should be: not a genre at all, but an adjective. One that describes the caliber of the writing. Using it like a catchall for those works of fiction without werewolves or elves or spaceships, it's dangerous, just because, at the back of our brains and in spite of what publishers and critics tell us, we still know "literary" is first and foremost an indication of quality. Meaning those things *without* werewolves and elves and spaceships, they're automatically quality. It's a dangerous little syllogism to let pass.

At the same time, of course, those werewolf and elf and spaceship books, they often get characterized uncharitably, by the very least of their kind. So I guess

* Originally published as the afterword to the SGJ *mixer* genre project. http:// mixerpublishing.com/?author=182

I can understand the impulse, the need to fortify, all that. But still. Just because you had a bad experience with a Ford Fiesta twenty years ago, that doesn't mean Ford's trucks can't be good today, right? And, though it should be otherwise, it's still and forever an insult when I hear somebody describe a book as "literary horror." What they're saying is, hey, *that* horror book's good enough to return to, *it's* deep enough for a second read. Which is a compliment. Just, one that insults the rest of the genre. In spite of the fact that it's using "literary" in its adjectival form, which should be proper.

I don't know. Things are kind of jacked on the shelves, I guess. It doesn't stop a lot of people from writing a lot of good stuff, though, so I probably shouldn't worry so much about what's finally just marketing categories.

As for my all-time favorite genre to read though? Depends on the day. Maybe on the hour. No, on the *book*. Near as I've found, I mean, I kind of just dig them all. I don't think there's a tighter novel than Scott Smith's *A Simple Plan*. The book I reread the most regularly, it's *Relic*. I'll die behind the chemical sheds for the cetology chapters of *Moby Dick*. The best book I read last year was N. K. Jemisin's *The Shadowed Sun*. Best thing I've read so far this year is Alan Moore's run on *Swamp Thing*. Book I'm reading right exactly now is *Gone Girl*.

Or how about the books I most wish I'd written—no, the books I most wish I could wipe from my head, so I could read them again for the first time. *Speaker for the Dead* and *Love Medicine* and *The Things They Carried* and *It* and *The Life of Pi* and Coover's *Ghost Town* and *The Magician of Lhasa* and *Bastard Out of Carolina*. Maybe *VALIS* and some Conan, but you have to trade a chunk of your mind in to do that and do it right, and I've done that trade-in a couple of times, and it's getting more and more difficult to put the pieces back together again.

I guess you could blame my genre wanderings on the people I take as models too. Joe R. Lansdale, Brian Evenson, Stephen King, Michael Chabon. Border crossers all. And, Robert McCammon, man. That dude could stick a spike through your eyes with horror, then break your heart forever, in the best possible way. And there's Vonnegut, PKD, Stanislaw Lem, Percival

Everett. There's Neil Gaiman, who I'm confident could, inside a couple of days, write the doors off any genre he got assigned. And not just because he's talented or well read or easy to dare. It's because he believes in story, whatever conventions it happens to be wearing. And it's also because his writing toolbox, it's got scalpels fitted for horror and it's got paintbrushes ready to paint the sunset in a western, and you can tell he knows the handles of all these just by touch. And that he sometimes uses the most delicate paintbrush for the monsters.

My toolbox isn't quite so organized. I'm always catching squirrels, stuffing them in while nobody's looking. At the time, it's the best idea ever. What it usually means, though, is that, unless solicited, I usually don't have a clue what "genre" my next piece is going to be. Just whatever the squirrel says. Wherever the day takes me. If I've just walked the gauntlet of a food court at the mall, then maybe I'm going interstellar, to some Mos Eisley, to try to identify all these alien life forms. If it's late at night and I'm too scared to brave the dark, dark stairs, then I might try really hard not to write horror, and end up with another high-school story about fighting. Because I need my blood pumping, to make it out of this room.

And there are other reasons for playing across the genre fields too, I guess. One is that I can't imagine how boring it must be to only write in one mode. At the same time, if I could be any writer in America, I'd likely choose C. J. Box, who only does mysteries. There's definitely something to be said for doing one thing and doing it very, very well. See Tolkien, right? I just can't do that. Hard as I try, I don't have that kind of focus, that kind of career-arching fascination with a single, single thing.

Which leads to the next reason, which is more of an accusation, really: dilettantism. I'm a perpetual amateur, a persistent dabbler. And I'm cool with that, though of course my spin is that a painting isn't very interesting when you only use only color. And then I fall back on my heroes, of course. Somebody who can give us both *The Body* and *Pet Sematary*. I respect decathletes, I mean: do it all, if you can. And even if you can't.

Nineteen years ago when I stumbled into grad school, the one promise I made myself was never to forget why I was doing this: to sneak in, steal some tricks for the Westerns and fantasy and horror and thrillers so close to my heart. In the course of that education, though, I discovered this strange beast people call "literary," and that was extremely interesting as well. And I had strong suspicions it could do with an injection of magic, of blood, of circuitry.

I don't know. I want to make my random wanderings all over the genre boards something noble, or at least intentional, but it probably just comes down to the simple fact that my toolbox isn't very organized. It's more of a nest, really. But if I dig around enough, I can usually find something that'll work. It's why I always buy old trucks instead of new cars: I love rolling down the road knowing there's just a beer can and some duct tape holding that radiator hose together. It makes me want to go faster and faster. Maybe even close my eyes. And I'm forever hot-wiring genres and modes. The trick is, when you're having those kinds of bad ideas, to not have them for that mad-scientist reason of "I wonder what would happen," but because it's the most direct and efficient way to get done what you need done. So you had to invent a tool, or mush a couple together, or reach back to Aquinas for structure. Great. And who cares. The only thing that matters, finally, it's the product. It's whether you were able to infect the reader with exactly what you're feeling and thinking. And in that order.

Finally, though, I'd guess the real reason I write across genre lines is just because I want to see cool stuff. No, because I *do* see cool stuff in everything I read, and that challenges me. I get sad that Vonnegut already evolved humans into seals, say, and I mope around a bit, but then I think, wait, what if we evolved into condors? And then got cast in *Buck Rogers*, with everybody thinking we were wearing a costume. What would that make craft services like on set? Same pecking order, or different? That's the kind of stuff I live for, the kind of stuff I'll never be able to stop doing. It's what's going in my head at any hour of the day. To make that cool stuff into something I can believe in though—isn't that what we all try to do in our writing? turn ourselves into the first reader?—I have to build it all into a world that's real, with real people. And because neither the world nor the people are my focus (I always want to fast-forward to the chrome-toothed werewolf, or, in "Fairies," say, to that excellent Cougar), all that other stuff becomes accidentally real.

It's some version of how poets use form, I think: as that thing that distracts your critical mind, so that what's real can maybe stand up from the grass without your too-guiding hand.

You don't teach somebody to play basketball, I mean. You give them a ball, leave them alone on court out in the middle of a pasture in West Texas.

Magic happens all the time.

So, all these stories here, yeah, they'd go in different magazines, different anthologies, and they probably don't all appeal to a single reader. But I secretly hope they kind of do. I so want there to be readers out there who read for story, who read to see cool things, who aren't locked into one shelf or another. Be as metal as you want, but don't lose the ability to hear a clarinet? That's all I ask.

A few years ago, Joe R. Lansdale said something on a panel that I've never forgotten, that I think's probably my religion. Somebody asked him what genre he writes in, and he shrugged, said it like it was the most obvious thing in the world: "The Joe R. Lansdale genre."

That's what I aspire to.

THE FAST RED ROAD

A Plainsong

(excerpt)

LITMUS WAS THE sixth one back from the register, which opened onto the buffet. "The goddamn gate to heaven," the bearded man behind him called it, and Litmus nodded his head back and forth, waiting. The bearded man was seven feet tall. Litmus drummed William Tell hard into his demo case, until the Indian woman directly ahead of him turned and grabbed his wrist just when his fingers were going their fastest, cadenced like horse hooves. He didn't tell her he wasn't her child, that he was old enough to be her father, but by the time he'd looked hard into her face and she'd turned away in apology, he was holding her hand there, under his own. *Silky Bird* it said on the back of her satin jacket, in thread. He asked her what it meant, and she stumbled through her childhood and her short motherhood and finally said "nothing, just nothing," then occupied herself smoothing Litmus's wispy forearm hair back down along his wrist. He was hungry, Litmus was. He'd spent the last two days trapped in a Folsom motel room, hobbled by his big toe, chained to a TV rerunning Jay Silverheels outtakes. He was here to eat and then eat again. He loosened his thin black belt in anticipation, looped his pale hair around his head and over an ear, where it was already falling down.

In front of him and Silky Bird were four cowboys straight from a beer commercial, each more beautiful than the last, their cheekbones chiseled sharp, collective dark hair cropped short against the Clovis sun. The high-school girl working the register was defenseless against them, a small nervous giggling thing with braids. When they were finally gone and Silky Bird was

1

digging through her purse for an elusive second party check, the waitress nodded her head down to Litmus's demo case and said she didn't think so.

"This is a buffet, sir."

"Yes ma'am," Litmus said back, talking slow and deliberate for her. "Pitch till you win."

The waitress ran her pen behind her ear, a violent motion. "This is a *buffet*," she said again, harder, pointing to his case now.

The line behind Litmus was quiet except for the breathing giant. Silky Bird was lining pill bottles up on the glass, no checkbook yet. Litmus told the waitress he wasn't going to sell a vacuum cleaner to her customers, for Chrissake, in the middle of the day like this, and she just said it again, like it was an answer, that this was a buffet. When she reached for the case Litmus shifted it behind his thick right leg.

"I'm here to eat, ma'am."

"And we're here to serve you, sir. But not with that."

Litmus made a sound to start the whole dialogue over, but saw in the tilt of her face it would run just the same. There were some three tons of people behind him. To his right was Silky Bird, an assortment of glass pipes and needles on the counter now, her on her knees, holding a tintype of her kidnapped son, making oval cooing sounds into the portrait. The giant palmed her head, patting gently, and his fingers came down to her jawline on both sides.

Litmus smiled to the waitress when he got it. "I'm not going to pack any of your precious food out of here, y'know."

"I don't much guess you'd tell me if you were." She said it with her voice flat like the edge of something, and Litmus laughed out his nose, because she was sixteen and there wasn't a thing in the world he could do. He had to eat. He finally just spun the twin combination locks in a grand gesture of defeat, surrendered the case.

It was eighteen seventy-six for him and Silky Bird and the giant. Business expenses, he explained, then collected the receipt and neatly covered the three steps to the end of the buffet, ahead of both of them. He didn't turn around when he heard his case being pried open either. He was going to eat, by God; as far as he could see were picnic tables with Purina-checkered tablecloths, and short Mexican busboys who, tub-less yet able, quietly collected the refuse by drawing the four corners of the tablecloths together, throwing the sack over their shoulders, and weaving themselves into the lunchtime crowd. The table-cloths were at least ten deep in places, and the walls in the distance were un-adorned, just adobe and chili stains and flies too slow to be all the way alive. The only noise was food: an orange-headed man cracking open a bone and sucking the black marrow out; a woman slurping gravy from a bowl and laugh-ing about something; a child with his lap wet from pee and his mouth attached to a doubled-together straw, the other end going from drink to drink around the deserted table, counterclockwise. He flipped Litmus off and Litmus smiled. He was just getting back to answering the kid in kind when the giant's index finger high in his back told him it was his turn, and then he was taking from each metal bin, heaping it on his plate, going by smell, letting the greases merge together then drip down his hand and off his knuckle, back into the bins.

A kitchen boy came with a new bin and refilled whatever was low. Litmus managed to slip him three dollars of appreciation, and the boy ducked away into the background noise, a background dominated now by a vacuum cleaner being slammed crudely together.

Litmus tried to ignore it.

He scooped more on his plate but it slid off the sides; he wasn't even half-way through the line yet, and already food placement had become an issue: only one more item was going to fit this time around, and even that was going to take a steady hand. Litmus nodded his head as little as possible, chased the saliva down his chin, and finally looked through the Plastiglass, for something that wouldn't slide off, something with balance, poise, the proper weight, and as his hand moved through the pork steam, searching, it became hard and harder to follow, indistinct, strobed, moving without him, hardly a part of him at all, and when he concentrated to track it, own it, direct the ladle foodward, the trough-style table in front of him suddenly and with no foreplay lost its horizontal hold and became flattened layers of itself, scrolling up and up, like there were birds on whatever antenna fed the diner, leather-skinned paleo-lithic things that should never have been able to fly so high. They screamed through the layers, right at Litmus, taunting, inviting, and in a clean snap the vertical went too, a little at first, but finally pushing everything side to side, leaving black at the edges, flecked with nothing. It was the black that made Litmus close his eyes. It made no difference.

He counted twice to what felt like a nervous three, and when he finally peeked out one lid at a time the hair on his forearm was still combed and the ladle was still heavy in his hand, still reaching, the diner and the bins before him were dialed back in, sweating grease, and he had only blinked. Home again home again. The ladle weighed the same, still had mass and even momentum, prior direction, and was still dowsing towards something in the centermost bin, dowsing like no one had blinked and no one would, so Litmus played along, followed its course under the glass, his hand behind but uninvolved, and that was when he saw what had been done, what he had counted into existence: in the bin closest to him was a selection of uncooked man-sized kidneys that had been blue dumplings the moment before last. On the opposite side of the trough an old and out of place Shoshone-looking man had speared a cross section of a tawny forearm and was balancing it across his plate like baby back ribs, his fork making no noise against the anchor tattoo. The blue ink was old, Spanish, *punta* or something, but the *u* had worn away into an *i*, for *pinta*, the disease, the ship. Scattered in the other bins were livers spotted scotch gold, fat sheathed backstraps, stuffed entrails, and more, parts without name, steaming and writhing, like a weak drive-in movie you're supposed to laugh at. But Litmus wasn't laughing. He wasn't even breathing. Five hundred years were slipping away. The giant poked him high in the back again, but this time Litmus didn't move. He couldn't. Everything was coming all at once: the marrow in his own bones, buried somewhere beneath the flesh, untasted; the flies on the wall drifting in and out of this world like small ferrymen; the fevered man in the bathroom, carving fevered words; even the dogs out back, fighting over leftovers as the three busboys huddled under the stoop passed a nervous joint between themselves, left to right. Two of them would be dead before the year was out, the third burying a small caliber handgun over and over, a different place each night, farther and farther out. Litmus watched the never-shaved area around the third one's mouth glow red with the joint, then go dim. He was aware again, of everything. For the first time in years, more than he cared to count. It was like waking up. And he didn't want to.

In a last effort to resist, he reached part of himself out, across the horror-show buffet, locked eyes with the old Shoshone man and pulled him in, forced him too to see what was on his plate, what he had been eating, what they had all been eating. The old man's lower lip trembled. His plate became heavy and fell to the ground. Nobody made to sweep it up. The old man tried to look away, to the sinking sound the anchor tattoo shouldn't have made, but Litmus held him there for a moment longer, because it hurt to know all alone, to have to be seeing through like this. For a moment then they were one, this random old man and Litmus, and instead of the sick buffet spread before them, Litmus tasted instead this old man's vision—Seth's vision—saw his daughter growing into a woman he didn't know, saw the many-hour drive to Clovis for this monthly ritual of food and medicine, but then too, buried deeper than the rest, right below the radio-talking days of WWII, was this scene all over: human flesh in bite-sized portions. Litmus could taste it washing back up his throat, up Seth's throat, and like that the visual tissue they shared tore, and the old man was shuffling away already, his shoulders caved around his chest, suspenders the only thing keeping his pants up.

On his own toilet that night the old man Seth sat reading the tabloid that'd blown up against his leg on the way out of the buffet. "It's not all crap," he told his wife, "come look for yourself," but she wasn't listening anymore. She had her shows, he had his reading. "It's not crap," he yelled hoarsely, and then more came out and he felt emptier than he ever had, hollowed out, pithed by the pharmacist. He raised the half-full milk jug of shit water to his mouth one more time and let it course through him, doctor's orders: in the morning they would sodomize him again with their oversized garden hose, just looking for something wrong, and then he'd break wind for days, sleeping behind their new trailer, cradling his tender bowels.

The buffet was supposed to have been his last supper before going to the Clovis doctor, a feast of BBQ beef ribs and honey-butter yeast rolls, but he hadn't even eaten his fill, hadn't even had time to smuggle chicken out in each of his pockets, for later, because there at the denuded buffet later hadn't begun to matter yet. His eyes had been haywired, looking thirty-four years backwards into a survivor's guilt he'd thought outrun by now, a deed he thought buried. Maybe it was something in the food, he told himself. Chemicals, preservatives, radiation, Clovis. Anything, even senility. Call it an episode.

More shit water. Just get it all out.

What remained of the tabloid had to do with a fledgling porn actor who'd broken his contract and disappeared into the Utah night with a twenty-seven-dollar supply check, going feral perhaps, keep an eye out. The silhouette of a watchful Mormon took up the rest of the page. Then too, further in, there was the creeping presence of Saint Augustine among eastern gardens, backlit by the recent outbreak of Saint Anthony's Fire in the Midwest. Geronimo, the

California reporter said, Jerome help us. Seth mouthed the words, *Ge-ron-i-mo,* and when the toilet water finally splashed onto his hairless inner thigh again he breathed out and flipped to the center section, the second to the last page. It was the predictions, Big Spring Sally's predictions, made from her padded cell. Seth smiled the side of his face that still smiled. He remembered her, or pieces of her, from way back when. The crazy-ass white girl. The color picture was of her holding both sides of her head, like she was trying to squeeze more out of it, or keep something in.

It didn't matter; she was beautiful.

This year's predictions weren't like last year's though; they didn't even bother with her hit-miss ratio. It was mostly just the same chest-up picture of her, from different sides of her room, a spider's-eye view, fractured angles hard to look from all at once. Except for one, of course, around which the rest revolved; it was centered across the fold, spanning the distance between staples. The back of a legal pad, the cardboard part. Thick magic marker words: *both of him are yet real.* The sideways happy face at the lower corner of the backflap was out of place, with its one lone feather reaching up from the back of its head. The reporter didn't even touch it. She was more interested in who the him was, or were, or whatever.

Seth stared at the non-prediction, looked hard to Sally for an explanation, then got nervous and turned the page, where a reader had written in that Sally was not only a pagan throwback, but a public menace; the reader was the health inspector for greater eastern New Mexico. She had included a computer-generated graph showing how Sally's "woefully inaccurate" eating-of-human-flesh prediction last year had temporarily lowered per capita dining out, not to mention overloading the postal service with health concerns, health concerns she in turn had to allay singly. She noted that she had done this survey on her own time, too, thank you. When Seth got to the end of the health inspector's letter, he dropped the tabloid then kicked it away, off his foot, out the bathroom door. He blew at it, trying to make it go farther. His hands were shaking. He hadn't seen anything, he hadn't seen anything. An episode, it had just been an episode. He tried to make out his wife's shows from pieces of words, but then he was in the diner again, the lights dimming from the vacuum cleaner being plugged in, whining high, inhaling the thin surface off reality, him staring across the buffet table at the pasty-faced man with the stomach, then looking down at his own plate, at what Sally had said would happen.

Get it all out.

He screamed for his wife and still she wouldn't come and hold his head by the temples and make him look away; he sang a song his grandmother used to sing in the fields, but it was no good against this. He was still in the diner, still dropping his plate and watching the pasty-faced man look down into the food bins and shape his mouth around the words once, then twice: *Not again, please, not again.*

This novel originally started with that hairy-handed gent line. That was back when every page had at least one direct rip from a song. But then Litmus Jones showed up in the clockwork a little bit in, so I figured he needed introducing earlier, maybe, since he was getting to kind of be the Puck here. So I wrote this cannibal-buffet opening mostly to get him on-page, in some way. But then as things kept happening, I kept stuffing more and more stuff into what I was coming to realize was a kind of prologue. I haven't read aloud from this novel much, but when I did, this is what I would usually read. The buffet part anyway. I just looked at it again too. I'll forever miss the way my head used to work. The things I used to think I could do. I was going to change the world, man, with just words. I'm not saying I'm not still going to. I'm just saying back when I wrote this, that was a lot more certain. I usually say Demon Theory's *my most autobiographical novel, and people always want to read* Growing Up Dead in Texas *like a memoir. This novel's both of those though. Like you sopped them up with a rag, then wrung that rag out into your cupholder, let it bake in the sun for a week. I would drink that.*

LONEGAN'S LUCK

LIKE EVERY MONTH, the horse was new. A mare, pushing fifteen years old. Given his druthers, Lonegan would have picked a mule, of course, one that had had its balls cut late, so there was still some fight in it, but, when it came down to it, it had either been the mare or yoking himself up to the buckboard, leaning forward until his fingertips touched the ground.

Twenty years ago, he would have tried it, just to make a girl laugh.

Now, he took what was available, made do.

And anyway, from the way the mare kept trying to swing wide, head back into the shade of town, this wasn't going to be her first trip across the Arizona Territories. Maybe she'd even know where the water was, if it came down to that. Where the Apache weren't.

Lonegan brushed the traces across her flank and she pulled ahead, the wagon creaking, all his crates shifting around behind him, the jars and bottles inside touching shoulders. The straw they were packed in was going to be the mare's forage, if all the red baked earth ahead of them was as empty as it looked.

As they picked their way through it, Lonegan explained to the mare that he never meant for it to be this way. That this was the last time. But then he trailed off. Up ahead a black column was coming into view.

Buzzards.

Lonegan nodded, smiled.

What was dead there was pungent enough to be drawing them in for miles.

"What do you think, old girl?" he said to the mare. She didn't answer.

Lonegan nodded to himself again, checked the scatter-gun under his seat, and pulled the mare's head towards the swirling buzzards. "Professional curiosity," he told her, then laughed because it was a joke.

The town he'd left that morning wasn't going on any map.

The one ahead of him, as far as he knew, probably wasn't on any map either. But it would be there. They always were.

When the mare tried shying away from the smell of death, Lonegan got down, talked into her ear, and tied his handkerchief across her eyes. The last little bit, he led her by the bridle, then hobbled her upwind.

The buzzards were a greasy black coat, moved like old men walking barefoot on the hot ground.

Instead of watching them, Lonegan traced the ridges of rock all around.

"Well," he finally said, and leaned into the washed-out little hollow.

The buzzards lifted their wings in something like menace, but Lonegan knew better. He slung rocks at the few that wouldn't take to the sky. They just backed off, their dirty mouths open in challenge.

Lonegan held his palm out to them, explained that this wasn't going to take long.

He was right: the dead guy was the one Lonegan had figured it would be. The thin deputy with the three-pocketed vest. He still had the vest on, had been able to crawl maybe twenty paces from where his horse had died. The horse was a gelding, a long-legged bay with a white diamond on its forehead, three white socks. Lonegan distinctly remembered having appreciated that horse. But now it had been run to death, had died with white foam on its flanks, blood blowing from its nostrils, eyes wheeling around, the deputy spurring him on, deeper into the heat, to warn the next town over.

Lonegan looked from the horse to the deputy. The buzzards were going after the gelding, of course.

It made Lonegan sick.

He walked up to the deputy, facedown in the dirt, already rotting, and rolled him over.

"Not quite as fast as you thought you were, eh deputy?" he said, then shot him in the mouth. Twice.

It was a courtesy.

Nine days later, all the straw in his crates hand-fed to the mare, his jars and bottles tied to each other with twine to keep them from shattering, Lonegan looked into the distance and nodded: a town was rising up from the dirt. A perfect little town.

He snubbed the mare to a shuffling stop, turned his head to the side to make sure they weren't pulling any dust in. That would give them away.

Then he just stared at the town.

Finally the mare snorted a breath of hot air in, blew it back out.

"I know," Lonegan said. "I know."

According to the scrap of paper he'd been marking, it was only Friday.

"One more night," he told the mare, and angled her over to some scrub, a ring of blackened stones in the packed ground.

He had to get there on a Saturday.

It wasn't like one more night was going to kill him anyway. Or the mare.

He parked the buckboard on the town side of the ring of stones, so they wouldn't see his light, find him before he was ready.

Before unhooking the mare, he hobbled her. Four nights ago, she wouldn't have tried running. But now there was the smell of other horses in the air. Hay maybe. Water.

And then there was the missing slice of meat Lonegan had cut from her haunch three nights ago.

It had been shallow, and he'd packed it with a medley of poultices from his crates, folded the skin back over, but still, he was pretty sure she'd been more than slightly offended.

Lonegan smiled at her, shook his head no, that she didn't need to worry. He could wait one more day for solid food, for water that wasn't briny and didn't taste like rust.

Or—no: he was going to get a *cake*, this time. All for himself. A big white one, slathered in whatever kind of frosting they had.

And all the water he could drink.

Lonegan nodded to himself about this, leaned back into his bedroll, and watched the sparks from the fire swirl up past his battered coffeepot.

When it was hot enough, he offered a cup to the mare.

She flared her nostrils, stared at him.

Before turning in, Lonegan emptied the grains from his cup into her open wound and patted it down, told her it was an old medicine man trick. That he knew them all.

He fell asleep thinking of the cake.

The mare slept standing up.

By noon the next day, he was set up on the only street in town. Not in front of the saloon but the mercantile. Because the men bellied up to the bar would walk any distance for the show. The people just in town for flour or salt though, you had to step into their path some. Make them aware of you.

Lonegan had polished his boots, shaved his jaw, pulled the hair on his chin down into a waxy point.

He waited until twenty or so people had gathered before reaching up under the side of the buckboard, for the secret handle.

He pulled it, stepped away with a flourish, and the panel on the buckboard opened up like a staircase, all the bottles and jars and felt bags of medicine already tied into place.

One person in the crowd clapped twice.

Lonegan didn't look around, just started talking about how the blue oil in the clear jar—he'd pilfered it from a barber shop in Missouri—how, if rubbed into the scalp twice daily and let cook in the sun, it would make a head of hair grow back, if you happened to be missing one. Full, black, Indian hair. But you had to be careful not to use too much, especially in these parts.

Now somebody in the crowd laughed.

Inside, Lonegan smiled, then went on.

The other stuff, fox urine he called it, though assured them it wasn't, it was for the women specifically. He couldn't go into the particulars in mixed company though, of course. This was a Christian settlement, right?

He looked around when no one answered.

"Amen," a man near the front finally said.

Lonegan nodded.

"Thought so," he said. "Some towns I come across . . . well. Mining towns, y'know?"

Five, maybe six people nodded, kept their lips pursed.

The fox urine was going to be sold out by supper, Lonegan knew. Not to any of the women either.

Facing the crowd now, the buckboard framed by the mercantile, like it was just an extension of the mercantile, Lonegan cycled through his other bottles, the rest of his jars, the creams and powders and rare leaves. Twice a man in the crowd raised his hand to stop the show, make a purchase, but Lonegan held his palm up. Not yet, not yet.

But then, towards midafternoon, the white-haired preacher finally showed up, the good book held in both hands before him like a shield.

Lonegan resisted acknowledging him. But just barely.

They were in the same profession, after all.

And the preacher was the key to all this too.

So Lonegan went on hawking, selling, testifying, the sweat running down the back of his neck to wet his shirt. He took his hat off, wiped his forehead with the back of his sleeve, and eyed the crowd now, shrugged.

"If you'll excuse me a brief moment," he said, and stepped halfway behind the ass end of the buckboard, swigged from a tall, clear bottle of nearly amber liquid.

He swallowed, lifted the bottle again, and drew deep on it, nodded as he screwed the cap back on.

"What is that?" a woman asked.

Lonegan looked up as if caught, said, "Nothing, ma'am. Something of my own making."

"We—" another man started, stepping forward.

Lonegan shook his head no, cut him off: "It's not that kind of my own making, sir. Any man drinks whiskey in the heat like this is asking for trouble, am I right?"

The man stepped back without ever breaking eye contact.

"Then what is it?" a boy asked.

Lonegan looked down to him, smiled.

"Just something an old—a man from the Old Country taught this to me on his deathbed. It's kind of like . . . you know how a strip of dried meat, it's like the whole steak twisted into a couple of bites?"

The boy nodded.

Lonegan lifted the bottle up, let it catch the sunlight. Said, "This is like that. Except it's the good part of water. The cold part."

A man in the crowd muttered a curse. The dismissal cycled through, all around Lonegan. He waited for it to abate, then shrugged, tucked the bottle back into the buckboard. "It's not for sale anyway," he said, stepping back around to the bottles and jars.

"Why not?" a man in a thick leather vest asked.

By the man's bearing, Lonegan assumed he was law of some kind.

"Personal stock," Lonegan explained. "And—anyway. There's not enough. It takes about fourteen months to get even a few bottles distilled the right way."

"Then I take that to mean you'd be averse to sampling it out?" the man said.

Lonegan nodded, tried to look apologetic.

The man shook his head, scratched deep in his matted beard, and stepped forward, shouldered Lonegan out of the way.

A moment later, he'd grubbed the bottle up from the bedclothes Lonegan had stuffed it in.

With everybody watching, he unscrewed the cap, wiped his lips clean, and took a long pull off the bottle.

What it was was water with a green juniper leaf at the bottom. The inside of the bottle cap dabbed with honey. A couple drops of laudanum, for the soft head rush, and a peppermint candy ground up, to hide the laudanum.

The man lowered the bottle, swallowed what was left in his mouth, and smiled.

Grudgingly, Lonegan agreed to take two dollars for what was left in the bottle. And then everybody was calling for it.

"I don't—" he started, stepping up onto the hub of his wheel to try to reach everybody, "I don't have—" but they were surging forward.

"Okay," he said, for the benefit of the people up front, and stepped down, hauled a half case of the water up over the side of the buckboard.

Which was when the preacher spoke up.

The crowd fell silent like church.

"I can't let you do this to these good people," the preacher said.

"I think—" Lonegan said, his stutter a practiced thing, "I think you have me confused with the k-kind of gentlemen who—"

"I'm not confused at all, sir," the preacher said, both his hands still clasping the bible.

Lonegan stared at him, stared at him, then took a respectful step forward. "What could convince you then, Brother?" he said. "Take my mare there. See that wound on her haunch? Would you believe that four days ago that was done by an old blunderbuss, fired on accident?"

"By you?"

"I was cleaning it."

The preacher nodded, waiting.

Lonegan went on. "You could reach your hand into the hole, I'm saying."

"And your medicine fixed it?" the preacher anticipated, his voice rising.

Lonegan palmed a smoky jar from the shelves, said, "This poultice, yes sir. A man named Running Bear showed me how to take the caul around the heart of a dog and grind—"

The preacher blew air out his nose.

"He was Oglala Sioux," Lonegan added, and let that settle.

The preacher just stared.

Lonegan looked around at the faces in the crowd, starting to side with the preacher. More out of habit than argument. But still.

Lonegan nodded, backed off, hands raised. Was quiet long enough to let them know he was just thinking of this: "These—these snake oil men you've taken me for, Brother. People. A despicable breed. What would you say characterizes them?"

When the preacher didn't answer, a man in the crowd did: "They sell things."

"I sell things," Lonegan agreed.

"Medicine," a woman clarified.

"Remedies," Lonegan corrected, nodding to her to show he meant no insult.

She held his eyes.

"What else?" Lonegan said, to all.

It was the preacher who answered: "You'll be gone tomorrow."

"—before any of our hair can get grown in," an old man added, sweeping his hat off to show his bald head.

Lonegan smiled wide, nodded. Cupped a small bottle of the blue oil from its place on the panel, twirled it to the man.

He caught it, stared at Lonegan.

"I'm not leaving," Lonegan said.

"Yeah, well—" a man started.

"I'm not," Lonegan said, some insult in his voice now. "And, you know what? To prove it, today and today only, I'll be accepting checks, or notes. Just write your name and how much you owe me on any scrap of paper—here, I've got paper myself, I'll even supply that. I won't come to collect until you're satisfied."

As one, a grin spread across the crowd's face.

"How long this take to work?" the bald man asked, holding his bottle of blue up.

"I've seen it take as long as six days, to be honest."

The old man raised his eyebrows. They were bushy, white.

People were already pushing forward again.

Lonegan stepped up onto his hub, waved his arms for them to slow down, slow down. That he wanted to make a gift first.

It was a tightly woven cloth bag the size of a man's head.

He handed it to the preacher, said, "Brother."

The preacher took it, looked from Lonegan to the string tying the bag closed.

"Traveling like I do," Lonegan said, "I make my tithe where I can. With what I can."

The preacher opened it.

"The sacrament?" he said.

"Just wafers for now," Lonegan said. "You'll have to bless them, of course."

Slowly at first, then altogether, the crowd started clapping.

The preacher tied the bag shut, extended his hand to Lonegan.

By dinner, there wasn't a drop of fox urine in his possession.

When the two women came to collect him for church the next morning, Lonegan held his finger up, told them he'd be right there. He liked to say a few prayers beforehand.

The woman lowered their bonneted heads that they understood, then one of them added that his mare had run off in the night, it looked like.

"She does that," Lonegan said with a smile, and closed the door, held it there.

Just what he needed: a goddamn prophetic horse.

Instead of praying then, or going to the service, Lonegan packed his spare clothes tight in his bedroll, shoved it under the bed then made the bed so nobody would have any call to look under it. Before he ever figured this whole thing out, he'd lost two good suits just because he'd failed to stretch a sheet across a mattress.

But now, now his bedroll was still going to be there Monday, or Tuesday, or whenever he came for it.

Next, he angled the one chair in the room over to the window, waited for the congregation to shuffle back out into the streets in their Sunday best.

Today, the congregation was going to be the whole town. Because they felt guilty about the money they'd spent yesterday, and because they knew this morning there was going to be a communion.

In a Baptist church, that happened little enough that it was an event.

With luck, nobody would even have noticed Lonegan's absence, come looking for him.

With luck, they'd all be guilty enough to palm an extra wafer, let it go soft against the roofs of their mouths.

After a lifetime of eating coarse hunks of bread, the wafer would be candy to them. So white it had to be pure.

Lonegan smiled, propped his boots up on the windowsill, and tipped back the bottle of rotgut until his eyes watered. If he'd been drinking just to feel good, it would have been sipping bourbon. For this, though, he needed to be drunk, and smell like it.

Scattered on the wood-plank floor all around him, fallen like leaves, were the promissory notes for yesterday's sales.

He wasn't going to need them to collect.

It was a funny thing.

Right about what he figured was the middle of lunch for most of the town—he didn't even know its name, he laughed to himself—he pulled the old Colt up from his lap, laid the bottom of the barrel across the back of his left wrist, and aimed in turn at each of the six panes in his window, blew them out into the street.

Ten minutes and two reloads later, he was fast in jail.

"Don't get too comfortable in there now," the bearded man Lonegan had made for the law said. He was wearing a stiff collar from church, a tin star on his chest.

Lonegan smiled, leaned back on his cot, and shook his head no, he wouldn't.

"When's dinner?" he slurred out, having to bite back a smile, the cake a definite thing in his mind again.

The Sheriff didn't respond, just walked out.

Behind him, Lonegan nodded.

Sewed into the lining of his right boot were all the tools he would need to pick the simple lock of the cell.

Sewed into his belt, as backup, was a few thimblefuls of gunpowder wrapped in thin oilcloth, in case the lock was jammed. In Lonegan's teeth, a sulfur-head match that the burly man had never even questioned.

Lonegan balanced it in one of the cracks of the wall.

He was in the best room in town, now.

That afternoon he woke to a woman staring at him. She was sideways—he was sideways, on the cot.

He pushed the heel of his right hand into one eye then the other, sat up.

"Ma'am," he said, having to turn his head sideways to swallow.

She was slight but tall, her face lined by the weather it looked like. A hard woman to get a read on.

"I came to pay," she said.

Lonegan lowered his head to smile, had to grip the edge of his cot with both hands to keep from spilling down onto the floor.

"My father," the woman went on, finding her voice, "he—I don't know why. He's rubbing that blue stuff onto his head. He smells like a barbershop."

Lonegan looked up to this woman, wasn't sure if he should smile or not. She was anyway.

"You don't see its efficacy," he said, "you don't got to pay, ma'am."

She stared at him about this, finally said, "Can you even spell that?"

"What?"

"Efficacy."

Now it was Lonegan's turn to just stare.

"Got a first name?" she said.

"Lonegan," Lonegan shrugged.

"The rest of it?"

"Just Lonegan."

"That's how it is then?"

"Alone, again . . " he went on, breaking his name down into words for her.

"I get it," she told him.

"Regular-like, you mean?"

She caught his meaning about this as well, set her teeth, but then shook her head no, smiled instead.

"I don't know what kind of—what kind of affair you're trying to pull off here, Mister Alone Again."

"My horse ran off," Lonegan said, standing, pulling his face close to the bars now. "Think I'm apt to make a fast getaway in these?"

For illustration, he lifted his right boot. It was down at heel. Shiny on top, bare underneath.

"You meant to get thrown in here, I mean," she said. "Shooting up Molly's best room like that."

"Who are you, you don't mind my asking?"

"I'm the daughter of the man you swindled yesterday afternoon. I'm just here to complete the transaction."

"I told you—"

"And I'm telling you. I'm not going to be indebted to a man like you. Not again."

Lonegan cocked his head over to her, narrowed his eyes. "Again?" he said.

"How much it going to cost me?"

"Say my name."

"How much?"

Lonegan tongued his lower lip out, was falling in love just a little bit, he thought. Wishing he wasn't on this side of the bars anyway.

"You like the service this morning?" he asked.

"I don't go to church with my father anymore," the woman said. "Who do you think swindled us the first time?"

Lonegan smiled, liked it.

"Anyway," the woman went on. "My father tends to bring enough church home with him each Sunday to last us the week through. And then some."

"What's your name?" Lonegan said, watching her.

"That supposed to give you some power over me, if you know?"

"So you think I'm real then?"

Lonegan shrugged, waiting for her to try to back out of the corner she'd wedged herself into.

"You can call me Mary," she said, lifting her chin at the end.

"I like Jezebel better," he said. "Girl who didn't go to church."

"Do you even know the bible?" she asked.

"I know I'm glad you didn't go to church this morning."

"How much, Mister Lonegan?"

He nodded thanks, said, "For you, Jezebel. For you—"

"I don't want a deal."

"Two dollars."

"They sold for two bits, I heard."

"Special deal for a special lady."

She held his stare for a moment longer then slammed her coin purse down on the only desk in the room, started counting out coins.

Two dollars was a full week's work, Lonegan figured.

"What do you do?" he said, watching her.

"Give money to fools, it would seem," she muttered.

Lonegan hissed a laugh, was holding the bars on each side of his face, all his weight there.

She stood with the money in her hand.

"I bake," she said—spit, really.

Lonegan felt everything calming inside him.

"Confectionary stuff?" he said.

"Why?" she said, stepping forward. "You come here for a matrimony?"

". . . Mary Lonegan," Lonegan sung out, like trying it out some.

She held the money out, her palm down so she'd just have to open her fingers.

Lonegan worked it into a brush of skin anyway, said at the last moment, "Or you could just—you could stay and talk. In the next cell maybe."

"It cost me two more dollars not to?" she said back, her hand to her coin purse again, then stared at Lonegan until he had to look away. To the heavy oak door that opened onto the street.

The Sheriff was stepping through, fumbling for the peg on the wall, to hang his holster on.

"Annie," he said to the woman.

Her top lip rose in what Lonegan took for anger, disgust. Not directed at the lawman, but at her own name spoken aloud.

"Annie," Lonegan repeated.

"You know this character?" the man said, cutting his eyes to Lonegan.

"We go back a long ways, Sheriff," Lonegan said.

Annie laughed through her nose, pushed past the lawman, stepped out into the sunlight.

Lonegan watched the door until it was closed all the way, then studied the floor.

Finally he nodded, slipped his belt off with one hand, ferreted the slender oilcloth of gunpowder out.

"For obvious reasons, she didn't bake it into a cake," he said, holding the oilcloth up for the lawman to see.

"Annie?" the lawman said, incredulous.

"If that's the name you know her by," Lonegan said, then dropped the oilcloth bag onto the stone floor.

The lawman approached, fingered the black powder up to his nose. Looked to the door as well.

By nightfall, Annie Jorgensson was in the cell next to Lonegan's.

"Was hoping you'd bring some of those pastries you've been making," he said to her, nodding down to the apron she was still wearing, the flour dusting her forearms.

"Was hoping you'd be dead by now maybe," she said back, brushing her arms clean.

"You could have brought something, I mean."

"That why you lied about me?"

"What I said, I said to save your life. A little courtesy might be in order."

"You think talking to you's going to save me?" she said. "Rather be dead, thanks."

Lonegan leaned back on his cot, closed his eyes.

All dinner had been was some hardtack the Sheriff had had in his saddlebag for what tasted like weeks.

Lonegan had made himself eat all of it, though, every bite.

Not for strength, but out of spite. Because he knew what was coming.

"You're sure you didn't go to church this morning?" he said to Annie Jorgensson.

She didn't answer. It didn't matter much if she had though, he guessed, and was just lying to him about it, like she had with her name. Either way there was still a wall of bars between them. And he didn't know what he was going to do with her anyway, after. Lead her by the hand into the saloon, pour her a drink?

No, it was better if she was lying, really. If she was a closet Baptist.

It would keep him from having to hold her down with his knee, shoot her in the face.

Ten minutes after a light Lonegan couldn't see the source of was doused, the horses at the livery took to screaming.

Lonegan nodded, watched for Annie's reaction.

She just sat there.

"You alive?" he called over.

Her eyes flicked up to him, but that was all.

Yes.

Soon enough the horses kicked down a gate or a wall, started crashing through the town. One of them ran up onto the boardwalk it sounded like, then, afraid of the sound of its own hooves, shied away, into a window. After that, Lonegan couldn't tell. There was gunfire, for the horse maybe. Or not.

The whole time he watched Annie.

"Mary," he said to her once, in play.

"Jezebel to you," she hissed back.

He smiled.

"What's happening out there?" she asked, finally.

"I'm in here," Lonegan shrugged back to her. "You saying this doesn't happen every night?"

She stood, leaned against the bars at the front of her cell.

One time before, Lonegan had made it through with a cellmate. Or, in the next cell, like this.

He'd left that one there though. Not turned, like the rest of the town, but starved inside of four days anyway. Five if he ate the stuffing from his mattress.

It had been interesting, though, the man's reactions—how his back stiffened with each scream. The line of saliva that descended from his lip to the ground.

"I've got to piss," Lonegan said.

Annie didn't turn around.

Lonegan aimed it at the trap under the window, was just shaking off when a face appeared, nearly level with his own.

It was one of the men from the crowd.

His eyes were wild, roving, his cheeks already shrunken, making his teeth look larger. Around his mouth, blood.

He pulled at the bars of the window like the animal he was.

"You're already dead," Lonegan said to him, then raised his finger in the shape of a pistol, shot the man between the eyes.

The man grunted, shuffled off.

"That was Sid Masterson," Annie said from behind him. "If you're wondering, I mean."

"Think he was past the point where an introduction would have done any good," Lonegan said, turning to catch her eye.

"This is supposed to impress me?" Annie said, suddenly standing at the wall of bars between them.

"You're alive," Lonegan told her.

"What are they?" she said, lifting her chin to take in the whole town.

Lonegan shrugged, rubbed the side of his nose with the side of his finger.

"Some people just get caught up when they're dying, I guess," he said. "Takes them longer."

"How long?"

Lonegan smiled, said, "A day. They don't last so long in the sun. I don't know why."

"But you can't have got everybody."

"They'll get who I didn't."

"You've done this before."

"Once or twice, I suppose. My oxen gets in the ditch like everybody else's . . ."

For a long time, Annie just stared at him. Finally she said, "We would have given you whatever, y'know?"

"A good Christian town," Lonegan recited.

"You didn't have to do this, I mean."

"They were asking for it," Lonegan said, shrugging it true. "They paid me, even, if I recall correctly."

"It was that poppy water."

Lonegan raised his eyebrows to her.

"I know the taste," she said. "What was it masking?"

In reply, Lonegan pursed his lips, pointed with them out to the town: that.

"My father?" Annie said, then.

Lonegan kept looking at the front door.

Her father. That was definitely going to be a complication. There was a reason he usually passed the night alone, he told himself.

But she was a baker.

Back in her kitchen there was probably all manner of frosting and sugar.

Lonegan opened his mouth to ask her where she lived, but then thought better of it. He'd find her place anyway. After tonight, he'd have all week to scavenge through town. Every house, every building.

Towards the end of the week, even, the horses would come back, from downwind. They'd be skittish like the mare had been—skittish that he was dead like the others had been, just not lying down yet—but then he'd have oats in a sack, and, even if they had been smart enough to run away, they were still just horses.

Or, he hoped—this time—a mule.

Something with personality.

They usually tasted better anyway.

He came to again sometime before dawn. He could tell by the quality of light sifting in through the bars of his window. There were no birds singing though. And the smell. He was used to the smell by now.

Miles east of town, he knew, a tree was coated with buzzards.

Soon they would rise into an oily black mass, ride the heat into town, drift down onto the bodies that would be in the street by now.

Like with the deputy Lonegan had found, though, the buzzards would know better than to eat. Even to them, this kind of dead tasted wrong.

With luck, maybe one of the horses would have run its lungs bloody for them, collapsed in a heap of meat.

With luck, it'd be that ornery damn mare.

They'd start on her haunch, of course, finish what Lonegan had started.

He nodded, pulled a sharp hank of air up his nose, and realized what had woke him: the oak door. It was moving, creaking.

In the next cell, Annie was already at the bars of her cell, holding her breath.

"They can't get in," Lonegan told her.

She didn't look away from the door.

"What were you dreaming about there?" she said, her voice flat and low.

Lonegan narrowed his eyes at her.

Dream?

He looked at his hands as if they might have been involved, then touched his face.

It was wet.

He shook his head no, stood, and the oak door swung open.

Standing in the space it had been was the Sheriff.

He'd seen better days.

Annie fell back to her cot, pulled the green blanket up to her mouth.

Lonegan didn't move, just inspected. It wasn't often he got to see one of the shufflers when they were still shuffling. This one, he surmised, he'd fallen down in some open place. While he was turning, too, another had fed on him, it looked like. His face on the right side was down to the bone, one of his arms gone, just a ragged sleeve now.

Not that he was in a state to care about any of that.

This was probably the time he usually came into work on Monday.

It was all he knew anymore.

"Hey," Lonegan called out to it, to be sure.

The thing had to look around for the source of the sound.

When he found it, Lonegan nodded.

"No . . ." Annie was saying through her blanket.

"He can't get through," Lonegan said again. "They can't—keys, tools, guns."

For a long time, then—it could sense the sun coming, Lonegan thought—the thing just stood there, rasping air in and out.

Annie was hysterical in a quiet way, pushing on the floor with her feet over and over, like trying to back herself out of this.

Lonegan watched like she was a new thing to him.

Maybe if he was just seeing his first one too though. But . . . no. Even then—it had been a goat—even then he'd known what was happening. It was the goat he'd been trying all his mixtures out on first, because it would eat anything. And because it couldn't aim a pistol.

When it had died, Lonegan had nodded, looked at the syrup in the wooden tube, already drying into a floury paste, and been about to sling it out into the creek with all the other bad mixes when the goat had kicked, its one good eye rolling in its skull, a sound clawing from its throat that had pushed Lonegan up onto his buckboard.

Finally, when the horse he'd had then wouldn't calm down, Lonegan had had to shoot the goat.

The goat had looked up to the barrel like a child too.

It was the same look the thing in the doorway had now. Like it didn't understand just how it had got to be where it was.

The front of its pants were wet, from the first time it had relaxed into death.

Lonegan watched it.

In its other hand—and this he'd never seen—was one of the bottles of what Annie had called poppy water.

The thing was holding it by the neck like it knew what it was.

When it lifted it to its mouth, Annie forgot how to breathe a little.

Lonegan turned to her, then to the thing, and got it: she knew what that water tasted like, still thought it was the water, doing all this to her town.

He smiled to himself, came back to the thing, the shuffler.

It was making its way across the floor, one of its ankles at a bad angle.

Now Annie was screaming, stuffing the blanket into her mouth. The thing noticed, came to her cell.

"You don't want to—" Lonegan started, but it was too late.

Make them take an interest in you, he was going to say.

Like anything with an appetite, jerky motions drew its attention.

Annie was practically convulsing.

Lonegan came to the wall of bars between them, reached for her hand, just to let her know she was alive, but, at the touch she cringed away, her eyes wild, breath shallow.

"You should have gone to church," Lonegan said, out loud he guessed, because she looked over, a question on her face, but by then the thing was at the bars. It wasn't strong enough to come through them of course, but it didn't understand things the way a man would either.

Slowly, as if trying to, it wedged its head between two of the bars—leading with its mouth—and started to push and pull through.

The first thing to go was its one good eye. It ran down its cheek.

Next was its jaw, then its skull, and still it kept coming, got halfway through before it didn't have anything left.

Annie had never been in danger. Not from the thing anyway.

She wasn't so much conscious anymore either though.

For a long time, Lonegan sat on the edge of his cot, his head leaned down into his hands, the thing in the bars still breathing somehow, even when the sunlight spilled through, started turning its skin to leather.

It was time.

Lonegan worked his pants leg up, slid the two picks out, had the door to his cell open almost as fast as if he'd had the key.

The first thing he did was take the shotgun off the wall, hold the barrel to the base of the thing's skull. But then Annie started to stir. Lonegan focused in on her, nodded, and turned the gun around, slammed the butt into the thing until its head lolled forward, the skin at the back of the neck tearing into a mouth of sorts, that smiled with a ripping sound.

When the thing fell, it gave Lonegan a clear line on Annie.

She was dotted with black blood now.

He might as well have just shot the thing, he figured.

"Well," he said to her.

She was crying, hiding inside herself.

"You don't catch it from the blood," he told her, "don't worry," but she wasn't listening anymore.

Lonegan pulled the keys up from the thing's belt, and unlocked her cell, let the door swing wide.

"But—but—" she said.

Lonegan shrugged, disgusted with her.

"*What?*" he said, finally. "I saved your life, Mary, Jezebel. Annie Jorgensson."

She shook her head no, more of a jerk than a gesture.

Lonegan twirled the shotgun by the trigger guard, held it down along his leg.

The easy thing to do now would be to point it at her, get this over with.

Except she was the cake lady.

For the first time in years, he wasn't sure if he'd be able to stomach the cake, later, if he did this to her now.

"What's the name of this town?" he said to her.

She looked up, the muscles in her face dancing.

"Name?"

"This place."

For a long time she didn't understand the question, then she nodded, said it: "Gultree."

Lonegan nodded, said, "I don't think I'll be staying in Gultree much longer, Miss Jorgensson. Not to be rude."

She shook her head no, no, he wasn't being rude.

"I'm sorry about your father," he said then. It even surprised him.

Annie just stared at him, her mouth working around a word: ". . . why?"

"The world," he said to her, "it's a—it's a hard place. I didn't make it. It just is."

"Somebody told you that," she said weakly, shaking her head no. "You don't . . . you don't believe it."

"Would I do this if I didn't?"

She laughed, leaned back. "You're trying to convince yourself, Mister Alone Again," she told him.

And then she didn't stop laughing.

Lonegan stared hard at her, hated Gultree. Everything about it. He was glad he'd killed it, wiped it off the map.

"Good-bye then," he said to her, lifting the fingers of his free hand to the hat he'd left . . . where?

He looked around for it, finally just took a sweated-through brown one off the peg by the door.

It fit. Close enough anyway.

For a moment longer than he meant to, he stood in the doorway, waiting for Annie to come up behind him, but she didn't. Even after the door of her cell made its rusty moan.

Lonegan had to look back.

Annie was on her knees behind the thing the Sheriff had become.

She'd worked his revolver up from his holster, was holding it backwards, the barrel in her mouth, so deep she was gagging.

Lonegan closed his eyes, heard her saying it again, from a few minutes ago: "But—but—"

But she'd drank the poppy water too. Thought she was already dead like the rest of them.

She only had to shoot herself once.

Lonegan narrowed his lips, made himself look at what was left of her, then turned, pulled the door shut.

Usually he took his time picking through town, filling saddlebags and feed sacks with jewelry and guns and whatever else would sell.

This time was different though.

This time he just walked straight down main street to his buckboard, folded the side panel back into itself, and looked around for a horse.

When there wasn't one, he started walking the way he'd come in. Soon enough a horse whinnied.

Lonegan slowed, filled his stolen hat with pebbles and sand, started shaking it, shaking it.

Minutes later, the mare rose from the heat.

"Not you," he said.

She was briny with salt, from running. Had already been coming back to town for the water trough.

Lonegan narrowed his eyes at the distance behind her, for another horse. There was just her though. He dumped the hat, turned back around.

Twenty minutes later, her nose to the ground like a dog, she trotted into town.

Lonegan slipped a rope over her head and she slumped into it, kept drinking.

All around them were the dead and the nearly dead, littering the streets, coming half out of windows.

Ahead of him, in the straight line from the last town to this one, there'd be another town, he knew. And another, and another. Right now, even, there was probably a runner out there from this town, trying to warn everybody of the snake oil man.

Lonegan would find him like he'd found the last though. Because anybody good enough to leave his own family to ride all night, warn people twenty miles away, anybody from that stock would have been at the service Sunday morning too, done a little partaking.

Which meant he was dead in the saddle already, his tongue swelling in his mouth, a thirst rising from deeper than any thirst he'd ever had before.

Lonegan fixed the yoke on the mare, smeared more poultice into her wound.

If things got bad enough out there this time, he could do what he'd always thought would work: crush one of the wafers up, rub it into her nostrils, make her breathe it in.

She'd die, yeah, but she'd come back too. If she was already in the harness when she did, then he could get a few more miles out of her, he figured.

But it would spoil her meat.

Lonegan looked ahead, trying to figure how far it was going to be this time. How many days. Whether there was some mixture or compound or extract he hadn't found yet, one that could make him forget Gultree altogether. And Annie. Himself.

They'd been asking for it though, he told himself, again.

If it hadn't been him, it would have been somebody else, and that other person might not have known how to administer it, then it would have been one half of the town—the live half—against the other.

And that just plain took too long.

No, it was better this way.

Lonegan leaned over to spit, then climbed up onto the seat of the buck-board. The mare pulled ahead, picking around the bodies on her own. The one time one of them jerked, raising its arm to her, Lonegan put it down with the scatter-gun.

In the silence afterwards, there wasn't a sound in Gultree.

Lonegan shook his head, blew his disgust out his nose.

At the far edge of town was what he'd been counting on: a house with a word gold-lettered onto the back of one of the windows: Wm. Jorgensson. It was where Annie lived, where she cooked, where she'd been cooking, until the Sheriff came for her.

Lonegan tied the mare to a post, stepped into Annie's living room, found himself with his hat in his hands for some reason, the scatter-gun in the buckboard.

They were all dead though.

"Cake," he said aloud, trying to make it real.

It worked.

In the kitchen, not even cut, was a white cake. It was smeared with lard, it looked like. Lard thick with sugar.

Lonegan ran his finger along the edge, tasted it, breathed out for what felt like the first time in days.

Yes.

He took the cake and the dish it was on too, stepped back into the living room.

The father was waiting for him, a felt bowler hat clamped down over his skull. He was dead, clutching a bible the same way the Sheriff had been carrying the bottle.

The old man was working his mouth and tongue like he was going to say something.

Lonegan waited, waited, had no idea what one of these could say if it took a mind to.

Finally he had to say it for the old man, though, answer the only question that mattered: Annie.

"I got her out before," he said. "You don't need to worry about her none, sir."

The old man just creaked, deep in his throat.

Walking across his left eyeball was a wasp.

Lonegan took a step back, angled his head for another door then came back to the old man.

If—if the buzzards knew better than to eat these things, shouldn't a wasp too?

Lonegan narrowed his eyes at the old man, walked around to see him from the side.

He was dead, a shuffler, but—but not as dead.

It hadn't been a bad mixture either. Lonegan had made it like every other time. No, it was something else, something . . .

Lonegan shook his head no, then did it anyway: tipped the old man's bowler hat off.

What spilled out was a new head of hair. It was white, silky, dripping blue.

The old man straightened his back, like trying to stand from the hair touching his neck now, for the first time ever.

"No," Lonegan whispered, still shaking his head, and then the old man held the bible out to him.

It pushed Lonegan backwards over a chair.

He caught himself on his hand, rolled into a standing position in the kitchen doorway. Never even spilled the cake.

"You've been using the oil," he said to the old man, touching his own hair to show.

The old man—William Jorgensson: a he, not an it—didn't understand, just kept leading with the bible.

Lonegan smiled, shook his head no. Thanks, but no.

The old man breathed in sharp then, all at once, then out again, blood misting out now. Meaning it was almost over now, barbershop oil or no.

Again, he started making the creaking sound with his throat. Like he was trying to talk.

When he couldn't get it out, and Lonegan wouldn't take the bible, the old man finally reached into his pocket, came out with a handful of broken wafers, stolen from the pan at church.

It was what Annie had said: her father bringing the church back to her, since she wouldn't go.

Lonegan held his hands away, his fingertips even, and stepped away again. Not that the wafers could get through boot leather. But still.

The bible slapped the wooden floor.

"You old thief," Lonegan said.

The old man just stood there.

"What else you got in there, now?" Lonegan asked.

The old man narrowed his half-dead eyes, focused on his hand in his pocket, and came up with the bottle Lonegan had given him for free. It was empty.

Lonegan nodded about that, got the old man nodding too.

"That I can do something about, now," he said, and stepped long and wide around the old man, out the front door.

The heat was stifling, wonderful.

Lonegan balanced the cake just above his shoulder, unhooked the panel on the side of the buckboard. It slapped down, the mare spooking ahead a step or two, until the traces stopped her.

Lonegan glared at her, looked back to the house, then did it anyway, what he knew he didn't have to: palmed up the last two bottles of barbershop oil. They were pale blue in the sunlight, like a cat's eyes.

He stepped back into the living room, slapped the wall to let the old man know he was back.

The old man turned around slow, the soles of his boots scraping the wood floor the whole way.

"Here," Lonegan said, setting the two bottles down on the table, holding up the cake to show what they were in trade for.

The old man just stared, wasn't going to make it. His index finger twitching by his thigh, the nail bed stained blue.

"I'm sorry," Lonegan said. "For whatever that's worth."

By the time he'd pulled away, the old man had shuffled to the door, was just standing there.

"Give it six days," Lonegan said, touching his own hair to show what he meant, then laughed a nervous laugh, slapped the leather down on the mare's tender haunch.

Fucking Gultree.

He pushed out into the heat, was able to make himself wait all the way until dark for the cake. Because it was a celebration, he even sedated the mare, cut another flank steak off, packed it with poultice.

He'd forgot to collect any water, but then he'd forgot to collect all the jewelry and guns too.

There'd be more though.

In places without women like Annie Jorgensson.

Lonegan wiped the last of the mare's grease from his mouth, pulled his chin hair down into a point, and pulled the cake plate into his lap, started fingering it in until he realized that he was just eating the sweet off the top, like his aunt had always warned him against. It needed to be balanced with the dry cake inside.

He cut a wedge out with his knife, balanced it into his mouth, and did it again and again, until something popped under his blade, deep in the cake.

It was a half a wafer.

Lonegan stared at it, stared at it some more. Tried to control his breathing, couldn't seem to.

Was it—was it from this Sunday's service, or from last?

Was what was in the old man's pocket the whole take, or just part of it?

Lonegan's jaws slowed, then he gagged, threw up onto his chest, and looked all the way back to town, to the old man in the door, smiling now, lifting his bible to show that he knew, that he'd known, that he'd been going to get religion into his daughter's life whether she wanted it or not.

Lonegan shook his head no, no, told the old man that—that, if she'd just waited to pull the trigger, he would have told her that it wasn't the poppy water. But then too was dead certain he could feel the wafer inside him, burrowing like a worm for his heart, his life.

He threw up again, but it was thin now, weak.

". . . no," he said, the wet strings hanging from his chin. It didn't—it couldn't . . . it didn't happen this fast. Did it? Had it ever?

His fingers thick now, he sifted through the cake for another wafer, to see if he could tell which Sunday it had been from, but all the shards were too small, too broken up.

Annie. Goddamn you. Which Sunday?

But—but . . .

The oil, the barbershop oil. Hell yes. It slowed the wafers.

Lonegan stumbled up through the fire, scattering sparks, the cake plate shattering on a rock, and started falling towards the mare. To ride fast back to Gultree, back to the old man, those two blue bottles.

But the mare saw him coming, jerked her head away from the wagon wheel she was tied to.

The reins held. The spoke didn't.

She skittered back, still sluggish from what he'd dosed her with, and

Lonegan nodded, made himself slow down. Held his hat out like there was going to be something in it this time, really, come on, old gal.

The mare opened her nostrils to the night, tasting it for oats, then turned her head sideways to watch Lonegan with one eye, then shied back when he stepped forward, shaking her mane in warning, flicking her tail like she was younger than her years, and when he took another step closer, leading with the hat, she ducked him, and in this way they danced for the rest of the night, her reins always just within reach, if he could just time his steps right. Or what he thought was his reach.

I have to suspect this came from Joe Lansdale's Dead in the West. *Well, I wrote this a few months after reading that for the first time anyway. And, Lonegan, that's kind of my corruption of Louis L'Amour's* Conagher. *And Conagher, he was serious bad, one of my favorites. But I figured he'd be even badder with zombies. My initial plan was for this to be the first in a series of Lonegan stories too (we all want to write the Sackett epic, yes). I had the next one planned out—it was a vampire kid who gets paid to take the place of men sentenced to hang—and one or two after. But then I just never got around to them. There's two distinct endings for this story too. The way it was in* New Genre, *then how it was in Steve Berman's* Shambling Through the Ages. *And I still half-suspect that I've somehow cheated. That the real and true ending is yet waiting in the wings. Which, that's probably why I never took Lonegan into other stories. I still don't feel like I'm done with this one.*

THE WAGES

An Argument

thesis

At twelve years old he was at the lake. Colorado. Playing hide-and-seek or war or something with his brother, lots of running through the bushes, getting farther and farther away from the truck. His brother who was three years younger than him. The shape of the part of the lake they were at was like a finger reaching into land, and all the green things grew right up to the water. He was twelve years old; he wasn't thinking anything, he was thinking maybe about his little brother, the way their hair was the same, dark and shiny and fine. It would make a ring in the sun that stayed level even when his head moved, his eyes always looking somewhere else.

They were running in the trees now.

He was ahead of his brother not by much, but enough that for a moment, when he stumbled out into tall grass and sunlight he was alone, blinking, and he could hear them coming, right out of the pages of *National Geographic*, manifesting first as heads balanced on long necks and then as things driven by men on horseback—llamas—and for as long as he stood there with them streaming by he could believe anything.

antithesis

At fourteen years old he was sitting at the breakfast table waiting for his pants to warm in the dryer. It was exactly eight days after his dad walked out of a bar and shot himself in the cab of his truck. At school no one talked to him. He could do whatever he wanted; he stared into his locker. His pants were tumbling four feet away, the only thing in this morning. His mother walked past them, past the dryer, to the porch with her first cup of coffee, then returned, waited for him to finish his cereal in a way that he knew that's just what she was doing. When he was done she told him their kitten had had a kitten of her own, evidently. Just one. It was on the porch. She told him twice that she couldn't do it. He nodded okay.

On the porch the kitten was still breathing. No hair no eyes.

His mom offered him the gun through the screen door but he couldn't, because it would spook the horses, and he had to get school. So he picked the kitten up with the flat-bottomed shovel and carried it to the burn barrels, where there was a small concrete pad. It was cold. His breath hung white in front of his face. Because he was wearing basketball shorts and boots without socks the kitten when he slammed the cinder block down was wet on his legs, and warm, and he didn't tell any of them about it.

synthesis

At twenty-six years old he was sleeping in a queen bed with his wife. He slept with his toe on her heel, the same trick he'd used with his brothers when he was young, to make sure they were there. His brothers were all in different states now; he had stayed within a hundred miles of home. He woke silently a little after two, and he lay there breathing until almost four. Telling himself to breathe. When his wife asked him if he was okay he told her yes the first two times, but then on the third he didn't answer, and she sat up and he didn't ask her if he'd ever killed anyone one drunk night with a trash-can lid, but he did tell her that he had that memory, all smeared around in his head. Of placing that person with a face in plastic under the kitchen floor of a rent house.

His wife told him that she was with him all the time back then, that that never could have happened, that, drinking, he wouldn't have planned ahead enough to take care of everything, that there would have been a smell, something, but then too she said that the only reason this seemed so real to him was that this is what he does, as a writer—that it was his job to anticipate all the details, all the excuses, anything that might expose the lie—and her voice coming at him across the darkness of the bed was the same as the llamas rushing past, only now they were going the other way.

I should stop pretending this one's fiction.

SO PERFECT

THE KILLERS HERE are Tammy and Brianne. They're seventeen. Well, Tammy's seventeen, but Brianne always lies that she's seventeen. They're both juniors at the new Danforth High School, "Home of the Titans," rah rah rah. As to where "Titans" comes from, none of the students really know. The complete name of the school is Susan B. Danforth High School. They're not really sure who she is either. The suburb they live in isn't old enough to have any history. The year Tammy and Brianne were born, the land their Geography class would someday sit on probably had a cow standing on it, if anything. No titans anyway.

As for Tammy and Brianne, you've seen them before, at all the malls and department stores. Here's a typical Tammy/Brianne conversation:

"And did you see her name tag?"

"Don't even start."

"Like I would be using somebody else's credit card though? Please."

"Shh, shh. She might be listening. Her dad's got to be in prison or something, right? To let her work at a register like that?"

"You're making excuses for her."

"No. I just don't want my car to get keyed. You know how these people—"

The girl they're talking about here is Joy Kane, known in the halls of Danforth as "Candy Cane" because of the red-and-white stockings she wears every day. Her job is adding tax to the purchases of her classmates, and checking identification. And her father isn't in prison; he's dead.

But Joy will be up soon enough. Right now it's Tammy and Brianne.

They're taking the long way out of the mall, to swing by the display window of the pet shop. Not because they want to hold the puppies or kittens, and especially not the birds or lizards, but so—this is a game they play—they can bend over at the waist to tickle the glass, like all they can think about are these cute little adorable animals.

The reason they do this is so they can waggle their peel-off lumbar tattoos. Today Tammy has the typical blue curlicues, Brianna a baseball with the word FOCUS as the brand, but they've also tried the IF YOU CAN READ THIS, YOU'RE TOO CLOSE one, to great effect.

On a good day they can fill the sitting area behind them in fifteen minutes, and then pretend to be oblivious, shake their way out to the parking lot to laugh and laugh in Tammy's car.

On a bad day, though, all they'll attract is the junior-high crowd.

Today is a bad day.

After the pet shop they glide through their favorite purse store, study themselves in the three-way mirror for an explanation.

"What'd you have for lunch?" Tammy asks Brianne.

This is also a typical conversation for them.

"Just coffee."

"You're lying. It had whipped cream on it."

"Pig."

"Slut."

"You wish."

Still, they leave together.

As for Joy, her shift goes over four hours later, and, walking to the corner where her mom will pick her up when she gets off, she doesn't key anybody's car, has forgotten all about Tammy and Brianne, really.

Two days later is a Friday. Tammy and Brianne are having a tanning contest on Brianne's back porch. Her dad, home early from work, is washing the Irish setter. The dog's name is Frederick.

Because it's funny to her, Tammy keeps arranging her bikini so as to make Brianne's dad have to look somewhere else.

"Did you see her today?" Brianne says, her voice bored and hot.

"Who?"

"Candy Cane."

"From the other day?"

"She remembered you, I think."

"Probably wanted to see my driver's license."

Brianne laughs about this, adds, "Like she doesn't know that horizontal stripes aren't really helping those tree trunks she calls legs?"

"They're probably supposed to distract from that sweater she always wears."

"Distract whom?" Brianne says, turning herself over on the chair, her skin glistening.

After that they just watch Brianne's dad wrestle with Frederick. It's the best kind of comedy, as it pretty much confirms everything they think about the class of people he represents.

"What's he doing now?" Tammy asks after about twenty minutes.

"He's not supposed to do it while the hair's still wet."

"Perfume?"

"It's for, like, ticks, I think."

Tammy sits up, lowers her glasses. "It keeps them off, you mean?"

"Something like that."

"Just from that part of Fred's neck?"

"It goes everywhere, I don't know. He's not supposed to do it while the hair's wet though," Brianne repeats louder, for her dad's benefit. "It waters it down or something."

Tammy keeps her sunglasses tilted to watch. She's never seen anything like this—shouldn't the gardener be doing it maybe? It is entertaining, though, Frederick squirming out again and again, his eyeballs white and desperate against all that shiny bronze fur.

But then Tammy has to turn over. Brianne follows. Now they're both staring through the plastic slat of their lounge chairs, into the grass.

"I've petted Fred though," Tammy finally says.

"What? No, it doesn't—you can't get it on you. It says so on the package, I think. Safe for children."

"You've done it . . . applied it or whatever?"

"Of course not. He keeps the box in the garage, by my mom's extra keys."

"Beamer or Volvo?"

"They're in the same place."

"But—you . . . he wouldn't need to put that on Fred if there wasn't a problem, right?"

"A problem?"

"Ticks," Tammy almost whispers, as if saying it might attract them, or make them real enough to hear her anyway.

Brianne laughs to herself, says, "He's a dog, T. Why don't you try to be paranoid or something for a change?"

Tammy shakes her head in mock amusement, but is really studying the grass, for bugs.

Where she should be looking is on her towel though.

One corner of it is trailing into the grass.

Crawling up it, still flat and brown and coppery, a tick.

That night while Tammy and Brianne are in the parking lot of the pool with all the other Danforth students, Brianne's dad starts throwing up, can hardly catch his breath.

Brianne's mom calls them, tells them to meet her at the emergency room.

This messes up everything they had planned for the night.

"You go on," Tammy tells Brianne.

She's standing by Bo Richardson, and never stops smiling as she says it.

"You're driving, T," Brianne says, smiling too, her eyes so pleasant.

"Show me later," Bo says to Tammy, pushing her lightly away, his hand large on her shoulder.

What he's talking about are the tan lines Tammy's promised him.

The whole way to the hospital Tammy doesn't say anything, and neither does Brianne.

"Well?" Brianne says to her mom, finally.

Her mom is eating a pastry from the snack machine. It sickens Tammy.

"It's poison," Brianne's mom says, leaning forward to touch both of them, as if she used to be them or something. "From the, y'know. Frederick."

"The tick medicine," Brianne says.

"He got it on his skin," Brianne's mom nods.

"He'll live though?" Tammy says.

"Yes, dear. Don't worry about—"

By this time they've already stopped listening, are already, in spirit, back at the parking lot with Bo and Seth and the rest, Joy at the edge of that crowd, rubbing out cigarettes with the toe of her Wicked Witch of the West boot. At least that's what Brianne calls it.

And of course, the rest of the weekend, except for when they sneak out, they're at Tammy's mom's house. Just because Brianne's dad is too gross to be around. The next time they see him is Monday morning, before school. They're only there to pick up Brianne's belt for Tammy to wear. Like every time, Tammy makes a production of cinching the belt in over and over again, like it won't get small enough for her.

"What have you been eating?" she says to Brianne, on the way down the stairs.

"Bo Richardson," Brianne tosses back quietly, and Tammy pushes her. It's in play—well, half in play—but Brianne stumbles forward anyway, into her dad, just rounding the corner.

"Girls, girls, girls . . ." he says, adjusting his tie.

It's the only thing he ever says to them anymore.

"Dad," Brianne says, stepping back, studying him up and down. "You look—how old are you?"

This has to be a joke though. Or an insult. Both. Her dad shakes his head like a sad clown and leaves. They get the story from Brianne's mom later: over the last forty-eight hours, Brianne's dad has lost thirteen pounds.

Thirteen pounds.

Neither of the girls can say anything.

At the fitting for their bridesmaid dresses two days later (Brianne's slut cousin Clarice is pregnant, and doesn't have any real friends), they have the seamstress pin their dresses tighter and tighter.

"It's supposed to hang, though, sweetie," the seamstress says to Tammy.

Tammy's studying herself in the mirror.

"It will," Tammy says back, and then her eyes catch Brianne's, and they look away.

In the ashtray of Tammy's car, now, where it's been since lunch, is the tick medicine.

In what should be Texas History the next day, a Thursday, they're standing in the girls' locker room together. Nobody else is there. It's just them and, on the plastic bench between them—wood would be unsanitary—one dose of Frederick's tick medicine.

"How much do you want to lose?" Tammy asks.

"From where?" Brianne says back.

They're talking like they're in church.

Tammy smiles, nods to herself, then, all at once, moving fast so she won't have time to think, she breaks the tip off the applicator and turns it over onto her fingertip, daubs a print of it behind each ear. Like perfume.

The fumes burn her eyes a little.

She blinks fast, pretends it doesn't hurt, and passes the applicator to Brianne.

"Thirteen pounds," she says.

Brianne, trying to be careful, turns the vial upside down once, fast, on the thin skin of each wrist.

And then it's over.

"Trig?" Tammy says, holding her breath a little.

"You can't smell it, can you?" Brianne asks, trying to nevertheless.

"'Safe for children,'" Tammy recites, and then it's Trigonometry, and, an hour later, the nurse. Because they've each started throwing up. From the Chinese food they ate at lunch.

The nurse doesn't smile, just sends them home.

By Saturday, the next time they see each other, Tammy's lost eight pounds, Brianne six.

"You've been eating," Tammy accuses.

"Could you?" Brianne says back.

The answer is no.

That night they float through the parking lot like runway models, their belly-button rings glinting in the moonlight, and, this time when Bo and Seth and Davis ask them if they want to hit the Yogurt Shack, they do, and order all they want, and even pretend that it makes them a little drunk.

Really it's the fourteen collective pounds they've shed.

From across the parking lot Joy watches them, and at one point Tammy sees her watching, and keeps smiling anyway, maybe even smiles more, then drapes herself across either Seth or Davis or that other guy from Ashworth or wherever.

It doesn't matter.

On Wednesday, they're going in for the second fitting for their dresses.

To make it to size, on Sunday night in Tammy's basement they lock themselves in the pool room and tap the tick medicine out from Brianne's hollowed-out old lipstick tube.

"The notes will still be good," Tammy says, the applicator in her hand again.

The notes are the ones the nurse wrote for them; they're good until they're well again.

"Like I'll miss Trig," Brianne says, smiling with one side of her face.

"Or ever need it," Tammy adds.

The blouse Brianne's wearing is Tammy's.

A week ago, she'd have been able to fit into it, sure, but it wouldn't have fit either.

Now, though—even Seth had taken a second look.

This time they each lose seven pounds in forty-eight hours, and Tammy doesn't ask if Brianne's been eating anything.

At school on Friday, Tammy sees Joy watching them again, and nudges Brianne.

They're in the cafeteria. *Eating.*

The only thing Joy's touched on her tray—she doesn't ever go off-campus for lunch—is her pudding. The foil is peeled back.

Tammy scratches at a spot under her hair and says, "I bet she's got a whole closet full of those tights. One for Monday, one for Tuesday . . ."

Brianne laughs into her coke, has to look away.

"Maybe she wants to kill us," she says behind her hand.

"By committing fashion suicide then hoping we catch it too?" Tammy says back, and then they have to leave the cafeteria altogether. Not to the bathroom though; this is an eating day.

That afternoon in their lounge chairs in Brianne's backyard—the pool boy's there, and he's even more fun to bother than Brianne's dad—Frederick keeps trying to chase a butterfly. Either the same one or the first one's twin, they can't tell. It always dives for the bushes though, then flutters back up a few minutes later, its shadow on the grass torturing Frederick.

It gets him thirsty enough that he has to come over, lick the sweat from the sides of their legs.

"The salt," Brianne explains.

"Pervert," Tammy says down to Frederick, scratching the top of his head with her long nails.

Frederick eats it up, finally creaks his body around to hook a hind leg up behind an ear, motorboat a furrow into his fur.

"I thought he was fixed," Tammy says, shaking her head away.

"I don't think you can get pregnant just by touching them, T," Brianne says, lowering her leopard-print sunglasses to see what Tammy's talking about.

"The stuff's supposed to keep him from scratching like this, right?" Tammy says, sitting up, her top starting to slide off, the pool boy suddenly very still.

"I told you," Brianne says. "It all got on my dad's hand. Not on Frederick."

"He didn't do it again?"

"You want me to remind him?"

"What, you think he counts how many he's got left?"

"He's kind of scared of it now anyway."

"Can't you make him stop though?"

By that time the pool boy's come to the rescue. Tammy just points down to Frederick.

"What's he doing?" she says to Brianne, drawing her legs up now.

The pool boy smiles, kneels down by the dog and comes up half a minute later with a plump grey tick, its black legs pedaling the air.

Tammy squeals and climbs the back of her chair. Brianne laughs.

"Kill it!" Tammy's saying, working up to a shriek.

"Why?" the pool boy says, holding it out before him—Tammy's forgotten about her swimsuit by now, and does have some stark tan lines—"When they're like this, they're full of babies, yeah?"

"Then—then—?" Tammy says, the back of her hand to her mouth.

"The toilet," Brianne says for the pool boy, who still hasn't looked away from what Tammy's not worried about. "Right?"

Which is when Brianne's mom steps out to see what's going on.

Instantly, the pool boy's posture changes and he's already heading for the bathroom they've let him use once before.

That night after dinner, stepping into the guest bathroom herself to check her face before Bo drops Tammy off, Brianne sees, smeared on the toilet seat, on purpose, the tick.

Without the medicine, even, she throws up into the sink until her eyes are hot.

When she steps into the dining room ten minutes later, Tammy's waiting.

"Start without me?" she says, touching the right corner of her mouth to show what Brianne's missed.

Brianne doesn't answer, just calls out to her mom that she's taking the Volvo and, instead of taking just one application from the shelf in the garage, she takes them all.

"Why?" Tammy asks, far enough away from Brianne's house that it's safe.

Brianne shakes her head no, doesn't say anything.

That Saturday between trips to Tammy's upstairs bathroom, her mom calls up to the girls that Jill is pregnant too, now.

"Slut," Brianne says, smiling, teasing a fleck of vomit from her hair.

"Three, two, one . . ." Tammy smiles back. It's the launch sequence; staying unpregnant is all about timing, they know.

As her mom explains to them the next morning, though, what this means is that Jill is out of the wedding party. Because she's only fifteen. "It wouldn't look right."

"She's showing?" Tammy says, stacking her plate with French toast she's not going to eat.

"It's the principle, honey," her mom says back, fixing both girls in her eyes for a second longer than absolutely necessary.

"Then it's off?" Brianne says.

"The wedding?" Tammy's mom falsettos, blinking fast to show what she's meaning here. "Heavens no. We just need an understudy."

"By Saturday?" Tammy whispers, incredulous.

"I'm sure you have just scads of friends . . ." her mom trails behind her, off to wherever. Church, maybe, after two hours of makeup and a handful of pills.

In her wake, Tammy and Brianne are silent, and then the bite of toast Brianne tried to sneak works its way up her throat and she's bent over the sink, dry heaving, Tammy guarding the door, waiting her turn.

That night, showering before the parking lot, and whatever might happen after the parking lot, Tammy's fingernail breaks off while washing her hair and the blood from her scalp seeps down over her face. The only reason she realizes its blood, even, is that it's gritty. And then she's throwing up again, and more, until her mom knocks on the bathroom door with the palm of her hand.

At her house, her hair still in her towel, her body too, Brianne walks through her living room to the garage.

What she's carrying is the box the tick medicine was in.

All that's left in it now is one half application. The other eight are in the secret pocket of her purse.

The pool boy's in the backyard again, too, doing his thing.

Brianne smiles to herself, holds the towel on her head tighter than the one on her new body.

In the garage it's easy to see where the cardboard box had sat for however many months. It's a small square of light-colored wood. The rest, all around it, is stained brown, and greasy. Brianne looks behind her, like the pool boy's suddenly going to be standing in the door, and then follows the stain up the wall to the next shelf, all the gardening stuff.

The bottle of fertilizer her dad bought off the infomercial is leaking.

"Surprise," she singsongs in her mom's voice.

It's why the cardboard was so greasy. It makes her look at her fingertips. With a spade she nudges the box into place, steps away, and then finds a reason to step outside. What she's pretending to look for is an earring she lost the other day.

What she's thinking about, though, on her knees in the grass with the pool boy, her towel barely there anymore—"Thinking about Tammy now?" she wants to say—is the blood on the toilet seat.

If he would do that when her parents weren't looking, what else might he do?

Ten minutes later, her towel all the way off now, she finds out, and wonders if he's even washed his hands since touching that toilet seat, and somehow that makes it even better.

At the parking lot an hour later, Tammy appraises her and finally says, "You've been eating again, haven't you?"

"Something like that," Brianne shrugs, no eye contact, and then the night swallows them again.

Three days later, the Wednesday before the wedding, Tammy and Brianne are standing at Joy's register again.

"Like you don't know me," Tammy is saying.

"It's, y'know, policy," Joy says back, watching a rounder of clearance shirts out by the aisle.

The *y'know* was funny to her anyway.

"I see you at school," Tammy says.

Joy doesn't say anything back.

"You could be pretty, y'know?" Tammy adds, offering her license, holding it like it's the most boring thing ever.

Joy takes it, compares it to the signature on the card, and hands it back.

"Gee, thanks," she says, wanting to drill a dimple into her cheek with an index finger. "Who wouldn't want to be prettier?"

"Thinner, I mean," Tammy says like a secret, flashing her eyes to Brianne. But Brianne's not following yet.

"How would you like to be in a wedding with us?" Tammy says then, now not letting Brianne catch her eyes.

"This is a joke," Joy says back, sliding the receipt across to Tammy.

"No," Tammy says. "The wedding's a joke. The dress is already ready though. It's—you. Just about ten pounds lighter."

"It would look good with your boots," Brianne adds, the muscles around her mouth tense like a smile.

Tammy kicks her a little where Joy can't see.

"Bo's going to be there," Tammy says. "And the rest of them."

"And I care about that?" Joy says, too fast.

"I wouldn't know," Tammy shrugs, signing the receipt, pushing it back. "Have you ever been in a wedding?"

Joy just stares at her.

Her mother's, Brianne just manages to hold back.

"Everybody's looking at you the whole time, you know?"

"At the bride," Joy corrects.

"Not this time," Tammy says. "Let's just say she's . . . carrying more baggage into the ceremony than—"

"The engagement photos were from the face up," Brianne interrupts, in step at last.

"It's the part of her most guys prefer, really," Tammy adds.

Joy rings the register open, stuffs the receipt in, says, "So what are you trying to say here?"

"I'm saying that you're not . . . what? 'Candy Cane?'"

"Right," Brianne chimes in, biting her top lip.

"I don't want to be like you, if that's what you're thinking," Joy says.

"Of course not," Tammy says, her voice a bit colder now. "I'm just saying. The final fitting is at seven tonight. Here."

She writes the address on the back of her customer copy, slides it to Joy.

"This is a joke," Joy says again. "You said the dress was too little anyway."

Tammy smiles. "No," she says. "The dress is just about the right size, I think. You just need to slender down a bit."

"By Saturday," Brianne says.

"Ten pounds?"

"It's not impossible."

"Look at us," Brianne says, striking a mock-glam pose.

"I'm not going to be there," Joy says, sliding the address back.

"Of course not," Tammy says, but doesn't take the address back either.

Thirty minutes after they're gone, Joy studies herself in the three-way back in the dressing rooms.

A bridesmaid?

She laughs at herself.

But then she remembers the way that Brianne one had angled her body over, to show how little extra she was carrying.

Joy looks in the mirror again, and then turns sideways to look, and then shakes her head no, just keeps collecting clothes from the stalls.

A bridesmaid, yeah.

Except—it's stupid and she knows it's stupid—what if Bo Richardson really is there?

It could be like all the movies, where the charity case loser girl finally puts on mascara, shows up at the dance, the air suddenly different around her, charged.

Which Joy laughs at as well.

She's not twelve years old, after all.

But what if she gets to keep the dress too?

This stops her.

Is that how it works at weddings? It would be cut specifically for her, after all.

Not that she would ever wear it again, of course.

But it might be fun to burn at the parking lot or something.

First she's going to have to fit into it though.

Just in case Bo's really there.

"What's that about?" her mom asks at five, nudging Joy's smile with the knuckle of her index finger.

"Nothing," Joy says.

Just to show that she's not taking it seriously, Joy shows up to the fitting twenty minutes late. With a friend, Lacy.

"So this is it?" Lacy says to Tammy, fingering a peach-colored spaghetti strap out from a rack.

"Where'd you get those boots?" Brianne asks back.

Everybody grins uncomfortably, and then Brianne keeps Lacy in the waiting room while Tammy leads Joy by the arm back to the curtained stalls and the fitting pedestal.

"So what do I do?" Joy says, smiling with one side of her face.

"Nothing," Tammy says, "this is all me . . ." and starts taking measurements with a tape from what looks like a tackle box.

"You mean I don't try it on now?"

"Not like—not like you are, no," Tammy says, her lips tight around a straight pin she's not going to be using.

"What do you mean?"

"We don't want to, you know, stretch it or anything."

"Listen, I don't—"

"No, I say that in the nicest way. But, you can make a dress smaller, but you can't really let it out. That's all. There's not enough material. That's why you always start big."

"Then I can't do this, right? Is that what this is about? God, I don't even know why I'm here."

"Because you want to be beautiful," Tammy whispers up to her. "Now, what size shoe do you wear?"

Joy stares down at her for a long moment, then finally looks away, to the idea of the waiting room.

"Seven," she says.

"Is that men's or women's?" Tammy asks, her voice syrupy with innocence.

Joy smiles with her eyes.

"Even if I don't eat for the next two days—" she starts.

"Leave that to me," Tammy says. "Did you see what I ate in the cafeteria today?"

"I wasn't watching, sorry."

"A piece of pizza."

"Crust and all?" Joy asks.

Tammy smiles, isn't stupid.

"I'm just saying," she says, measuring from the point of Joy's shoulder to the round bone of her wrist, "there are ways."

Joy looks down along her arm.

"I thought they were sleeveless," she says.

"Just being sure," Tammy says back, and then does the other arm. "You're naturally dark, too, so that's good. It'll be a nice contrast against the fabric."

"It?"

"Your sk—Your tan."

"This is a joke," Joy says again, after the necessary lull.

"If you're not coming, you might let us know," Tammy shrugs, stepping back, threading the pin from her teeth. "I mean, I know another girl."

"She needs to lose ten pounds too?"

"No. She's perfect."

"Then why me?"

"Because—I can't be telling you this. But . . . God. I saw Bo looking at you the other day. I think he likes your tights or something. He said something about—it was gross. Licking, and a candy cane?"

On accident then, Joy smiles.

"So tell me," she said. "If I were going, I mean. What's this trick?"

"To what?"

"Ten pounds," Joy says, her voice perfectly even, and Tammy looks up, as if to make sure she's serious.

Tammy had come up with the plan in the department store, right there at Joy's register, and then whispered it to Brianne in the aisle before they were even out of the store.

All she had at first, standing there having her license checked, was the image of Joy, throwing up in the middle of the ceremony. Because Clarice was a slut of a bride, obviously. Because of the example she definitely wasn't (to say nothing of Jill, the whore), Tammy's mom had been tightening the reins the last few days. Joy throwing up during the vows, then, it would be like a sign. Like revenge, or justice. Same thing.

The problem was getting to that image though.

Like Brianne said all the way to the car, it was complicated. If they were in a movie maybe. But this was real life. Susan B. Danforth Detention Unit and Vomitorium. It was a word she'd heard in World History last year.

Tammy knew it was complicated, she said. But she knew Joy too. Her kind. She was jealous of what Tammy and Brianne had, of how Bo and Seth and Davis would all lift their chins and smile when they walked in.

She didn't want to be Tammy and Brianne, so much, but she did want Bo to notice her like that. At least once.

Anybody would, right?

He was Bo after all.

There was nothing complicated about that.

After the measurements, Tammy leads Joy into one of the fitting rooms and pulls the curtain shut behind them.

"What?" Joy says. "This where you cut my arm off?" She holds it out as if weighing it in her mind.

"This way's better," Tammy says, flashing the applicator between her thumb and index finger.

Joy narrows her eyes, then has to squeeze over against the wall as Brianne wedges herself in.

"What is it?" Joy asks.

"Just some diet stuff," Tammy says, nodding to Brianne. "We stole it from her mom. She got it in Greece or somewhere."

"On a cruise," Brianne chimes in.

"Then it's not legal?" Joy says, her eyes watering from the fumes.

"You're really worried about illegal substances?" Brianne says back.

"FDA illegal," Tammy clarifies. "Not DEA illegal."

Joy smiles. With them, for the first time.

The punch line of the joke is supposed to be giving Joy enough antacids or something the day of the wedding that she stops throwing up, and then give her another just before the ceremony. Only that last tablet is something else. Red food dye, maybe, so it looks like she's dying, turning inside out at the altar.

It's going to be perfect.

"Well?" Tammy says, holding the applicator up, and, to show it's not dangerous, she dots her fingertip with it, swirls that finger behind each ear.

"That's all?" Joy says.

Brianne has it now, is rubbing a drop between her wrists. "We just need to, y'know, burn off a couple of pounds by Saturday, yeah? I mean, I lose any-more, I'm going to be back to an A cup. Freshman year all over again."

Joy takes the plastic applicator.

"Greece?" she says.

"They don't wear tops to their bikinis over there," Tammy says, like that can be the clincher: Greek women, proud enough to go topless.

Joy laughs to herself about this, studies the applicator, and says, "So, what? One drop is two pounds?"

"Here," Tammy says, and pinches the applicator away, upends it on Joy's wrist until her skin is slick with it, "now just hold it and count to twenty."

At ten seconds Joy starts coughing from the fumes, but doesn't let go.

"Ten pounds," Brianne's saying, smiling.

By Friday morning, the stomach bug the nurse had diagnosed Tammy and Brianne with again has run its course again, and they make it to school in time to breeze through lunch.

Sitting on her side of the cafeteria, hunched over the table, is Joy. She's pale, looks clammy even from this far away, and, Tammy and Brianne can't be sure, but it looks like her tights aren't even so tight anymore.

"She'll thank us," Tammy says, holding her books tight to her chest.

"If she keeps it off," Brianne adds.

They don't talk to her, though, and Joy doesn't look up to see that they aren't talking to her.

"Maybe her dad makes her come to school anyway," Brianne says on the way to Trigonometry.

"What, he makes that call from prison?" Tammy asks with a smile, then slows for Seth at his locker, which turns into Davis and Bo as well, which turns into being five minutes late.

Brianne glares at her when she finally waltzes in.

Tammy glares back, adds some oomph to it.

On the other side of the classroom, hiding, is Joy. She isn't lifting her head from her desk.

Tammy shrugs to Brianne about it and Brianne shrugs back, makes the *eeek!* shape with her mouth.

Halfway through class is when it happens, the thing that will spark an investigation that will span four high schools and never once interrogate either Tammy or Brianne, the real killers here.

All at once, in the middle of Mr. Connors taking up last night's problems, Joy slings her head up from her desk. A line of vomit strings down from her lip. And there's more coming.

She's trying to hold it down though. Trying just to look over at Tammy and Brianne for help, her fingers clenched around the edge of her desk.

When she can't talk, she finally lurches to a half stand of sorts, lifts her arm to point across the room. At Tammy.

Tammy opens her mouth as if to say something then looks behind her, at the chalkboard.

"Wha—?" she starts to say, her fingertips touching her chest now in consternation, but then Joy is losing everything she's been trying to hold down, only it isn't just the bile and whatever that Tammy and Brianne already know so well. This time it's blood, like's supposed to happen at the wedding, clumpy and dark, and when her throat isn't big enough to turn her inside out, it starts seeping from the corners of her eyes too, and her nose, maybe even beading up through her scalp.

For a half second Tammy is too shocked to react, but then her instincts kick in and she slams her open palms onto her desk and screams. Not in terror so much as in protest. Of having to be witness to this. It infects the classroom, the hall, and even the nurse when she gets there.

Though Joy is unconscious by now, there's still blood gurgling past her lips, her sides contracting over and over.

Somehow Brianne thinks to raise her hand, ask without being called upon if what Candy—what Joy has is catching, or what?

The nurse just keeps staring down at the blood, finally has to support herself with the chalkboard, which gives under her weight, sends her toppling into the brown metal trash can.

By two-thirty, classes are cancelled.

It's so the paramedics can carry Joy down the quiet hall and out the door, a sheet draped across her face because it doesn't matter anymore if she has air.

Tammy and Brianne watch, their eyes saucers, and then they get in the car and put their seat belts on and creep away, both Tammy's hands on the wheel.

"Shit," she says, minutes later.

"Exactly," Brianne says back, then looks over to Tammy. "Can Deborah still fill in, you think? She Candy Cane's size?"

"Deborah?"

"Tomorrow," Brianne says, her tone all about how obvious this is.

Tammy nods once, then again, yes: Debbie, her sister's ditzy friend.

53

The ride home is silent, no radio even, but then, standing from the car, using it to steady herself, Tammy gets out a shaky "Hungry?"

Brianne laughs, doesn't even answer.

The day of the wedding is also the first day of Joy's viewing. There's going to be more of a crowd at the wedding, though, Tammy and Brianne know. And anyway, except for Lacy, who's already been kicked out of Danforth twice in the short time it's existed, nobody knows that they've ever even known Joy, much less stood in a dressing room with her. And anyway, it had been mostly to help her, really. It wasn't their fault she'd turned out to be a pig, slopped so much of the stuff on.

And, while Tammy had promised Bo a show at the wedding if he showed up, she's confident she can still give him something to remember anyway.

All days are salvageable, if you're really committed. If you can still smile.

Of course, Tammy doesn't know what Brianne doesn't even know she knows: the super fertilizer compound from the infomercial.

At the bottom of the leaky container is a warning not to eat any of the fruit this fertilizer has helped grow. It's for pageants only. The fruit and vegetable kind.

Brianne's late to the dressing room of course, but that's just because her mom's made her go stand around the flagpole at school and hold a candle.

Because Joy was in Tammy and Brianne's grade, Clarice of course cancelled the rehearsal dinner last night. "In honor."

Tammy had thanked Clarice for both of them and then gone to the parking lot alone. It was empty, everybody already at one of the memorial services.

Twenty minutes later Brianne showed up in the pants she was only just now fitting into right. She stood from her mom's Volvo, smoothed her pants down along her hip and looked across all the empty asphalt. Even the pool was in mourning.

"They think she was a saint or something," Tammy said when Brianne was close enough.

"Maybe I should try some red-and-white tights," Brianne said back.

Walking through Brianne's living room an hour later, Frederick growled at them like he knew.

But that was stupid.

"It won't . . . she must have been on something else too," Brianne finally whispers to Tammy, the next morning. Not over breakfast—they're going to be on *display*, after all, right?—but at the long vanity in the holy holy dressing room at the church.

"At least they'll be able to keep the flies off her now, yeah?" Tammy smiles back in the mirror, then turns before Brianne can register the joke.

Their dresses fit so perfect they each almost cry.

"Well?" Tammy says, shrugging in anticipation, her eyelashes tittering.

Brianne takes Tammy's hands in hers and bites her lower lip, and then the music's started and their groomsmen—nothing special—are walking them up the aisle, and every note the organ plays is for them.

It's perfect. Even better than that. Like bathing in the silvery flash of cameras, in the powdery scent of groomed flowers. The ashy taste in the air is candles.

Tammy scans the audience for Bo, and he's there with the rest. But, on their lapels, they're all wearing black—*ribbons*?

For Joy. Of course.

The bitch.

She can't even let Tammy and Brianne have this one day.

"Bend your knees," Brianne whispers to Tammy and Tammy just keeps smiling. In heels like she's got on, what other choice does she really have?

Moments later Clarice is waddling up the aisle on her father's arm, and Brianne is laughing without smiling, and Tammy almost gives in as well, at the corners of her mouth. Instead her eyes just cry a little, but that's to be expected.

Except—and this is where things start going wrong—as Clarice gets closer, Tammy looks over to Brianne to be sure they're seeing what they're seeing: under Clarice's dress, her lace and ivory wedding dress, is she really wearing motorcycle boots?

No wonder she got pregnant.

But there's something . . .

Tammy closes her eyes.

Joy again. The boots are the same. "In *honor*."

Tammy grits her teeth, smiles past it, then, when it's time to rotate forty degrees over, to witness this travesty, she sees a flash of red-and-white stripes somewhere in the pews, but can't keep her eyes there without drawing attention.

She's dead, though, Joy.

Dead dead dead.

Maybe not next year, but the year after that anyway, the kids are even going to be calling her "Killjoy" or something, Tammy knows, and then she'll just be a plaque in front of a tree that probably won't even make it two summers.

So, instead of being paranoid, Tammy smiles and stares past Brianne's hair, up to Clarice and her catch of the day, and is only just starting to get bored with all the preaching that comes before anything can even happen—the reception is what matters, she keeps telling herself—when she sees something shiny and brown grope out from under the left strap of Brianne's dress.

A tick, its body impossibly flat.

Tammy looks away, dipping her chin as if swallowing.

Five seconds later, the tick's gone.

But.

Tammy closes her eyes, holds her tissue to her nose as if trying to control herself. Or, not as if, just not for the reason everybody thinks.

In her hair in the shower that day.

The reason she could never find the scratch in her scalp was because it hadn't been a scratch at all, but one of those pregnant ticks, bursting. The grittiness in the blood, in the tick's blood, had been—it had been baby ticks.

Tammy lowers her tissue to her mouth, is breathing faster than she wants to. Finally she has to reach out for Brianne's back just to keep from losing her balance.

Brianne turns around pleasantly, sees the danger Tammy is in, then turns back around just as pleasantly. Takes a polite half step forward even.

Tammy shakes her head no, just a little—there are two hundred and twelve invited guests, after all—but then it starts to rise in her throat anyway, everything she hasn't eaten that morning.

"I can't—" she starts, and loses the rest all over the back of Brianne's peach dress, and it's red, even, and she was right: it does look perfect against that silk. Classic.

For a second Tammy tries to believe that she's imagining all this, torturing herself, that this is a side effect of Frederick's drops, but then the blood still coating her teeth, it's gritty.

Tammy shakes her head no, her hand rising to her mouth.

For the worst instant of her life, Tammy looks out to the crowd again, for Bo to . . . she doesn't know. Help her? Not see her? Please?

But, instead of Bo or Seth or Davis or any of them, what she sees instead, staggered in a pew behind an old couple, is Joy. Just sitting there alone, her milksop hair tucked behind each ear.

Slowly then, so Tammy has to see, Joy opens her mouth, her head turned just sideways enough for Tammy to see that she's lifting her tongue, trying to show Tammy something.

"What?" Tammy says weakly, and is on her knees now, her fingertips to the front of her own lower teeth like Joy's showing, and then past them, to where the floor of her mouth meets the base of her tongue.

Lined there like pigs at a trough are the engorged bodies of nine ticks. And they're bigger than the one from Frederick, too, are like grapes, or cherry tomatoes, or plums, or, or—

It doesn't matter.

All that does is that they have to come out.

Starting at the left, Tammy pulls on the first one until it pops, flooding her mouth with blood, and then the second one's torso tears away as well, and she's crying now—two hundred and twelve people!—and by the time the first of the groomsmen's fathers are able to rise from their pews, offer medical assistance, Tammy has pulled her tongue out by the root, and has started on the large tick hanging by its mouth from the back of her throat.

Standing above her, Brianne is in a kind of shock, she knows. Like this is all happening on the other side of thick, soundproof glass.

For her there's no stockings or boots or faces in the congregation.

Instead, in her lower stomach, there's just a—not a kick, but a surge of sorts. Like life, raising its wet head. From the pool boy, she knows. Out in the grass, which had to have been infested.

How could she not have remembered that?

Over the next few months of therapy and sympathy and dieting she'll try to hide it, of course, her stomach, and then, with the last application, she'll even try to kill it, but the only thing that finally works is Frederick, lunging for her in the kitchen one afternoon, trying to dig it from her swollen midsection with his teeth and his claws. It's a suicide mission for him, of course—Brianne's dad has him put down that afternoon, in a ceremony nobody attends—but it also makes things awkward for a moment in her curtained room at the hospital, when the doctor steps in with the blood results. Behind him on wheels is an ultrasound machine.

Brianne firms her lips and looks away.

When the image resolves on screen, instead of the hazy outline of a giant tick like Brianne expects, it's a baby girl.

"Just like Joy," Brianne's mom whispers, her hands in cute little grand-motherly fists under her chin, her eyes wet.

"Joy?" Brianne hears herself say, all other noise suddenly gone.

"Clarice's girl . . ." her mom says, her voice hesitant like how could Brianne not know this? "Fattest little thing you've ever seen."

Brianne breathes in deep once, twice, thinks of Tammy in her padded room, and then the doctor has the ultrasound all over her slick lower stomach, trying every angle.

The noise that was suddenly gone a moment ago was the heartbeat.

Brianne's mom stands, the stool clattering away behind her.

"What?" Brianne says.

"It's—it's . . . I'm sorry," the doctor stammers, looking at his ultrasound wand like it might really have been a knife. "It wasn't even in distress. I don't—"

Brianne smiles a sleepy smile, like she's more drugged than she is.

"It's okay," she says, "just . . . do you get it out now?"

Already she's thinking of the jeans she wore to the parking lot that last night. Because of Tammy, everybody's going to crowd around her.

The doctor focuses in on her, then on a spot beside her, Brianne is pretty sure.

"In cases like this," he says, "your body just reabsorbs the—the . . ."

Brianne's mom is already crying, though, her dad pulling her close, hiding her face in his chest.

Brianne swallows, nods, and looks up to the doctor.

"How many—" she starts, unsure how to phrase it even though it's the most obvious question in the world, "how many calories is that, do you think?"

When nobody answers she decides it must be a lot, a truly unmanageable amount, so, later that week, locked in the basement, hunched over with an art knife, she does the procedure herself, and then decides that she might just want to shorten those intestines too, maybe even loop them together front to back, so they're a closed system.

It makes so much sense that Brianne laughs a little, and then looks up when the light above her lowers to almost nothing.

It means the garage door is grinding up on its long chain. Her parents are home.

But she still has time.

"Just . . . here," she says to the assistant she can see now, in the dark. The assistant is standing beside her, holding a silver tray, her red-and-white tights inadvisable against that nurse dress, except—except she's kind of pulling it off too, no?

Brianne doesn't let herself think about that, just balances a piece of her lower intestine on the blade of the knife, deposits it on the tray with a plink, and then pushes the sharp point deeper into her stomach, her assistant leaning down over her shoulder to help, saying over and over there, and there too.

There's more fat than Brianne ever would have guessed.

Things will be better once it's all out though.

She'll be perfect then.

"There," the nurse says again, pointing to a section Brianne really should have seen, and Brianne smiles—of course—reaches down for it with the knife just as her parents' footsteps are crossing the ceiling above her, a world away.

When my kids were in strollers, I used to take them to the pet store in the mall in Lubbock, Texas, a lot. My wife worked up at the mall, so we'd kill time waiting for her by looking at bunnies and puppies. But there were these high-school girls who would sometimes show up to titter at the animals through the glass too. They didn't care about the animals though. They were flirting with the boys who hung out on the planters. How could I not write these girls' twisted story? As for the ticks, the poison—I know someone (Hi, Dad) who had a very, very bad weekend from injudiciously applying that stuff to his dogs' necks one Friday. Stuff'll seep right into you. And then you're on a bad, bad roller coaster. I should also cite this one story from Jeremy Robert Johnson's Angel Dust Apocalypse. As my end for this story is pretty much a direct steal of it, I mean.

STATE

THE FIRST TIME I saw Slowpoke take somebody down in his particular fashion, it was the second to last weekend before our senior year got officially going. I was still in two-a-days, was still puking halfway through each one and cussing Borde, who should have been there with me. He'd got special permission to start in with the team the first day of class, though, because he was going to be roughnecking all summer with one of his uncles down towards Big Lake. As far as Coach knew, Borde—that's short for "La Borde," my best friend since second grade—he was going to be on the rig until the very last Saturday before class, one day after our last two-a-day. What Coach had told him right before he left was not to get his thumbs pulled off, yeah? And then he'd mimed guiding a chain down into the hole.

Borde had turned around in the hall, kind of jogged backwards like he owned the world, and Fonzed his hands back at Coach, and then we'd exploded into summer.

This year, we were all returning, were going to make a run for Regionals, at least. Maybe all the way, if all the promises we'd made last November had been real.

Some of those promises included not drinking beer behind the Sonic and not driving our trucks through anybody's fields at night and not sneaking into the community pool after hours, with the girls, and Coach hadn't been smiling when he laid all this down, but still, right?

You can always keep a promise later, I mean.

And, if Borde did manage to come back whole, a "man" now, if everything his dad wanted to happen on the rig happened, then his tight-end hands, yeah, they might just carry us to Regionals, where the college scouts watched, clipboards in hand.

It was the dream.

I didn't need the season to be good so much, had my grades to fall back on, but if Borde had to stay around Midland, he was one of those guys you could already see his life story: he'd bounce around from rig to rig, girl to girl, truck to truck, fight to fight, and then wake up one morning thirty-five years old, a warm beer in his hand, feeling cheated. He'd become his dad, I mean, and start glaring at his own son, a resentment building in them both that would poison each dinner, each game, each everything.

It wouldn't be a bad life, don't get me wrong. But I'd known Borde since we were nine, trying to save baby birds' lives with eyedroppers, and what I wanted for him was for that nine-year-old to grow up, as stupid as that sounds.

Not that I'd ever tell him this.

His girlfriend though?

Yeah, maybe. In not so many words.

With Borde gone the summer through, he'd told me to watch out for her. I'd told him sure, watch out, quadruple quote marks, and he'd tackled me and I'd slung him around into the fence and then he was gone in his uncle's truck.

Lacy didn't need watching out for though. She hadn't known Borde since elementary—hadn't moved here from Rankin until freshman year—but she'd seen something in him, I guess. That nine-year-old maybe. And she still saw it. So, sure, she'd hit the pool at three in the morning with the rest of us, but she'd have a bikini on under her shirt too. And anyway, she was Borde's. You'd have to be a walking suicide, right? The La Bordes were known throughout Midland County for taking crowbars and pipes to people in public places, then doing their thirty days in lockup with a grin. Coach had kept Borde from this so far, but that was just because most of the cops wanted us to make it to Austin. That would all change once we graduated.

But, Slowpoke. Real name, Johnny Vasquez. He was a junior, just transferred over from Permian. Didn't play ball, just had *S L O W P O K E* airbrushed on the tailgate of his truck. And, we'd never known him before, but we knew the truck, had seen it cocked at the corner of the Odessa drag, all of us just staring as we eased past. He wasn't a football player either. As near as I could pick up over the summer, the Vasquezes were the La Bordes of Odessa, pretty much. And, though we'd never say it out loud, never admit it, you never went to Odessa alone, at night. Even if your girl'd just dumped you and you were looking for a fight, somebody to take it out on, still—not Odessa. A friend of ours, Scott, he'd been trying to clamp a heater hose back onto his Trans Am over there one night, on the way to pick up his cousin, and some Permian guys had pulled up, held him down against the hot intake manifold while they slammed his hood over and over.

Scott carries a gun under his seat now, yeah. And his dad does too. It's not going to end well. Coach has advised us to stay clear, if we can.

Yes, sir.

As for why Slowpoke had to leave Odessa, that's the mystery right there. And, none of us knowing, the reason he had to come here, to Midland, it gets worse and worse.

And, because Slowpoke didn't play football, that second-to-last weekend before school started, it was the closest I'd been to him.

The guy he was fighting was Manuel Garcia, who, because of his twin brothers Raymond and Ramone, was pretty much off-limits, untouchable. And Manuel knew it too, had probably been brushing shoulders with Slowpoke every weekend for the last two months. But Raymond and Ramone had probably always been sitting back in their low-slung Impala, watching this situation.

This weekend, though, it was just Manuel.

And I don't have any idea what really started it, but I knew what it came down to: Slowpoke and Manuel looked too much like each other, had the same grown-out hair in back, wore the same clothes, walked the same way.

I was mostly there because I'd always kind of wanted to see what Manuel could do, having grown up with Raymond and Ramone, who maybe even the La Bordes would have thought twice about jumping.

Not much, it turned out.

Manuel was big, and strong from working on cars, and knew how to wrestle his brothers off, but Slowpoke took him apart. And it wasn't pretty, not even a little. Some fights, you watch because they're exciting—exciting because you're not in them, you're not there, getting pounded, don't have to deal with the consequences.

This wasn't like that.

Slowpoke drove Manuel back into the cinder-block fence, chocked his left elbow up under Manuel's chin, and slammed his fist into Manuel's side over and over. Not wild playground swings either, but all in one place, until, when Manuel coughed, it was red, frothy.

Slowpoke nodded, and, when Manuel kind of staggered forward, Slowpoke stepped aside, as if to let him fall.

It was all part of the dance though.

When Manuel brushed past, broken in some important way inside, Slowpoke stepped in, his left boot standing halfway on Manuel's shoe, heel-on-toe.

Some girl in the crowd of us screamed then, knew somehow what was about to happen, but I didn't. Could just watch.

The reason Slowpoke was holding Manuel's foot in place like that, it was so the knee would really break when Slowpoke came down on it from the side.

Manuel folded, is going to be one of those old Mexican men with a wooden cane someday, and when Slowpoke looked up to us, to each one of us in turn it felt like, what he was asking was if we had any problems with this?

Nobody said anything.

That next morning, Borde knocked on my door. His dad had been right: "You, what, twenty-two now?" I asked, pushing his dumb ass off my porch.

Borde was brown with sun, and thicker than he had been. More raw.

"I mean, not counting the brain," I added, and he tackled me and what we were saying was hey, hello, where you been.

In the garage I stole two of my dad's beers—he knew, let it slide—and we sat in the shade and I sketched out the new defensive coach for him, all the drills and sets he was bringing in from Monahans.

Borde nodded, sipped. Watched the street, like Midland was too small for him now. After living out in an eight-by-twelve orange doghouse in a pasture with five other guys for three months, yeah. But still. I'd shagged parts in an air-conditioned truck all summer, yeah? Scraped gaskets and listened to the radio in the downtime. I knew every song this town had to offer.

"What about that sophomore, Melissa?" Borde asked then, doing his hands in front of his chest to show, and I kind of tongued my lower lip out and shrugged, and by lunch we had no choice but to leave the house, just because we'd drunk all my dad's beer, might laugh too much through our noses if my mom offered us milk and cookies.

Out at Wallace's in Greenwood, we bought more beer—my dad's brand—then just kind of coasted around town, neither of us saying how good it was. How this last week, now, it was ours, so long as Borde could keep off Coach's radar. Or even if he couldn't.

After we put the beer back, careful to make sure two were missing from the original count, we fell into our usual places in the street, spiraling the ball back and forth, going longer and longer, like a thousand Thanksgivings.

That night—because of something with his dad—Borde ate with us, and my mom announced to us all how I'd moped around all summer without my old running buddy.

"And what about Lacy?" my mom asked then, pouring us more tea.

Twenty minutes later we were gone, on the drag in the parts truck I still had the keys to. It was a mini, for the mileage, and had the stupid sticker on the door, but it had a tank I didn't have to pay to fill too.

"She know you're back yet?" I asked, and, when Borde didn't answer right away, just looking into the milling bodies at the Western Auto, I understood: we were on a spy mission.

It had been nearly three months, after all.

We followed Lacy from the Sonic to the Whataburger three times, other cars and trucks screaming past, slowing down, shirts hanging out windows, beer spilling into defrosters, but the windows of our tiny little truck were up, and dark, the air conditioner on because this gas was free.

"Uh-oh," I finally said, at a light.

We were right behind them.

"She know this truck?" Borde said.

Before I could shrug a maybe out, Christine Gentry's passenger door opened, Lacy spilled out, and Borde stepped down, right into the street, the light turning green and everything. And then they both just stood there, like waiting for the director to yell cut.

All the cars behind us were honking, of course, but Borde just smiled, that involuntary kind of smile, like he was caught, he was here, here I am, and then Lacy was shrieking across the distance between them, launching up onto him, and, because Lacy's parents were moving one of their parents into a nursing home in San Angelo all week, that was the last time I saw him for four days.

The next morning at practice, I threw up again, but was able to make it off the field this time, so nobody would slip in it.

"Well?" Coach said to me when I was done.

I pulled my helmet back down, leaned back into it.

Friday, the call came in to the shop: the guys down at the Avis needed a D40 filter, stat. That was the way Gerald always said it: "stat."

He tossed me the dusty filter and a case of belts they had on order and I was gone, the air conditioner on against the hundred and ten degrees Coach had even said was ridiculous. Not that getting lectured in the locker room about grades and behavior and life after school was any less ridiculous, but still.

When I showed up at Avis, though, Borde ambled up from the pit, tossed a broken wrench into the rag drum.

"You're not dehydrated?" I said.

"Ask her," he said back, and shouldered into me, walked out into the sun.

Neither of us were saying anything about his dad. He'd called once, on Tuesday, but my mom had managed to answer all his questions with questions, her eyes asking me more questions across the kitchen. Now Lacy's parents were probably coming back, though, meaning Borde's camping trip in her bedroom was over. She was probably already checking all the trash cans and laundry piles for rubbers.

"Davy?" I said, tilting my head down into the pit, and Borde chewed his cheek. Of course Davy. Our quarterback, learning the family business in case he tore his shoulder out some Friday night, or tweaked his elbow slinging the ball sideways like Coach was always telling him not to.

Borde leaned over, spit into a grate and wiped his mouth.

"She's different," he said. "Lacy. Somehow, I don't know."

"You just haven't seen her," I told him. "What?"

"Nothing. It's nothing. You were watching out for her, I know."

"And Melissa Stephens," I said, lifting one shoulder to punctuate it. "And Mandy Watson."

"She graduated, right?"

"Missy too," I added, having to smile to say it.

Borde looked to me, raised his eyebrows.

"The Missy?"

"One and only."

66

Borde nodded into the Avis, said, "Davy know?"

Missy was Davy's twin. We were a town of twins on every block. Something in the brown, brown water.

"Was it like, you know, was it like . . ." Borde had to lean in, whisper the next part: "Like you and Davy? You got a crush on him you need to tell me about, man?"

"Exactly," I said back, right up against Borde's ear, and he pushed me away, and, after hitting the tackle dummies all week—we'd started full pads, Monday—it gave me a gauge for how much muscle the rig had put on Borde. He'd always been bigger than me, even in second grade, but the few times we'd had to really fight each other, he'd always held back, I thought. In seventh grade in the cafeteria, everybody chanting in a circle around us, and that time in ninth, when Lacy was still the new girl.

Now, though, it would be one of those two-hit fights, and neither of them would be mine.

Not that I didn't push him back with everything I had, here.

It threw him a few steps back, right into the grille of a truck neither of us had seen ease up.

The trunk honked, just a short blast, and Borde turned around, his teeth set, hands balled, and then he smiled.

It was Coach.

He stepped down laboriously, like he was barefoot, and felt Borde's arms, looked at his head from each side then knocked on it with his middle knuckle.

"Shit," he said. "Was hoping you'd got some brains while you were gone."

Borde turned away, embarrassed, and while Coach's truck was getting serviced, he bought us barbecue sandwiches next door, and ate without talking, and then afterwards, using the sugar packets and the salt shakers, Coach laid out some of the new plays on the booth's table, and the way he would strike a Sweet'N Low forward all at once, breaking through the line into open field, we could see it too, the whole season before us. How this was the year.

We were supposed to go out that night, our second-to-last night of summer, but Coach managed to mention Borde to Lacy's dad somehow, so we wound up over there for a napkin-in-your-lap dinner, Borde editing his roughneck stories on the fly, me playing some made-up card game with Lacy's little brother, their dog barking in the backyard, Lacy's rotary-club dad shaking each of our hands when we left, looking us in the eye.

After that we just wound up at the pool with my dad's beer, but nobody even showed up, so we just sat there in the plastic chairs and listened to the pump and tossed our empties into the water, waited for them to sink.

The next night, Lacy sitting between us in the cramped parts truck—my dad still hadn't asked for the keys back, but hadn't really given me run of the truck either—we made the loop around the drag like everybody else, Borde a star now, especially with one of my white T-shirts on, so you could tell he'd worked in the sun all summer, not hid under hat brims and awnings like the rest of us.

Because the truck was a stick, I had to keep my hand down on Lacy's knee practically, but she was clamped onto Borde, and it's not like we hadn't done this a thousand million times before.

We hit the Whataburger, stopped to shoot the bull at Western Auto, made the slow U around Sonic twice, looking for a slot, then wound up in a game of catch with a Nerf football in the Furr's parking lot, Davy barking out plays, Borde rising up to snag that red-and-yellow ball out of the sky, me on the bench like always, my beer going warm in the floorboard.

"Missy?" Lacy asked me, then, from Borde's part of the seat.

I let my shoulders kind of chuckle up. Reached down for the beer I didn't want.

That fight me and Borde had had in ninth grade? Lacy hadn't not been a part of it, anyway, even if she hadn't been in the gym that afternoon.

"I told him you checked up on me every day," she said.

"Why?" I asked.

She shrugged, ashed out the window after checking to see if her dad was binoculared in on her, or maybe dressed up like a federal mail box.

"He say anything about me?" she said.

"I know about that birthmark."

She hit me with the heel of her hand, flared her eyes out.

"Who would be the male equivalent of Missy anyway?" she said, taking another long drag.

"Equivi-what?" I faked, watching Davy rainbow one up, a real Hail Mary, the kind Coach would crucify him for.

"I know, I know," she said, leaning forward, breathing smoke right into my face, looking past me where I was already looking: Davy.

I pushed her back and she grabbed my pushing hand, and we wrestled like that, my beer doing its usual spill thing, so we didn't even hear the deep growl of the Trans Am when it pulled up, nosing into the parking lot that was a football field now.

Scott cocked his door open.

Borde looked to Davy about it and they just shrugged, but then somebody from the other group of cars said something.

"What?" Scott asked, standing up.

It was Slowpoke.

He wasn't in his truck, was riding with somebody else tonight.

He stood up and up from the hood he'd been leaned against.

"I was enjoying the game," he called across in his way, where the words were kind of clipped.

Scott just stared, stared some more, his face still scarred up from his own intake manifold, and my breath kind of caught: would Slowpoke have been one of the guys crashing that hood down on him that night? Was just being from Odessa enough to make that not matter?

Yes, and yes. And it doesn't matter either.

Scott sat back down into his captain's seat, kept his left foot out the door, and gunned his Trans Am out a length farther. Chirped to a stop then just idled, his racing cam loping in place, that two-inch exhaust throaty.

Slowpoke shook his head like he couldn't believe this, and nodded to himself, stepped out onto the field as well.

"Hey, hey," Davy said then, always the quarterback, the ball back in his hands somehow.

He patted it against his other hand for attention, looking from Scott to Slowpoke, but this wasn't his game anymore.

"Just going to sit there, punk?" Slowpoke said across the field, his eyes boring through the Trans Am's windshield. "I have to drag ass all the way over there, you're not going to like it, I promise you that."

In response, Scott fired his big 455 up, buried his foot in it and dropped down into first, his other foot on those front disc brakes, so just smoke and sound welled up, like he wanted the cops here now, not later.

Slowpoke laughed, rubbed his mouth with the side of his wrist, and didn't step aside even a little. Just kept coming.

Finally Scott rose to meet him, Davy still calling something out, Borde just watching, trying to track this, almost missing the ball when Davy underhanded it over, like he was about to need both his hands, here.

But, because Davy was the quarterback, had been since elementary, none of his fights ever went all the way. Somebody always stepped in, between, wanted to save him.

It's what happened this time too. Borde snagged the ball Davy had lobbed and hooked a hand on Davy just as Davy was about to step out, try to be the peacemaker.

Davy had been counting on that, of course.

By then Scott was to the sharp front of his still-idling Trans Am, the parking lights on, and, when Slowpoke still had maybe three steps to go, Scott's arm came up, the elbow never bending.

In his hand, that pistol from under his seat.

This time, Slowpoke did stop.

He looked around to all of us, so we could each see that Scott was asking for this. That it was out of Slowpoke's hands, now.

"This really the way you want it?" he said to Scott. "Baby can't take his medicine, that it?"

Scott's lips were writhing, his chest heaving, and he was crying too, some. I could even tell from back in the crowd where me and Lacy were, her left hand digging into my right wrist, leaving a line of blue half-moons.

"Hey, hey!" Davy said then. But louder, deeper, with more authority.

And not Davy at all.

Borde.

Like this happened every day on the rig, he stepped in, palmed Scott's gun down like the legend he was already becoming, tossing it back to Davy without looking, Davy catching it with the flat parts of his hands, where there were no fingerprints.

Then Borde, with the football, pushed Scott back so he almost tripped over his car, and kept pushing him, got him all the way into the seat and reached in, dropping it into reverse. Or, trying.

Finally, Scott lit the asphalt up with his brakes and the engine growled lower, the transmission engaging, and Scott was still crying and trying to suck it in, and if I could write a check from Scott's dad to Borde, it would be for everything in the world.

When Scott backed up, the crowd kind of relaxed, looked to each other and nodded.

Except Slowpoke.

When Borde turned around, Slowpoke was right there in his face. Johnny Vasquez in the flesh.

"Woah, woah," Borde said, holding his hands up, sidestepping.

Slowpoke stepped with him, never breaking eye contact.

They were the same height, the same build. Same everything.

Borde narrowed his eyes, changed the football to his left hand.

"What?" he said.

"You," Slowpoke said.

"Me," Borde said back, smiling for the crowd, holding his arms out to the side, and Slowpoke slammed both his hands into Borde's chest.

It caught Borde unexpected, drove him back onto his ass, the ball tucked into his ribs like he'd had drilled into him.

"No," Lacy said, and I looked across to her, realized it could have been her who yelled that *No* out last weekend, for Manuel Garcia.

I creaked my head back over to Borde, the night coming at me in frames now, in pictures all stacked on top of each other, a stack I was never going to be able to climb, never going to be able to get over.

"No," I said too, and stepped forward, to the front edge of things.

Borde was the one shaking his head from side to side now. Smiling to himself.

Slowpoke just waiting for him to stand.

He did, coming to a three-point stance first to collect himself.

Lacy tried to fight past me but I held her, knew better.

Knew better for her anyway.

But I'd known since the second grade.

"La Borde!" I called out, using his full name so he'd know this was serious.

Borde looked over, his jaw already set the way I'd seen it set before in the fourth quarter, when some defensive end had had him targeted all game.

I shook my head no, my most serious no, that he didn't want to do this. That this was a mistake, and it was going to stay a mistake for the rest of his life.

Slowpoke was looking over at me too.

"Need to ask permission from your bitch?" he said to Borde, about me.

In reply, Borde tossed the football away. To nobody. To the ground.

What we needed here were cops, and dads, and coaches.

What we had was just us.

I broke from the ring of people, stepped in.

"Don't do this," I said again to Borde.

"Get back," he said to me, not breaking eye contact with Slowpoke.

Slowpoke smiled, limbered his shoulders up, did that thing with his neck that killers always do.

"Good," he said, his voice deep.

Borde nodded yes about this too, licked his lips to step in, and then, because I had to, I said it, just loud enough for him to hear: "You said she was different somehow, right?"

Every person in that parking lot looked to me. Every person in Midland, Texas.

I nodded, held my hands up, to count down: "Melissa, Mandy, Missy," I said, dropping a finger for each one. "But what comes before *M*, La Borde? They still teach that in remedial?"

Borde was just staring at me now, his hands fists.

"*L*," I spat out, smiling behind it to make it true.

Now Slowpoke looked from me to Borde, and back again.

"His woman?" he said.

"He thought," I told him, "yeah," and stepped in, right up against Borde, chest to chest. "You were right about that birthmark too."

Borde pushed me away, hard. Right into Slowpoke.

Slowpoke pushed me back into Borde, and Borde grabbed me by the shoulders, was going to slam his head into my nose, I knew—I'd seen him do it, seen the results, was ready—but then he guided me to the side, said, "I know what you're doing here."

The one fight of his my dad ever told me about, the part I never understood until now was how he said he never remembered the first punch, that he only really knew about it because he felt the shock in his hand, coming up his arm. But it's true. I know that now. You can kind of just wake up, find yourself already swinging, already committed, already putting your whole entire life square against somebody else's jaw, and praying it'll be enough.

Borde fell back, to the side a bit, but caught himself on his fingertips. Stood again.

"Thanks," he said, looking around me to Slowpoke, "but my dance card's full tonight, I think."

And then Slowpoke planted his meaty hand on my shoulder, pushed me out of the way.

"Been hearing about you," he said to Borde.

"Likewise," Borde said, turning to the side to spit, keeping his eyes on Slowpoke, random hands clamping onto me, keeping my narrow ass out of this, for my own sake, but also because they were embarrassed for me, I think. That punch, it had been the most tender, obvious thing I'd ever tried.

"No!" I screamed anyway, still fighting, my own saliva a mist in front of me, and Slowpoke reached out slow like, just one hand, and pushed Borde in the shoulder.

"Oops," he said, and Borde did that movie thing, kind of dusted his shoulder where Slowpoke had smudged it, and then he breathed in deep to swing, to kick, to head-butt, to wrestle and bite and tear, to do whatever he needed to tonight, never mind tomorrow, or the rest of his life, which was when Lacy's voice split the night.

What she said at a volume I didn't even know she had in her was "Three months!"

Borde looked over to her, then to me.

"Three months," she said again, lower. More real.

"Shit," Slowpoke said, and pushed Borde again, but Borde walked through it, his eyes narrow on Lacy.

"That's right," she said, stepping up beside me, "you were gone, what? Three months? Know how many times my mom had to go to San Angelo? Left me alone at the house? Want to take a guess?"

"No," Borde said.

"Fuck you, Derek La Borde," she said, then turned, took my face in both her hands, and kissed me long and deep, my mouth pushing her away at first but then not, then getting it. I brought my hands up to cup her head, pull her deeper into me, and, no lie, it was good. Lacy was Lacy, God.

"You wouldn't," Borde said when we were done. "This is—"

"Except that birthmark, man, it's not really shaped like a—" I started, never got to finish.

It was the night I lost two teeth, the night I still carry in three faded lines around my left eye, the night my best friend sat on my chest and pounded my face to pulp, his girlfriend hanging off his back, trying to take it all back. It was the night my mom could never understand, the night Coach just shook his head about all season, but it was also the night the Garcia Twins eased up alongside Johnny Vasquez in their primered black Impala, stepped out onto the asphalt as one person. And, sure, it was the last night Lacy and Borde were really together and good, and it was the last night for me and him as well, but when I see him now at the hardware store or at the games on Friday night, where the announcer still introduces him sometimes, the way Borde keeps his hand on his son's shoulder, trying to guide him here, or there—last Friday I saw Lacy watching him too, her second husband right beside her, still new to all this small-town stuff, and she kind of smiled and pulled her lips into her mouth at the same time, nodded once across the stands to me, and I had to turn back to the game again, focus in on these seniors, my lips just like hers.

I'd been writing a lot of horror, and I suddenly got nervous that I'd forgotten how to do it without monsters or evil. So I wrote this story right quick. And it's one of my favorites ever. I mean, it's me and my friend Randy, cruising the drag in Midland, Texas. I used to live on that drag. And I nearly died on that drag a few times. Most of the people here, they're people I used to know. And the cars and trucks are definitely cars and trucks I knew, that I raced, that I worked on. The football's all fake though. I don't know anything about football. But I've got friends who know stuff about it. Anyway, the seed of this story, I think it's one night at Sonic. I was with Randy and another friend, Teddy, and I did something stupid to make somebody in a truck mad. Nothing new. Except then this guy stood from his truck, and he just kept standing and standing and standing. Before he could wade back to me, though, I remember Teddy rushing forward, to take this for me. It was the same thing Randy'd done time and again, for no reason I could ever figure out. No, it's because we were friends. It's good to have friends. I always wanted to pay them back for saving me so many times. In this story, I tried anyway.

CAPTIVITY NARRATIVE 109

HIS NAME WAS Aiche, like the letter. And all he ever meant to do that day was drive down to Great Falls and pawn the rifle, fold the ticket in a piece of plastic and hide it in his wallet for a couple of months. But things happen. Arson. Kidnapping. Gunplay. Aiche, stuck behind an early-morning school bus in residential, his truck too tall and too red to try swinging around. So he pulls forward each time the bus does, stops when it stops, watches the mothers bowl their children out into the yard and then stand there after the bus pulls away, their robes held tight to their throats. They stand there until there's nothing else they can do, and then they go in. Aiche nods at them in turn. The third one nods back, waves as she's already turning away. Aiche takes another drink of his coffee, and then another mother waves at him, holding her hand up long at the end, her arm slowing, eyebrows coming down. Aiche resettles his cup on the dash in what could be taken as a wave back, then rubs a smudge off the blue of the rifle by his leg, because he needs to get sixty dollars out of it. Four houses down, another robed woman waves at him, and now Aiche is burrowed down into the tall collar of his coveralls. One corner and six houses later is when it happens, when it starts happening: two children—eight, eleven—rolling off their front porch, aimed for the bus, the girl leading the boy across the two snows built up in their drive, the boy leaving perfect white breaths in the air, then looking up, pulling back at his sister's arm.

They look at the tall red Ford together, then back to the porch, and Aiche looks with them, to the mother, snapping her head away now, to the bus. It's rolling back, crunching through the slush. Aiche lets off his own brake, rolls back too—careful, careful—and the girl, her mitten already lifted for the door handle on that side of the truck, shakes her head like this is a game, like Aiche is playing with her. And then she gets it, the door. The wind fills the cab, sucking the steam from the coffee on the dash. Aiche has one hand on the wheel, the other on the shifter, and before he can do anything the two children are up, in. Looking at him. The straggly black hair. The skin.

"You're not Uncle Jay," the girl says.

Aiche shakes his head no, says it—*H*—and the mistake he makes is that, instead of touching the brake to stop rolling, he touches the gas, to ease back up to where he was. But it's like there's a chain between his truck and the bus, he's been following it for so many blocks now. When it pulls away, he's behind it, trying to look through his sliding back glass at the children's mother, still there.

"You're Indian," the girl says.

Aiche nods, asks her what school they go to.

She smiles—glitter on her lips—shakes her head. "Different ones," she says.

Aiche purses his lips, nods, nods. Drinks more of the coffee than he means to, just idling down the road now, still craning back for the children's mother. When he looks back in front of him, the bus is gone. Left, right, up. Behind him, the children's mother is standing on the porch again, the phone stretched out with her. Aiche closes his eyes and lets the clutch out, for the long roll downhill. Where the bus had to be going. Because this can still work.

"Here?" he says. "This way?"

The girl shrugs.

The boy isn't saying anything. When Aiche isn't shifting, he rests his hand on the scope of the rifle. He's going to tell the pawnshop owner that the scope alone is worth one-fifty. He drinks the coffee until it's gone and still there's no school, just a convenience store, standing up out of the road.

Aiche tells the girl to stay there, starts to close the door, then comes back for the gun. Because the boy's only eight.

He hooks the strap onto his right shoulder and leans into the glass door, gets two honey buns for the children, more coffee for himself, and sets it all on the counter. The clerk surrounds it with his hands, palm down, fingers spread. Aiche looks at them, looks at them, then follows the arms up to the clerk.

The rifle.

Aiche smiles, looks out to the blond heads of the two children, just there over the line of the dash, then turns back to the clerk.

"This isn't what you think," he says.

"And those are your kids," the clerk says. "I know the drill, man. Just take it easy."

"I'm trying to," Aiche says.

He leaves two dollar bills on the counter and gets into the truck again.

The girl flattens her voice out and tells him Aiche isn't his real name. That it's just a letter, that he's probably Horace or Harry or something.

Aiche nods, backs out, nods some more.

"Where's your school?" he asks her.

She takes him there with her index finger. They pull into the parents' lane. Someone in a sports jacket at the double doors of the gym waves at him, Aiche. At the truck. Aiche looks down at the girl.

"Can't you just take him with you?" he says—the boy.

"It's not his school," she says, then shuts the door hard enough that the ice caked on the glass calves off. Aiche ducks away from the clear view the man in the blazer has to have now, pulls down along the curb, into Great Falls. For legal purposes he tells the boy in as many ways as he can that he's not kidnapping him. The boy says he knows, he's been kidnapped once already, by his dad. His voice isn't shaking.

"Your dad?"

"He's in Arizona."

"Did he take you there?"

"No. We went to a hotel and watched cartoons and then called Mom."

"You know your phone number, don't you?"

The boy nods. Aiche smiles, asks the boy how he'd like to just go home today, skip school, take an Indian holiday? The boy shrugs, looks once at Aiche and then away. "The one with the Manimals," he says.

"What?"

"The cartoon."

"Oh."

"They have guns, too."

And then the next thing happens. It's like driving into a mirror: Aiche pulls out of the parents' lane, into the school zone stretching two hundred feet in either direction, and coming at him in the road is his own tall red Ford, right down to the grill. Aiche rotates his head, watching the truck slip past.

Uncle Jay.

The only difference in the two trucks is that Uncle Jay has a red light on top of his cab, a power cable running from it into the door, down to the cigarette lighter. A volunteer fireman.

In Aiche's rearview mirror Uncle Jay slides sideways a bit, trying too hard to turn around. Aiche lets off the gas, to wait, but the truck behind him stops, and Uncle Jay steps down to lock the hubs. In his hands is another rifle.

Aiche looks over at the boy.

The boy's staring straight ahead.

Aiche tells him to put his seat belt on.

"It is," the boy says.

"Good," Aiche says, and then they're driving as fast as the roads will let them, Uncle Jay a block behind, finally spinning out in some mother's yard, Aiche already coasting farther downhill, his coffee percolating into the vents of his defroster. The boy tells him he shouldn't say bad words. Aiche agrees, says he's sorry, and then noses the truck behind the double dumpsters of a thrift store, kills it. There's nothing to say, not really. Just Aiche, coming around to open the boy's door, guiding the boy down, leading him by the hand into the store, past the staring clerks and the secondhand lingerie to the back, where he can think. They stand there while he does, and finally he nods, asks the boy if he still knows his phone number. The boy nods. The pay phone is in the hall with the restrooms. Aiche dials the number the boy recites.

"Who are you?" the mother asks.

"He's okay," Aiche says.

"You can't just do this," she says.

"I'm going to leave him . . ." Aiche says, looking around, looking around, until he doesn't know the name of the place. He closes his eyes. ". . . Can't you just tell me where his school is?" he says, and when the mother starts crying he hangs up as gently as he can.

The boy's looking at him.

Aiche smiles.

"She said to buy you something," he says, and they do, a Manimal action figure from a bin—half man, half puma, with a looped string out his back to hold him by, or hang him with, something.

As they're crossing the parking lot, the boy reaches up for Aiche's hand,

and then Aiche lights a match to the rag he cleaned the gun with last night, drops the rag in the dumpster. Because Uncle Jay is a fireman.

Four minutes later, they're back up in residential, Aiche out in the street looking for stadium lights, the kind that schools have. The picture of him that makes the paper the next morning is of him doing that, even: standing at the front of the truck, the rifle leaned across the hood, his right eye held close to the scope, his breath held in, so it won't fog up the lens.

Nothing though. Just Uncle Jay, climbing the road behind them.

Getting back into the cab for the rest of the chase, Aiche looks north, to the reservation, to Browning, still four hours away, ten minutes of that town, five of that ten residential, and, in residential, six stop signs to slide through. At the second stop sign the near collision is a pale-yellow house, because they have to make the downhill turn, and at the fourth the near collision is another red truck, Uncle Jay. The locked hubs of Uncle Jay's truck pop like gunfire as he turns wide in the rearview, rooster-tailing through a lawn.

Aiche starts smiling like it hurts.

"What's your name?" he asks the boy, but the boy doesn't answer, and over the next two miles he tells the boy everything he knows—about sneaking into Glacier with his grandfather to hunt, how they just shot an old moose who wouldn't leave them alone; about the time his best friend in junior high stood out in the road by Starr School all day once, trying to get run over, just to go somewhere else; about how his cousin Natt in Seattle only robs places with water guns, because you don't get in as much trouble if you don't have bullets; about how his plan this morning had been simple—to pawn the rifle and pay back the gas money he had to borrow to get to Great Falls in the first place; about how he thought all this land they were driving through maybe used to be Prickly Pear Valley or something, a long time ago. The boy watches the yellow grass whip by, asks if they're going to a motel room like last time, and Aiche looks out the window with him, out to where the grass is still in relation to them, a fixed point.

"You're supposed to be in school today," he says, "right?"

"Indian holiday," the boy says back, quiet.

Aiche smiles his best tragic smile, nods, and takes his right foot off the accelerator, coasting to a stop. Uncle Jay does the same, blocking the road fifty yards closer to Great Falls. Aiche tells the boy who doesn't have a name that he's sorry, and then the wood stock of the gun is in his hand.

The boy asks Aiche if he's going to turn into a wolf now.

Aiche looks at him, looks at him.

"A wolf?" he says, and then sees, gets it: Manimals, Indians.

He shrugs, looks back to Uncle Jay, says maybe, yeah.

Through Uncle Jay's scope—his rifle eased into the crotch of his door and cab—all there can be is an Indian of some kind, a nephew kidnapped at gunpoint. Motion in the cab, for too long, an action figure getting left behind on the dash, and then the door opening, the nephew on the Indian's knees, the Indian holding the rifle barrel up, its butt against hip bone.

They step down as one.

The Indian keeps the rifle well away from his body, the nephew on his other arm. He stares at Jay, says something that doesn't carry, and then sends the nephew walking over, looking back once and getting waved on for it. Whatever the Indian's saying, he says it again, and this time points, back to where a dumpster is billowing black smoke up into the sky. Like that should be enough.

Aiche. That was his whole name, like the letter.

And already, then, he was pulling away in second gear, picking the action figure off the dashboard, looping it over his rearview mirror so that it blocked the highway patrolmen converging behind him, pulling him over for Driving While Indian, more or less, but unable in the end to charge him with anything worth the ride back into town because the rifle he'd carried onto school grounds and then used on a convenience store clerk had no shells the troopers could find, shells they begged and bargained existence for, tried to dig out of ashtrays and door panels and headliners and every other possible place except for the pockets of my school jeans as I walked from one red truck to another, moving between letters, the smoke marking my return, leading me deeper into town than I ever wanted to go.

This truck in here, it's mine. A 1979 F-250 4WD, faded red. I miss that truck. I've had a whole string of '79 Fords, but this one lasted the longest. I drove my son home from the hospital in it after he was born. My daughter too, I think. Those kinds of things matter. Anyway, the reason I bought that truck? Because I love '79 Fords, sure—that body line is absolutely timeless—but more than that, it's because I was coming through Great Falls in the leftover snow one spring, and this tall Ford chugged across an intersection in front of me, and I fell in love with

*the perfect narrowness of its tires, with its rust, with its bed rails. So I went back
to Texas, found one just like it. Except red. Oh, too, this story comes from following a bus in Shallowater, Texas, one afternoon after school, and having a kid run
up to my door like he knew me. Kind of freaked me out, as I was the only one in
Shallowater with this truck. But it made me wonder what if I wasn't. I think this
story was called something else when it was first published, too. Can't remember
what now though—no, I do: "Action Figures."*

EXODUS

---

1. Annabella. Because of her my mother thinks I'm on drugs. Of course I am, but that's not the issue. The issue is that now she knows: I had to tell her even. It was better than the alternative.

2. Annabella is taller than me by one inch, has hair so dead she doesn't have to use hair spray anymore, and actually cares whether I eat or not. Her parents are never home either. Sometimes I picture them after a long day at work, lying side by side in their king size bed, hands laced over their lower stomachs, eyes fixed on the ceiling. They can't be comfortable.

3. Crabs. The Romans called them *pediculosis pubis*. Annabella gave them to me to remember her by. I didn't ask her where she got them.

4. My first sexual encounter with her ended before it began. We were at her house. I was back from the refrigerator, vaulting over her mother's cedar chest at the foot of the bed. The leading blade of the ceiling fan caught me on the bridge of the nose, and for a moment my body leveled out in the air—legs rising, head falling—and then it was just blood and my face pressed to Annabella's pale stomach, my eyes already swelling shut, both of us trying not to laugh.

5. The day I told my mother I regularly used a wide variety of drugs is the day I call the Day of the Goat. Because through the thin wall of the bathroom I

could hear the news about a goat that had gotten loose downtown, was hopping from car to car, up to the occasional diner or café to bray. The after-work crowd were running behind the cops, who were chasing the goat. It was a mob. My mother was on the other side of the door from me. I fed her names she knew from her pamphlets: marijuana; crystal meth; ecstasy; yellow jackets. She cried. In the other room my father leaned forward in his recliner (I could hear it) to see the goat better.

6. The Day of the Goat was also meatloaf night. In the weeks ahead I would think of the meatloaf we'd left on the table smothered in ketchup, with cross sections of green bell peppers draped across it, and then return to my duties: sneaking every piece of linen and every article of clothing and every scrap of cloth into the washer and boiling them, then using my old T-ball bat to transfer them to the dryer. I don't know what my mother thought was going on: drug-induced psychosis; paranoia; doing laundry for crack. Every towel in the house was folded differently. None of the curtains reached their sills anymore.

7. You can rent a SteamVac with fake identification too. It's easier than buying beer. My father opened the door on me with it, the carpet lathered, rising, and we looked at each other across the living room, and he closed the door, sat in his car until I was done.

8. Annabella told me about the crabs over the phone. They were grey unless they'd eaten, and then they were reddish brown. Lindane was the cream I needed, the shampoo. Lindane was my friend. I had to get it at the pharmacy myself, though, tucked into the cuff of my winter coat. On the way back my headlights washed over her house—Annabella's—and there on her curb was her parent's mattress, my nose blood sprayed over it. The crabs were feasting on it. It made the itching worse somehow.

9. The Day of the Goat I smelled like medicine. Like I had dandruff, or arthritis. The scent of meatloaf filled the house; I stood on the back porch and smoked the fattest joint in the history of fat joints. It was more of a cigar, really. Like a paper towel tube stuffed with one of my mother's hip euphemisms: Mary Jane; loco weed; tea. Annabella had rolled it for me. Her fingers

were like that—able to do perfect things while the rest of her fell apart. She said it was so quiet at her house, it was good to hear me talk. I told her they still weren't gone. She told me to use a comb.

10. The vision I had on the way to the table that night was Annabella and me, only Annabella was my mother. Which I know isn't my fault. We were in the living room; the sun was streaming in around the miniature shades and we were naked on the coffee table, picking nits out of each other's body hair and flicking them to the carpet. Above us the ceiling fan turned slowly, like in detective movies where the detective has to follow a clue to South America. I was so hungry.

11. My father cut the meatloaf with the big knife. It was a formal affair. Or maybe I just wasn't to be trusted with sharp objects. Maybe they knew I was stoned. One thing I noticed was that everyone kept one hand under the table while we ate. Because they itch. I excused myself to the bathroom, applied the shampoo without water. There was no lather. The bottle said the eggs of pubic lice can live six days. It hadn't even been a week, then. In the next room the news wasn't on, but still I knew about the goat somehow—bounding ahead of a teeming mass of police. I smoked the rest of the joint out the open window behind the toilet, and then exhaled down the front of my pants once, for good measure. The dog was clawing at the door, whining for me to come out.

12. In the cartoons, all the fox has to do to rid himself of parasites is find the right stick, hold his breath, then jump in the pond. The ticks and lice all gasp for air, climb towards the sunlight, perch on the stick, and then he flings it away professionally, rises light-headed on the bank; shakes, each droplet of water animated to perfection, arcing off his red body into the sky.

13. On the way back down the stairs I realized that my mother's tea was just another way to pronounce THC. I wanted to tell this to them so bad.

14. At the table the meatloaf had been done up like a ham: all in slices laying on each other. Healthy slices. Like it had been dropped into a piano. We ate without talking and I sang lyrics in my head. My father commented on my apparent thirst and I commented back on the quality of the tea. My mother

looked at him with her look. The lindane was burning a chemical hole in my jeans. I dropped my napkin six times just to adjust, and then set it on my lap, smoothed the wrinkles out like a sheet I was spreading. They were both already watching me.

15. The goat as it turned out was a visual aid gone awry. From one of the business towers. I felt sorry for it when they got it cornered on the bridge downtown, but then my father went to another station. It could have been an accident though: alone in the room, he could force his hand into his pants, his fingernails. His elbow could have just changed channels and he never even knew, his eyes rolled back to the whites, and for an unusually clear moment I realized he was terrified. That he'd brought them home. I leaned against the tile wall of the shower and smiled. My mother had her face to the space beneath the locked door and the carpet. She was reading the bible to me.

16. Because my eyes were still swollen I didn't trust them at first. And because I was stoned. It was all Annabella's fault too. The joint had been an apology. I'd held it and looked to her and then she was walking away, the wind trying to blow her stiff hair, having to go around instead. She'd said they could get in your eyebrows. That the higher the egg is up the hair shaft, the longer you've had them. Her hairs were ripe with pale eggs, follicle to split end. She was sorry. I smiled, looked at the sky in the best way I knew how, and then stroked a match head on the concrete, slow enough that it didn't catch until the end. The whole time I was watching her.

17. What happened—what I didn't believe at first—was that the crabs were finally leaving. At the dinner table. Genesis, Exodus, all that. One of them leading the rest up out of my jeans, out of the oppressive haze of lindane. He was a hero. The first thing they had to cross, though, was my white napkin. And it wasn't a neat, single-file thing. It was panic. Like the soccer game was over, the theater on fire. I looked up to my mother and laughed, and the already-downturned corners of her mouth turned down some more. Somebody's meatloaf fork clattered to the table. I had no idea what to do with the napkin either. Just to run.

18. Weeks later, the house sanitized, all my stashes off-property, lindane still

under my fingernails, I saw her again, Annabella. In the fluorescent light at the convenience store at the end of our street. Her father was idling in their car in the parking lot, a newspaper spread between him and the world. I was in line behind her. Her hair was beautiful—healthy, full, lustered: like the commercials say. I touched it, weighed it, and she straightened her back under her leather jacket, and then the hair shifted. It was a wig. I pulled my hand back, looked at it. This was the Day of the Hair of the Dog: earlier I'd chased our dog down, scrubbed the crabs off him while my father watched, beer in hand. Because I was old enough he had been telling me about how the pretty ones, how they're always broken, how that was something I was going to have to figure out, and I told him not to worry, this wasn't going to happen again. He raised his beer to me, father to son. Another successful talk. We never made eye contact.

19. In the convenience store the clerk was pretending he didn't know what was going on. That I had called my mother from the pay phone outside and made up drug after drug for her, then licked them, inhaled them, cooked them up, shot them into my arm, between my toes, the tear duct of my right eye, because I'm right-handed. The thing was that the dog was white now. Our Irish setter. You're not supposed to apply lindane in the sun; it says so right on the bottle. Later I planned to corner him with the wet-dry vac, get all the eggs off him. Because they can live six days. What I was buying at the convenience store was a pig's ear, because dogs like them. I hadn't expected Annabella though.

20. Remember me? she said, looking directly into my eyes then fast away. She was buying lip gloss and low-salt peanuts. Her boots touched each other then didn't. She had no eyebrows. My last sexual encounter with her would be on the trampoline in her backyard, three years later. Stepping off to adjust their motion-sensitive security light I would break my arm, and her father would have to hold the steering wheel with both hands and drive me to the emergency room, and standing with her in line at the convenience store I knew all this somehow, too, could see it. But my hand was already holding the side of hers. Her dry lips smiled. The lindane had burned all the hair off her body. I leaned close, closed my eyes, and said into her ear that I wanted whatever she had, it didn't matter, and her hand tightened around mine and she led me out

the door, past her father, across the parking lot, through the remains of my mother's heart, and once out of the light she leaned on me, removed her boots, her hair, and I did hesitate, yes, but it was only to take a mental snapshot before we exploded into the night like birds

21. only birds don't know what it's like to really fly, to jump into that perfect space between a downtown bridge and the wide roof of a recreational vehicle heading out of town and then just float for an impossible second, your veins shot full of drugs both imaginary and real, with names like ecstasy and love and gonorrhea and speed and apology and innocence and acid and guilt and music and peanuts and crystal and crank. But there's never any rush like the first time, a fan blade rushing towards your face. Until I caught Annabella's father watching me in the rearview the Night of the Trampoline, I never knew that either.

So fiction. All made-up. Completely just only a story. And, I wrote it specifically for 5_trope. I was scoping out their guidelines one day, and saw how they were insisting upon "No flashcard fiction." I remember leaning back from that, wondering what flashcard fiction could possibly even be? Like, blocks, paragraphs, what? Something that would fit on an index card, I guessed, and then get dealt out one card at a time. So, immediately, I sat down and wrote that. And then, as thanks to them for getting me to write it, I mailed it off to them. And they accepted it, crazily enough. Anyway, this story should be dedicated to Diane Womack. Not for reasons in the story. Just because. And, since this story, I've done a few other of what I would call list stories. It's my most natural form for a story, I think. Second person is my most natural angle, but this is my most natural form.

NOT FOR NOTHING

FOR ONE 1978 quarter, the cold rinse at the car wash cleans you up. You spray the leftover pressure in a silver mist out towards 137, then hook the dripping wand back into its rack, duck behind the car wash when a patrol car eases by, feeling the stall out with a dummy light. You close your eyes against it like that'll hide you, and, your hands balled at your sides, have to accept the real reason you let Dan Gates go at you: it wasn't because you're a good person or anything special, but because that righteous way he was feeling, you've always wanted that.

Walking back from lockup the first time—yesterday?—you've already stopped at the corner of your father's street once. His living room window was blue with television. What you did was hold your mouth in the shape of a word like *hello*, just one that somehow says everything else too.

You remember thinking, on accident, that maybe he'd even kept your old bicycle in the garage. You saw again Rory Gates, your childhood enemy, shadowboxing with his grown son on the caliche in front of Aardvark Custom Economy Storage. The way they ducked and weaved. How you had to look away.

Maybe *that's* all Dan wanted really: the shadowboxing, the reaching across with your fist, not to hurt.

You touch your ear where he tagged it, cock your head over in appreciation, and are glad this happened here, anyway, instead of at the funeral tomorrow. Not that anybody there would be likely to pull him off you. They'd probably start digging a second hole even.

Stanton, Texas, in the middle of July. The clown parade. You step out into it again, point yourself south down 137 and almost make it to the Caprock parking lot before the headlights come back.

You don't turn around this time, just stand there.

The truck, not diesel, eases up alongside.

It's Thomas.

"Your mom know you're out?" you say to him.

"Gonna rat me out?" he says back. "Where you going?"

You point with your chin.

"Liquor store's closed," he says. Then, looking closer, "What happened to you, man?"

You climb in.

He pulls away, going nowhere. On the floorboard on your side is a ratty phone book, *Martindale, James* probably in there somewhere.

You look away from it, out the side window. Ease past Dairy Treat on 80, then the elementary. "So you just wasting gas out here, or what?"

This novel is built out of moments like this excerpt. I mean, out of my memories of growing up in Stanton. Slipping into that car wash, digging for quarters because you've got a date tonight, and whoever it is, she won't want the truck to be all dusty. Except that high-powered wash, you've got so much rust that the metal starts to flake away from the bottom half of the door, and the windshield leaks onto the dash, and now you've sprayed the air filter too so the truck won't even start, and you want to ether it alive, but you always get carried away, end up with the whole engine on fire. I'm still standing in that stall, I mean. The night's still there before me. Anything can happen. Everything can happen. It usually did.

FATHER, SON, HOLY RABBIT

BY THE THIRD day they were eating snow. Years later it would come to the boy again, rush up to him at a job interview: his father spitting out pieces of seed or pine needle into his hand. Whatever had been in the snow. The boy had looked at the brown flecks in his father's palm, then up to his father, who finally nodded, put them back in his mouth, turned his face away to swallow.

Instead of sleeping, they thumped each other in the face to stay awake.

The place they'd found under the tree wasn't out of the wind, but it was dry.

They had no idea where the camp was, or how to find the truck from there, or the highway after that. They didn't even have a gun, just the knife the boy's father kept strapped to his right hip.

The first two days, the father had shrugged and told the boy not to worry, that the storm couldn't last.

The whole third day, he'd sat watching the snow fall like ash.

The boy didn't say anything, not even inside, not even a prayer. One of the times he drifted off, though, waking not to the slap of his father's fingernail on his cheek but the sound of it, there was a picture he brought up with him from sleep. A rabbit.

He told his father about it and his father nodded, pulled his lower lip into his mouth, and smiled like the boy had just told a joke.

That night they fell asleep.

This time the boy woke to his father rubbing him all over, trying to make his blood flow. The boy's father was crying, so the boy told him about the rabbit, how it wasn't even white like it should be, but brown, lost like them.

His father hugged his knees to his chest and bounced up and down, stared out at all the white past their tree.

"A rabbit?" he said.

The boy shrugged.

Sometime later that day he woke again, wasn't sure where he was at first. His father wasn't there. The boy moved his mouth up and down, didn't know what to say. Rounded off in the crust of the snow were the dragging holes his father had made, walking away. The boy put his hand in the first, then the second, then stood from the tree into the real cold. He followed the tracks until they became confused. He tried to follow them back to the tree but the light was different now. Finally he started running, falling down, getting up, his chest on fire.

His father found him sometime that night, pulled him close.

They lowered themselves under another tree.

"Where were you?" the boy asked.

"That rabbit," the father said, stroking the boy's hair down.

"You saw it?"

Instead of answering, the father just stared.

This tree wasn't as good as the last. The next morning they looked for another, and another, and stumbled onto their first one.

"Home again home again," the father said, guiding the boy under then gripping onto the back of his jacket, stopping him.

There were tracks coming up out of the dirt, onto the snow. Double tracks, like the split hoof of an elk, except bigger.

"Your rabbit," the father said.

The boy smiled.

That night his father carved their initials into the trunk of the tree with his knife. Later he broke a dead branch off, tried sharpening it. The boy watched, fascinated, hungry.

"Will it work?" he asked.

His father thumped him in the face, woke him. He asked it again, with his mouth this time.

The father shrugged. His lips were cracked, lined with blood, his beard pushing up through his skin.

"Where do you think it is right now?" he said to the boy.

"The—the rabbit?"

The father nodded.

The boy closed his eyes, turned his head, then opened his eyes again, used them to point the way he was facing. The father used his sharp stick as a cane, stood with it, and walked in that direction, folded himself into the blowing snow.

The boy knew this was going to work.

In the hours his father was gone, he studied their names in the tree. While the boy had been asleep, his father had carved the boy's mother's name into the bark as well. The boy ran the pads of his fingers over the grooves, brought the taste to his tongue.

The next thing he knew was ice. It was falling down on him in layers.

His father had returned, had collapsed into the side of the tree.

The boy rolled him in, rubbed his back and face and neck, and then saw what his father was balled around, what he'd been protecting for miles maybe: the rabbit. It was brown at the tips of its coat, the rest white.

With his knife, the father opened the rabbit in a line down the stomach, poured the meat out. It steamed.

Over it, the father looked at the son, nodded.

They scooped every bit of red out that the rabbit had, swallowed it in chunks because if they chewed they tasted what they were doing. All that was left was the skin. The father scraped it with the blade of his knife, gave those scrapings to the boy.

"Glad your mom's not here to see this," he said.

The boy smiled, wiped his mouth.

Later, he threw up in his sleep, then looked at it soaking into the loose dirt, then turned to his see if his father had seen what he'd done, how he'd betrayed him. His father was sleeping. The boy lay back down, forced the rabbit back into his mouth then angled his arm over his lips, so he wouldn't lose his food again.

The next day, no helicopters came for them, no men on horseback, following dogs, no skiers poling their way home. For a few hours around what should have been lunch, the sun shone down, but all that did was make their dry spot under the tree wet. Then the wind started again.

"Where's that stick?" the boy asked.

The father narrowed his eyes as if he hadn't thought of that. "Your rabbit," he said after a few minutes.

The boy nodded, said, almost to himself, "It'll come back."

When he looked around to his father, his father was already looking at him. Studying him.

The rabbit's skin was out in the snow, just past the tree. Buried hours ago.

The father nodded like this could maybe be true. That the rabbit would come back. Because they needed it to.

The next day he went out again, with a new stick, and came back with his lips blue, one of his legs frozen wet from stepping through some ice into a creek. No rabbit. What he said about the creek was that it was a good sign. You could usually follow water one way or another, to people.

The boy didn't ask which way.

"His name is Slaney," he said.

"The rabbit?"

The boy nodded. Slaney. Things that had names were real.

That night they slept, then woke somehow at the same time, the boy under his father's heavy, jacketed arm. They were both looking the same direction, their faces even with the crust of snow past their tree. Twenty feet out, its nose tasting the air, was Slaney.

The boy felt his father's breath deepen.

"Don't . . . don't . . ." his father said, low, then exploded over the boy, crashed off into the day without his stick even.

He came back an hour later with nothing slung over his shoulder, nothing balled against his stomach. No blood on his hands.

This time the son prayed, inside. Promised not to throw any of the meat up again. With the tip of his knife, his father carved a cartoon rabbit into the trunk of their tree. It looked like a frog with horse ears.

"Slaney," the boy said.

The father carved that in a line under the rabbit's feet, then circled the boy's mother's name over and over, until the boy thought that piece of the bark was going to come off like a plaque.

The next time the boy woke, he was already sitting up.

"What?" the father said.

The boy nodded the direction he was facing.

The father watched his eyes, nodded, then got his stick.

This time he didn't come back for nearly a day. The boy, afraid, climbed up into the tree, then higher, as high as he could, until the wind could reach him.

His father reached up with his stick, tapped him awake.

Like a football in the crook of his arm was the rabbit. It was bloody and wonderful, already cut open.

"You ate the guts," the boy said, his mouth full.

His father reached into the rabbit, came out with a long sliver of meat. The muscle that runs along the spine maybe.

The boy ate and ate and then, when they were done, trying not to throw up, he placed the rabbit skin in the same spot he'd placed the last one. The coat was just the same—white underneath, brown at the tips.

"It'll come back," he told his father.

His father rubbed the side of his face. His hand was crusted with blood.

The next day there were no walkie-talkies crackling through the woods, no four-wheelers or snowmobiles churning through the snow. And the rabbit skin was gone.

"Hungry?" the boy's father said, smiling, leaning on his stick just to stand, and the boy smiled with him.

Four hours later, his father came back with the rabbit again. He was wet to the hips this time.

"The creek?" the boy said.

"It's a good sign," the father said back.

Again, the father had fingered the guts into his mouth on the way back, left most of the stringy meat for the boy.

"Slaney," the father said, watching the boy eat.

The boy nodded, closed his eyes to swallow.

Because of his frozen pants—the creek—the father had to sit with his legs straight out. "A good sign," the boy said after the father was asleep.

The next morning his father pulled another dead branch down, so he had two sticks now, like a skier.

The boy watched him walk off into the bright snow, feeling ahead of himself with the sticks. It made him look like a ragged, four-legged animal, one long since extinct, or made only of fear and suspicion in the first place. The boy palmed some snow into his mouth and held it there until it melted.

This time his father was only gone thirty minutes. He'd had to cross the creek again. Slaney was cradled against his body.

"He was just standing there," the father said, pouring the meat out for the boy. "Like he was waiting for me."

"He knows we need him," the boy said.

One thing he no longer had to do was dab the blood off the meat before eating it. Another was swallow before chewing.

That night his father staggered out into the snow and threw up, then fell down into it. The boy pretended not to see, held his eyes closed when his father came back.

The following morning he told his father not to go out again, not today.

"But Slaney," his father said.

"I'm not hungry," the boy lied.

The day after that he was though. It was the day the storm broke. The woods were perfectly still. Birds were even moving from tree to tree again, talking to each other.

In his head, the boy told Slaney not to keep being on the other side of the creek, but he was; the boy's father came back wet to the hip again. His whole front side was bloodstained now, from hunting, and eating.

The boy scooped the meat into his mouth, watched his father try to sit in one place. Finally he couldn't, fell over on his side. The boy finished eating and curled up against him, only woke when he heard voices, like on a radio.

He sat up and the voices went away.

On the crust of snow, now, since no more had fallen, was Slaney's skin. The boy crawled out to it, studied it, wasn't sure how Slaney could be out there already, reforming, all its muscle growing back, and be here too. But maybe it only worked if you didn't watch.

The boy scooped snow onto the blood-matted coat, curled up by his father again. All that day, his father didn't wake, but he wasn't really sleeping either.

That night, when the snow was melting more, running into their dry spot under the tree, the boy saw little pads of ice out past Slaney. They were footprints, places where the snow had packed down under a boot, into a column. Now that column wasn't melting as fast as the rest.

Instead of going in a line to the creek, these tracks cut straight across.

The boy squatted over them, looked the direction they were maybe going.

When he stood, there was a tearing sound. The seat of his pants had stuck to his calf while he'd been squatting. It was blood. The boy shook his head no, fell back, pulled his pants down to see if it had come from him.

When it hadn't, he looked back to his father, then just sat in the snow again, his arms around his knees, rocking back and forth.

"Slaney, Slaney," he chanted. Not to eat him again, but just to hold him.

Sometime that night—it was clear, soundless—a flashlight found him, pinned him to the ground.

"Slaney?" he said, looking up into the yellow beam.

The man in the flannel was breathing too hard to talk into his radio the right way. He lifted the boy up, and the boy said it again: "Slaney."

"What?" the man asked.

The boy didn't say anything then.

The other men found the boy's father curled under the tree. When they cut his pants away to understand where the blood was coming from, the boy looked away, the lower lids of his eyes pushing up into his field of vision. Over the years it would come to be one of his mannerisms, a stare that might suggest thoughtfulness to a potential employer, but right then, sitting with a blanket and his first cup of coffee, waiting for a helicopter, it had just been a way of blurring the tree his father was still sleeping under.

Watching like that—both holding his breath and trying not to focus—when the boy's father finally stood, he was an unsteady smear against the evergreen. And then the boy had to look.

Somehow, using his sticks as crutches, the boy's father was walking, his head slung low between his shoulders, his sticks reaching out before him like feelers.

When he lurched out from the under the tree, the boy drew his breath in.

The father's pants were tatters now, and his legs too, where he'd been carving off the rabbit meat, stuffing it into the same skin again and again. He pulled his lower lip into his mouth, nodded once to the boy, then stuck one of his sticks into the ground before him, pulled himself towards it, then repeated the complicated process, pulling himself deeper into the woods.

"Where's he going?" one of the men asked.

The boy nodded, understood, his father retreating into the trees for the last time, having to move his legs from the hip now, like things, and the boy answered—hunting—then ran back from the helicopter forty minutes later, to dig in the snow just past their tree, but there was nothing there. Just coldness. His own numb fingers.

"What's he saying?" one of the men asked.

The boy stopped, closed his eyes, tried to hear it too, his own voice, then just let the men pull him out of the snow, into the world of houses and bank loans and, finally, job interviews. Because they were wearing gloves, though, or because it was cold and their fingers were numb too, they weren't able to pull all of him from the woods that day. Couldn't tell that an important part of him was still there, sitting under a blanket, watching his father move across the snow, the poles just extensions of his arms, the boy holding his lips tight against each other. Because it would have been a betrayal, he hadn't let himself throw up what his father had given him, not then, and not years later—seconds ago—when the man across the desk palms a handful of sunflower seeds into his mouth all at once, then holds his hand there to make sure none get away, leans forward a bit for the boy to explain what he's written for a name here on this application.

Slade?

Slake?

Slather, slavery?

What the boy does here, what he's just now realizing he should have been doing all along, is reach across, delicately thump the man's cheek, and then pretend not to see past the office, out the window, to the small brown rabbit in the flowers, watching.

Soon enough it'll be white.

The boy smiles.

Some woods, they're big enough you never find your way out.

There's two versions of this one as well. As it was in Cemetery Dance, *then how it is in* The Ones That Got Away *and* The New Black *(which are slightly different from each other as well). But, I'm working on a comic-book version of it right now as well, and, after hours and hours of scripting and rescripting and looking at my artist's thumbnails for it, I think I finally, finally, after all these years of having this story bouncing around in my head, figured out how to make the end work. But I don't think I could make it happen in prose. Only in panels. So, maybe that'll come out someday. Anyway, this story mostly comes from me being lost in the woods once while I was carrying a bloody white rabbit and, I think, a gnawed-on moose antler I'd stole from a wolf den. And there was grizzly bear scat like every fifth step, and it was supercold, it was getting dark, and my son was born then but not old enough to come hunting with me yet. But still. You take your kids with you, don't you? You try to find the edge of those big woods, because that's how you get back to your kids. I keep myself warm with stories, I think. This one's always kept me good and warm.*

CARBON

AND THE DRUGS me and Casey did.

I mean goddamn.

All the usual stuff, yeah, but there was the Freon cold in our heads, the aerosol fertilizer staining our faces lawn green, the moonshine shit we drank that time in the dark when we couldn't even tell what color the flame burnt. Blue or yellow, it didn't matter. We were already blind. It was like we were running from one pool of mercury to the next in some old Chinese picture book, nobody chasing us. Only us.

We were skinny too, bone thin. Casey a joke of a girl, only one period in eight months, her eyes black and snake flat in the low times, waiting.

But when we weren't waiting. When we were awake four days straight and our hands shook around our cigarettes and the sun came up and made a day for us, for the two of us. Sometimes she'd look at me and my teeth would be chattering around my sawed-off filter and she'd tilt her head back and laugh a little, breathing out her nose, and I'd know that there was nothing else in the world except for her and me.

Her and me.

A man walks into a bar. This is not a joke. I was there.

A man walks into a bar, nothing under one arm, nothing in the other. Just a need. The skin and bones girl, she can see it in the hollows of his eyes, his need. She has a bottle before her, before everything. It's what she does, the only thing. Him and her and the bottle make three, and they sit there through the morning hours and he smiles when she says she's sleepy. He smiles and comes back from the bathroom with three blue pills in his hand. They swim seedlike through the white contents of the bottle, and when the white is gone the blue remains on the glass neck, the threaded lip, and when she smiles, afraid her heart is going to explode, her teeth are watery blue and he takes her.

Just like that.

By the hand. They walk out of the bar and she wants a bed, a couch, a car, a corner dark enough for the two of them to forget each other, but he just kisses her. He tells her that's not what this blue is about. It's something softer. Feel it. Soon they find themselves down where the tall grass meets the sky. They laugh and he tells her all the money he has in the world wouldn't buy them bus fare to Wisconsin even.

"Wisconsin?" she says, "I don't want to go there anyway," and when they wake they're holding hands and he leads her wherever he goes.

It was a waiting time, flat black, then the waiting was over, but we knew it would come again. We were right at the end of what felt like five days, looking over into a dry sixth and a hurting seventh. Casey asked me about the bible.

"What did God make on the fifth day anyway?"

I looked around. We were in a grey-tiled garage with a golden eagle Trans Am and on the back wall a huge black velvet painting, a bleached white tiger caught there somehow. Animals all around us. It was nobody's house we knew. They didn't care if the purple holes under our fingernails dripped blood on the concrete, if we wrote our names on the silvery dash of the Trans Am, if we started the car and let it idle all around us like the sonorous thunder of creation.

"On the fifth day . . ." I said minutes after and too late, but couldn't think of anything except the sixth, tomorrow. We were going dry. This was it, again. Casey knew. When we were both in the car she said she could feel it coming already, the waiting. She looked up at me and her eyes were glossy black and going flat. She said she wished tonight was the last night of all, and I stared until I knew she was serious, until I wasn't afraid.

She held my hand up at dash level for me and the watery blood from under my fingernail traced the lines of my hand. She followed one with her fingernail.

"That's your life line," she said, that last word sculpted from the carbon monoxide staining my vision a sable veldt.

Life
line. And I'm not sure what became of her finger.

Imagine the shadow of a bleached white tiger and lose yourself somewhere in
it. Not the shadow, but the looking. It's distance is what it is, the spaces between whatever you are and whatever lack of light there is on the ground,
feeling inexorably up one blade of grass and then the next, like a sunrise in
negative, developing softly, the smell of chemicals all around, the tail moving
slowly back and forth. Watch it and feel it, smell it, and when the tiger leaps
silently over the golden-lined hoodbird for you as it must, try if you can to
remember those spaces, the distance between you and it, the tiger, how it can
never reach you because it's chained down to each velvety blade of savanna
grass, and each individual blade must bend before you'll ever feel the hard
ivory of its mouth.

Sometimes you can even slip into those spaces, find the door and hide.

Don't be fooled though.

Things have been killing each other long before you were born.

It was the tiger that got us. Its eyes pooled silver and deep, the standing-up
hair on its back white, not from birth or breeding but from age, from the
weight of eons of light.

It just came through the blue smoke for us and all we could do was smile,
it moved so slow.

Yes, Casey was dying.

The story. Her dad wanted to hear it over and over, every night at dinner while
she was in the back breathing heavy oxygen in the room where they tell me
she grew up alone. He'd point his chicken leg across the table at me (this is the
same guy Casey told me felt her up at her eleventh birthday) and I'd swallow
and then I'd tell him about her hair, how when I woke in the Trans Am, my
shirt wet with whatever I had eaten last, I could still smell the tiger musty and
heavy all around.

"I've smelled her myself," Casey's father would say, the tiger, and I'd ignore
whatever he was really saying and keep going, getting to her hair but not listening to myself anymore. He knew the story. Instead I'd be half in the dream
I'd had every night sleeping on his once-plaid couch, about Casey as a little

girl, her hair more red than the strawberry it was now, more alive. In the dream all she did was stand there, looking pretty much the same, her arms by her side. I told myself she was waiting for me, waiting to know what to do.

For her dad her hair was where the story ended. When I got to the part where it was morning and the Trans Am bird was back in the hood, he'd start smiling, and then I'd say it, draw in his mind a picture of how the only way I knew something was wrong was that Casey's almost-red hair looked all wrong strung across her lips, which were pale blue like the middle pages of a phone book. He'd smile and lean across the table and bury his index finger in my chest, and with his chicken breath he'd say she was damn lucky he gave her that red hair, wasn't she?

He was a big man.

Every time I said yes.

But that's not where the story ends. That's only where he quits listening.

At the hospital that morning when I was bringing Casey stolen mints to line her bleeding gums with, she went into some close-eyed sort of seizure thing and they took her down for more tests, all the tests, and they told me before they told her. The results. By bad luck they'd found deep in her bones a thing that was killing her, hollowing her out from the inside.

"But she's okay," I argued. "She just breathed some exhaust."

They shook their heads together no and then said yes: "It *was* the toxic levels of carbon monoxide in her blood (among other toxins) that got us looking, yes—and maybe that was a strange blessing of some sort?—but the fact is that those same tests found the thing that was killing her. We're sorry. At least now she can be . . . treated. More comfortable. You know."

An intern hung around after the big guns were gone. He gave me a cup of Styrofoamed coffee. He told me he didn't really want to be a doctor, and I told him I wished Casey and me had died the night before. He stared. He tried to say something, tried to get me to imagine a world where me and Casey were Pacific great white sharks and this thing couldn't touch us, but I looked at him and made him know that the blind hunger would remain, if nothing else, and that would still kill us. He didn't say anything more, and pretty soon the coffee was gone and I was alone.

After a while I started hanging out in the back bedroom with Casey, hiding from her dad and his football, watching Jeopardy and Love Connection and holding her head up while she drank, trying to get her to forget what that charcoal stuff in the emergency room tasted like when it was pumped from her stomach. It was a good time. It was like we were a unit of some kind, standing there in our last holdout, against the world. But her eyes. She was waiting. She'd found that she could breathe fast in her oxygen mask and hyperventilate. It only lasted a few seconds, a minute at most, but it was something.

They'd stopped the pain pills some time back, doctor's orders.

But we found ways.

The rain. That's what she said she needed, and so that's what I got her. Out on the lawn with her dad, him naked to the waist and hairy red all over. Out on the lawn with me sitting on the porch with my thumb over the nozzle and the hose water arcing up as high as the roof and falling down on them, no rainbows. An Irish song. When she came over she called me the Opposable Thumb of God and I smiled, and then two nights later we were in an alley talking to a friend about the price of gold, and whether we had any credit left. As always, we were shit out of luck, and as always, we found ourselves hours later floating on something, we didn't care what.

"Am I going to die too?" I asked her, and she showed me her lawn-green teeth and said not if she could help it, no, it's not a catching thing.

"Death?" I asked her, thinking of how my family fell dead like dominoes after my dad left us his illegible note, and she laughed and said what else?

That night we slept in the bathroom of a hardware store with quart cans of paint opened all around us, glue on the walls, and we dreamt of living in the radio songs low on the dial, with a two-car garage, kids, a station wagon, everything, everything normal.

We woke and her hair was stuck to the floor, but it came out without even pulling, and we left it there in remembrance of her, of us.

The bald man in the waiting room is praying and praying hard, so that when I close my eyes I see angels up in heaven singing to God with everything they have, singing until their throats bleed and still they sing, afraid of ever stopping.

I can almost hear them. We all almost can, there in the waiting room, Casey getting bombarded somewhere beyond the lead-lined doors, trying not to scream anymore. We know about radiation now, me and her. In the past three months we've read every last one of her little brother's Incredible Hulk comic books. We know what the radiation can do, and what it can't.

The praying man takes my hand in his and looks into my eyes for a long time, asks me who I'm waiting for, is it somebody dear?

I nod.

"The first time you saw her, do you remember that?" and I say that I do, I remember: "She was working on a bottle and I showed her something else. Something in blue."

"When did she find out?" he asks, and I know he's talking about the disease. I look past him hanging on my next word and see a cowboy sitting quiet in the corner, acoustically positioned so that all conversation in the room will funnel towards him and be collected by the large dish of his hat. I know he's listening. It's like I'm talking to him, right to him.

And so I confess. I tell him that in a way *I* told her she was dying, that if anybody's killed her it's me, I'm the killer here, dammit, she never had to know, and then I stand and someone tries to pull me down but I'm mad, getting stronger, walking, following my voice to Him.

"What?" I yell at Him, the Listener with the Cowboy Hat, because I know he's God. What? And the next thing I know my sin is an anvil black in my chest and somebody is holding me facedown in the bathroom and I'm crying, and before I leave I've been down on one knee for some time, praying with the praying man, praying for God to go back to Texas and leave me and Casey the hell alone, please, just stay away. Look somewhere else.

Three on a bridge, and the water it is cold, yes, but this isn't a joke either.

The man is pushing the girl in the wheelchair and the disease—dis-*ease* as she calls it—rides for free, taking what it wants here in the land beyond symbiosis. The water below laps hungrily at the support posts. Somewhere far above a silver plane hangs suspended. In the middle is this bridge, and it's moving with the world around and around and it doesn't care.

The man parks the girl where she can see over the rail to where the sun will go down. He spits over the edge and it falls end over end into the water. He watches the spit merge and imagines himself doing this once a day every day, until the water rises and swallows him and takes him away, back to his childhood, so he can start over. Maybe back to when he met her, so he can crawl out that bathroom window and never know what they can be together.

Two people on a bridge, the third in its daily remission. None of them are thinking of jumping. There are much easier ways. They both know them all, weigh them in grams, balance them in the empty parts of spoons.

When they leave this bridge the wheelchair will float by its cushion in the running water and then be gone. Two weeks from now the nurse at the front desk of the Place will call looking for them but they'll be gone, *lost*, her dad will say, *regressed*, some sort of remission, probably dead by now. Four months from now she'll be a side story in a tabloid in the grocery store, and people will say she's a miracle, search for her everywhere; she will have forged an unholy alliance with heroin, one that's a deeper green than radiation, stronger. Forty-seven people will die with needles in their arms, most of them senior citizens. Right now though, they hold hands, him and her.

He tells her he's so sorry about all this, it didn't have to happen, and she says, "Who are we to say? I never thought of growing old anyways, you know. People don't last forever."

"Not by theirselves, they don't," he says, acting like he's in a movie too (they both want the happy ending), and pulls her up to hug him. For a moment there's one person on the bridge there in the middle of everything, no shadows, no spaces, nothing between.

A man in a cowboy hat sees them from across town and doesn't cry or smile. He just tells the cab driver to drive, drive, man, anywhere.

Time passes, builds up behind us like a dust cloud. I save my nosebleeds in a cup because I'm afraid of the finality of dying. I imagine giving Casey my kidney, my lung, my heart, becoming her, taking her place. Me and her. We lie. We steal. We cheat. Anything to achieve the height we need, to maintain it. We feel guilty for beating a man so we trade for weak cocaine that makes us sick, and we call it justice.

We laugh. All the drugs we did because we were afraid of each other. It's a joke.

Everything.

Like that time we had the Freon and our synaptic pathways were so icy slick there was zero resistance for the current of thought and everything was happening in a silent montage, I remember Casey finger-drawing on a table and whispering to me like it was secret that we were the Kite People, that we weren't supposed to ever come down, that we were together up here forever, in the sky-blue clouds with the silver mercury lining, up here where nothing could touch us.

I think it was love.

My nose blood in the cup has been trying to coagulate into a scab lately, and when it finally does I'm going to leave it in a tide pool somewhere (wherever the oceans are), so at least some of me can have another chance.

Tigers should run so fast.

My favorite story I've ever written, by far. By miles. By leagues. By orders of magnitude. Closest I've come to it again is The Bird is Gone, *I think. Maybe "Venison." But this is more direct. And it's very post–*Big Lebowski, *for me. Or, I was still very impressed with* Big Lebowski *when I wrote this one anyway. That's Sam Elliot with the radio-dish cowboy hat. When this was first published in* Blood & Aphorisms, *too, I was spelling "tiger" with the "y," like Blake did. Or like I thought he did, I don't know. I only knew Blake through Thomas Harris, I think. I still prefer that spelling too. But, when some editor came at me asking what's up with this antique spelling, my only defense was that it felt right, it felt perfect. It felt like the only way it could be. And that's never good enough, I don't suppose.*

TO RUN WITHOUT FALLING

WE CAME UP out of the streets like we'd slept there all day, the underbellies of delivery vans and police cruisers passing silent, huge, and black through our field of vision. Our joints pounded with it still. When we looked back the sewers were exhaling steam, and it was rising, so we leaned into the night and ran, the slap of our feet filling the empty spaces around us until it all fell behind and we were there again: the handicapped park, its gentle yellow slide arching up nearly as high as the rocket. Josh rolled over the tall fence in stages, leaving part of the skin of his hand in the chain link, and Mike perched on top, pulling me up after him, and Tim was already there somehow, riding the metal duck into oblivion, his forehead kissing the gravel each time he leaned the spring forward, his mother's prayers the only thing keeping him alive.

Another Friday night.

We huddled in the nose of the rocket and passed a joint counterclockwise, and then Tim's bottle, and when Josh couldn't remember if the guy had said to never take more than two or always take at least two, we swallowed three yellow pills each. It was better living through chemicals. It was something at least. We were fourteen. In the silence after the rush, the gravity acceleration of the rocket pushing our faces into the steel floor as we shuddered towards escape velocity, I saw Josh seeing what he always said he saw: the men of the cocktail party retiring to the porch after dinner to pass the needle, the ladies gossiping into the drawing room with their marijuana cigarettes and snifters of vodka. We were the gentlemen. Josh didn't know none of this would last. I saw what I saw even without the chemicals: a kite's-eye view of a boy as he runs across a backyard, melting over fence after fence, whatever it takes to keep the kite aloft. Mike just stared through the bars of the rocket into the unforgiving irises of the great metal duck. He was the oldest of us. When Tim raised his head to track down Mike's line of sight his glass eye stayed behind, gummed to the floor, some second grader's saliva reactivating long after his bedtime.

We left the eye. Tim didn't care.

"It's all fun and games," Josh said in his adult voice, leading us down the switchback ramp, back to earth, "until Tim's goddamn eye falls out."

He pushed Tim in jest and Tim fell in earnest, took the rest of us with him, end over end.

Later, dawn already a smell, we would become magnetic ghosts of ourselves on a security tape as we floated up one aisle of a convenience store and down another, touching the gauze and the disinfectant with sticky fingers, professionally gauging the distance from pharmaceuticals to the front door, the parking lot, our passenger curled in the backseat. It would be too late for first aid, though, and we would be large and obvious in the convex mirror anyway, gravel still in the cuffs of our pants from here, from the dipping action of the wheelchair seesaws we used as catapults, seesaws greased so quiet that we had to make up for it by screaming our presence, that we existed. Our voices didn't come back to us, but for one perfect moment Mike ran after his, down the full length of the balance bar, his arms out like wings. The deserted park was his, then and maybe forever, but the bar was only twelve feet long, and there I was at the end of it. He slammed headfirst into my gut, the vertebrae piling up in the back of his neck.

We rolled through the gravel to the merry-go-round, and the three of them pushed me on it faster and faster until the green beans I'd swallowed whole at dinner became the reaching arms of a spiral galaxy, the delicate tips trailing behind, the rest whipping ponderously ahead, around and around. It turned me inside out. Tim's chin split like a plum when he dove to the ground to avoid the pale-green plane of vomit, and when he lay sideways on the special swings, Josh could move the red cut like a little mouth. We made a puppet show. We crept to the nose of the rocket to check on Tim's eye, and it was still there, the grey strands of gum attached to its back side like a mass of optic nerves, and his chin said something to it none of us could understand.

On the way down—back to earth—Josh looked around as if just waking and said *my brother*, but then couldn't take it any further. We knew which direction he'd been going though: this was his brother's park. How we'd found it. Just now was the closest he'd ever come to talking about it to anyone but me.

"I had become as one bored with television," he said then, louder, correcting himself in deep falsetto, leading us down the wheelchair ramp a second time, "and was as yet too young to properly appreciate AM radio, so I entertained myself with various and sundry substances of foreign manufacture."

"Emphasis on the *sundry*," Mike said, flashing the yellow husk of one of the pills on the blunt tip of his tongue, and by the time Josh turned to push him in the chest Mike was already in motion, racing for the swings. We all chased him there, got belly down on them and absolutely flew, the chains slack each time we rose, until Mike lost it and caught his heels on the downswing. It flipped him up, the plastic seat suddenly at his armpits, his eyes cartoon-size, and then he flopped back, hard and awkward. Because Tim's dad was a doctor, he held Mike's head in his lap and pulled the gravel out, and we gave him the last of the bottle then threw it shattering into the monkey bars, where we didn't go anymore. Now we wouldn't go on the swings, either, probably. Maybe.

Somewhere in the city below us a dry-cleaning van and a police cruiser were passing going opposite ways, eyeing each other across the dividing line and nodding acknowledgment, that yes, they always see each other here, now, like this, their headlights only showing where they're about to go, never any farther. "Don't watch too long," Tim said, his hand on my shoulder, and I nodded: soon enough it would be us in the dry-cleaning van, keeping it in second gear, a delivery schedule on the clipboard on the dash, all neat and proper, the starched-stiff uniforms swaying behind us like husks of what we used to be, what we are now.

"Space suits," I said, in wonder, a rocket-shaped swath of stars missing behind us, looming black over our shoulders, and then Josh kicked at a moth and his boot went end over end off his foot, and just before it disappeared a bat or a bird or some flying thing slammed into it beakfirst. They fell together, at the same rate, and then our boots rained down out of the sky, trying to get some repeat action, but there wasn't any. Just us, laughing, waiting, holding our breath. Even Mike, the back of his hair matted with blood. We didn't walk the same afterwards, would spend thirty minutes in the car with masking tape even, drawing stripes onto our black socks so they'd look enough like shoes for the convenience store, where there was a sign about proper footwear. They wouldn't have tread, though, so when we had to run we'd spin out instead, taking shelves and shelves of dry goods down with us, never making it back to the parking lot.

Because the gravel hurt Tim's feet he climbed onto one of the special swings and said he needed a wheelchair for this one, and Josh shook his head no, told him not to say that, not to ever say that. It almost turned into a fight except for me, throwing myself down the yellow slide in distraction, the second hump releasing me from gravity.

Josh smiled one side of his face in appreciation, seeing us at forty remembering this maybe, looking fondly up this hill at ourselves, and he had just locked his elbow to push his hand deeper into his pocket for a pack of cigarettes when a pale beam of light fell across the playground, the broken glass from our bottle glittering. At the top of the beam was a flashlight in a hand, the hand attached to an arm, the arm cradled around a boy or girl, it was hard to tell. Skinny, though, and twisted at the hips. Our age.

The father kept the light low enough that we could see in his other hand the special key, the one he needed because they couldn't go over the fence, and it had been a bad night for them, whatever was happening. And now there was us.

Josh was our talker, so he stepped forward, the gravel crunching under his socks. He didn't know what to do with his hands though, his shoulders, any of it. He said something like *sorry*, something like *sir*, but from my place at the spooned-out bottom of the slide, it didn't matter: the man—the father—was still trying to place us, imagine that we could exist in the same world as his child. That there were people who threw it all away. Nothing Josh could have said would have helped. We stood still to not show off how we could move like deer when we needed to, flit off into the night on our straight hips, and finally the man turned the flashlight off, showing us how dark it was, and then deliberately locked the gate behind him, and I could see Tim already couldn't wait for the convenience store, getting caught, paying for all this somehow, but that was still hours away, and it was Friday night, so we tried to play some more, pretend nothing had happened. We leaned back far enough in the normal swings that our hair dragged the earth. We rode the wheelchair seesaw in weak imitation of ourselves. Soon enough Mike climbed onto his metal duck and I spiraled up the rocket to wait for morning, for the warm asphalt to embrace me, obliterate me, the traffic pounding up and down the length of my body. Tim was already there somehow, too, watching his glass eye, not yet touching it. We split the last pill, wasting most of the powder, then touched fists like we'd seen them do in the movies, and then watched as Josh materialized behind Mike and the metal duck, pushing him like they were children, like they belonged here or could have, but then harder, like they were who they were, until Josh was crying without sound and Mike's face was red with gravel, the blood from his mouth slinging up after him, trying to get back in.

"Let go," I whispered to him through the bars, "please," but Tim, who always took care of us, wrapped his hand around my wrist in a way I'd never let anybody else see, and I could feel it rising, the certainty that the man with the special key had locked a part of us in here, and Tim in his way knew it too, so we stood together into the cone of the rocket, as high as we could get, plate steel all around, where we couldn't see anything anymore, just Tim's eye at our feet, staring out across the city. No kites, no sirens, just our bones creaking as we grew into the men we never thought we'd be, chasing our children across the slick grass of April, the fences melting out of the way, the neighborhood playground yawning before us too soon, the bright new equipment hulking in its bed of gravel. Last Friday I saw Josh there. With his son, over in the corner, on the purple dinosaur bolted to the car spring. He had one hand on his son, the other on the burnished steel head of the dinosaur as it rocked back and forth, barely moving. I don't know what his son's name is, but I know what Josh was calling him. We pretended not to recognize each other, that our eyes were just painted on, but then on the seesaw with my own son gravity called in its marker, pulled me back to earth too hard, my son almost catapulting up into the blackness of space.

"Do it again," he said when it was over, his hair resettling strand by strand, and I saw what I always see: the automatic door of the convenience store opening for us as we ran, our shirts full of medicine and candy, each of our sons curled in the backseat of the car waiting for us.

This is me and my friends in Midland, Texas, at seventeen or so. I was living in town for a bit, and there was this cops and robbers game everybody was playing, which works about like you'd suspect, just with about fifty or sixty kids, some in cars, some on foot. We were on foot this night, and we won, but it was that kind of win where nobody knows you won, they just think you quit playing. My friend Steve got on this spring-loaded cartoon animal to ride it, and I'll never forget him slapping his head forward into the gravel over and over. Or maybe that was me. I honestly don't know. There was blood anyway. Lots and lots of blood. And then there was a father there at the proper gate, with his son. And there was us, standing as one, giving him the playground back. We didn't win that night, now that I think about it.

DISCOVERING AMERICA

BECAUSE I'M INDIAN in Tallahassee, Florida, the girl behind the counter feels compelled to pull the leather strap ($1.19 per foot) around her neck, show me her medicine pouch, how authentic it is. "Yeah," I say, "hmm," and don't tell her about the one-act play I'm writing, about this Indian in the gift shop at the bottom of Carlsbad Caverns. His name isn't Curio but that's what the lady calls him when she sighs into line with her Germanic accent and her Karl May childhood. "You should do a rain dance or something," she tells him, she's never seen heat like this, like New Mexico. In the play she's sweating, he's sweating, and there's uncounted tons of rock above them, all this pressure.

In Tallahassee it rained all the time.

I stayed there for eleven months, nineteen days, and six hours.

Because I'm Indian at a party in Little Rock, Arkansas, a group of students approaches me out of a back room of the house, ceremony still thick on their breath. In a shy voice their leader asks me what kind of animal my spirit helper is, and when I can't quite get enough tact into my mouth to answer, they make a show of respect, say they understand if I can't tell them, really. They tell me theirs though: a grasshopper, a dragonfly, three wolves, and somewhere in there I become that tall, silent Indian in Thomas Pynchon's "Mortality and Mercy in Vienna," right before he goes cannibalistic in the middle of an otherwise happening party. The working title of the play I'm still writing is *The Time That Indian Started Killing Everybody*, and standing there with my beer I don't revise it.

In Little Rock there were all kinds of bugs I hadn't seen before.

I stayed there for five months, four days, and twenty-two hours.

Because I'm Indian in Odessa, Texas, the guy who picks me up off the side of the road asks me what kind. He's an oil-field worker. His dashboard is black with it. When I say *Blackfeet* he finishes for me with *Montana*, says yeah, he drilled up there for a while. Cold as hell. "Yeah," I say, thinking this is going to be an all right ride. He drives and tells me how when he was up there he used to ride a helicopter to the rig every morning, it was that cold. In trade I tell him how the National Guard had to airlift hay and supplies a couple of winters back. He nods as if this is all coming back to him, and then, with both arms draped over the wheel real casual, asks me if they still run over Indians up there? I turn to him and he explains the sport, even hangs a tire into the ditch to show me how it's done.

In Odessa the butane pumps go all night, and it's hard to sleep.

I stayed there for three months, fourteen days, and fourteen hours.

Because I'm Indian the guys at the warehouse in Clovis, New Mexico, add a single feather to the happy face that's been carved into the back of my locker ever since I got there. It's not like looking in a mirror. Every time it's not like looking in a mirror. My second week there we're sweeping rat droppings into huge piles, and when I lean over one to see what Butch is pointing at he slams his broom down, drives it all into my face. That weekend I start coughing it all up, become sure it's the hantavirus that's been killing Indians all over. My whole check goes into the pay phone, calling everyone, talking to them one last time, reading them my play, the part where Curio kills one of the gift-shop people the old way, which means he hits him across the face with a log of Copenhagen, then follows him down to finish it, out of mercy.

In Clovis they don't turn their trucks off so you can talk on the phone, so you have to scream.

I stayed there for four weeks, one day, and two and a half hours.

Because I'm Indian in Carlsbad, New Mexico, the crew I'm working with calls me Chief, motions me over every time there's another animal track in the dirt. "I don't know," I tell them about the tracks, even though I do, and for a couple of hours we work in silence, up one row, down another. Once I find strange

114

and cartoonish tracks in my row—traced with the sharp corner of a hoe—but I pretend to miss them, pretend no one's watching me miss them. All this pretending. Towards the end of the day I pass one of the crew and, without looking up, he asks if I've scalped anybody today, Chief? I unplant a weed from his row, look up for the briefest moment, long enough to say it: "Nobody you know." He doesn't laugh, and neither do I, and then later that night in a gas station I finish the play I started writing in Florida. It starts when the clerk wipes the sweat from his forehead, says how damn hot it is. And dry. I neither nod nor don't nod, just wait for him to say it.

In Carlsbad, New Mexico, the law is sluggish, slow to respond.

I stay there for sixteen hours, nine minutes, and fifty-two seconds, and when the rain comes it's not because I danced it up, but because I brought it with me.

Except for the very last section, this is all what happened, like, word for word, breath for breath. This is me, working my way back to West Texas, from Florida. New Mexico's a bit out of order, but I spent a lot of time working the fields there. And I've spent a lot of time getting rides out on the highway. And some of those rides, I wish I'd just kept walking. When I read this one out loud, I never say that early parenthetical, either, though for me it's always very core to the proceedings. And I never say "Karl May" with the right bitterness, either, I don't think. This one was first published as "Life in These United States." I wrote it right after writing this long e-mail to my then classmate Adam, about how I was going to write this essay about being Indian, how it was going to be perfect. And this e-mail, man, it had to be longer than whatever essay I was thinking I was going to write. Adam came back with something like, "Well, write this, then." So I think I sat down to try. But I don't know how to do essays. Only stories. They don't have to be lies though. I figured this out early.

THE GOSPEL OF Z

(excerpt)

CHAPTER FOURTEEN

Fifteen feet from the jeep that wasn't really for him, Jory stopped. The driver. It was the same guy from the training session. The guy who'd been cocked up against the back wall, punctuating Voss's walk-through with sneers. The distant chuckler, up close now.

"You," Jory said.

"Me," the driver said back, burning the clutch a bit to show they needed to be gone.

Jory kept his eyes on the ground in front of him, then on the side of the jeep, then on the dashboard.

"Mayner," the driver said, offering his hand.

"Jory Gray," Jory said, not taking the hand. "No need to commit it to memory, right?" "Think I picked this job?" Mayner said back.

"Said the ferryman."

"This is your first call, right?" Mayner said, and backed them up, jerked them forward, onto the road that led to the gate.

"Don't give up, do you?" Jory said, holding on to the dash.

"Yeah, *I'm* the stubborn one," Mayner said back, taking the first curve too fast. "Everybody's new in there," Jory said. "J Barracks. Attack of the rookies."

"That a question or an answer?"

"Observation."

117

"*J* is for ghost . . ." Mayner nodded, anticipating Jory's next line. "Last week's been"—his signature chuckle—" unfortunate."

"For torches."

"For humanity."

"Humanity?"

"Reason you had your pick of the beds in there's that everybody got coded, the last few days. The dead aren't staying dead anymore. Even less than usual, I mean. Like a whole 'nother wave." Another turn, another near-death experience. "Bonefaces are even making some special robe to protect themselves, I hear."

"From the dead?"

"From us. From you. From getting coded."

Mayner rested his forearms on the top of the steering wheel, mimed a small explosion over his instrument cluster.

"Have to believe in a robe pretty hard for it to protect you in a firestorm," Jory said, turning to watch base slip past.

"Got to have faith, faith, faith."

"I don't even have a key."

"Key?"

"For a footlocker. They never issued me one."

"You bring something valuable? What?"

Jory touched the small pocket Linse's ID was stashed in.

"What were you?" Mayner said, braking hard for the gate. "Before?"

"Does it matter?" Jory said, his hand on the fold-down windshield now. He turned, studied Mayner. "What were you?" he asked.

Mayner saluted their way through the gate, said, "So you know how to use the torch, right?"

"Feels like a funeral, doesn't it?" Jory said back.

"Funerals have this?" Mayner said, and popped the glove compartment, a tangle of wires and circuits, a chrome disc spinning in there, its skeletonized player resting on a bag of sand. Some kind of pop music lilting out at them. A girl, maybe sixteen, trying to reach into her soul, pull out a hit.

Jory couldn't help but smile.

It was his first call.

Like Jory had been told to expect, their destination was deep in one of the restricted zones. The places that hadn't been cleared yet. Nowhere you'd want to be after dark.

A derelict public restroom, the landscape around it so reduced that Jory couldn't tell if this had been a park, a rest stop, or what. The only reason the restroom was still standing was that it had been built like a bomb shelter. Even so, it was creaky, tilting, had a year left, two at the outside.

Lined all along its roof, and high-stepping it on the ground like old men with delicate feet, were the pharaoh vultures that had shown up again not long after the plague. Before, there'd been rumors of maybe three breeding pairs. With the feast the postapocalypse had been for them, these rumors were like pigeons now. Just with wingspans of eleven to fourteen feet, the grandfathers reaching out nearly to twenty. Black feathers oily to the touch. A digestive system able to process whatever fell down into it, evidently. The best survivors.

The two on the ground raised their wings in warning, but Mayner pulled right up to them anyway, leaning forward for the jeep's dust to drift past, Jory only clueing into this at the last moment, the last gritty breath.

"Thanks," he said a few moments later, coughing.

Mayner smiled, his face right up against the steering wheel.

"Helmet's behind you," he said to Jory, then sat on the hood while Jory strapped the armor on, fitted the helmet down, adjusted the strap on the torch and moved his arm on that side, to be sure he still could. Then his fingers. Then the tips of his fingers.

Stall, stall.

Finally Jory stepped in beside Mayner, and the two of them studied the broken-down restroom. Its shifting black wainscoting watched them back.

"They can't get in," Mayner said, about the vultures. "They can smell it, but they can't get to it. They don't want to be anywhere without the sky above them."

Jory didn't say anything. Four of the vultures had metal bracelets on their right ankles, those tiny lights blipping green with radio signals.

"Just one?" Jory said, about what he was apt to find inside.

"Probably," Mayner said, shrugging one shoulder. "Out here, it's—why be out here, right? Unless you're smuggling."

"Black market," Jory filled in.

"Probably a grocery store buried out here somewhere. Find that storeroom, grab as many cans as you can, and"—with his sideways hand Mayner zipped a fast path back to the fence.

"You've seen that one they have in the glass box in old downtown?" Jory said, pawing his pocket for his pack, hitting armor instead.

"The mime?" Mayner asked, looking over, then playacting he was lying down in an invisible box, testing its limits gingerly.

"More like a coffin," Jory said.

"You've seen it, like with your own two eyes?"

Jory shrugged.

"It's not real," Mayner said. "Control'd never let the virus circulate like that."

"They're pretty good at keeping expired canned goods off the streets too?" Jory said, trying to unstrap his chest plate, to get at his cigarettes.

Mayner stopped him, threaded a red-striped straw up from his shirt pocket, the straw tied at both ends.

"Menthol," he said, at important-whisper level.

Jory took the straw reverently. It was one of those milkshake ones, from back when milkshakes were real. Just, with a menthol preserved inside now. He ran it under his nose, trying to smell that green taste.

"Serious?" he said. "Where?"

"Just don't tell Voss."

"Because I'm definitely seeing him again."

"Toss the butt out when you and his holiness are ready for the big boy. I'll be watching for it. Won't give him the signal until then. Not that they always listen so well."

"'Big boy'?" Jory said.

"And his pet dog," Mayner answered.

Jory got it—the handler. Throw the menthol butt out when he was ready for the handler. When the priest was ready for the handler and his walking, slobbering bad idea of a laboratory rat.

"What if I'm not done with it yet?" Jory asked, holding the straw out before him.

"You can save the world or you can smoke a cigarette, right?" Mayner said.

Jory studied the straw again, considering. Inside was maybe the only menthol left in the postapocalypse. Maybe his last smoke ever.

"It'll help with the smell," Mayner said, nodding inside.

"So we're the first ones here?" Jory said.

"Except Señor Deadalo in there," Mayner said back.

"And whoever made him dead."

"Unless he died of happiness," Mayner said.

"Lot of that going around these days," Jory said, then pushed off with his butt from the jeep.

Mayner chin-pointed down to Jory's torch. "You know what to do with that, right?"

"Pull the trigger. Point. Spray."

"Maybe in a slightly different order, but, yeah. Okay. And"—keying his own headset on—"you can hear me, right?"

Jory flinched from Mayner's voice in his helmet, dialed it down.

Then, leaning away, into his own unlit funeral pyre, Mayner's hand on Jory's shoulder kept him there for one more moment.

"Don't make me code you," he said. "Be the one that lives this week."

Jory looked around at the ravaged sky one last time. The jagged horizon. Then he clapped his hand down on top of Mayner's.

"Thanks for the—" he said, lifting the red-striped straw, walking backwards into his story, his torch at port arms, the pharaoh vultures lumbering up into the air behind him, fifteen birds at once, so that for a few moments Jory was in shadow.

And then he ducked through the door.

This novel took so long to write. I mean, first time, like, I don't know, some amount of weeks, not more than four months, but the second time, the redo, like ten months. I'm glad I didn't give up though. There were moments like this waiting to be unearthed. And, the same way I wrote Demon Theory *so I could teach myself dialogue? I wrote this one so I could try to learn to accommodate "gray" with that ugly, barbaric "a." So I said it over and over again, I typed it until I could do it telekinetically, from the other room, while sleeping. But it never stuck. I still feel evil if I say "gray." I've got standards, I mean. Lines I won't cross. Two of those are leaning against each other at the top.*

THE PARABLE OF THE GUN

WE LOCKED HIM in the old fitting rooms because he said he was Jesus. And because it was the end of our shift.

"Save them," Marco said to him through the louvered doors, and swept his hands to all the naked mannequins the fitting rooms were already storing, their arms in every posture of worship.

Jesus pulled his face over the top of the door, rested his bearded chin on the backs of his fingers, and watched us. He wasn't even mad about the way we'd tackled him off the cosmetics display pad. How the customers had laughed and clapped and then turned away, embarrassed. What Marco had threatened to do to all that long hair. What I had done with the leather sandal that had been left on the display pad, as if Jesus had just been transubstantiated up to the second floor. Lingerie, probably.

It was as close as there was to heaven at Dunlap's.

In the security booth we spent the rest of our shift with sticky notes, putting one on each monitor, telling Jarret and Kale, the night shift, that Jesus was their problem now. Through the walkie-talkie Marco had left keyed open by the fitting rooms, we could hear Jesus humming. It wasn't even a hymn, just a song from the radio.

"We should throw him to the lions," Marco said, smiling to himself, wheels turning in his head that hadn't turned in a long time.

"You mean Delaney and Gale?" I said, after checking behind me.

Delaney and Gale were the area coordinators, the bosses when the manager wasn't on the floor. They took it very seriously. Marco hissed through his teeth, dotted an *i* on some complicated insult he'd been writing to Jarret and Kale, then fixed it on the last empty screen. He nodded to himself, satisfied with his work, and leaned back in the ergonomic chair we'd had to make special requests for.

Jesus still humming, the dial tone of his voice starting to break into words in places. The lyrics would be next.

"He didn't have headphones, did he?" Marco said.

"Gale's going to hear him," I said back, nowhere to put my eyes now that all the monitors were covered.

Marco focused his attention on the walkie-talkie again.

"Watch this," he said, and palmed it, thumbed the line open. Said in his deepest, most resounding voice, "Son, this is God, your father. Don't make me come down there again."

The humming trailed off, got swallowed.

I shook my head, looked out the small, wire-mesh glass window set in the steel door of our security booth.

"We're going to hell now," I said to Marco. "You know that, right?"

Marco laughed, stood. Said, "This place isn't hell, I don't want to see it, man," then started unpacking his belt into his locker, shouldering into his jacket. I fell in, standing my pepper spray on the top shelf of my locker, hanging my stick from the hook. Charging the batteries on my handheld. The one we'd left by the fitting rooms with Jesus was Jarret and Kale's problem now. Let them charge it.

Walking out, my foot stopping the door for Marco to ease through, I almost saw something on the monitors, I thought. All the sticky notes though. I couldn't be sure.

"What?" Marco said.

"Good night," Jesus said, clearly, through the walkie-talkie. As if his beard were right up to it, rustling into the receiver holes.

"Shit," Marco said, drawing his lips up from his teeth. "I see a donkey in the parking lot, my dumb ass is calling in tomorrow."

I pulled the door locked behind us.

Jesus was Jarret and Kale's problem now.

Part of the end of rounds—what the OP called it when security was clocking out—was making a final circuit of the store, to be sure what you were handing off to the next shift was as safe and secure as you could make it. It was a useless procedure, of course: on the way to the time clock, not only were we in our civvies, but our spray and sticks and walkie-talkies were back in the box. It kind of made any kind of walk-through useless. Except for Jeanine, of course, the built-for-sin holy roller in Misses, who for some reason thought we were real cops, or cops in training, or something. It didn't matter. If we got there at 8:45, she'd already be zoning her area, squaring all the shirts onto their aisle displays, fluffing collars, refolding pants. To one degree or another, of course— because of Delaney and Gale—everybody at least went through the motions of zoning. Not everybody wore blouses as loose and low-cut as Jeanine's though. All you had to do while she folded was stand there, and, bam, suddenly the last eight hours had been worth it.

"Guess you heard we caught your boy today," Marco said to her, his right arm cocked up on a rounder, "Jesus, I mean."

Jeanine looked up to him, then me.

I nodded, said, "The real one."

She shook her head, smiled, and said we must be real Philistines then, right?

Over her shoulder, Marco bored his eyes into me, waiting for a signal, to know if being a Philistine was good or bad.

"That a commandment?" I said to Jeanine.

In reply she hit me lightly on the shoulder and I acted like it was a roundhouse, folded over the register in fake pain, then, walking through Housewares minutes later, realized that I should have played along, gone farther, should have spun her around by the wrist, her arm behind her, as if I were apprehending her. It would have pulled her right up against me.

That's why I was working security at a department store though: because my whole life had already been a series of not thinking of things in time, when they could have done some good.

At the end of the Housewares, the final stretch to the time clock, me and Marco both saw the trench-coat guy, already turning away from us, the tails of his black coat swirling around like the cape of a superhero.

Marco pretended just to be looking straight ahead.

"You care?" he said.

"Amateur," I said back, about the trench-coat guy, and like that we let him slide, didn't want to do the paper work he was obviously going to require. All he was stealing was plates or saucers or something anyway. For his grand-mother, what? It didn't matter. Fine china wasn't why the store had gone full-time with security last year. There wasn't really a market for hot saucers, nice forks. What there was a market for, however, always, was electronics. It's why we kept them in a chain link cage in back now, locked with a set of key codes that the computer kept track of somehow. It didn't stop the handheld stuff from walking out of the store, but it did make it walk slower anyway. Sometimes in our pockets even, which management had gone to special workshops about, learned to expect. The way they dealt with it was to try to buy our loyalty, show we were part of the family—that it was our stuff too. What they tried to buy our loyalty with was a 20 percent discount on all elec-tronics that weren't on clearance. To get that 0 percent though, we had to use a charge card. Which is to say the store owned us now, more or less. Had even cut off the 10 percent discount all the floor employees got, for work clothes. Cut it off and still made us stick to their stupid-ass dress code: black slacks, shirts with at least three buttons, not counting the sleeves.

What we could have done with the trench-coat guy, I guess, was lock him up with Jesus.

What we did instead was home in on that time clock, lean against the wall around it with unlit cigarettes in our mouths, the third shift cleaning crew waiting there as well, to clock in.

"Say a prayer," Marco told me, lifting his chin to the time clock that was taking hours, not minutes.

I looked at it hard, nodded, and said, "I wish I may, I wish I might—" and then didn't get to finish.

From the floor, a woman was screaming.

Marco closed his eyes, thinned his lips, and shook his head no, please, but it didn't matter: we were still clocked in.

Before following him back through Hardware, I balanced my cigarette on top of the time clock, shook my head no to the custodial staff. That that was *my* cigarette.

When I turned to take the impact of the aluminum doors Marco had left swinging though, my cigarette was already gone, the custodial staff all just standing there with their hands in their pockets, no eye contact.

Of course I didn't believe our guy in the old fitting rooms was really Jesus.

In my eight months at Dunlap's, the eight months since the other security crew had gone up on grand larceny charges, there'd been a total of two screaming women. Just absolutely hysterical I mean, unstoppable. If we could have restrained them, we would have maybe. Instead, because the women had been screaming due to some bad or good news they'd just got on their phones—a death the first time, an engagement the second—we'd let the women on the floor talk them down. Sit with them until they were just sobbing, then lead them away. Knowing the girls on the floor, sell them something along the way.

This third screaming woman was a whole different scene.

It was Gale.

She was on her knees at the intersection of the two main aisles, where the tile was still rough from the watch stand that had been pulled up from there my first week on.

She was screaming because the man in the trench coat was standing behind her, a large chrome pistol held to the back of her head.

I slowed down my run.

"Do it!" the trench-coat man called out across Misses, and I followed his voice to Delaney.

Her key was in the console that dropped the cages on all the exits.

She turned it, the ceiling shook, and the trench-coat man smiled, and together we watched all the rounders move like savanna grass, when you know the small, tasty animals are moving away just beneath it.

In turn, one by one, the trench-coat man waited for the shoppers to make their last scuttle from the makeup counter to the freedom of the mall, and lined up on them. It was fourteen feet, I knew. How far the salespeople were supposed to keep their merchandise from the exit.

Because the trench-coat man's pistol was a revolver, only had so many bullets, he just held it on each person who escaped and fake shot them, the barrel rising with the sound his mouth was making.

The last of the shoppers to slide under the door on their stomachs wasn't a shopper at all either. It was Marco.

He splashed through the fountain, silver and copper rising behind him, and was gone.

Trench-coat man came back to me, scratched his forehead with the sight of his pistol, and said, "You should have gone with him, yeah?"

Story of my life.

Six minutes later—I could tell because my ears were so tuned into the time clock, which cut the hours into tenths, into six-minutes sections—the trench-coat man had all of us down on our knees. Not in a single-file line, but two single-file lines that crossed where the aisles crossed. From the top of the escalator, that's what we had to be too: a cross.

It wasn't accidental.

When the bottom of the cross, the base where I was, had needed a little more length, the trench-coat man had scared up two more bodies from Misses. One of them was Jeanine. Her fists were balled tight, her skin glistening.

I put my hand on her shoulder and the trench-coat man smiled, nodded me on.

"Get some," he said. "It's the end of the world, man. For you I mean."

I lowered my hand.

When the trench-coat man had passed, was inspecting his work, how even we were, how much like dominoes, Jeanine shook her head no to him. Said, "It doesn't matter what you do to us, y'know? It won't be as bad as what you'll have waiting for you."

The trench-coat man nodded, smiled a gap-toothed smile at her, and produced a bible from his right pocket. Waggled it like a revival preacher.

"Talking about this?" he said, stepping in.

Jeanine just stared at him.

"Thou shalt not kill," she said, her voice so even now I thought maybe she was channeling or something. Possessed.

I could feel myself pulling away from her, from the line of fire.

The trench-coat man leaned down to her, to her ear, his eyes locked on mine, to keep me in place.

"You're right about that, missy," he said. "But you forgot one too."

She angled her body away enough to face him.

He nodded, opened the bible. Cut into the pages was a box. In the box was a small automatic pistol.

"Why are you doing this?" Jeanine said, shaking her head at him, in disgust.

"Me?" he said back, doing some fake-offended shuffle, then stopping, looking down the line at the rest of us. "More like you, I'd say."

Jeanine held his eyes for maybe three breaths, then turned forward as if he weren't there at all, and started praying.

The trench-coat man nodded, fingered the gum from his mouth, and fell into Jeanine's prayer with her. Knew it as well as she did.

It shut her up.

He trailed off as well, then held the automatic in front of her, for all of us, and loaded a single shell in, pulled the slide back.

"Don't give it to me," Jeanine said. "I don't want to go to hell for shooting you."

The trench-coat man shrugged, stared at her, then said, "You're part right anyway."

It made Jeanine turn to him.

"You are going to hell," he clarified. "But not for me. No. Thou shalt not kill, right? But there's another one. Kind of an automatic deal, like. Don't pass go."

Jeanine smiled now, said it: "Suicide."

Yes.

She closed her eyes, opened them again. Said, "You mean, you're going to hold one gun on me, so I'll shoot myself? And your threat is that, if I don't shoot myself, then you go to hell?"

The trench-coat man just stared at her.

Jeanine shrugged, held her hand out. Said, "So give it to me then."

This made the man smile, look down the line at the rest of us. To see if we were getting it, if we could see the joke here.

When we couldn't, he pulled the punch line out from behind the counter.

An eight-year-old boy. The pistol to his head.

"Now what do you say?" the trench-coat man said, and slid the automatic over to Jeanine.

"You don't pick it up," he said, "bang, I go to hell, he goes the other direction. You point it at me . . . bang. Get it? Make sense?"

Behind us, Gale lost it again, started sobbing, having some sort of attack.

The trench-coat man sneered at her, pushed the barrel of his chrome pistol deeper into the boy's blond hair.

Outside now, sirens. And Marco, probably still running.

Inside, us, on our knees, in the form of a cross.

It's the best way to be when Jesus comes down from Lingerie.

As you would expect, Jesus wasn't one of those people who walked down the already moving escalator. Maybe because of his robes, or the sandals he had to have just lifted. It made him look like he was floating, anyway, the way he didn't use the rubber banister. His eyes locked on each of ours in turn, his face so—there's no other word—serene.

The trench-coat man watched him descend too, swallowed whatever he'd had in his mouth.

From somewhere in Men's Casual, a man threw a package of dress socks up against the tile ceiling, to herald Jesus's arrival. The plastic of the sock bag clung to the rough ceiling for three impossible seconds, then the socks tumbled back down in what felt like slow motion, made no sound when they hit the carpet.

Jesus smiled about it, as if in thanks, then folded his arms the way people do in the bible: with his hands up his own wide sleeves.

The teeth at the bottom of the escalator were nothing to him. The whole world.

Instead of keeping to the wide aisle, he navigated through the rounders and T-bars, looking at each of them in turn, finally touching them as he passed, leaving the palm of his hand on them long enough that I knew they were holy now. Cured. Blessed.

I was crying maybe, I don't know.

Jesus fixed the trench-coat man in his benevolent stare and held him there, turning the pages of his soul, reading the book of his life. When he was done, he nodded, looked down to us again, the corners of his mouth ghosting up a little at me, in recognition. And forgiveness. Then he came back to the trench-coat man. Said, "You're sure you don't want to reconsider?"

The trench-coat man moved his mouth but didn't have any words.

Oblivious of the chrome pistol, Jesus stepped in, close to the trench-coat man, then lowered himself to one knee. Not to wash the man's combat boots, but to pick up the cored bible.

"You know why they put my words in red in here?" he said, paging through, amused. He shrugged, looked up to the trench-coat man. "Supposed to be like blood," he said. "As in, this is my body, this is my—?"

The trench-coat man gave one nervous nod.

Jesus shut the bible. "I can see you believe," he said, tracing the cross we were all arranged in.

The trench-coat man nodded again.

Jesus nodded with him, chewed his cheek some. Didn't need to have the ridiculous who-was-going-to-hell-for-what thing explained to him. The way the trench-coat man was clinging to the eight-year-old boy, the whole scheme was obvious. Undeniable.

"Would you do it?" Jesus said then, focusing in on Jeanine suddenly, intensely. "Would you sacrifice your eternal soul to the save this boy you don't even know?"

Jeanine closed her eyes, nodded. Was crying now.

Jesus looked up to the trench-coat man and smiled, satisfied. Did something vulgar with his eyebrows it seemed, then shrugged the temptation off. Raised his hand to his beard instead, a tic the bible never said anything about.

Finally, to the trench-coat man, he said, "You were going to let her do it, too, am I right? Let her make that sacrifice?"

In reply, the trench-coat man flared his eyes and his nostrils both, and took a long step back. Pushed the barrel of his pistol even harder against the side of the boy's head.

Jesus nodded as if to himself, didn't press the trench-coat man about it anymore. Said instead, looking back across the store, as if savoring it, "Good thing I showed up then," then came back to the trench-coat man all at once. "Sacrifice is kind of my thing, y'know?"

Somewhere in her sobs, Jeanine was laughing too now. With joy.

She couldn't see what I could though: Jesus, lowering himself to the loaded automatic, weighing it in his hands.

"I'm here to take your place," he said to Jeanine, then, looking along the line, at each of us. "All of your places. This sin, what he's asking, it's . . . it's too much for you. And anyway"—winking once at the eight-year-old—"Jesus loves the little children, right?"

The boy nodded and Jesus liked it, bobbed his head forward as if it was time now. No more stalling.

He raised the automatic to chest level, held it sideways to study it, the trench-coat man stepping back again, into a rack of blouses, his eyes all over Jesus's automatic.

Jesus smiled.

"Don't worry," he said, and lifted his face as if hearing something, focused again over the tops of all the clothes, all the merchandise. At the cage bars over the mall entrance, it seemed.

He nodded, shrugged. Said it again, to himself now: ". . . if there were just one person, willing to take all that sin upon himself . . ."

He was talking himself into it.

I opened my mouth when I understood, turned all the way around to him, to Jesus, and was too late one more time: already, at the right arm of the cross, Jesus was lowering the small automatic to Gale's left temple.

He didn't close his eyes when he fired, then held the automatic there until Gale had slumped down.

"One," he said, holding his hand back to the trench-coat man, for another shell. He thumbed it in like it was second nature.

Next was a shopper, still gripping her bag, then another shopper, then up the post part of the cross for Delaney. By this time I wasn't even hearing the small, wet popping sounds anymore. Just Jesus, killing us so we wouldn't have to kill ourselves. Saving our souls, becoming a murderer himself so we wouldn't have to.

Jeanine, singing quietly, perfectly. A hymn, it sounded like. I hummed along as best I could, felt the woman behind me lean forward into my back, dead weight, and closed my eyes for what was coming, what was here, even felt the hot barrel hiss into my hair, and then the shot, the sound, filling the store years before I was ready.

The automatic jerked down to my ear, then my neck, leaving burns in both places, and I turned to see: Jesus was still standing over me, but the center of his robe was red, and spreading.

Opposite his chest, a hundred and fifty feet away, was the mall entrance, the wall of aluminum bars. Resting at shoulder level on one of those bars the thick barrel of a sniper rifle.

Before Jesus could even fall, the trench-coat man was dead too, the eight-year-old boy just standing there.

I started to stand, to help him, to shield him—I was *security*, for Chrissake—but then Jesus was slumping over me, pushing me down, the smell of his hair spray harsh against the back of my throat, his blood washing over me.

From the second floor, Lingerie, we would have been the bottom of the cross, where it's buried in the ground.

I closed my eyes, saw the silk and satin of the teddies up there undulate away from something huge, moving among them. Saw them undulate away and then reach out, after it.

Four months later, I said my first cuss word since the shooting. It was *god-damn*. One of the bad ones.

"Lord's name in vain," Jeanine ticked off for me.

We were in the food court, trying to reclaim our lives.

I slung my finger back and forth where the napkin dispenser had snagged it, said it again: "Go*damn*it, I mean."

Jeanine leaned back in her waffle chair, raised the straw of her red ice drink to her lips. Didn't approve.

Because the sex we'd had two weeks after the shooting had been premarital, and kind of just compulsive, and had started with her explaining the bible to me anyway, she was pretending it had never happened. Repressing me. A mental virgin.

I didn't care.

She wasn't pregnant, I knew, but I was. Not just with the halfway-disappointing memory of her breasts, but with something else, something not quite religion, or faith, but having to do with how Jesus's name turned out to be Harold Gaines. How, in those last moments before he started shooting, he, Harold Gaines, had looked across the store to the mall entrance, what was waiting for him, and then done it anyway, lowered the automatic to Gale's head.

How, because of that, I think, I had tried to stand, to save that eight-year-old boy.

How, eight months after signing on, I had become security.

Because Jeanine was still watching me, waiting for me to apologize for breaking the third commandment or eighth amendment or whatever the hell it was, I looked away, over her shoulder. Focused on the shape walking up to our table from the pizza place after four months gone.

It was Marco.

For the briefest possible moment our eyes locked, and I read the pages of what he was here for—his old job, how I could get it for him, because I was a hero, how it would be just like old times—and then I lowered my face. For once in my life did something in the moment, instead of just after: stood, turned, and walked back to the store.

This is from me working at Sears for so long. Always the warehouse, as I'm hardly fit for customer interaction. Pushing a dolly all day long, you get to thinking. I did anyway. And my thoughts, they're always of two varieties, even still: What if a lion runs through here, chasing a kid? or What if somebody here pulls out a pistol? So then all I had to do was put this pistol in Jesus's hand—oh, wait, now I'm remembering: this is a complete redo of another story, about a guy divorcing his wife, a guy who encounters a homeless dude at a stoplight who may or may not be Jesus. There was a sailboat involved, though, and writing that story, it quickly became apparent to me that I don't know jack about the water, or boats, or sailing. So I quit that story, ported Jesus across, put a pistol in his hand to see what would happen. It was fun. I've always really liked this story. The way it ends, it felt like I was figuring something out about story there. About what you could do, and what you didn't always have to do.

PALEOGENESIS, CIRCA 1970

I.

This is how I say rain, in little grey drops of noise that roll down the face of the page, a silent patter that has been falling for years. But it's not raining now. Listen.

This is how I say truck stop: a finger of neon light on the horizon; the feel of idling rigs in the stained concrete; the smell of diesel, grease, chiliburgers, toys bought that will someday be the only thing a child has left. My toy is the rain, my setting is the truck stop, and the trucker sitting in the corner booth and the waitress sneaking him a thermos of steaming coffee have been here since only moments before me.

They're always here, at this truck stop, the neon all around them getting softer and softer.

Sometimes I sit in this booth and write for hours and drink coffee until I shake inside, and I can't look away.

They're my parents.

II.

The waitress pulls the silvery thermos from under her apron and the trucker takes it. The cook doesn't see all this through his order window, he's not really even there. That's why nobody ever orders food, why none of us ever eat, but just sit here going through it all over and over. And starving.

The trucker looks up at the waitress and tips his hat. Black? he says, and she nods, smiles. They know each other already, enough so that he whispers *I love you* to her, makes her eyes water. But no, he doesn't say *I love you* to her, he says, It's been a while Rosie, I been 'cross this country four times since I seen your pretty face.

The waitress smiles and does her eyebrows up in a V, her letter for everything. And Rosie is her name, the name she always made me call her because she said she wasn't a real mom like a real mom should be. Rosie. She fiddles with her name tag and says, Has it been that long, really? The trucker's name is on his hat: Peterson. Just a greasy patch, a trucking operation that went under years ago and left no real records. By his plate a rubber snake with the price tag still on. He directs her eyes down to it, grabs it by the tail, whips it, breaks its rubber neck.

Rosie takes a step back and he laughs.

That damn snake'd be dead if it were real, he says, that's how we did it when I was a kid. He drags kid out into *ke-id*, like maybe there's a *y* in the middle somewhere, floating around. Rosie sits down opposite him in the booth, takes a drink of his coffee and swallows it too hot, lights a cigarette.

I dreamed about you last night, she lies, you were there working behind a counter somewhere.

Must have been somebody else, he answers back, maybe my dad or just somebody that looks like me.

Rosie shakes her head. No, I've never seen your dad anyways. It was you, you were wearing that same yellow hat as last time, that first Christmas. Peterson laughs and stands and whips the snake again. The price tag circles slow to the ground. Rosie puts her foot on it when Peterson reaches for it, and he wraps his hand around her calf, runs it up to her knee.

In my booth I look away, lose myself in the telling grains at the bottom of my cup, cough. Rosie hears and puts her hand on his through her waitress dress. He doesn't see me, never will. When she rises to bring me another refill he walks over to the jukebox and stands there dragging the rubber snake's head through the air like a pendulum.

I look up at Rosie while she pours me coffee. She's younger than me by a few years.

I'll bring you some more of that cream, she says, motioning at the eight empty little cartons I've scattered on the table. I put my hand over my cup, shake my head.

I take it black, I tell her, and when she can't hear me and asks me to say it again my voice is trembling and I can't. Finally I get it out—Like his, ma'am—and she smiles and asks me if everything is all right. I look away, find Peterson's Kenworth outside the plate glass.

Where you going anyways, mister? she asks.

I take a drink of the coffee and feel it black inside me, getting cold already. Here, I say. Here. Been coming here for twenty-six years already. My whole life.

She laughs, says she's only been working here for four herself, but she's still never seen me. I want to tell her that's not what I meant, want to tell her to listen to my words, but Peterson is dropping silver into the jukebox and the snake is hanging limp by his leg, dead, and she walks over to him without asking me if I want anything else.

III.

Peterson pushes the wrong buttons on the jukebox and the same song plays over and over, burrowing its way into me. Into us. Finally he stands up out of his booth and starts trying to move the jukebox, so he can unplug it. His hands are shaking, trucker speed racing through his veins, looking for a way out, any way. Rosie looks back at me, smiles, her eyes telling me to just ignore him, to look somewhere else.

I rub my eyes. I can't look anywhere else. This is the only place I see anymore.

IV.

Peterson stands after the record in the jukebox finally stops spinning, the voice winding down and finally forgetting itself deep in the middle of a word, in the middle of two l's. He stands and holds the snake out to Rosie, asks her if she wants to kill it for a while, he's bored. She motions no with her cigarette, the smoke tracing half-moons in the air that float up into the ceiling and disappear.

This is the only way I know to say her name the way it sounds to me: she stands and walks barefoot over to Peterson, her cigarette held behind her, her feet whispering across the floor, and with her other hand lets her hair down; it falls golden brown like molten strands of copper down her back and moves with her every step, like the down-hanging branches of a willow I saw once years ago that had a car and a dead person wrapped around it.

Peterson watches her walk to him and whistles low. I look away again, at his idling rig. He's wearing heavy steel-toed boots, maybe from when he was a roughneck somewhere, maybe just because he likes the way they sound. He drags the heel of the left one when he walks, and this is what I hear after he kisses her in front of the jukebox, when he walks to the bathroom, already fiddling with his belt buckle.

When the bathroom door closes Rosie sits down in the booth by the door and starts doing her lipstick in the shined-up part of a napkin holder. She holds her mouth in an O and traces it out: her whole life has been letters that never spelled anything for her. She told me this once when I was seven when we were staying with her sister in Arizona, and I didn't understand for a long while. But I hung on her every word.

While she fixes her lips I stand and go to Peterson's booth, give my fingers time to play across the silver of his thermos, feel the heat inside, trace sworls in the steam that melt back to nothing. When the toilet flushes I shuffle away, look out the front window, see through my reflection, all the nights I haven't slept but have sat here drinking coffee and burning my eyes.

Peterson walks behind me and I hold my breath. He doesn't say anything, only drags his heel across the floor. The vinyl of his seat creaks as he sits down, and then Rosie is by my side again.

You waiting for somebody? she asks, cupping her hands around her face to see outside. I shake my head, don't say that I'm just waiting for her and him to walk out to the sleeper of his rig together. That's all.

Where's the bathroom? I ask like I've never been here, and she motions her head. I thank her and retrace Peterson's dragging footsteps, hear the record in the jukebox finally fall, minutes too late. I had forgotten about it I was watching them so closely. The little things get away sometimes, don't seem to matter when they really do, more than anything maybe.

The vinyl doesn't crack though. I won't let it.

In the bathroom I sit on the counter and look at the dead rubber snake by the sink, pink drops of slow soap dripping by its head. I pick it up, hold its lifeless body across my thighs, hold the tail to my nose for the grease on Peterson hands. It just smells new, like the inside of an inner tube. I swing it in an arc and slap its head against the counter. It dies again, and again, and again, and then I see myself twisted in the metal mirror, see my cap greasy like his, my eyes just as red. The wall behind me washing-machine green and deep and empty. I wash my hands until they hurt and then leave, the snake's tail hanging out my pocket as I walk to the end of the hall and into the break room.

I find Rosie's locker in the corner like always. I open it and place the rubber snake on the top shelf, on her carton of menthols and her astrology bible she used to read to me while I was still in her stomach, breathing heavy water like ink. She told me that's where she found it—the rubber snake—on top of her bible, that's how she knew about me and Peterson.

The stars don't lie about things like that, not to her.

Once when I was eleven and they had puts locks on our trailer so we couldn't get in anymore, she drove both of us out into the country until the car coughed and died, and then we laid out in a field and she pointed out stars to me and told me for the first time about my dad and about this night at the truck stop, cried and told me how she heard he had jack-knifed his rig on a wet road and didn't make it out, drowned facedown in the ditch. I fell asleep listening to her talk, dreamed of voiced bubbles rising through the murky water, and woke to a world I had never known, woke to the blank stare of cows set up in the dry grass around us like chess pieces, flies already blanketing their shoulders black.

But this isn't a story about me. Not like that. It can't be. It's about her, Rosie, the way she didn't really like waitressing that much, how her whole life had just come down to that somehow; it's about how she scribbled the zodiac crude on the back of her order pad, trying to figure it all out in penciled lines; it's about him, the trucker, Peterson, the way he got down on his knees to unplug the jukebox when he couldn't listen to the same thing over and over anymore. It's about why she sneaked him that thermos of hot coffee when there wasn't even a cook to catch them doing it.

V.

Of course when I walk back from the break room they're both gone. The dining room is empty. I missed whatever Peterson said to lure her out to his sleeper, missed the way she must have said yes not with her mouth but with her eyes, missed seeing how she just went with him because she couldn't stand being alone at the truck stop tonight, the neon was blurring the edges of her shadow so much she couldn't make it out anymore.

It's just me.

I run out behind them, stand in the door and pull them back through the years, watch Rosie follow Peterson to his rig, see the way his yellow running lights play with the soft contours of her face, how the wind whipping around the nose past the round headlights lifts her hair and lays it out across her shoulders. But no, that's not enough, I pull them back further.

To here: as they're walking across the smooth concrete towards his truck a song they both know drifts down out of the speaker in three-four time. They stop in the halflight of the pumps. They hold each other awkwardly, and then better, closer. They shuffle back and forth, a slow waltz, and afterwards hold each other's hands as they walk together to his Kenworth, and *then* the running lights caress her face and the wind plays with her hair. The door opens and closes and they're gone. That's the way it has to be. The way I see it.

The sleeper behind the cab moves gently now, like a child on his father's back, running across a yard that goes forever. It rocks back and forth on rubber bushings that cost $172 each. Maybe the same country station is on in there. Maybe they have their own song he keeps above the visor in eight-track, puts in when he's with her. Yes, they do. They have this song, at least. I can almost hear it. Something real for them, maybe "Moody Blue," maybe just some soft jazz that was playing when they first met, maybe Johnny Norton singing "Slow Dancing," just for them. Just for them. Johnny Norton.

"Slow Dancing" comes down out of the speaker now, touches where they were just dancing, touches me standing alone with the pumps and the bugs falling golden like rain all around.

Three-four time everywhere.

VI.

A lifetime later Rosie walks back into the dining room, straightening her hair. I've been getting my own coffee, three cups so far and there's no more. My hands tremble. She smiles at me and I smile back, and then she pulls her bottom lip into her mouth and bites it.

Something wrong? I ask across the two tables between us.

She says, No, and motions her head outside.

He just had to check something under the truck, she says, he'll be in in a little bit. But she doesn't believe it. He always has to check something under the truck, always remembers to bring his thermos with him when they walk out to the parking lot together.

It doesn't matter, I say, and she smiles her waitress smile that means nothing. I want to tell her that everything will be okay, that she's got me now and we'll keep everybody else away from us for the next fourteen years, moving from state to state, until I decide to stay once when she moves on.

Rosie. That's her name. It says so right on her name tag. I say her name without thinking and she starts brewing some more coffee, her duty, and becomes a waitress again. I let her. It's easier. When she starts pushing the jukebox back up to the wall I slow things down and try to see her only at the truck stop for a moment, try to keep her there in that liquid drop of time before Peterson pulls away, that handful of minutes when she still thought he might come back in and talk the night away with her, listen as she read his story in the sky. Drink coffee and say, More than anything when he asked if she didn't want to ride to the East Coast with him. Call the radio station and get them to play their song over and over while they slow danced out by the pumps. Fall asleep in a booth and let their cigarettes dwindle down to ashes.

It's still just a handful of minutes though. And now that she's alone she can only take the weight of my stare a few lines longer.

VII.

After she gets the jukebox plugged back in and the first song is spinning she comes to my table in bare feet and balances tears in her eyes and pours my coffee, and when the headlights of the rig cut through the window at her she lets her head down and her tears spill out, for me writing this story every night in logbook pencil, for my father driving away to his wet road. For the way the stars never line themselves up in the sky for her.

I look up to her and in the afterglow of headlights I see something real in all these words, and then I look away before the image is gone and scribble into my napkin, say, *This is how I say rain, in clear little drops that roll down her face, hang onto her chin, and fall.*

The original of this is "The Ballad of Stacy Dunn," a story I wrote to death in grad school. I don't know why, but for some reason one of the most permanent images rattling around in my head, it's of a couple slow dancing at a truck stop at night. Behind them are the quilted steel doors of a forty-foot trailer. And it's a perfect moment. Too, this was the first story I ever had published, I think. Or, published in a big place: Black Warrior Review. *And it's hardly at all like the "Stacy Dunn" version. That one's got all kinds of stuff going on, as I recall. This one's just me sitting in a booth. Or, "me," I should say; putting that "1970" into the title at the last moment, that's my super-hiding abilities (I'm born in '72). I think this is the story where I figured out what would become one of my principles with fiction too: "grey" is spelled like that. But also, the way the rain falls, in words, that's also something I'm very attached to. I'm very interested in the bridges between fiction and this place. Permeable membranes, yes. I'm always trying to look through. And, I'll forever remember* BWR *calling on the phone to accept this piece, and to say I was getting $175 for it. It was amazing. I stood there in my new, just-married apartment with my hand on the phone and I honestly felt like it was all beginning, like this is where it starts. And then the phone rang under my hand. I held it up to my ear. It was the police. My mom had just been in a head-on collision in Midland, Texas. Right directly in front of the emergency room of the hospital, so they could just wheel her gurney right in from the street. When that call was done, I held my hand on the phone for a little bit more, waiting for whatever was going to happen next.*

INTERSTATE LOVE AFFAIR

THE DERIDDER ROADKILL
Unidentified, controversial remains discovered on the side of Highway 12
just outside Deridder, Louisiana, in 1996, and subsequently either lost or taken.
According to the Dequincy News, *the remains expressed both canine and pri-*
mate characteristics. The photographs support this. For many, the Deridder
Roadkill established that the Cajun werewolf (loup-garou) wasn't just legend.
For others, the roadkill was a skunk ape, or chupacabra, even a misplaced ba-
boon. To the Louisiana Department of Wildlife and Fisheries, the photographs
are just morbid documentation of a large, brown Pomeranian dog.

That's one explanation.

1.

William drank three beers in his truck in the parking lot, just to get ready. He lined the cans up on the dash, looked through the second and third at the metal front door of the pound. The animal-control trucks were nosed up to the building; it was almost five o'clock. William peeled the tab off a fourth beer, looked into it and shook his head no, because he knew he shouldn't. Four was too many. He told himself not to be stupid. That there was no room for error. And then he laughed, killed the beer.

The fifth and sixth were nothing, not after four, but then, balancing the sixth on the dash like a wall, William straightened his legs against the floorboard, pushing himself back into the seat: for a moment the cans had quit being cans, had become the cushions him and his brother used to build forts with in the living room.

William hit himself in the side of the head until he was sure he wasn't going to cry. He used a baby wipe from the glove compartment to stop the bleeding. Most people don't know about baby wipes. William held the wet paper—fabric, almost—to his temple. It was cool, perfect. Then he held it over his mouth, breathed through it until he could breathe evenly again.

The fourth beer was a mistake, he knew that now, but it was too late. It had to be today.

Instead of leaving the cans on his dash, he dropped them over his shoulder, through the sliding rear glass. They landed in the bed. Any sound they made was muffled by the fiberglass camper shell. But they didn't make any noise.

William stepped down from the front seat and was almost to the wheelchair ramp of the pound when he had to go back, check to see if he'd locked the door of the truck. And then, just because he was there, he checked the passenger door too, and its vent window, and then the handle on the camper, then the camper itself.

If he put his hands around his eyes, his nose to the black glass, he could see the silver cans in the bed of the truck, and if he looked into the cab, there were the classifieds, still open to Pets, four of the ads circled in blue, but he couldn't spend all day in the parking lot.

The same way William knew about baby wipes, he knew about this.

He smiled and stepped away from the glass, faking a shrug for anybody watching, as if he'd just settled something with himself. There was nobody out there to see him. Just the same number of cars and animal-control trucks there had been when he first pulled up.

It was time.

He nodded to himself, moving his neck the way he imagined someone with the last name Pinzer would, then remembered to keep the tips of his fingers in the tops of his pants pockets. Because if he didn't, the pound attendant would keep looking at his hands, at William's hands, and then William would start looking down to them too, until that was all he could do.

Smile, he said to himself. People trust an easy face.

He hooked the door open with his forearm, caught it with his shoulder, stepped in sideways.

It was the usual waiting room—cast-off chairs, metal tables salvaged from the county's overflow warehouse. The lamp was one that an attendant's mothers had probably given them years ago, when she was updating her sitting room. The too-green plant would be from another attendant, who had pretended she'd bought it with the coffee money but had really paid for it herself, to liven the place up, keep her from slitting her wrists one night.

William took it all in in a dismissive glance, noticed that his hand was in his beard.

He lowered it slowly, his teeth set with the effort.

Behind the desk, nobody. On the wall, certificates, awards, letters of thanks framed twenty years ago. Near the hall leading back to the barking, two clipboards. One from today, Monday, and one for the weekend.

William swallowed, leaned toward the lists.

The dog column for the weekend had thirty-nine dogs, each identified first by location, then tag, if there was one, then just description: *25–30 lbs., black, white tail tip. Probably Lab, Lab-mix.* The dead, the run over, the already burned in the incinerator.

William smiled, found his hand covering his mouth again, made it go back down.

The girl who opened the door beside the lists stopped, pulled her breath in sharp, had to crane her head back to see all the way up to William's face.

William opened his mouth, stepped back, holding his hands up to show, to show her—

She was looking to the metal door in the waiting room now though. Then back up to William. "It was open?" she said, crinkling the corners of her eyes about how that shouldn't have been the case.

William nodded. She was twenty-three maybe, a rich caramel color, silver chain around her neck, holding a pink stone to the hollow of her throat. Otherwise, she was a nurse: green scrubs, yellow rubber gloves. Hair pulled back. It made her eyes better.

Hands, William said to himself.

They went back to their pockets, and he could tell from the way the caramel girl's features softened that this was better. That what his hands in his pockets did to his shoulders, how they were round now, making him look stooped, embarrassed of his height—a lifetime of standing in the back row, a thousand old ladies asking for help with the top shelf—that he wasn't a scary man in a flannel jacket anymore. Just William. Bill, Bill Pinzer.

The girl nodded to the list with her mouth.

"Any luck?" she said.

William knew to pause before answering, and then not to answer anyway, just shake his head no.

The girl was looking at the door again.

"We close at five, y'know?"

"Sorry," William said, looking over her shoulder at the wire glass in the door behind her. As if looking for his dog. ". . . I just—my work. Five. You know."

The girl looked at him for maybe four seconds, then shrugged.

"Thad was supposed to lock the door," she said, finally. "Not your fault."

William nodded.

"You seen him up here?" the girl asked.

"Ted?"

"Thad—don't worry. Listen. Your pet, sir. When did it—"

"Saturday. "

The girl turned to the door, zipping her keys out from her belt, towards the lock. William felt his lungs burning with air, made himself breathe, breathe.

"What kind?" she asked, not looking at him.

"Not sure," William said, shrugging in case she could see his reflection somewhere. "I only got him last week."

The girl opened the door, turned up to William.

"This is an adult dog?"

"Yeah, yes."

"Did you check the prior owner?"

William nodded. When the girl gave the door to him, she flipped it a bit so they weren't quite touching it at the same time. Like it would conduct something between them. Something more than she wanted. William's lips thinned behind his beard but he closed his eyes, stepped, stepped again, until it became a walk.

"Color, then?"

"Kind of . . . brownish. Black maybe. I'll know him."

"Husky, bull, Lab?"

"I don't—you want me to call my friend?"

The girl looked back to William, stopped in the hall, as if to go back to the front desk, and then she looked ahead of them too. William could see it in her eyes: it was already past five, right?

"Maybe you'll see him," she said, turning around again.

She came up maybe to William's sternum.

At the first corner she palmed the radio she had on her belt, said into it that she was taking a gentlemen back into "Large Dogs." William watched her thumb the radio back off, hook it to its plastic clip.

"Thad?" he said.

The girl nodded, shrugged like she was sorry.

William shook his head no though. "It's good you do that," he said.

"We had something happen—it's nothing. Couple of years ago. Listen. We're going to go through the forty pounders first, all right?"

William nodded, took the next corner with her.

Two years, then. It had already been two years.

Every few steps there was a drain, and every forty feet maybe, a twenty-foot hose coiled on the concrete wall.

The first dog they got to exploded against his chain link, his saliva going arm over arm down the metal.

The girl held her hand out—this one?

William shook his head no without even looking again, and they went on, run after run, until they came to an obviously pregnant dog. Mastiff, maybe, two generations back.

"That her?" the girl asked.

William hesitated a moment before shaking his head no.

"She's going to have puppies," he said.

The girl shook her head no, shrugged like an apology. One with calluses on it.

William looked to her for an explanation.

"We'll—our doctor . . ." She was searching for words, falling back on what sounded like a pamphlet: "Any stray we release, we fix, right?"

William nodded, looked to the bitch again. Got it: "So I can't have her?"

"Not today," the girl said, looking at the dog too, then away, as if she had to. "After the procedure though . . ."

"I should find Lobo first," William said, remembering.

The girl zipped her keys out, a nervous thing, and they moved on. Lobo was four runs down, a large Rottweiler with scarred eyebrows.

William smiled, wrapped his fingers around the chain link, and dropped to his knees.

The dog crashed into the fence then fell back onto his hind legs. They collapsed under him. Bad hips.

"Nothing to do about that, is there?" he said.

"Acetaminophen for the pain," the girl said. "You're sure that's him though?"

Because of the snarling, the snapping.

William shrugged, squinched one side of his face up.

"I didn't—my friend. I shouldn't even tell you this. He doesn't know I have him, Lobo."

"You *stole* him?"

William closed his eyes, as if controlling his voice.

"He kept him chained to a telephone pole all day." He shrugged. "Not even shade, y'know? The kids after school, I'd see them . . . Doesn't matter."

The girl was watching the dog now. Again.

"So Lobo's not his name?"

"It's his new name."

The girl didn't smile, didn't nod, just looked to the dog, on one side of the wire door, William on his knees on the other.

"I—I . . ." she started, then pulled the radio back to her mouth, thumbed it open, but finally didn't say anything.

"What already?" Thad snapped back, in the middle of what sounded like a bad scene with a large cat.

Instead of reporting, the girl smiled over her hand. At William.

William smiled back.

"Nothing," she said, lowering the radio back to her belt. "This isn't procedure, you know that, right?" she said.

William shrugged. "Don't want to get you in trouble," he said, reaching back, touching his wallet.

The girl shook her head no.

"It has to cost something," William said.

"Twenty-five," the girl said, taking down the rainbow leash from its hook by 24B, Lobo's run. "If there was going to be any paper work, I mean," she added. "Twenty-five for shots and neuter."

William nodded, watching her.

"If there was going to be paper work," he repeated.

She nodded with him, watching Lobo.

"Not like I'm on the clock anymore, really," she said, shrugging, passing the leash over. "Right?"

William worked the clasp on the leash, the skin on the side of his index finger alive where it had brushed her hand.

Behind the chain link, Lobo was growling now, just a steady rumble.

"Thanks," William said.

The girl smiled. "For what? I'm not even here, right?"

William didn't let himself smile, then stood in the door of the run with her when she opened it. Like, if Lobo had anything bad, any violence he'd been saving up for the last thirty-six hours, William was going to be the one to take it here.

He was an old dog with bad hips though. Used to being the biggest, sure, his head a cinder block he could clear a room with. But William had been doing this for years, from Florida to Texas. All along I-10.

When the dog slung his head around, William popped his knee to the side, rattling its teeth, then, covering it with his flannel body, he popped the dog once with the heel of his hand, hard, at the base of his spine. Just enough for the back legs to give. Then it was just a matter of leaning down onto the thick neck, working the rainbow leash around, clasping it to itself.

The dog's—*Lobo's*—eyes shot red almost immediately with the pressure, the lack of air, and William kept his hand close to the clasp, so he had to walk hunched over.

The girl was on the other side of the hall now, a can of something defensive in her hand.

William smiled.

"Not his fault," he said, urging the dog along.

"He won't—he won't get out again . . . ?"

"The fence—" William said, making more of the struggle than there was, "fixed, yeah . . . don't worry," and then left the girl there like that, never even had to use the Pinzer name, or Pinker, or whatever the hell it had been.

Two dogs later—a shepherd mix and a golden retriever, each from the classifieds, families he'd had to make earnest, shuffling promises to—William pulled into a gas station, checked all his doors, and asked the clerk for the bathroom key.

"Have to buy something," the clerk said, shrugging that it wasn't his rule, but hey.

William looked down the candy aisle behind him, came back to the clerk.

"I will," he said.

"*First*," the clerk added.

He was five-eight maybe. A smoker.

William stared at him, stared at him, then lifted an air freshener off the revolving display by the register. Ninety-nine cents. He laid down a dollar, counted out one nickel and two pennies.

"Bag?" the clerk asked.

William shook his head no.

The air freshener was an ice cream cone, pink. It smelled like bubble gum. William tucked it into the chest pocket of his flannel jacket and took the key the clerk held across the counter. It was chained to the rusted steel rim of a go-cart maybe. Or a kid's old three-wheeler. Nine inches across, four-hole, maybe eight pounds.

William held it easy, nodded to the clerk, and chanced a look out to his truck. It was parked against the shattered pay phone.

No plates visible, just a side shot, a profile. Hardly even a real color.

William stepped away from the security camera, rounded the corner of the building for the bathroom. When the door wouldn't lock behind him, he set the key with its ATV rim down on the concrete, as a doorstop. And then he unrolled his leather case, let the water run until it was hot, and started applying the razor to his face, to his beard.

Because the door wasn't shut all the way, the mirror didn't steam up. William took note of this. Mirrors were always a problem. Scratched in this one were years of names and profanities and lopsided shapes—stars, crosses, lines that were going to be something complicated but got interrupted when the door had opened.

Something complicated: William smiled, pulled the skin tight against his jaw, his six-week beard collecting in the drain, then froze, his elbow out like a bat wing.

A noise, at the door?

In the mirror, William was distant, his face lathered in the pink soap from the dispenser. Distant but coiled.

It was nothing. Raccoon nosing the base of the closed door. Blow-by from the big trucks.

William returned to his beard, stopping with just a mustache for a bit— his father's, silver the farther it got from his mouth—then going fast over it, deep enough that, near the lip on the left side, the razor burn he could already feel welled up into tiny points of blood. Like he was sweating it.

Outside, a car or truck rolled across the hose attached to the bell.

Past that, the interstate, its steel-belted hum.

William closed his eyes, let it wash over him, then slammed his open hand into the side of the sink, told himself he wasn't alone, that this could have been it—that you can't do that, close your eyes in public places. Alone maybe. But even then.

William rolled the razor back into its pack, tied the string and ran the water until his beard was gone, and then he peed on top of it. Because the urine, leeching through whatever the hair was going to ball up against in the pipes, the urine would corrode the hair into something else.

After the beard, William took his shirt off, held it up to the light over the mirror. It was clean, so he didn't burn it, but he didn't put it back on either. Just the jacket. Driving at night was better with no shirt. And he was going to make Beaumont by dawn.

First, though, the clerk.

William picked up the key and its ATV wheel, his middle finger in the groove where the wheel had been welded together. So it would roll off when he threw it, the key slinging around it on the chain like a fast, tiny moon.

The car that had pulled up to the gas tanks was a Chevette. Kids, one of them standing at the rear bumper. William looked down, away from any eye contact, then walked far enough around the side of the building to lift the wheel behind him like a bowling ball, like a disc. But then the kid was calling something out to him.

William turned to him.

The kid hooked his head into the gas station.

"He said I'm next."

William looked through the unbroken plate glass, to the small image of himself on the security monitor, and nodded, held the key up, showing he was surrendering it. The kid started across the slick concrete to take it. His arm was covered in blue tattoos. William took a half step back then set the wheel with its key down on the curb, and he was already walking away, already disappearing.

His truck was a 1981 F-250, and it was legal: stickers, registration, insurance. Each light worked, except the cargo. The wire that fed it was tied into the dome light, inside the cab, just over the back window. To get it to work—the cargo— William just had to take the plastic case off the dome light, pull the bulb, and set the raw wire into the socket, work the bulb in with it like a fuse.

He was forty-two miles from the gas station when he started working the plastic bubble off. It was cold, stiff, would break easy if he wasn't careful, then everybody would see the bare bulb, know something was wrong. He couldn't heat it up with the light though either; if you were driving with your dome on, the state cops had to assume it was to find another beer, or to see the nudie mag on your passenger seat. So William edged the plastic bubble out one corner at a time with his right hand, his left steady on the wheel, and had been seeing it for maybe two seconds before it registered: a dark lump, stretched out along the shoulder of the interstate.

He smiled, forgot the dome light. Replayed the dark lump in his head.

When his rearview was clear he eased over, then turned his lights off and backed up twenty yards at a time, letting the tractor trailers sweep past. If they saw him, none of them blew their horns, though something did move in the grass once, which could have been a bottle, whipped out the passenger side at seventy miles per hour, the way the truckers liked to do it. William knew this from his father, had learned it at ten years old, how to sit perfectly still every few miles, his back pressing into the seat, a wine-cooler bottle spinning past his face, connecting with a mile marker, his father watching in the side mirror then slamming the heel of his hand into the top of the wheel in celebration.

William never thought about it on purpose, but sometimes it came unbidden, all on its own. Not the bottles so much as the high-up seat, how still he had to sit in it, how he had to push on the legs of his jeans to stay like that long enough for the bottle to slice by his face. And how, even though he didn't want to, he'd listen along with his dad, for the chance of shattering glass behind them.

Sometimes, ten years old again, he would be in the seat listening, and other times he would be in the ditch, waiting for the bottle to slam into his head.

He was in the truck now though. *His* truck.

It was important to always remember that.

He stopped alongside the dark lump and watched it for long minutes. The way none of the people driving by even noticed it.

He nodded that the world was a good place, a good place for someone like him, then opened his door, the dome light sputtering, the bulb half-out. He reached back in, tapped it into place, the current running through him to the ground for an instant. It was nothing.

He approached from downwind, to get the smell, know the whole animal, the blood, the feces, the fear if there'd been any, if it had looked up into the headlights. Because of the slant of the ditch he had to go on three points—both feet and one hand, the other shielding his eyes from the traffic.

Driving by, he'd thought it was a deer, maybe, its coat matted with blood, making it black, but now, now it was a dog, just too big.

He made himself move slow, just walk.

From his truck, no barking. Night falling down all around him.

He stepped up onto the shoulder and already there was blood. Just spatter, like a mist that had settled. He stepped around it as best he could, caught an air horn for his effort. It straightened his back, took his breath in the best possible way.

And then he smiled an accidental smile: a *bear*. A little black, a cub maybe. That was what it was.

William lowered himself to it, running his hand along its thick coat.

A bear.

He had never touched one before.

Its shoulder and head were shattered, one of its forelegs missing, burned off on the asphalt. But a *bear*. William could feel himself getting hard in his pants, looked to the interstate just in time for a dummy light to blaze across his face.

The hand he'd had at his crotch came up to his eyes.

The cop walked up out of the light, his hand to the butt of his pistol, his flashlight feeling out through the ditch, splashing against William's truck.

William stayed with the bear. Just touching it.

"What you got?" the cop said.

William shrugged, almost said *Billy Pinzer* but instead just watched a cabover like his father's push past. Pulling silage, it smelled like.

What he had to do now was breathe evenly. Not run. Remember to swallow.

The cop eased around the bear so he was facing traffic, played his light across the bear, then up to William again.

"You hit it?" he asked.

William shook his head no. "Just saw it, I guess."

The cop kind of laughed. "And you—you *stopped*?"

William shrugged. "Thought it might be . . . you know. Hurt."

The cop didn't nod but didn't quite keep his head still either. He trained the light down onto the bear again.

"Probably endangered," he said. "You want it, that it? The skin, teeth, that shit?"

William shook his head no, stood.

"What'll—what'll happen to it?" he said.

The cop watched a pair of headlights long enough that William turned. They were bouncing off the yellow line. The cop exhaled through his nose.

"Can't leave it here," he said. "Buzzards'll come, and—shit. They're endangered too, yeah?"

William pretended to suppress a disgusted laugh.

"I'll call it in maybe," the cop said. "Biologists like this kind of shit. Hell if I know why."

William nodded, made himself keep not looking to his truck. The cop was though. His light was already playing on the windows of the camper.

"What about—about like, dogs and stuff?" William said. "Deer? What do you do with them?"

"Not endangered," the cop said, taking advantage of the break in traffic to step back around the bear, towards his car. "Some people eat the shit, I've heard, I don't know." He hooked the brim of his stiff hat to his car. "We've got shovels, y'know. If it's impeding traffic, we help it into the ditch."

William nodded.

"Him?" he said, about the bear.

The cop looked down to it too.

"Was it in your way as a motorist, Mr. . . . ?"

William looked away.

"Pinzer," he said, like he'd been saying it his whole life. Then he shook his head no, it hadn't been in his way.

The cop flashed his light down onto the truck again.

"You've got four-wheel drive on her?"

William nodded.

The cop shrugged. "This is Louisiana," he said. "I mean, I'd never advise leaving the blacktop unless I had to, know?"

"I'm careful," William said.

The cop nodded, spit.

"Where to?"

"My sister. Shreveport."

The cop touched something off the right lens of the glasses he had hooked in his pocket.

"Fucking bear," he said.

"I know," William said back, and they smiled together.

Two minutes later, the cop was gone.

William looked at the bear for maybe thirty seconds more, thanking it, then pushed it as far into the road as he could. He hadn't lied to the cop though: he didn't want it. A bear would draw too much attention.

The first truck that hit it caught it across its hindquarters, forcing all the air and gases in its body up past its throat, past its voice box.

William screamed with it.

Three miles after the next rest stop—Louisiana, still—next to a burned-out trailer house with trees growing all around it, William hung his bubble-gum pink ice cream cone from the rearview, turned the cargo light on.

Lobo was there, and the shepherd mix he was supposed to call Max and feed canned food twice a day, and the golden retriever with the red handkerchief tied around his neck like a cartoon dog.

They were dead, of course, lined up against the naked body of the woman as if nursing.

Her name was M-something, William didn't know.

She had been an accident. Not on purpose. From Birmingham.

William stepped up into the camper with her and laid sideways behind her, stroking the top of her arm, getting hard again.

But there was no time for that.

William closed his eyes, told himself that, that there was no time, then let his hand fall to the soft muzzle of one of the dogs, and came anyway five minutes later, his hand against the dog's dry tongue, the place where the girl's nipple had been, then he cried into her matted hair, apologized. Hit the side of his hand again and again into the bed of the truck, until that hand was numb. And then the rest of him too. Just cold, nothing.

He was ready.

Twenty miles deeper into Louisiana, at a truck stop, he pulled over, walked back to his passenger-side rear tire, and popped the camper shell open.

In the dead space between trucks pulling out of second gear, building speed for the interstate, he slung Lobo out into the ribbon of shiny asphalt, where the tires ran. He weighed half again as much as he had, was pregnant with the girl now. Pieces of her anyway.

In the back of the truck, on the tarp, William had laid out her arms, all four pieces of her legs, and the four quarters of her torso. From biggest to smallest. The head he ran over with his truck again and again, until there was nothing left of the teeth or any of it, and then he buried it, peed a circle around it to keep guard.

Then it was back to the tarp.

Working in the dim glow of the cargo lamp, he opened the three dogs from sternum to asshole, cleaned them out, and tried to fit what he could into each: an arm, part of a ribcage, a lower leg. When he was done, the dogs sewn up with pig string, William had nodded, stood from his work, and caught the shadow of something in the door of the burned-out trailer behind him.

He turned the cargo light off—everything calm, no problem—folded the tarp up, pushed the dogs carefully back under the camper, then stood facing the trailer for twelve minutes.

Nothing moved. He dared it to, but nothing did.

Finally he nodded, narrowed his eyes, and marked the place in his mind, so he could come back sometime when he could leave what was in his truck in his truck.

Not tonight though.

Four miles back, he'd already been seeing the signs for the truck stop, could feel a flat coming on.

He didn't even have to get the jack out this time. Just opened the tailgate, positioned Lobo on the road, then closed the tailgate, pulled away. At first, years ago, he'd always had to wait, to see the trucks come, watch them flatten all the bones at once, human and canine, but now, now he knew it happened whether he was there or not. The only other choice would be someone stopping to autopsy this dog that had already been hit. Or to move it out of the way. But only the state cops did that, and this was a county road, or parish, whatever things were in Louisiana.

The next dog he left on an exit ramp, in the intersection, where everybody was supposed to yield.

The golden retriever with the red handkerchief he simply stood up with a dry branch in a low spot on the service road, eighteen miles down from Lobo. Stood him up, circled back, then ran him down, leaning into his horn at the last minute, closing his eyes to the thumping from underneath, the crunching—*Marissa*, that had been it—then downshifting for the hill ahead, for Beaumont.

2.

Four months later—Houston—William tried for the third time to balance his empty beer can on the four-wheel-drive shifter of the Chevy he had now. For a moment, maybe, it held, staying there for him, but then fell into the passenger-side floorboard with the rest.

He was sitting in the first visitor row of the downtown hospital parking lot.

The Chevy was because that state cop had caressed the Ford with his flashlight. William had tried to forget it, tried not to feel the heat the flashlight had pulled across the skin of his truck, the sharp-edged shadows the trim and fender flares had cast, but it was too much. Each time since then that he'd walked up on the truck from that angle—after work (stacking transmissions), after the bar, after buying all the newspapers he was in—it had been the same: that night, the bear. And because it was like that for him, it had to be for the cop too. So the Ford had to go.

William had sold it to one of the mechanics at his work, Al, who never looked anybody in the eye but had told William once that he'd started out at the shop scraping gaskets too. That if William just stuck around long enough, a sentence he finished by studying the insulation chicken-wired to the metal walls.

William had shrugged, looked out at the traffic, Al peeling up a line of the seal that had been under the camper shell. Then, William had been saving it, the shell, for his next Ford, but that was what he'd sold the first Ford for, right?

Now it was in his efficiency apartment, the camper, leaned up over the window.

He didn't know what to do with it.

The Chevy was one the garage across the street had applied for the title for, in lieu of payment for services. The title had come back salvage; the manager let William have it for eight hundred. Alone in the parking lot after hours, William sifted through the cab, the gum wrappers, beer caps, and dimes that had settled behind the seat. The stack of magazines by the seat adjustment: *Shaved, Bare, Lassie.*

William dropped them into the asphalt, backing away, shaking his head no, he wasn't like that anymore.

But then the magazines started opening by themselves, in the wind.

After three weeks, William made himself throw them away in fourteen separate dumpsters. It was too late though; his beard was thick again, full. He replaced the magazines under the seat with clippings of himself: a missing girl in Pensacola, another just outside Hattiesburg. Sixteen over the last nine and a half years, the first two still buried in plastic drop cloths, soaked first in ammonia, then pesticide, then gear oil. So none of the gas of decay would work its way up through the soil.

He'd put them side by side, east and west, faceup.

The first time he'd gone back to see them, grass was growing everywhere but the two rectangles where they were.

William had started breathing hard, too hard, and returned with fertilizer, Bermuda grass seeds, finally flowers. They all died, until he understood: the ground was dead, it needed life. William had nodded, unzipped his pants, and, over the course of five weeks, left enough of his seed on the graves that the soil took on a richer color, and then a plant of some sort raised its head. William named it Baby Green, thought about it when he wasn't there, then watched it stand up straight, establishing itself.

Once, William reached down to touch it, just once, but then saw something watching him across the field.

It was a dog, her teats heavy, dragging.

William stood, and she didn't move, didn't move. Like she knew.

Four weeks after that, going back to check on Baby Green, sure that a raccoon was digging the girls up for their silver rings, William's headlights caught eleven perfect little puppies walking across the road. Their shadows were taller than his headlights could reach.

William opened his door, stepped down, and the mother dog came for him from the tall grass, and it was all slow motion, overfull with meaning, with detail.

At the last moment he pushed her aside with his boot, stepped back into the truck. Rolled forward carefully, respectfully.

After that, he started noticing all the dead animals along the interstate.

Baby Green was still out there too, William knew. A fairy tale beanstalk he could never see again, because the graves were probably staked out by patient men with mirrored sunglasses.

In the parking lot of the hospital, William opened a fifth beer. Some of it splashed onto the leg of his jeans and he stood up. It made it to the seat of his pants anyway. The crack of his ass.

She would never talk to him now.

Her name was Julia. A caramel-colored nurse.

William had got her name off her nameplate by timing his entrance with her exit a week ago, then done it again, in case she'd just been borrowing somebody's ID that night.

Julia.

She got off every night at eleven. Wore a series of headbands, probably to keep her hair out of patients' faces. Or to keep them from falling in love with her.

Tonight, William watched the waist of her aquamarine scrubs for a zip key, a handheld radio. The best forty-five seconds of the night were her, stepping across the crosswalk, dipping her head down for the cell phone, the call she only made once she was outside the magnets and radiation of the hospital.

There was never any blood on her scrubs, never anybody walking with her. Just Julia, Julia.

William smiled, nodded, and turned his truck on just after she'd passed, so his brake lights could turn her red in his side mirror.

She never looked back.

William drank the fifth beer down, eased out of Visitor Parking, past the security booth, which pulled the blinds down at five-thirty, and out into the road. For a moment at thirty-five miles per hour, there was a squirrel in the road, flattened to the pavement.

William said it aloud: "Squirrels."

They didn't hold anything.

What he needed now, and what he knew he didn't need, was a camper shell for the Chevy. The one in his apartment he had pieced up with a hacksaw and a pair of tin snips, then finally just carried the last four big pieces away in the bed of his truck, left them in four different alleys, upside down to catch rain, become a nuisance, a mosquito pool, the edges sharp enough that only the garbage men with their thick, city-bought gloves would be able to lift them. And garbage men didn't care about anything. William knew; it was one of the jobs his father had taken, after the army, before all the wine coolers that didn't count as drinking, that didn't break any promises.

Again William remembered building forts with his brother in the living room.

Their father was always the Indian. The one who had taken their mother away.

William slammed his fist into the horn of the Chevy. It honked. The man in the leather vest behind the counter of the pawnshop ratcheted his head around to the sound, then up the hood to William.

William looked away, pursed his lips. Backed out.

The paper had said they had camper shells, but it was just to get the hunters in, sell them a gun. William didn't need a gun though. He used his blinker to get in front of a blue El Camino. What he needed was a camper shell. Because if he didn't get one, he would be back to tarps, and wouldn't be able to drive on the interstate anymore, because the truckers would see, radio ahead.

Because because because.

William had $300 dollars in his pocket, part of it an advance on his pay-check, part left over from selling the Ford.

That was another reason he was leaving Houston: every day, he had to see his old truck across the road, cocked at an angle against the chain link, by the parts cars.

Finally, in the classifieds, William found a camper shell. It was supposed to be north of town, and east. Tomball, in the crotch of I-10 and I-45. He had to call twice for directions, then listen for real the second time. Each time, the man who answered the phone thought William was calling about a help wanted ad, somebody to replace his son. One hour later—eight miles—William turned up the long driveway of the farmhouse, slowed alongside the camper shell. It was on an old Gentleman Jim, had been painted black and gold to match the truck, then had the paint baked on.

William stepped out, ran his hand over the warm fiberglass, then looked at his palm. It was glittering. Past it, the old man, picking his way through all the other junked cars. He held his hand out, looked over William's shoulder at his Chevy. It was gold and white, the colors of some oil company from West Texas.

The old man nodded.

"It matches," he said. "The gold, right?"

The old man was sixty-eight, maybe seventy-four. A house twice as old as him, at the end of a series of dirt roads that were better than any fence. Most of the land around the house was weeds, some of it on the downslope spongy with swamp water, thick with frogs.

William looked to the Gentleman Jim then raised one cheek, narrowing that eye. He shook his head no.

"You don't think it'll fit," the old man said. "It will."

"I know," William said. "But—the paint, I mean. You can't just spray fiber-glass yourself."

The old man agreed.

"Seventy then," he said, no eye contact.

William shrugged, looked to the shell again. The ad in the paper had an *OBO* after the *$100*. "I don't know," he said.

Overhead, one small airplane whined just as another—yellow—broke from the line of trees down the hill from the man's house.

William flinched backwards, stumbled into the grass.

The old man looked to the plane to let William avoid the embarrassment of trying to stand as if nothing had happened.

"Maniacs," he said. "There should be a law."

It was a crop duster. The racks of nozzles, the bitter smell in the air, then, just all at once, no smell at all. William knew the herbicide had numbed his nose. He still couldn't talk.

"Fifty," the old man said, toeing the ground.

William opened the envelope from his shirt pocket, counted out the three bills, and then the old man insisted on a receipt, was gone for ten minutes to the house, for pen and paper.

William ducked again the next time the plane came, but this time saw a roll of toilet paper trail down from it. It was how the pilots flew when they didn't have a spotter—how they marked their passes.

"Maniac," William said to the plane, low, smiling, then got the wrenches and pliers and flat-head from his truck, started getting the camper ready to move off the Gentleman Jim.

When the old man came back with his receipt the SOLD TO part was blank. William wrote in *Bill Dozier* then laid on his back in the bed of the Gentleman Jim, placed the soles of his boots against the underside of the camper shell. At first, pushing with his legs, it just rained fiberglass down onto him—spun light—but then the foam seal on one side gave, then the other, and the camper shell shifted towards the rear of the truck. The old man stepped forward to take its weight, and, behind him, looking between his legs, there was a large, dark dog, loping through the grass.

The old man followed William's eyes, turned, then called something out to the dog, a name William didn't quite catch. *Blanco? Blackie?*

"He didn't hear you," William said.

The old man laughed without smiling. "He heard me," he said.

Moments later, the black dog was there. A puppy in an adult-dog body, unable to stand still. Excited just to be alive for another perfect day.

William let himself pet it between the shoulder blades. The dog craned its head around, to lick the sweat from William's wrist.

William looked up, for the plane he was hearing again. It was what the dog had been chasing probably. The shadow coursing along the ground, blackening a tree for a moment, so that it looked new again when the plane was gone.

William understood.

He stepped down from the tailgate of the Gentleman Jim, all his weight on his left arm for a breath, the shoulder there forever torn.

"What?" the old man asked.

William realized he was making a noise in his throat.

"Nothing," he said, then took the old man's eyes away from that side of his body, ran his other hand along the side window of the camper, in appreciation. All that was left now was to back his truck up, work the camper from one to the other, and screw it down. The foam kit, he would get in town. Then he could back the truck into the empty bay at work, chock the shell up on blocks, sand down the bed rails.

But that was all later. Everything was later, nothing was now. Just the sound of that crop duster, the black dog streaking across the field.

William was sure the plane wasn't going to clear the trees this time.

He opened his mouth to tell the dog, but the old man was still watching him, following his arm out to the dog, an acre away already.

"Need one?" he said.

It was a joke.

Across the field, the yellow plane crashed up into the sky again, tearing away from the earth.

"Not yet," William said, swallowing his smile.

Not yet.

Three six-packs later, William sat up against the sink of his apartment and cried and cried. Like a baby, like a goddamn girl.

The one name he never gave anybody was William H. Bonney. Billy the Kid.

Surrounded by couch cushions in the living room, he had been Billy the Kid, his brother Jesse James, because his name had started with a *J*.

Their father's Indian name was Bites All the Way Through, was Kicks Open the Door Until the House Falls Over, was Born With Teeth, was Custer. This was when they didn't understand, thought Custer was Indian.

William rubbed heat into his shoulder and drank another beer, promised Julia that it was going to be all right this time. That he didn't have to do anything. And then he said it out loud, like a defense, like the only logical answer—cowboys and Indians, Dad—but heard again his shoulder tearing, like the sound had never even left his body after all these years, had just been traveling back and forth along the guitar-string tendons of his neck, burrowing into his inner ear.

The reason his dad had been jerking him up from the couch was because they weren't supposed to play on the couch like that anymore. Because their mom was going to be home soon.

William reeled his pocket watch up, studied it.

Julia was in the eighth hour of her shift probably. Holding the pad of her middle finger to a patient's pulse, counting under her breath. The clock ticking, moving, each second two cents to her maybe, or more—a nickel? William had no idea how much a nurse made.

He said it again, cowboys and Indians, then put himself back into the pound. As Pinzer. Walking down the hall behind the caramel-colored attendant who's already off the clock. The pound where she has her keys zipped out from her belt, is twirling them around her index finger, letting them swing back to her palm again and again.

William follows, follows, all the dogs in their runs barking and barking, but no sound.

"This one," he says, about a Husky, then, about a chocolate Lab with child eyes, "No, this one."

The attendant in front of him smiles, keeps swishing back and forth, *knows*, and William follows her around one corner, then another, and then she's waiting for him with a hose. It's on, just trickling because she knows how to work it. She asks if he's thirsty and he says *yes*, drinks. When he looks up, she's unlocking an empty run.

He walks in behind her because she wants him too. She's already stepping out of her scrubs, using her feet to pull the loose pants down each leg.

William smiles at the tan lines he wouldn't have expected on her, how close the top line of her bikini dips to her nipple, how close her aureole is to the sun—how wide it is, spreading like a stain, like she was dipped in something then laid out on her back—then sees that his hand is in his pants, like he told himself to do in the parking lot, and then she comes to him, hooking one brown leg around his side, grinding her warmth up against him, breathing into his ear, and that was the way he came back to his kitchen: hard, all the air in his apartment compressed in his lungs. Pushing with his heels on the linoleum.

He barely made it to the hospital in time, then came just as Julia stepped into the crosswalk, gushing onto his chest and stomach so much he thought that maybe he was bleeding somehow, that he was shooting spinal fluid, then gagging from the thought of it, splashing hot vomit into the tilted well of the speedometer, down along the steering column to the fire wall. Crying still, because he knew from the way he'd taken the caramel-colored pound attendant, from the way he'd been about to take her, the way she turned around for him, resting the tips of her fingers on the stained concrete, he knew she was pregnant now with a litter of puppies that were going to eat her the first chance they got.

Two days later Al called him from the shop, to ask where he wanted his check mailed. What there was of it, after the advance.

"I'll come get it," William said.

"Not a good idea, hoss," Al said back, low enough that William knew Mitch was standing in the bay by the phone.

"Sorry," William said, when it seemed like Al was waiting for him to say something.

"Where you been?"

"My shoulder," William lied.

Al laughed—shaped his breath into a laugh, it sounded like. So he wouldn't have to smile.

"This a workman's comp issue?" he said, quieter, the punch line.

William shrugged.

After that, Al said something, William said something—none of it mattered, was like other people talking—and then William put the phone back on its cradle.

He hadn't been back to the hospital since the night he'd thrown up all his love for Julia, then fingered it back in. Off his chest too, the strings matting his beard. Since the night he'd started his truck when it was already running, the metal-on-bone sound of his flywheel jerking her head around in his side mirror, her hair in the brake lights sideways from her body for one perfect instant—a communion. A moment they'd shared, the rabbit recognizing a blind spot in the trail it had been walking for weeks now.

An accident.

William leaned into the wall by the phone and apologized to her again. Because now he had no choice—she knew his truck, had marked how the black-and-gold camper shell didn't fit the oil-field pale body. Because now she was trying to remember if it had been there the night before, or was it last week? She was probably making up a history for him, even, William: that his brother was in ICU, that he was driving up from Galveston each night just to sit by the hospital bed, struggle through the day's paper out loud.

Like that could have saved James. Like anything could have.

In his apartment, William smiled.

Now that he had to do it, it would be easy.

He spent the rest of the afternoon wiping down his apartment, even the underside of the toilet lid, the inside of the P trap in the kitchen, then an hour trying to fit the magnet from the mouthpiece of the phone up into the earpiece, then two minutes locking the door behind him, then dusk at a filling station, for the Chevy's two tanks, then lining the camper shell with black RTV sealant, because he hadn't had time for the foam kit. All that was left was answering an index card that had been posted at the animal clinic with a red tack in the shape of a heart. An index card that had been posted just for him.

The woman who answered the door was a girl. Eleven, twelve. Her eyes tracked all the way up William. His hands were already in his pocket, his sunglasses hooked into his flannel shirt.

"Hello," he said.

The girl called behind her, for her mother.

She was even better. William looked down along the porch, steadied himself on the wall.

"Yes?" the mother said, one hand on her daughter's shoulder, ready to pull the girl into the house, step between.

William felt his eyes heat up about this.

"The—the Lhasa," he said, like a question.

The mother tried looking past him, for his truck, but it was down the street where some Mexicans were working a lawn.

"You're . . ?" the mother started.

William opened his mouth, stepped back in apology.

"Just—sorry, sorry. I just . . . my daughter, I'm seeing her this weekend."

The mother looked up to him, to his eyes.

"Her birthday," he explained, and then it was there, the Lhasa, yapping, its tiny forepaws edging past the weather-stripping on the floor.

The mother nodded. A cordless phone in her hand. William wondered how anybody ever strangled anybody anymore.

The index card had said FREE TO GOOD HOME.

The mother nodded down to William's left hand. His naked ring finger.

In return, he shrugged, squinted away, down the street, to the sound of a weed-eater or an edger.

"She looks like her," he said finally, lifting his chin to the daughter.

The daughter shrank to her mother's leg some.

Inside, William smiled. Outside, he shrugged again, shook his head no. Arranged his face into an outside smile too.

"I'm lying," he said, like it had been going to come out anyway. "She's—Kimbo. She's not mine. My brother's girl. Niece. I just like to . . . y'know. Pretend."

"Maybe your brother can—" the mother started, but William closed his eyes tight, shook his head no.

"He can't," he said.

That part wasn't a lie.

Two minutes later, the mother calling her husband, "to let him know about Vanessa," the dog—really just an excuse to leave the phone on, to let William know the phone was on—William stepped into the house, felt like he was balancing on the welcome mat. He looked back, where he'd just been, on the porch: there was no one watching.

Twofer Tuesday, he said to himself, a thing he'd been hearing on the radio, and stepped off, onto the pale, absorbent carpet of the living room.

This time he parked in the second row of Visitor's, first the other way, nosed away from the hospital, so she would just be seeing the top of the camper, the tailgate, but then realizing in a desperate rush that that's what she'd already seen when he'd started his already-started truck last week. He backed out, turned around and reversed into the slot, scratching the tires with each gear change, then didn't let himself drink any beer except one, and then another to hide the first, to stop his hands from shaking, and finally just three, to get it over with.

From the floorboard with all the cans, Vanessa stared at him.

He smiled down to her, patted her on the head.

Her bowl and extra collar and her favorite pink ball were in three dumpsters on three different streets. The mother and daughter had insisted William take them. The only thing he'd kept was the rhinestone leash, but then, walking away from their house, he hadn't even used it. Instead, he'd carried Vanessa like a baby, like they wanted him to, whispering down into her left ear that he knew what she tasted like, yes he did yes he did.

Everything was falling into place. Like always.

Ten thirty came and went, then 10:32, then 10:35. Two hours later, it was almost 11:00. William stroked his beard down along his jaw, blinked too much, and rocked in his seat, went through the checklist again, making sure.

When she walked out all at once, looking into her purse, he straightened his right leg hard, washing the cars in his side mirrors angry red, look-at-me-I'm-the-I-10-Killer-give-away red, but then knew it was now, it was now. Because once she got her cell phone open—

It was the only reason he wasn't simply parked by her car, out in B.

Now, now.

He stepped from his truck, pulled Vanessa down to the end of his row, opposite the truck. Knew the rhinestones were going to give him away, that he should just—

But no: now.

This.

It was why they were alone here in the middle of the city, charmed, nobody walking in from the parking lot, nobody pushing through the exit doors.

William smiled, nodded.

She was four long steps from the crosswalk now, the phone in her hand, her finger to the call button, she was four, three steps from the crosswalk when

William choked up on the leash with his right hand, still holding the loop in his left. Like that, he could lift Vanessa, swing her, her collar already tightened then double-checked.

One time around, then two, the soft Lhasa body stiff at the end of the leash, then more slack, like a hammer throw, then he let her go into the sky, followed through with his right arm.

Five seconds, then Vanessa fell into the crosswalk Julia should have been using, for safety.

Julia stopped, the cell to her ear, ringing probably, and she looked at it, the dog, then looked up into the sky, lowered the phone.

There were maybe one thousand things that could happen now.

William knew she would accept any of them too: a man in an almost-white truck with a black camper, pulling out of the Visitor's lot, stopping at the small, white, twitching dog, stepping out, locking eyes with Julia, asking her without words what happened, his truck too loud so she has to take a step closer, another step, and by then she's already started dying.

From a phone booth at a gas station at the Texas state line, William called to confess, to tell her everything, the caramel-colored pound attendant, that he loves her, that he was confused, that he's sorry, that she doesn't understand, but then he didn't know her name. So he explained her to the pound's night attendant, explained her too well—her nipples under her scrub shirt, how she was one of those girls who wore a tank top instead of a bra—then asked about the pregnant dog. If her puppies were running around the waiting room already, pulling all the stuffing from all the chairs. If their eyes were open yet or if they were still blind.

The attendant on the other end laughed through his nose.

"Blind," he said, "yeah. Technically, I mean. If you count dead."

William leaned deeper into the phone booth.

"And the—the mother?"

The attendant laughed again, said William wasn't shitting about Charla, there, the house pointer, then laughed some more, hung up while he was doing it so that William had to picture him sitting there, alone in the pound, eyes teared up from laughing. At William.

He turned to his truck, knew suddenly in the way he knew things that he was parked too close to the trash can. That the clerk or the clerk's manager or a homeless person or a monkey escaped from the circus was going to reach into the trash, pull out the three strips William had just cut the junk license plates into.

William shook his head no, wiped the phone down, then almost ran across the concrete to the truck, to the trash can, pushing his arm as deep as he could into it, deep enough that he had to turn his head away, point his chin up. The clerk standing at the glass door, watching.

William raised his other hand, waved, made himself smile as if this were all some big mistake—the credit card itself, instead of the receipt, the beer bottle instead of the cap.

The clerk raised his hand back hesitantly, his face wrenched into a fake smile as well.

William left with two of the license plate strips, a cut finger wrapped in electric tape, and Julia, asleep in back, tied and gagged under the tarp, the tarp held down with toolboxes with real tools in them (Mitch's), and a cooler with bumper stickers all over it, beer inside.

She wasn't awake yet.

William apologized to her again, for how cold the tarp was going to be for her, naked like that. The tips of her breasts stiff against the black, woven plastic.

Drive, he told himself. Miles, miles, go go go.

Louisiana was a familiar bog of smells and alligator eyes.

William held the wheel with both hands, accidentally looked up to a cab-over passing him slow in the left lane, and knew for an instant it was his father, straightened his back into the seat for the coolness of the wine-cooler bottle, whooshing by.

When it never came, the truck driver just nodded, pulled ahead in a way that William knew he had read the last number called on Julia's cell phone. It was open on the seat beside him, its small screen glowing green, a beacon.

William made himself slow down to sixty, spit the taste of adrenaline out the window. He turned the radio up.

The last person he'd seen in Texas, the last person who could identify him, had been a paramedic pushing an empty gurney across the Emergency lane, from one red curb to another. William had stopped, and the paramedic had raised his fingers on the aluminum tubing, in thanks.

"No problem," William said, both in the Emergency lane and in Louisiana, then nodded instead of waving back, because her hair had still been in his fingers, from pulling her into the cab, slamming her face into the dashboard three times fast.

All she had left behind was one shoe, but he'd backed up, leaned down for it, then pulled away, no headlights.

Three miles past a rest stop—always three miles, because by then the truckers would be into their tall gears, be making too much time to stop—three miles past a rest stop, he finally climbed back through the sliding rear window he'd fed her through in Houston.

The radio was still on, the old, nasal country William hated drifting in from the cab.

But Julia.

He lay down beside her, the tarp still between them. Used his finger to find her mouth then pushed the very tip of his knife through the tarp and through the duct tape stretched across her lower face.

She was awake. Just a small hole in a piece of black plastic.

William said her name and she didn't say anything back.

The tape across her lower face was parallel to the tape across her forehead, keeping the back of her head to the bed of the truck. William had pushed her bangs out of the way as much as he could.

He came on her stomach and she never felt it.

Julia.

If he did everything right this time, she might last four days, maybe even five. Six was the record but he knew better than to go longer, that they would get a power over him then.

"You're a nurse," he told her, instead of everything else.

She moved. It was maybe a nod.

William nodded with her, cut a hole over her left eye but messed up, had to do the right instead.

He held the green display of the cell phone up to the hole, at all the distances between two inches and a foot.

"Who's Robert?" he asked, using the same voice he'd used to tell her she was a nurse.

Robert was from her message log. Robert Mendes.

Julia moved again but this time it was no, a plea with the length of her body.

William smiled, laid back beside her, staring at the roof of the camper shell, and told her to look at all the fiberglass threads, how they made a cocoon, how that meant that the two of them were moths, about to lift up into the hot air over I-10, and then he put the mask he'd bought at the store over the shape of her face, straddled her hips, cut a hole over the tip of one breast, and fed.

Two days later William took her down to see the water, the ocean. Because sunsets on the Gulf are romantic.

He carried her from the bed of the truck to the busted sand, to the line of darkness that meant it was wet, and even took the new tape off her mouth. There was no one for miles. He watched her watch the light on the water. She was shivering. There was nothing he could do for the fever. Once he'd tried, feeding a girl named Roberta aspirin at regular intervals, but it thinned her blood so much that she bled out on the second day, and then kept bleeding, long after her heart wasn't even pushing the blood anymore.

But Julia.

William smiled. His knees were up on either side of her, his arms around them, hands clasped between his knees.

They were still in Louisiana. William had decided that the first night: that she was going to be a Louisiana girl. That she would be more comfortable there—the humidity, the green. It would be like Houston for her. They weren't calling him anything there yet. Last year in Florida, in one paper he'd been the I-10 Killer, and in another, on the same day, he was Ponce de Leon. He'd looked it up in a public library in Jacksonville that afternoon: Ponce de Leon, traveling along what would become the interstate, looking for the fountain of youth.

For four days at a time anyway. Six if the girl was strong enough.

In the dying sun, William saw that Julia's wounds were healing. Something about the melanin of dark girls probably. Her foot was in the sand though. Deeper than the sun could reach. And she wasn't going anywhere with that foot. The one time she tried, slumping sideways away from him, he had to hit her with the back of his hand, was already catching her fast enough that the tips of her hair just left ghost lines in the sand.

So she wouldn't choke, he cradled her head in his lap, stroked her hair away from her face, along his leg, the weight of it on his thigh no more than a shadow.

It wasn't too late to take her to a hospital. Or to call 911 from a pay phone, leave her there. Or sit her down at the bus stop, her silver little phone blinking Robert Mendes.

William closed his eyes, swallowed. In her breast closest to him there was a hole. It was leaking. Not blood, but something thicker, more clear. William smeared it around the edge of the hole, then, half on accident, slipped his finger in to the second knuckle, saw his brother James for a flash and clamped his eyes shut against that, curled his finger deep enough in Julia's breast that she straightened out, standing on her heels and the back of her head.

William opened his mouth to tell her to stop this, to keep James and his chicken-wire chest out of this sunset, that she didn't even know about it, or about their dad poking his finger into it too hard, and the way her head nodded forward on her neck, he knew she understood. She was telling him it was all right, that it had always been all right.

Breathing too hard, his eyes wet, William forced another finger into that hole, and then his hand, the skin stretching to swallow him, and then he flexed his fingers inside the warm wet insides of her breast so that his knuckles were like little dome-headed puppies waking up in there, their eyes not even open yet.

William's other hand dealt with himself, urgently.

They were the only two people in the world.

When it was over and done with, he arranged Julia's hair all in a line, like it had been combed. Her head eased over into his lap again, some muscle in her neck drawing tight. And William wasn't crying. He thinned his lips so anybody could see that he wasn't crying.

He looked out to the water again, his fingers still in Julia's hair.

"You like dogs?" he asked her, and when her head moved again, that one stubborn muscle giving up, he smiled, told her good, that was good. Maybe he would have to get her a dog, then. A big one.

3.

The mask he made her wear when she was under the tarp was Little Bo Peep, only he'd pulled the hair away from it, so it was just those baby-fat cheeks, the red Shirley Temple lips he kept having to lipstick over. It was hard, though, getting the lipstick straight, not smearing it on the porcelain skin, and no matter how long he let it dry, it still made his mouth look like he'd just eaten a cherry lollipop.

Julia was in her third day.

After he'd told her about James on accident, and after she'd figured out that she was in a Gentleman Jim camper, he'd had to reach in through the tear duct of her bad eye with a coat hanger, pull everything he'd told her out, swallow it back down.

She was a doll now.

Then it was her fourth day. The cab of the truck was rolling with Weimaraner-pit puppies. They had been in a box by a vegetable stand. William had paid eight dollars for each of them, eighty-eight dollars in all. This was before the coat hanger, when he was sure Julia was going to live months and months, and happily ever after. When it made sense to buy the dogs young, wait for them to grow.

Now he was going to have to get an extra dog just to hide them in. Like the unborn. Maybe he could even sew their eyes shut again, or superglue them, or—

William shook his head no. That he was never going to do this again. That it was wrong. That Julia didn't count because she was an accident, a victim of his weakness.

But then he remembered James and his friends, catching farm dogs and starving them down for three or four days, then putting them in the cotton trailer with a fat little cottontail. Watching that cottontail run around and around the trailer and finally climb the wire fence, making the kind of sounds a rabbit only ever makes once.

It was too complicated for Julia to ever understand. For any of them to.

Going back to the rabbit days after, after the dog had caught her and didn't know what to do with her. Going back to her and the boy that was standing there, watching through the fence. Maggots roiling out of the carcass, the boy smiling, saying they were babies, that she was having babies, that he was going to catch one, keep it.

William nodded, veered off the road, corrected the right amount.

The rabbit babies. It was funny. Maggots, worms, like the blind white things wriggling in the puppies' shit now.

William kept the windows up to punish himself, teach himself a lesson.

Tried to drink a beer but gagged on it, spit up onto his chest. Called out to Julia through the sliding glass, no answer.

The sign on the side of the road said to yield.

William backed up to it, threw beer cans at it until his floorboard was empty.

Above him, the clouds were musty, motionless. His headlights giving him a shadow with a head shaped like the yield sign, like he was an alien.

He turned them off, backed into the trees, and tried to get the smallest of the puppies to feed from a slit in the plastic he cut over Julia's good breast, then held its mouth there until his arm was trembling. Until his whole body was.

Beside her still was the coat hanger, black from the lighter he'd held all along it, to clean it. Because she was a nurse: hygiene would be important to her.

William nestled into the plastic alongside her, kept his eyes open until the fifth day.

At a gas station, the truck parked by the propane tanks, locked and double-locked, William shaved earlier than he ever had before, saw himself in the mirror so clean. A different person. A new one.

He cupped his chin in his hand, tilting his head left then right.

On the door by the clerk—already—was a black-and-white photocopy of Julia. Julia Mendes.

William pretended it wasn't there.

For six hours now he had been thinking about the boy and the rabbit, the boy saying how he was going to keep one.

William kept saying it to himself like that, trying it on: *I'm going to keep one.*

Not Julia, it was too late for her. But the Weimaraner-pit puppies. One of them. A boy one. He would ride shotgun with William, guard the truck for him when he couldn't be with it.

William didn't know how he hadn't thought of it years before.

He walked the two aisles of the store for canned dog food, or beef stew, but it was just oil and paper plates and chips.

"Where is it?" he asked the clerk.

"What?"

"Dog stuff."

The clerk smiled, shook his head no.

"For a puppy, I mean," William said, tapping himself on the side of the head to remember better. "Puppy food."

The man studied William now.

"Like milk, you mean?" he said.

William brought the largest puppy in to show. The clerk took it over the counter, holding it expertly, in a way that made William immediately know he was going to trust this clerk forever.

The clerk turned his attention to the pup, held it up to his face and put his nose to the sharp little mouth.

"Sweet," he said. "Weaning?"

William forgot to blink for too long, made himself, then suddenly couldn't stop, just shook his head no. "She doesn't have any—she's dry, I mean," he said.

The clerk shrugged.

"Milk, then," he said, handing the puppy back. "Who knows, right?"

William paid for two gallons, left, but the puppy wouldn't drink any of it, even when he pulled over, leaked it into the cup of flesh that had been Julia's nipple. Even when he leaked it onto his own.

He shook his head no, no, then just drove faster than he knew he should have, fast enough to get caught and deserve to get caught, but no blue lights flashed, everyone knew he was charmed, probably even wanted him doing what he did.

But the puppies.

He smiled, told them it was going to be all right, then, taking a road around some nothing town, found himself easing through a ditch where a livestock trailer had overturned days ago. The cows were still there. William nodded, didn't have to look to either side to see his father, moving among them right after the wreck, his sickle glinting moonlight.

Just past the cows were the dogs that had come to the smell. Green eyes in the tall grass, one of them moving to chase the truck, then all of them moving.

William nodded like this was the way it was supposed to be.

A quarter mile down, after the most long-winded of the dogs had fallen away, William saw what had to be there: one of the dogs, already run over.

He watched it in his headlights until he was sure it wasn't going to rise, then stepped down, inspected. It was huge, a Rott like Lobo maybe, but bigger, with some shepherd or something in it. Big like the bear cub.

William cradled its stiff body to his chest, peeled it from the asphalt, and put it on Julia's feet, to keep her warm.

It was tonight. The dog had been a sign.

Three hours later, dawn not even a smell yet, William had two more dogs in the camper shell. Both spaniel size. The third he had to go into town for, run down the address. It was a Lab, though, would hold enough to be worth the trouble.

Now all he needed was a place to work.

He stepped back up onto the interstate, knew immediately where he was, where the rest stops were each way, and it was comfortable, right. He kept the Chevy at sixty-five, let the big trucks slam past him for Florida, and blinked his lights, letting them pull back into his lane.

It was during one such black moment—headlights off—that the lightbar flared up behind him.

He touched his brakes, pulled his lights back on, and coasted to the side.

The cop followed his flashlight along the side of the truck, stood at an angle to the window William had already rolled down. The light played across both of William's hands, gripped onto the wheel in plain sight. The back of them was white, dusted with the same hair his forearm was. The palms were black with blood, from the Lab.

"Sir," the cop said.

"Officer?" William said back, turning his eyes from the light.

It was the same cop from the bear. The cop who knew the Ford. It was his county, his stretch of the interstate.

"I do something . . ?" William led off.

The officer had his beam of light shining pale through the tinted side window of the camper. And then he got the smell from the cab, stepped back, his hand falling to the butt of his gun.

"What the hell—?" he said.

William shrugged.

"Dogs," he said, and pushed back into the bench seat, giving the officer a better angle on the puppies in the floorboard. The cardboard barrier William had cut, to keep them from the pedals.

The cop was breathing hard now, trying to.

"Where—where?"

"Weimaraners," William said, a half lie. "Delivering them for my sister."

"Your sister?"

William hooked his chin up the road.

"Not crossing any state lines," he said. "Don't worry."

The cop blinked, wiped his eyes with the back of his sleeve, and tapped his flashlight against the camper.

William kept his hands on the wheel, looked through the sliding glass behind him.

The other dogs were back there. They were moving, undulating, as if asleep: Julia, kicking slow under the tarp. "Those ones are mine," William said.

"All of them?"

Through the tinted side glass, the blood on the two smaller dogs' coats would be the liver stains of a springer spaniel. And the bigger two dogs were black.

William nodded.

"Shouldn't they be—awake?" the cop said, tapping the glass again.

William smiled, caught.

"Benadryl," he said. "I should give them Dramamine, I know, but shit. You know what that costs?"

"Allergy medicine?"

William nodded, almost snapped, pictured the blood from the Lab spattering from his fingers to his face.

"Knocks 'em dead," he said, shrugging.

"Serious?"

"You should try it."

The cop flashed the light along the dashboard, to the one silver can. He held the light there, looked at William.

"Do I need to check your license, sir?" he asked.

"It's old," William said, then took a chance, dropped one hand into shadow and leaned over to the window, as if reaching for his wallet. "But if you want . . . ?"

The cop started to step closer, breathed in the puppy shit again, and gagged, stepped out into the highway, and, without even thinking about it, William reached out through the window, pulled him back over, a Kenworth sucking past, its chrome mirror nearly skimming the camper shell, rocking the truck.

The cop tried to breathe, couldn't.

There was blood on his sleeve, now, from William's hand. On the black fabric.

He finally sucked in enough air to talk. His eyes wet, swimming.

"I know you," he said, leaning on the truck, watching the road behind his cruiser.

"The bear," William said.

The cop nodded.

"Whatever happened to it?" William said.

The cop lifted his head at the interstate, the truckers. "Them," he said, his lips already thinning. "It must have been alive, crawled back up there for one more round or some shit."

William nodded, leaned over to spit. The cop almost stepped back to let him, then just moved a little farther along the side of the truck instead.

It was all William could do not to smile.

The cop felt it too, just at the corners of his mouth, then patted William on the arm, told him to be safe, and extended his hand for a shake. But the twelve-inch light was still in it. Still on. And then he held it there.

William followed the pale beam.

Maybe sixty feet out, where the light started scattering into motes, was a tall black dog, her teats heavy with milk.

She was staring back along the beam of light.

The cop hissed through his teeth then took the light back, and told William to be safe. William nodded, watched the cop in the mirror, feeling along the side of the truck then disappearing behind it, walking as far in the ditch as he could back to his cruiser. Crawling in the passenger side.

He rolled the lights across his bar once in farewell, accelerated evenly into the night.

Minutes after he was gone, William pulled his headlights back on.

The dog was still there, watching him.

"Okay then, little momma," William said, and started easing the Chevy forward.

She was another sign, led him first onto the service road then to a copse of trees. Buried in the trees was a trailer house, burned out. The same one.

William shook his head no, no, that you don't do this, you don't ever come back to the same place, even if it's a perfect place, but she wasn't listening, had already lowered herself under the trailer's torn skirt.

He backed the Chevy to where he'd backed over Marissa's head three times. There were ruts from it almost—a shallow depression, like the earth remembered.

No lights, no nothing.

Just fast. It had to be fast.

But not like before either. Not like when something had been watching from the front door of the trailer.

In six trips, William carried in the four dead dogs, the armful of puppies, and Julia. She was still breathing, but it was like she was having to remind herself to.

William nodded, kept nodding, and rested her down onto the mildewed couch. The dogs were already on the floor, the shepherd's head lolling most of the way off, both ears still alert. A sorry state of affairs, but William would make do. He always had.

The seventh trip he made was for a six-pack of beer.

He stood over the hole where the sink had been and drank them one by one, dropping his cans down into the cabinet then digging them out to wipe his prints off. Walking back and forth from the shepherd on the floor. Trying to fit the head back on. Telling himself it wasn't important but then caping it out some anyway, like a trophy. Reaching up into the skull to drag more out, enough that a section of leg might fit up there now. Always room for more.

He was on the fifth beer, breathing hard, almost ready, telling himself he didn't have time for Julia anymore but rubbing himself all the same, when one of the puppies rolled into her couch and he understood the whole, stupid night: the mother dog under the trailer, she was the one from the pound. The one whose puppies had been taken away. They'd killed her but she'd lived through it, and now here he was, with a whole, starving litter of ghost pups.

William smiled, left the beer half-full on the counter.

He stepped down from the front door, off the wood somebody had stacked up as a staircase, and lowered himself to look under the skirt, snapped his fingers for her to come. She wouldn't though. Wouldn't even growl, didn't care about whistles or promises.

William stood, not mad. Not anything, really.

"Julia," he called through the front door, singsong, "Julia, I think she's hungry, dear," then stepped up, cut a perfect coin of meat from the palm of her right hand. Like a slice of pepperoni. He stood and her hand closed over the pain, and he thanked her, really meant it.

Down at the skirt again, he held the coin of meat into the darkness, but still the little momma wouldn't come, even when he left it there. So he kicked the trailer and hit it and spit on it. When he lowered himself to the skirt again, though, the coin was gone, and he smiled.

She understood.

William nodded, tuned in for a moment to a recap flapping on the interstate; his radio, leaking country music; his beer on the counter inside, fizzing down.

This was going to be even better, this was the next thing: before, he'd just been putting the girls in the dogs. Now, though—now he could feed them to the dogs. Julia, at least. And then, and then she could nurse the puppy he chose, and in that way it would be a perfect circle.

William knew he was rubbing himself again but couldn't help it, this was so good.

But then the skirt of the trailer, the very edge of the tin, dipped down into the surface of the ground.

William cocked his head to the side, not getting it, then followed the skirt up to the trailer, then to the door. The perfect pair of caramel legs there. The one breast pointing out into the night.

"Julia," he said, in his other voice, "I was just about to—" and then saw all the way up her, and fell back, never felt the ground.

It was Julia, but not. Julia, naked but for blood. Julia, with the dog head that had lolled off. The shepherd. She'd pulled it down over her own somehow.

William felt his breath tremor in his chest, tried to smile, couldn't come close.

"Julia," he said again, and then she was stepping down, the black dog under the trailer exploding from the darkness, the square-headed grey puppies spilling around Julia's feet, down the rotten steps.

William pushed himself back through the dirt, tried to laugh at himself, at this, at her. Her gone breast was leaking down her body, the fingers of the hand he'd cut the coin from dripping black. The eyes of the dog head watching him like a god, unblinking.

William laughed through his nose, wiped his eyes, and shook his head no to her now.

She had a hand to each side of the doorjamb, was stepping down.

Laughing with no sound, William slashed the air with his razor but it was weak, nothing.

She lowered herself from the doorway to the dirt, leading with her good foot, the placement so deliberate that William suddenly felt what was happening here. Why. That it was time. That, after sixteen, seventeen girls, it was time. He nodded his head to her—yes, yes, this. He was ready.

"Please," he said to her, lifting his chin so she could have his throat, "please, I'm sorry," and then the dog head looked down at him with its dry eyes, knew him all at once, saw him in his cowboy hat, hiding in all the cushions of the couch, and he started throwing up down his chest, pushing back again, away from her, from it, and the body that had been Julia took one more step, no doorway to lean on now, and folded over the bad foot. Onto William. Her warm breath on his inner thigh, through the denim. The dog head nosing into his navel. William's whole body trembling, neck jerking, cheek stubble wet with tears.

He was alive.

She had spared him. She was forgiving him.

He breathed in, out, made a sound with his voice just to see if he still could. Felt his own nipples swelling with a sort of milk he could feed her with if she wanted.

Everything made sense.

Except then she growled.

From the shepherd's mouth.

Instead of standing up like the woman she'd been, she pushed up onto her bowing-out arms, raised her heavy head to study him. To taste the air for him.

William kicked out from under her and she stayed crouched like that, on all fours. The shepherd head just watching him.

"No, no, no," William said to it quietly, and the little momma dog under the trailer snarled back there in her wet darkness, and the puppies boiling in the doorway screamed with the voices of sixteen women, and William drew a sharp line across his left nipple with the razor, his own fluids spilling down his front, into his lap, in offering.

She just stared at him.

"Julia?" William said.

In reply, she took her first step, her right arm reaching out for the ground.

William pushed back farther, still shaking his head no, and a second before she lunged forward off her hind legs, he was turned, crawling into a blind run.

Billy Billy Billy the Kid, she said in his head, in her dog voice, and William leaned forward, deeper into the night, and the puppies and the trailer and his truck fell away behind them, and the one time William looked back, Julia's new mouth was moving, her teeth shiny wet and curving in and in, and this isn't one of those stories where the killer is chased by his own guilt out into the road to get run down by a truck his father could be driving, it's one of those stories where you understand that no matter how fast a man runs, a dog can run faster. Especially when she's hungry.

I used to burn up I-10 between Texas and Florida. These twenty-two-hour drives where I'd forget what's real, what's for sale, all that. And somehow it mixed itself up in my head with being lost in the hills above Santa Fe one night, on what I call a UFO road (these are roads I completely expect to get abducted on), and my headlights flashed on this tall, tall dog over in the ditch, just waiting for me to pass, so he could continue on with his nightly perambulations. Which, I would swear to this in court or wherever else, involved trucking a human arm from one side of the road to the other in its mouth. I didn't stop. But, every roadkill I ran over for a while after that, I kept feeling other kinds of bones in it, like. And I still do. Anyway, William in here—oh, man, I guess this is just the first time I've used that name for a serial killer, right? Oops. Or maybe they're instantiations of the same personality, nodes on a continuum. Yeah, that. Anyway, I wrote him because I'd been reading a lot of killer lit, and I was less and less impressed with how much these killers seemed to belong in Batman's rogue's gallery, what with all their scheming and themed-up parties and all. I wanted to strip all that off, if I could. Just write somebody pure. I went on after this, too, wrote an eighty-thousand-or-so-word novel with this as part 1. I don't think I've found the proper way to close it out yet though. Or the right title, for that matter. So it sulks in the drawer, trying to bleed all over my other novels.

UNCLE

———————————————————————————————————————

IT MUST HAVE been just about the very last thing Teresa ordered before she died.

A handheld laser infrared thermometer.

The packaging made it look like a ray gun, complete with a red beam shooting out across the room. Even thinking about holding it, I could feel the fingers of my left hand spreading away from each other like in a Western when the camera's focused down alongside the thigh of a quick-draw artist.

I figured it was the last thing she ordered because it didn't show up until two weeks after the funeral. On some slow boat from Malaysia probably. Meaning sending it back was going to be a headache, especially since she'd used her credit card.

Returning it too—I don't know. I guess it would have felt like a betrayal, sort of. Like I was passing judgment on this one last thing that was supposed to have somehow made everything better. Like I was telling her it was going to take more than something she saw in an infomercial to fix our marriage.

Before she died, we'd been sleeping in separate rooms for three months already. Keeping our takeout on different shelves in the refrigerator. Only using the ketchup at different times, using our cells instead of the landline, all that.

Neither of us wanted to say it out loud, but it was over, me and her. Not because of any particular revelation or event, though I could name a few if pushed—her too, I'm sure—but, stupid as it sounds, it was more like we'd just started going through different drive-throughs. Our tastes had changed. I mean, you need difference, you need friction in a marriage, sure, this is talk-show gospel, but what it came down to was that I was perfectly content to let her keep on with her chicken tacos with sour cream thing, and felt zero need to convert over to the goodness of Caesar salads with a small bowl of chili. I didn't care what she was eating, and I don't think she felt particularly sorry for the heartburn the chili kept leaving me with.

Soon we were watching different shows in different rooms, changing our own batteries in our separate remotes, then falling asleep apart, waking up on our own.

And then, as if to complete the process, she drifted into a busy intersection under the false safety of a green light.

The police came to my office to tell me about the accident, took me to the morgue.

I identified her, I called her parents, we buried her, and now I had a hand-held laser IR thermometer to show for our three-year marriage.

I unboxed it, batteried it up and held it to my forearm like a science-fiction hypodermic, pulled the trigger: 98.4 degrees.

Perfectly normal.

According to the packaging, home inspectors were big on these handheld thermometers. It made their job worlds easier.

Supposedly you could use it to double-check the temperature in your oven, or track pipes in the wall, or do something I didn't understand with the hot-water heater. You could find air leaks around windows, too, especially in winter. The living room might be a balmy, draft-free seventy-two degrees, but run this dusty red light around that dried-out caulk line in the sill, and you'll see where your electricity bill's really being spent.

I took it to work, checked the heat on the electric pencil sharpener, on the copy machine, on the coffeepot, on my supervisor when he was walking away. My desk mate Randall shoved it down the front of his pants before I could stop him, pulled the trigger to prove how hot he was.

The microwave was nearly the exact same temperature off or not. The only difference was its light bulb probably.

On the bus a woman across from me screamed when I pulled it from my pocket.

I got off at the next step, my hand still on the pistol grip.

When Teresa and I had first been dating it had been winter. One of our things was to walk to the liquor store seriously bundled up in scarves and jackets and stocking caps, so that, cutting across the parking lot, we'd joke about how we were going to stick the place up—at least that's what the clerk was going to think when we walked in.

Walking home after the bus, I stopped by a different liquor store, paid for a six-pack, the thermometer's grip warm against my stomach.

The beer was Teresa's brand. I didn't even notice until my first drink.

I drank it anyway, had two gone by the time I made it home.

Later, I settled my red pointer on the late-show host's cheek. It made me feel like a sniper.

And then I checked the living room out.

The walls were warmer behind the set, cooler by the door. The lamp that I'd had on while eating was still comparatively hot. The doorway to the kitchen was the same as the wall. My foot was the same as the wall. The late-show host was on fire. The window was the Arctic, the ceiling indifferent, the carpet the same.

I tried to write my name on the wall but wasn't fast enough.

Finally I was able to draw a heart, slash an arrow across it.

The audience on television exploded with laughter.

I nodded in acknowledgement, sighted along the top of the gun down the hall, to my bedroom, but stopped at Teresa's instead.

Everywhere else in that darkness, the temperature was hovering around seventy.

There was spot right in her doorway though.

It registered as body heat.

I sucked the red light back into my hand.

The next morning I called in when I knew I was going to be late if I tried to make it. One more tardy and I'd have to talk to somebody about it. I was a widower now, though, right? Surely they'd give me a day or two extra.

After the sun was up and the neighbors gone to work, I strolled around the front yard to make sure I was alone and then checked the faucet under the window, followed the hose—frozen solid—around the side of the house, where I was aiming.

I peeked through Teresa's window.

Her room was just her room, her doorway her doorway.

So I aimed the gun in.

Nothing, no one.

I nodded that this made sense, this was right, thank you, and spent the day at the movies, and walking around, and buying more batteries.

We hadn't had insurance on each other, but the other driver's policy had given me a big enough check, I suppose. Not enough to buy a person, but I could buy an ATV if I wanted. Maybe two. Or all the batteries I could carry.

I would have felt guilty taking the money, as she was kind of a careless driver, even if she had been in the right this time, but we had bought that car together. I told myself it was kind of like getting my investment back. And out of the marriage to boot.

When I got home, a package was waiting for me on the stoop.

It was a little handheld movie camera, with NightShot.

I left it in its box.

Three days later, the thermometer had lost its novelty. And I wasn't turning the light in the hall off anymore.

Sitting in my chair in the living room, I could lean over, have a clean line all the way down to my bedroom—to the one I'd claimed in the bad old days. Those days being the ones when Teresa was alive, yeah.

Now, in these good and unawkward days, I could stake out the master bedroom again.

Except I wasn't.

The morning after the camera came, I'd finally pulled Teresa's door shut, nodded to myself that this was good, that it wasn't my job to clean it out.

That afternoon, it was open again.

And that doorway, it was always a few degrees warmer than the hall. And the curtains over her window had shifted, so I couldn't stand in the bushes and see inside anymore.

I filed it all under Things You Never Expected to Know, and went to work, the camera in my bag.

Randall bought it from me for a hundred and fifty, half to be paid next check, half before summer.

That night he called me for a refund.

"You didn't pay me anything," I told him, still trying to watch the show I had on.

"I mean on owing you," he said.

He dropped the camera off, stood on the porch like I was supposed to invite him in, and finally looked to the street behind him like somebody was waiting, sloped off for the bus stop.

I fiddled with the camera over a second microwave dinner.

Three beers of the six-pack I'd bought were still in the refrigerator. They weren't an offering, but I couldn't seem to drink them either.

At work they'd asked if I wanted to see a grief counselor. I'd said thanks, but no. Because there was just show grief, not real loss, real sadness.

As hard as I tried, even at the funeral with her parents and little brother there, still, it felt like more like relief than sorrow. Like I'd hit the lottery without even buying a ticket. Game over, reset, start again.

There was no way what had happened was my fault. And, as far as everybody knew, we were happily married, pretty much. As happy as anybody. Except for the debt she'd been piling up, mail-ordering stuff, we didn't even have anything to argue about, really. And the card was in her name.

Instead of throwing the camera away—the invoice said it had cost her three-fifty—I flipped through the manual, arguing with Randall in my head that it was brand-new, no way could it be broke.

I fell asleep with it in my lap, woke to a distinct pop.

The kids in the street, cracking baseballs into the horizon.

I dragged my blanket to the couch, sat on it backwards, on my knees, and parted the curtains, watched them.

They were letting the new kid swing. And he could. He so could.

Without thinking, I raised the camera, zoomed in on him, and, like I hadn't been able to make the camera do all last night, the little red record-light glowed on in the eyepiece.

Because nobody had catcher pads, the kids had rigged a soccer net behind the batter.

The new kid didn't need it though.

He lofted ball after ball into the sky, everybody craning to track it each time, run it down, his little brother—they were like different stages of the same kid—ready to collect the ball, if any of them made it over the imaginary plate.

I left them to it, trolled the refrigerator for the nothing I already knew was there, then skirted Teresa's door, aiming for my own.

And it hit me, the smell.

From her room.

It was one of those thick smells that are like particles in the air, that feel like an oil on your skin.

I fell over dry heaving, trying to hold it in because I didn't want to clean it up.

After throwing up in the toilet, I hitched my shirt up over my lower face and stood in her doorway—it didn't feel warm—flicked her light on, but it was dead.

I came back with the flashlight, cruised its yellow beam over her magazines and pillows, her shoes and purses. Over me in her dresser mirror, standing there in my boxers. Nobody staring over my reflection's shoulder, even though my skin was crawling.

That dead-raccoon smell though. I could feel it settling on my face.

And then, over my shoulder, the skin there sensitive in a way it hadn't been since childhood, something crashed.

At first I thought it was a hand, clamping down.

Then, rationalizing at a furious pace, I told myself it was one of the beers in the refrigerator, exploding.

Wrong, wrong.

It was the shorted-out doorbell, hanging right behind me. Pile-driving into my ear, the sound straightening my back so fast that it was going to be sore.

Somebody was at the door.

I made myself smile.

Probably the new kid. He'd fouled a ball into the backyard, wanted to walk through.

Sure, sure.

I opened the door.

It was another package.

I stood there, opened it, the white peanuts drifting down to the floor, some clinging to my legs.

Air freshener. Twenty-four cans of it.

This was all because I'd faked my way through the funeral, I knew. Or, it was all in my head, was just coincidence—she'd ordered all this weeks before—but, if it was all in my head, was just guilt, then that meant I could fix it too.

Right?

I took the remaining three beers to the cemetery, poured them into her dirt, drinking the last drink of each like we were sharing. Like I was letting her go first. Because it hadn't been all bad. There had been a time when we—well, we weren't going to conquer the world, show them how it was done. But we were going to close the front door of our house, and do whatever the hell we wanted in there. Wear pajamas all day, eating chips and playing video games. We weren't going to play by the world's rules, we were going to make our own. Screw the rat race, all the pressure to be upstanding, start a family, leverage our way to a bigger house, better car. We could fake it for work, sure, but after we left our cubicles, we were just us.

Because we felt the same about all that, I guess we figured that was love. Or close enough. And I'm not saying it wasn't. That it couldn't have been.

I stood at the bus stop to go home but then crossed the street, went the other way instead. Just walking.

I left the camera on the slanted-frontward brick ledge in front of a liquor-store window, the manual folded back as well as I could, tucked under. The world could thank me later for that.

Then, when I finally made it back to the house, the baseball kids stalling their game so I could hunch-shoulder past without getting beaned in the forehead, I came back onto the porch with a screwdriver, pried the middle two numbers out of our 1322, put them back as 1232.

And I pulled Teresa's door shut again, and this time looped a bungee cord over the handle, tied it off on a cinder block I dragged in from the backyard, and when I shouldered it open enough to reach in, make sure the light switch was off, I was pretty sure there was a shape in the mirror that had two shoulders, couldn't have been me.

I let the door click shut quietly, didn't want to draw any extra attention.

My heart just slamming in my chest.

I went to the refrigerator to reload and stopped a couple of steps away.

The floor was tacky.

With beer. It had come from the refrigerator. No empties in there.

I laughed, rubbed my smile in with my hand and turned on all the lights in the house, even the front and back porch lights, then set there with my thermometer pistol, checking each bulb from my chair.

Teresa's door never opened. Exactly like it shouldn't have. And none of the light bulbs exploded for no reason at all.

It was just me, sitting awake all night. The kids out there playing night ball, the baseball dipped in rubbing alcohol and lit with blue flame, just like some big brother had showed them.

With NightShot, it would have looked so excellent.

I thought I was dreaming it until the two police cars rolled in, to keep the city from burning down.

Or maybe we were all dreaming.

By now I was carrying the thermometer in my pocket at all times. And calling in for the week.

Randall messaged me but I let it slide. I had enough cash from Teresa to ride it out for a few weeks if I needed to. If it came to that.

In a way, it was being loyal to Teresa, really. I wasn't playing the world's game, wasn't doing what it expected me to do.

Or, I was being loyal to the Teresa I'd married. Not to the one who I'd kind of started thinking was looking in a different way at my sisters maybe. At their perfect, reasonable, cookie-cutter lives. Their husbands and their nice neat families. Their living rooms that were grown-up living rooms.

We didn't want all that though. It's not what we'd signed on for.

I sat the day out, cleaning my recorded TV shows off the DVR, telling myself this was a chore I had to get through. That I wasn't hiding, I was doing stuff, I was taking care of things.

Because I still didn't trust the refrigerator, I ordered a pizza.

Thirty minutes later the doorbell chugged in its diabolical way.

It wasn't the pizza delivery guy but one of those respectable dads. With a letter for me that had shown up in his box—two houses having the same address had short-circuited the mail guy's brain, I guess. It would have mine.

I nodded thanks to the dad and he reached past me, tapped the street numbers by my door.

"This is why," he said.

I turned as if just seeing them.

"Kids," he explained, and we laughed together and he asked if I needed help getting his address off my house, and the question under that was about his mail, if I'd been getting it.

I told him I'd flop the numbers, it was nothing, and thanked him, stepped inside, left him there.

Behind me, the whole house was dark. For the first time in days.

Finally the dad stepped away, walked down the sidewalk instead of crossing the grass.

I aimed my thermometer at the letter. It was just normal.

I aimed it at all the light bulbs, knowing where they were by instinct now. They were all cool, like they'd never been on.

The letter was from the city, had never touched human hands, was just machine-printed, machine-stuffed, machine-stamped, and machine-mailed.

It was a traffic ticket.

Teresa was being cited for the light she hadn't run. When the other driver had run it, it had triggered all the traffic cameras in the intersection.

The picture—black and white and grainy—was down in the corner of the ticket, supposed to be proof that she'd really done this.

I didn't look, didn't look, and then I did.

The camera had her from above, of course, and from the front.

And it was her, no doubt. That wasn't the part that made me try to step away from what I was holding.

What made me step away was what she was clutching to her chest. Over her shoulder.

A baby.

To show I could, I left all the lights off, slept curled up in my chair, the thermometer pistol gripped in my hand, pressing into my face.

Once when I woke I'd been pushing the trigger in my sleep, the beam lasered straight down the hall. Not making it all the way to the end. Stopping at something there.

I clicked the gun off, didn't look at the temperature. Made myself close my eyes again.

She was telling me something.

I shook my head no though. That I didn't want to know. That no way was I going to call the coroner, ask if that woman from the wreck had been pregnant.

It wouldn't mean she'd been seeing somebody else. Six weeks ago, like a game of chicken, like we were each daring the other to enjoy it less, each waiting for the other to call it off, say it wasn't worth it, call uncle, we'd had sex and ended up laughing afterwards. At ourselves.

So she *could* have been pregnant. I guess. Her parents could have been grandparents, had she not pulled into that intersection. My sisters could have been a gaggle of perfect aunts.

No.

Even if she was, it's better the way it happened. Even if she was secretly thrilled about it, it's better she pulled in front of that car. That he was late to wherever he was going.

It's wrong to say it, I know, but it's the truth.

If three people bit it in that wreck instead of two, then okay. Now her and that unborn baby, they could be together forever, I guess.

Which covers no distance at all in explaining why she's still here.

The doorbell rang again and I slammed the door open.

It was my pizza.

I took it, ate it with water from the tap. Remembered splitting pizzas with Teresa.

Our first date had been pizza, then the arcade in back.

When we were going to make it forever.

I don't know if I missed her, but I missed that, I guess.

I nodded thanks to her, stood with a mouthful of the past, went to her door and pushed it open, the bungee cord humming with tension by my leg.

The heat billowed out like a rancid breath.

I came back with the air freshener she'd thought to send, sprayed two cans' worth, until I was coughing and laughing, my hand leaving tomato-sauce stains on the wall by her door.

Somewhere in there, I cried. I tried to tell myself it was for her, for us, for what we'd had, what we'd meant, but I don't know. It just hit me, that I was here, now. Alone. That this was it. That everything was just going to keep getting worse now, from here on out.

I cried and cried, just sitting there on my knees in the hall, holding Teresa's door open the whole time. Like telling her I was sorry, and *meaning* it now.

Like isn't this *enough*?

No.

The doorbell rang its broken ring.

I shook my head no.

I stood in the hall. The doorbell rang again. Then again.

"Wait here," I said to Teresa's open door, and let it close gently, made my way to the front door, to whatever this next punishment was going to be. From the Philippines, from China, from Kentucky.

It was from six doors down, on the other side of the street.

The new kid's little brother. He was holding a bat, shuffling his feet.

Behind him the street was empty. Just the soccer net.

He'd come out alone to practice. To get good enough to play with the big kids.

Until now.

"Let me guess," I told him, and he nodded, couldn't make eye contact, and I saw him through the camera again, from a distance, with NightShot.

The way Teresa would have.

I stepped aside, shrugged, and he leaned his bat against the porch wall, came in.

In the living room now, some of the lights were on, some off. In the whole house. Perfectly normal.

"I think it went—" he started.

"I heard it," I told him, leaving the front door open, and ushered him down the hall, pushed against Teresa's door with my fingertips.

"What's that smell?" the boy said.

Teresa's room was as scattered as it had been, just me and the boy's dim outlines in the mirror, but, in the direct center of the bed, like the bed was a nest, was a baseball, the curtains in the now-open window rustling like it could have come through there, sure.

"If anything's broke, my dad will . . . I'm sorry," the boy said, about to cry.

"No worries," I told him, "it happens," my hand to his shoulder, and guided him in like Teresa had to be wanting, held the door open just long enough for him to get to the edge of the bed, look back to me once. And then I let the bungee cord snick the door shut, collected the bat from the front porch and settled back into my chair. There wasn't even a muted scream from down the hall. Just the sound of forever.

In it, I aimed the gun into my mouth, pulled the trigger.

The readout said I was still alive, still human.

As far as it knew anyway.

Wrote this one for Paula Guran. All I remember knowing was that it needed to involve a ghost in some say; the anthology was Ghosts: Recent Hauntings. *And, I'd always wanted one of those laser-pointer thermometers, but had never been able to justify the price, as it would just be a toy to me, not a tool. So, like usual, if I couldn't buy it, I could write about it anyway. At which point things got darker and darker. The end to this one, too, man. Surprised me. I was pretty fresh off watching* Monster House, *I think. This ending is from how that house works, I think. But it's also from trying to figure out people who play video games. I'm always trying to figure that out. At the time I wrote this, a lot of my friends were always talking about* World of Warcraft. *Because I couldn't understand the fascination, I figured I'd write from the angle of somebody who did, and maybe then I'd get it. But I still don't.*

RAPHAEL

BY THE TIME we were twelve, the four of us were already ghosts, invisible in the back of our homerooms, at the cafeteria, at the pep rallies where the girls all wore spirit ribbons the boys were supposed to buy. There was Alex in his cousin's handed-down clothes—his cousin in the sixth grade with us—Rodge, who insisted that *d* was actually in his name, Melanie, hiding behind the hair her mother wouldn't let her cut, and me, with my laminated list of allergies and the inhaler my mother had written my phone number on in black marker. Three boys who knew they didn't matter and one girl that each of us fell in love with every morning with first bell, watching her race across the wet grass to make the school doors by eight.

"We're the only ones who can see us," Rodge said to me once, watching Melanie run.

I nodded, and Alex fell in. When Melanie burst through the doors we each pretended not to have been watching her.

It was true, though, that we were the only ones who could see us. And there was a power in it. It let us live in a space where no one could see what we did. The rules didn't apply to us. Maybe that freedom was even supposed to balance out our invisibility somehow. The world trying to make up for what it had failed to give us. We used it like that anyway: not as if it were a gift, but like it was something we deserved, something we were going to prove was ours by using it all up, by pushing it farther and farther, daring it to fail us as well.

Or maybe we pushed it just because we'd been let down so many times already, we had no choice but to distrust our invisibility, our friendship.

Anything this good, after everything else, it had to be the opening lines of some complicated joke. We were just waiting for the punch line. By pushing what we had farther and farther each day, testing each other, we were maybe even trying to fast-forward to that punch line.

But, too, it just felt so good to be part of something, finally, and then act casual, like it was nothing. Even if it was the rejects club, the ghost squad. Because maybe that was where it started, right? Then, next, weeks and weeks later—homecoming—maybe one of us would understand in some small but perfect way what it felt like at the pep rally, to give a girl a spirit ribbon then watch her pin it onto her shirt, smooth it down for too long because suddenly eye contact has become an awkward thing. Or, maybe one of us would be that girl. Or, just get swept away for once in the band's music. Believe in the team, that if they can just win Friday night, then the world is going to be good and right.

More than anything, I guess, we wanted to be seen, given a chance. Not on the outside anymore. That's probably what it came down to.

And the first step towards getting seen is of course being loud, doing what the other kids won't, or are too scared to do.

The days, though, they just kept turning into each other.

Nobody was noticing us, what we were doing. Even when we talked about it loud in the cafeteria, in the hall.

It would have taken so little too.

A lift of the chin, a narrowing of the eyes.

Somebody asking where we were going after school.

If we just could have gotten that one nod of interest, maybe Alex would still be alive. Maybe Rodge wouldn't have killed himself as a fifteenth birthday present to himself. Maybe Melanie wouldn't have had to run away.

Even if whoever saw us didn't want to go with us, but just had a ribbon maybe. For Melanie. Because she really was beautiful under all that hair. The other three, then, we would have faded back into the steel-grey lockers that lined the halls, and we wouldn't have gone any farther, ever.

But we were invisible, invulnerable.

Nobody saw us walking away after final bell. We were going to the lake. It was where we always went.

In a plastic cake pan with a sealable lid, buried in the mat of leaves that Rodge said was just above where the waves the ski boats made crashed, was Alex's book. It was one of a series off a television commercial; his mom had bought it then forgot about it. And we didn't hide it because we thought it was a Satan's bible or *The Anarchists Cookbook* or anything—because it was powerful—we hid it simply because we didn't want it to get wet. If my mother ever missed her cake pan, she never said anything.

"Where were we?" Melanie said, not sitting down but lowering herself so the seat of her pants hovered over the damp leaves. She balanced by hugging her knees with her arms. She'd told us once that her father had made her take ballet and gymnastics both until the third grade, when he left, and the way she moved, I believed it. We were all invisible, but she was the only one with enough throw-away grace that you never heard her feet fall.

Sitting back on her heels like that, her hair fell over her arms to the ground.

The rest of us didn't care about our clothes. Just the book.

What we were doing was trying to scare ourselves. With alien abductions, with unexplained disappearances. Ghost ships, werewolves, prophecies, spontaneous human combustion.

The person reading would read in monotone. That was one of the rules. And no eye contact either.

The first entry that day was about a man sitting in his own living room when the television suddenly goes static. He reaches for the mute button, can't find it, but then the screen clears up all at once. Only it's not his show anymore, but an aerial view of . . . he's not sure what. And then he is: his house, his own house. Ambulances pulling up. He opens his mouth, stands, his beer foaming into the carpet, and then doesn't go to work the next day, or the next, and finally starts getting his checks from disability.

"That's it?" Alex said, when Rodge was through.

"What's the question?" Melanie said.

Part of the format of the book was that the editors would ask questions in italic after each entry.

"Was he stealing his cable?" I offered, my voice spooky.

Alex laughed, not scared either.

"Was it a warning?" Rodge read, following his index finger. "Was TJ Bentworth given that day a prophecy of his own death, and the opportunity to avoid it? And, if so, who sent that warning?"

Melanie threaded a strand of hair behind her ear, shook her head, disgusted.

The test now—and we'd sworn honesty, to not at any cost lie about it—was whether or not, that night, alone, we'd think twice with our hands on the remote control. If we thought, even for a microsecond, that that next station was going to be us.

Melanie shrugged, looked away, across the water.

"This is crap," she said. "We need a new book."

I agreed.

Alex took the book from Rodge, buried his nose in it, determined to prove to us that this book was scary.

I left him to it, was prepared to go to Rodge's house, raid his pantry before his brother got home from practice, but then Alex looked up, said it: "We should tell our own stories, think?"

Rodge looked down, as if focusing into the ground.

"Like, make them up?" he said.

Alex shrugged whatever, smiled, and clapped the book shut.

He was three hours from the Buick that was coming to kill him.

The story I told was one that I'd already tried hard enough to forget that I never would. It was one of my dad's stories. I was in it.

The first thing I told Alex and Rodge and Melanie was that this one was true.

Alex nodded, said to Rodge that this was how they all start.

"It should be dark," Melanie said, swinging some of her hair around behind her. There were leaf fragments in the tip ends. I looked past her, to the wall of trees. It was night, in a way. Not dark, but still, with the sun behind the clouds, the only light we had was grey. It was enough. I nodded to myself, started.

"I was like ten months old," I said.

"You *remember*?" Alex interrupted.

Rodge told him to shut up.

"My dad," I went on. "He was like, I don't know. In the bedroom. I think I was on the floor in the living room or something." I shrugged my shoulder up to rub my right ear, stalling. Not to be sure I had it right, but that my voice wasn't going to crack. The first time I'd heard my father tell this, I'd cried and not been able to stop. I couldn't even explain why, really. Just that, you look at enough pictures of yourself as a baby and you imagine that everything was normal. That it doesn't matter, it was just part of what got you to where you are now.

But then my dad took that away.

The story I told the three of them that last afternoon we were all together was that I was just sleeping there on the floor, my dad in his refrigerator in the garage, getting another beer or something, my mom asleep in their room. The television was the only light in the room. It was wrestling—the reason my mom had gone to bed early. Anyway, there's my dad, coming back from the garage, one beer open, another between his forearm and chest, when he feels more than sees that something's wrong in the living room. That there's an extra shadow.

"What?" Melanie said, her eyes locked right on me.

I looked away, down. Swallowed.

"He said that—that—" and then I started crying anyway. Twelve years old with my friends and crying like a baby.

Melanie took my hand in hers.

"You have to finish now," Alex said.

Rodge had his hand over his mouth, wasn't saying anything.

When I could, I told them: my dad, standing there in the doorless doorway between the kitchen and the living room, looking down into our living room, past the couch, the coffee table, to me, on my stomach on the floor.

Squatted down beside me, blond like nobody in our family, a boy, a fourth grader maybe, his palm stroking my baby hair down to my scalp.

My father doesn't drop his beer, doesn't call for my mom, can't do anything.

"What—?" he tries to say, and the boy just keeps stroking my hair down, looks across the living room to my father, and says, "I'm just patting him," then stands, walks out the other doorway in the living room, the one that goes to the front door.

". . . only it never opens," Alex finished, grinning.

I nodded as if caught, pressed my palms into my eyes and stretched my chin up as high as I could, so the lump in my throat wouldn't push through the skin.

"Good," Melanie said, "nice," and, when I could control my face again, I smiled, pointed to Rodge, his hair straw yellow, and lied, said that it was him patting me, somehow.

Rodge opened his mouth once, twice, shaking his head no, please, but, when he couldn't get out whatever he had, Alex clapped three times, slowly, and then opened his hand to Melanie, said, "Ladies first."

"Guess I'll have to wait then," she said back, flaring her eyes, but then shrugged, wrapped a coil of hair around her index finger like she was always doing, then walked her hand up the strands, each coil taking in one more finger until she didn't have any more left.

It was one of the things Alex and Rodge and I never talked about then, but each loved about her—how she was so unconscious of the small things she could do. How she took so much for granted, and, because of that, because she didn't draw attention to the magic acrobatics of her fingers, to the strength of her hair, she got to keep it.

We didn't so much love her like a girl, desire her, though that was starting, for sure. It was more like we saw in her a completeness missing in ourselves. A completeness coupled with a kind of disregard that was almost flagrant. But maybe that's what desire is, really. In the end, it didn't matter; none of us would ever hold her hand at a pep rally, or tell her anything real. It wasn't because of her story, either, but that's more or less where it starts.

"Four kids," she said, looking to each of us in turn, "sixth graders, just like us," and Alex groaned as if about to vomit, held his stomach in mock pain.

Rodge smiled, and I did too, on the inside.

A safe story. That was exactly what we needed.

"The girl's name was . . . *Melody*," Melanie said, arching her eyebrows for us to call her on it. When we didn't, she went on, and almost immediately the comfort level dropped. Alex flashed a look to me and I shrugged my cheeks as best I could, didn't know. What Melanie was telling us was the part *before* the story, the part we didn't want and would have never asked for, because we all already knew: the thing between her and her stepdad. What they did. Only, to amp it up for us, maybe, make it worse, Melody added to the nightly visitations Melody's mother, standing in the doorway, watching. Mad at this Melody for stealing her husband.

Desperate to not be hearing this, I latched onto that doorway as hard as I could, remembered it from my own story, and nodded to myself: all Melanie was doing was reordering the stuff I'd already laid out there. Using it again, because it was already charged—we already *knew* that bad things followed parents standing in doorways.

Or maybe it was a door I had opened, somehow, by telling a real story in the first place.

After the one rape that was supposed to stand in for the rest, Melanie nodded, said, "And then there was . . . *Hodge* . . ." at which point Rodge started shaking his head no, no, please.

"We only have an hour," Alex chimed, tapping the face of his watch.

Melanie turned her face to him and raised her eyebrows, waiting for him to back off. Finally, he did. As punishment, his character didn't even get a name. Mine was *Raphael*, what Melanie considered to be a version of *Gabriel*, I guess. But Gabe, I was just Gabe back then.

I couldn't interrupt her though. Even when her story had the four of us walking away from school, to play our little "scare" game.

But this one was different.

In the Lakeview of Melanie's story, Lake*ridge*, there wasn't a book buried in a thirteen-by-nine Tupperware dish, but an overgrown cemetery. It was just past the football field.

Over the past week, she told us, her face straight, the dares had been of the order of lying faceup on a grave for ninety seconds, or tracing each carved letter of the oldest headstone, or putting your hand in the water of the bird-bath and saying your own name backwards sixty-six times.

"They were running out of stuff though," she added.

"I *get* it," Alex said, holding his mother's book closer to his chest.

Melanie smiled, pulled a black line of hair across her mouth and spoke through it: "But then *Raphael* had an idea," she said, looking to me.

"What?" I said, looking behind me for no real reason.

Melanie smiled, let the silence build—she had to have done this before, I thought, before she moved here, or seen it done—and told us that *Raphael*'s great idea was to take some of the pecans from the tree over in the corner, the tree that (her voice spooking up) "had its roots down with the dead people, in their eye sockets and rib cages."

"Take them and what?" Rodge said, worried.

"Look at you," Alex said to him.

"And what?" I asked, at a whisper.

"Take them to one of your basements," she said. "Then put them in a bowl with water for six days, then turn the lights off and each eat one."

The lump was back in my throat. I thought it might be a pecan.

"That it?" Alex said, overdoing his shrug.

"Six days . . ." Melanie said, ignoring him, drawing air in through her teeth, "and the four of them collect back in the basement, turn all the lights off except one candle, and then, that too."

"At midnight," Alex added.

"At midnight," Melanie agreed, as if she'd been going to say that anyway, and then drew out for us the cracking of the shells in the darkness, how they were soggy enough to feel like the skin of dead people. Then she placed the pecan meat first on the Alex stand-in's tongue—he throws up—then on the Hodge-character, who swallows it, gets stomach cancer two days later, then it's Raphael's turn. All he can do though is chew and chew, the meat getting bigger in his mouth until he realizes that, in the darkness, he's peeled his own finger, eaten *that* meat.

I laugh, like it.

And then it's Melody's turn to eat.

With her thin, beautiful fingers, Melanie acts it out for us in a way so we can all see Melody through the darkness of the basement, not so much cracking her pecan as peeling it, then setting the tender meat on the back of her tongue, only to gag when it moves.

In the darkness she's created, we all hear the splat, then, unmistakably, something rising, trying to breathe. Not able to.

The lights come on immediately, and running down Melody's chin is blood, only some of it's transparent, like yolk, like the pecan was an egg, and—

"C'mon," Alex said. "You don't try to outgore the gore of Gabe here eating his own *finger*, Mel."

"I'd expect that from you," Melanie said, smiling through her hair, "it was you who was born from that dead pecan," at which point Alex hooked his head to one side, as if not believing she would say that, then he was pushing up out of the leaves, tackling her back into them, and we were smiling again, and I finally breathed.

When Rodge wouldn't take his turn, saying he didn't know anything scary, Alex went. Instead of telling a ghost story, though, he opened his mother's book again.

"Cheater, " I said. "They're supposed to be real."

"Wait," he said back, "I was just looking at this one the other—" and then he was gone, hunched all the way over into the book.

I lifted my face to Melanie, said, "Where'd you hear that piece of crap?" and she pursed her lips into a smile, said, flaring her eyes around it, "You listened."

"I heard it with a walnut, not a pecan," Alex chimed in, turning pages, only half with us.

"A walnut?" Melanie said, crinkling her nose. "Nobody plants a walnut tree in a graveyard."

Looking back, now, I can hear it—how she'd used *cemetery* in the story, *graveyard* to Alex—but right then it didn't matter. What I was really doing anyway was saying it *had* scared me.

"You heard it at Dunbar?" I said.

Dunbar was her old school.

She opened her mouth to answer but then stopped, seemed to be fascinated by something out on the lake.

I followed where she was looking.

"What?"

"I don't know where I heard it," she said, still not looking at me, but out over the lake. "Somewhere, I guess."

"No, what are you looking at?" I said, pointing with my chin out across the water, and she came back to me."

"Nothing."

We were twelve years old, going to live forever.

When Alex finally got the book open to the right place, it was about witch trials all through history. Salem, the Spanish Inquisition, tribesmen in Africa. A whole subsection of a chapter, with pictures of the devices used to torture confessions out of people, pointy Halloween hats, all of it.

"I'm shaking," I said to him, trying to chatter my teeth.

"Can it," he said, following his finger to the next page.

It was one of the blue boxes framed with scrollwork. The stuff that was supposed to be footnotes, but was too important.

"How to test for a witch," he read triumphantly.

"This is scary?" I said to him.

Already, one of the blue boxes from two weeks ago had given us a list on how to become werewolves: roll in the sand by water under a full moon; drink from the same water wolves have been drinking from; get bitten by a werewolf without dying. Our assignments that night had been to try to become werewolves. Or get grounded trying, yeah.

"Weigh her against a *bible*?" Melanie read, incredulous.

"Her," Alex said, quieter, an intensity in his voice I knew, and knew better than to argue with.

By this time, Rodge was rocking back and forth, looking up to the road each time a car passed. When the noise got steady enough, that would mean it was five o'clock, and this would be over. On a day the sun was shining, the sound of cars would slowly be replaced by the sound of boat motors, but that day, if there even was a boat, Melanie had been the only one to see it. If she'd seen anything.

"Her," Melanie repeated, not letting it pass.

Alex smiled one side of his face, looked up to her. "How do we know?" he said.

"I'm a witch," Melanie said, "yeah."

Alex shrugged.

Melanie shook her head without letting her eyes leave him. "What do you want to do, then?"

Alex looked down to the blue box and read aloud: "Devil's mark . . . kiss of—do you, if I cut you, or stick you with a needle, will you, y'know, bleed like a real person?"

Melanie just stared at him.

"C'mon," I said, standing, pulling her up behind me. She didn't let go of my hand after she had her feet under her either. Alex saw, looked from me to her, and, even though I was just twelve, still I understood in my dim way what he was doing here: he wanted to be the one holding her hand. And, if not him, then, at least for this afternoon, nobody.

"Do you?" he said, again. "If I stick you with a pin, will you bleed?"

"Do you have a pin?" she said back.

Alex scanned the ground as if looking for one, or trying to remember a jackknife or hypodermic one of us had in a pocket.

He shook his head no.

Melanie blew air out and then held the sleeve of her right arm up, cocked her elbow out to him. It was the wide scab she'd got three days ago, when, to scare ourselves after reading about the jogger who disappeared mid-stride, we'd each had to run one hundred yards down the road, blindfolded.

Alex curled his lip up.

"What?" he said.

"You asked," she said. "It's blood. Want me to peel it?"

"But that's not—scary," he said.

Melanie lowered her elbow, let her sleeve fall back down.

Ten seconds later, Alex raised his face from the book. He was smiling.

"How about this?" he said, and I stepped around, read behind his finger.

"We can't," I said. "It's too cold."

Alex shrugged, let his voice get spooky. "Maybe we have to, for her own sake."

"What?" Melanie said, her arms crossed now.

"Tie your hands and feet," Rodge said from below, where he was still sitting. "Tie your hands and feet and throw you in the water."

"Bingo," Alex said, shooting him with his finger gun then blowing the smoke off, the thing the football players had all been doing during class lately, because it made no real noise.

"Excuse me?" Melanie said, to Rodge.

"He's been reading it after we leave," I said. "Right, Rodge?"

Rodge nodded. I'd caught him doing it early on. It wasn't because he wanted to know, to be more scared, but because, if he'd already read it once, then hearing it again wouldn't scare him so much. He'd made me promise not to tell. In return, I'd walked to what had been my spot in the leaves that day, dug my inhaler out, held it up to him like Scout's Honor.

"Well?" Alex said.

"It's cold," Melanie said.

"More like you just know you'll float," Alex said back, daring her with his eyebrows.

Melanie shook her head, blew a clump of hair from her mouth.

"Just tie my feet then," she said, and already, even then, I had a vision of her like she would have been in 1640 or whenever: bound at the wrists and ankles, sinking into the grey water. Not a witch but dying anyway.

Because we didn't have any rope like the blue box said we should, Alex sacrificed one of his shoelaces. Melanie tied it around her ankles herself.

"It's only a couple of feet deep out there," Rodge said.

He was standing now, facing the water. A defeat in his voice I would come to know over the next three years.

"Then I won't sink far, I guess," Melanie said, to Alex.

"Then we can tie your hands too," he said back.

Melanie took the challenge, offered Alex her wrists.

"Not too tight," I told him.

He told me not to worry.

"This gets me out of homework for two weeks," she said, having to sling her head hard now to get the hair out of her face, then lean back the other way to keep from falling over.

"Three," I said back.

"A month," Rodge said.

Alex didn't say anything. Just, to Melanie, "You ready?"

She was. Alex should have asked me though, or Rodge.

All the same, he couldn't lift her all by himself.

"C'mon," he said, stepping in up to the tops of his laceless shoes. The water sucked one of them off, kept it.

"Cold?" Melanie said.

"Bathwater," he said back, grimacing, then, because her feet were tied together, giving her his hand.

"Thanks," she said.

"It's in the book," he said, smiling.

He was on one side of her, me on the other, both of us trying to pull her along, not dunk her yet. Rodge still on the bank.

"Not too deep," I said, but Melanie jumped ahead of us, splashing me more than I wanted. "It has to be a little deep," she said. "I don't want to hit bottom either, right?"

Right. I just thought it, didn't say, because I knew she'd hear it in my voice: that this didn't feel like a game anymore. It wasn't like rolling in the sand under a full moon or running blindfolded down a part of the road that had one of us standing at each end, to watch for cars.

Something could really happen, here.

It was too late to stop it, though, too. Or that's what I tell myself.

We followed her out until the water was at our thighs, and then Alex nodded, and she turned sideways between us, so one of us could take her feet, the other her shoulders. She leaned back into me and I held her as much as I could, but she was already wet, her hair in the water so heavy.

"If she's—" I started, taking her weight, trying not to hurt her, and when Alex looked up to me I started over: "She walked out here, I mean. Like us. Didn't float. Is that enough?"

Alex refocused his eyes on the water and silt we'd just disturbed.

"Doesn't matter," he said, "it wasn't a test, then. It was her doing it herself, not getting thrown. 'Cast,' I mean. Getting cast into the water, to see."

"But you know she's not—"

"On three . . ." he interrupted, starting the motion, setting his teeth with the effort, and I shook my head no but had to follow too, like swinging a jump rope. One as thick and heavy as a young girl's body.

If I could go back, now, I would count to three in my head and never look away from Melanie, I think. But I didn't know. Instead of watching her the whole time, I kept looking up for boats, for somebody to catch us, stop this. Meaning all I have left of swinging her is a mental snapshot of her face, all of it for once, her hair pulled back, wet, inky, her skin so pale in contrast it was almost translucent. And then we let her go, arced her up maybe two feet if we were lucky, and four feet out. Not even high enough or far enough for her hair to pull all the way out of the water.

It was enough.

Without thinking not to, I raised my right arm, to shield my face from the splash, but then—then.

Then the world we had known, it was over. Forever.

Instead of splashing into the water, Melanie rested for an instant on the surface in the fetal, cannonball position, eyes shut, all her weight on the small of her back, her hair the only thing under, and then she felt it too—that she wasn't sinking—and opened her eyes too wide, arched her back away from it, her mouth in the shape of a scream, and flipped over as fast as a cat. Once, twice, three times, until she was out over the deep water, where the gradual bank dropped off into the cold water. She was still just on the surface, writhing, screaming, whatever part of her that had been twelve years old dying. Finally, still twisting away, she lowered her mouth to the laces at her wrists, then her hands to the laces at her ankles, and then she tried to stand but fell forward, catching herself on the heels of her hands, her hair a black shroud around her.

She looked across the water at us, her eyes the only thing human on her anymore, pleading with me it seemed, and then whipped around, started running over the surface on all fours, across the mile and a half the lake was wide there, leaving us standing knee-deep in the rest of our lives.

Thirty-two years later, now, the two hours after Melanie ran away are still lost. There's an image of Alex, falling back into the water on one arm, of Rodge, just standing there, limp, and then it's trees, maybe, and roads. The redbrick buildings of town; an adult guiding my inhaler down to my mouth. Alex running up the side of the highway to meet his Buick.

At his funeral, Rodge held my hand, and I let him, but then I couldn't hold on tight enough, I guess. Three years later, on his birthday, he bungee-corded car batteries to his work boots, stepped off a stolen boat into the middle of the lake.

Leaving just me.

Geographically, I moved as far away from Lakeview as possible. There are no significant bodies of water for fifty miles, and my children, Reneé and Miller, they each got through their twelfth years unscathed somehow. Probably because I stood guard in their doorways while they slept. Because I only allowed history and political books into the house. Because, finally, they were each popular in their classes, unaware of the kids standing at the back walls of all the rooms they were in, their faces a combination of damaged hope and hopeful fatalism, ready to break into a smile if somebody looked their way, *at* them instead of through them, but knowing too that that was never going to happen. I didn't tell them that that kid was me. The day Reneé came home with a spirit ribbon on her sweater—SKIN THE BOBCATS—I almost cried. When she forgot about it, the ribbon, I took it from the dash of her car. It's in my sock drawer, now. One Saturday morning I woke to find my wife, Sharon, studying it, but then she just put it back, patting it in place it seemed, as if putting it to bed, and I pretended not to have been awake. It's a good life. One I don't deserve, one I'm stealing, but still, mine. Last Sunday I dropped Miller off at basketball camp two towns over, then, on the way home, bought Reneé some of the custom film she said she needed for the intro to photography course she's taking at the local community college.

Three nights after that, a Wednesday, I took her to the carnival. Because she's seventeen, and I won't get many more chances. I even broke out the

Bobcats ribbon; she remembered it, held it to her mouth. At the carnival she took picture after picture, washing the place in silver light—clowns, camels, the carousel—and at the end of the night put her hand over mine on the shifter of my car, told me thanks. That she wouldn't forget.

Like I said, I don't deserve any of this.

When I was twelve years old, I helped kill a girl. Or, according to the doctors, helped her kill herself, punish herself for what her stepfather had been doing to her. I never told them about the dead pecans though, or about how her hands had been tied. Just that we'd been daring each other farther and farther out into the water, until her hair snagged a Christmas tree or something. At first, I'd tried the truth, but it wouldn't fit into words. And then I realized that it didn't have to, that, with Rodge clammed up, catatonic, I could say whatever I wanted. That I'd tried to save her even. That something like I thought I'd seen just couldn't happen, was impossible, was what any twelve-year-old kid would insist he'd seen, rather than a drowning. Especially a twelve-year-old kid already in a "scare" club, a book buried in a cake pan under the leaves that nobody ever found, that's probably still there.

I told it enough like that that sometimes I almost believed it.

But then I'd see her again, running on the surface of the water, and would have to sit up in bed and force the sheets into my mouth until I gagged.

When I finally told my wife about her—the girl I'd had a crush on who I'd seen drown when I was in the sixth grade—I'd even called her Melody, I think, like the story, and then not corrected myself. The main thing I remembered was her hair. The sheets I stuffed into my mouth were supposed to be it, I think, her hair. An apology of sorts. Love. The way your lip trembles when your best friend from elementary tells you he's moving away forever. Or your mother tells you they found him out on the highway, crammed up into the wheel well of a Buick.

The story I told myself for years was that her body was still down there, really tangled up in a Christmas tree or a trotline. That Rodge was down there now for all of us, trying to free her, but his hands are so waterlogged that the skin of his fingers keeps peeling off. Above him, a mass of fish backlit by the wavering sun, feeding on the scraps of his flesh.

"Keep her there," I'd tell him, out loud, at odd moments.

"Excuse me?" Sharon would say, from her side of the bed, or table, or car.

Nothing.

The other story I told myself was that I could make up for it all. That I could be the exact opposite of whatever Melanie's father had been—could be kind enough to Reneé that it would cancel out all the bad that had happened to Melanie, and that Melanie would somehow see this, forgive me.

So I go behind Sharon's back, buy her film she's supposed to buy herself. I take her to the carnival and hold her hand. I sneak into her room the morning after and—a gift—palm the film canister off her dresser, so I can pay for the developing as well, then can't wait twenty-four hours for it so go back and pay for one hour, leave the prints on her dresser without looking at them but then have to, when she leaves for a date. Like Rodge, I'm reading the book in secret, preparing myself, cataloging points to appreciate when she finally shows them to me, proud: the angle she got the man on stilts from; the flag on top of the main tent, caught mid-flap; the carousel, its lights smearing unevenly across the frame. The . . . the *tinted* or heat-sensitive lens or whatever she had on her camera, to distort the carnival. And the shutter speed—it's like she has it jammed up against how fast the film is, so that they have to work against each other. Like she's *trying* to mess up the shots, or—this has to be it—as if it might be possible to twist the image enough that it would become just another suburban neighborhood. Maybe it's part of the project though. They're good, all of them. She's my daughter.

Saturday, deep in the afternoon, Sharon gone to get Miller from camp, I walk into the living room and Reneé's there. On the glass coffee table, she has all the prints out, the table lamp shadeless, lying on its side under the glass, making the table into the kind of tray I associate with negatives, or slides. I see why she's done it though: it filters out some of the purple tint in the prints, and makes everything sharper.

She's in sweats and a T-shirt, her hair pulled back to keep the oils off her face. No shoes, her feet curled under her on the couch.

"Date?" I say.

She nods without looking up.

I'm standing on the other side of the coffee table from her. "These them?" I ask.

Again, she nods.

"They're—wrong," she says, shrugging about them, narrowing her eyes.

I lower myself to one knee, focus through my reading glasses, pretend to be seeing them for the first time.

"What do you mean?" I say.

"Daddy . . ." she says, as if I'm the thicko here.

"They're . . . purple?" I say.

"Not that," she says, and points to one of the carousel shots that, with her lens/shutter speed trick, has come out looking time-lapsed. I lift it delicately by the edge, hold it up to the light, my back old-man stiff.

"See?" she says.

I don't answer, don't remember this one from when I flipped through them the first time. It's one of the carousel shots, when she was figuring out how to move her camera with the horses. The effect is to keep them in focus, more or less. Not the children—their movements are too unpredictable to compensate for—but the horses anyway. And some of the parents standing by the horses, holding their children in place.

I shrug.

"*Look*," she says.

I shrug, try, and then see it maybe, from the corner of my eye, as I'm giving up: what's been waiting for me for thirty-two years. I relax for what feels like the first time. Don't drop the picture.

"Right?" Reneé says.

I make myself look again. Tell myself it's just a trick of the light. The special film. It was a carnival, for Chrissake. I even manage a laugh.

What Reneé captured and the drugstore developed—maybe that's where the mistake was: an errant chemical, swirling in the pan—is two almost-paisley tendrils of iridescent purple breath curling up from one of the wooden horse's nostrils, the horse's eyes flared wide, as if in pain.

Somebody with a cigarette, maybe, I say, a mom or dad standing *behind* the carousel, smoking. Or cotton candy under neon light. But then I follow the high, royal arch of the horse's neck, to the crisp outline of a perfect little child sitting on its back, holding the pole with both hands.

Standing beside him, out of focus, is his mother, her hand to the horse's neck. Patting it.

All I can see of her is her hair, spilling down the side of her legs.

This time I do drop the picture.

After Reneé's gone on her date, her mouth moving, telling me her plans but no sound making it to me, I take the flashlight into the backyard.

Buried under what Sharon insists will be a compost pile someday is a cake pan I bought at the discount store. In it, a book. Not the same series, not the same publisher, but the same genre: an encyclopedia of the unexplained.

The carousel horse isn't going to be in there, I know. Because it was an accident.

But Melanie.

That's the only page I read.

Her entry is in the chapter of unexplained disappearances. The woman jogger who disappeared is on the opposite page from her, like an old friend. The title the jogger gets, because of a later sighting, is "Green Lady Gone."

The title of Melanie's entry is "Roger's Story." They forgot the *d*; for the thousandth time, I smile about it, then close my eyes, lower my forehead to the book the way Alex used to, in class. It was a joke: by then we both knew enough about Edgar Cayce that we wanted too to be able to just lay our heads on a book, absorb it.

Like every time, though, it doesn't work. Or, now, this book is already in my head. All closing my eyes to it does is bring Melanie back. Not as she was on the water, but as she was running across the wet grass for the last bell, fighting to keep her hair out of her face.

Did she even leave tracks in the dew?

If she hadn't, and if we'd noticed, it would have just been because of her ballet training, her gymnastics. That she was made of something better, something that didn't interact with common stuff like grass and water.

But that wooden horse, breathing.

The mother I always knew she would be, this is the kind of gift she would give her child, I know. If she could. If it wasn't just a trick of the light.

Rodger's story is what he left as a birthday card to himself. Not word for word—it's been edited into the voice of the rest of the entries—but still, I can hear him through it. It starts just like Melanie's, with four social outcasts, creating their own little society. One in which they matter. How none of the four of us knew what we were doing, really. How we're so, so sorry. We never meant for . . . for her—

Rodger places us by the lake. The reason I've never been able to stop reading his version is the same reason I was never able to forget my father's story about me as a baby, sleeping on the floor: because I'm in it, just from a different angle.

In the light-blue box framed with scrollwork, the way Rodge tells it is he was just watching us, not as if he knew what was going to happen, but as if, in retelling it, reliving it, he had become unable to pretend that the him watching hadn't been through it a hundred times already. The way he watches us, he knows about the Buick coming for Alex, about Melanie, writhing on the surface of the lake. How a car battery changes the way a boat sits in the water.

Maybe the gases that escape from the cells of the battery on the way down are iridescent, are the last thing you see, before the strings of moss become hair, smother you.

According to Rodger, Melanie *asked* us to tie her hands and feet, throw her in the lake. I shake my head: he's protecting Alex. Protecting me. And then our stories synch up, more or less, the viewpoint just off a bit: instead of an image of Melanie's face just as I let her go, I see her rising from, slipping out of mine and Alex's hands the way a magician might let ten doves go at once.

And then she hisses, throws her hair from her face, and crawls across the lake, her hip joints no longer human. Her body never recovered.

The question after the entry is *What was Melanie Parker?*

I close the book, set it on the island in the middle of the kitchen, then look down the hall when the noise starts, but don't go to it.

It's the bathtub. It's filling.

I raise my chin, stretching my throat tight, and rub my larynx, trying to keep whatever's in me down, then am clawing through Sharon's cabinets in the kitchen, spice jars and sifters raining down onto the counter.

Finally I find what I know she has: the three tins of nuts, from Christmas.

The first is walnuts, the second two pecans, still in their paper shells.

I raise the blackest one up against the light, to see if I can see through it. When I can't, I feel my chest tightening the way it used to—the asthma I've outgrown—and know what I have to do. My head wobbles on my neck in denial though.

But it's the only way.

I place the pecan on my tongue, shell and all, afraid of what might be inside, then work it over between the molars of my right side, close my eyes and jaw at once. Make myself swallow it all. Fall coughing to the floor, have to dig out one of Miller's old inhalers, from when he had asthma too.

The mist slams into my chest again and again, my eyes hot, burning.

At the end of Rodger's birthday card to himself, which the editors chose to encase in their version of the blue box, are the words *She's still down there.*

I envy him that.

When I was twelve, I helped kill a girl I thought I loved, helped give birth to something else, something she didn't even know about. Something that saw me before crawling away. What makes it real, maybe, undeniable, is the way, that last time she looked up, she spit out the piece of Alex's shoelace she had in her mouth. Had to shake it away from her lip.

Her tongue was any color. Maybe the same it had always been.

Because I don't know what else to do, I sit with my back against the wall, behind my chair, every light in the living room on, random muscles in my shoulder and right leg twitching, as if cycling through the sensory details of letting Melanie go that day, above the water. My lap warms with urine and I just sway back and forth on the balls of my feet, hugging my knees to my chest, Miller's inhaler curled under my index finger like a gun

An hour later, eleven, midnight, something, I try to tell the story to the end, name the out-of-focus kid on the carousel Hodge. Give him a good life. And then the front door swings in all at once and I know I'm dying, that this is what death is, and have to bite the knuckle of my middle finger to keep from screaming.

From behind the chair, all I can see is the top of the door. It closes and my vision blurs, a grin spreading from my eyes to my mouth—that this will be finally be over, after so long—but then a sound intrudes: keys, jangling into a brass bowl. The one on the stand by the coat rack.

Reneé.

She swishes past me in slow motion, for the mess the kitchen is. Never sees me.

I stand in the doorway behind her, my slacks dark enough that she won't see the stain maybe.

Instead of putting stuff back into the cabinets, she's looking through the book I left out. Opening it to the place I have marked—marked with a spirit ribbon.

Slowly, she cocks her head to the side, studying the ribbon, then holds it to her mouth again, breathes it in.

I cough into my hollow fist to announce myself, there behind her already.

She sucks air in, pulls the book hard to her chest. Turns to me, leading with her eyes, and looks at me for too long it feels like, then past me, to the living room, so bright.

"You okay?" she asks.

I nod, make myself smile.

"How'd it go?" I ask—the date.

"You know," she says, opening the book again. "Sandy and his music."

I nod, remember: Sandy's the one with the custom stereo.

"What is this?" she says, about the book.

"Just—nothing," I tell her. "Old."

"Hmm," she says, leafing through, wowing her eyes up at the more sensational stuff. Aliens maybe. God.

"She did it to herself," I say, all at once.

Reneé holds her place in the book, looks up to me.

"She was . . . she was sad," I say. "She was a sad little girl. Her dad, he was—you've got to understand."

Reneé shrugs, humoring me I think. I rub my mouth, look away, to all Sharon's cooking utensils, spilling onto the floor. When I don't look away fast enough, Reneé has to say something about it: "A surprise?"

"Surprise?" I say back, trying to make sense of the word.

"Reorganizing for Mom?" she tries, holding her eyebrows up.

I nod, make myself grin, feel something rising in my throat again, have to raise my shoulders to keep it down. Close my eyes.

When I open them again, Reneé's sitting on the island, the book closed beside her. Just watching me.

"I could have stayed home tonight," she says, an offering of sorts, but I wave the idea away.

"You need—need to go out," I tell her. "It's good. What you should be doing."

The heels of her hands are gripping the edge of the countertop. I can't not notice this.

"Okay," she says, finally, "I guess—" but then, sliding the book back so she won't take it with her when she jumps down, her hand catches on the stiff, upper part of the spirit ribbon, pulls it from the book. "Oops," she says, doing her mouth in the shape of mock disaster, "lost your place."

I shake my head no, it's all right, I *know* where my place is, but then she has the ribbon again, is studying it. Remembering too.

We were ghosts, I want to tell her. And then the rest, finally.

Instead, I watch as she pulls the stick pin from the head of the ribbon.

"Stacy showed me this," she says, holding her right arm out, belly-up, in a way that I have to see Melanie's again, waiting for Alex to tie his shoelace around it.

"No," I say, taking her hand in mine, but she steps back, says, "It's all right, Daddy."

What she's doing is placing the pin in the crook of her elbow, the part of her arm that folds in.

I shake my head no again, reach for her again, but it's too late, she's already making her hand into a fist, drawing it slowly up to her shoulder.

I feel my eyes get hot, my mouth open.

When she unfolds her arm, the pin slides out of her skin like magic. No blood.

"That's—" I say, having to try hard to make the words, "in a blue box, that's the—Devil's Mark."

She looks up to me, not following.

I smile, touch her arm. Say, "You didn't bleed," and then I'm crying, trying to swallow it all back, but it's too late: the pecan is coming up.

I step back from her and throw up between us, and was right: it's not just a pecan, but bits of shell and meat and blood. Not red blood, like the movies, but darker. Real.

Reneé steps back, raising one of her shoes, to keep it clean maybe, and I look up to her, wipe the blood from my lips with the back of my forearm.

"Daddy?" she says, and I nod, sad that it's come to this, but there's nothing I can do anymore. With trembling hands I pin the ribbon to the chest of her shirt, through her skin maybe, I don't know. It makes her pull back anyway, look up to me, her eyebrows drawing together in question.

"Skin the Bobcats," I whisper to her, unable not to smile, then, when I pick her up in my arms like a little girl, say it at last—that I'm not a good person, that I've done bad things. She doesn't fight, doesn't know to. Doesn't know that we're going down the hall to the bathtub, which is already full.

Afterwards, my shirt wet like my pants, I stand again in the kitchen, hardly recognize it. Have to go outside, onto the balcony, my face flushing warm now like my eyes, my teeth chattering against each other.

Standing at the wood railing, then, I feel it: the tip ends of hair, silky long hair, lifted on the wind, trailing down from the roof.

She's up there I know, one knee to the shingles, her long fingers curled around the eave.

"Reneé?" I say weakly, unable to look around, up, and it's not so much a question as a prayer. That this isn't real. That it's Reneé on the roof maybe. Trying to scare me.

But then Melanie speaks back in the breathy, adult voice I knew she was going to have someday: *No, Raphael.*

I nod, see my shadow stretching out over the gravel drive, how it's split, doubling from two sources of light, and I know that this is all right, finally, as it should be, as it's always been ever since that day, and then Sharon pulls in under me, my son in the passenger seat, and I'm invisible again, a ghost. Able to do anything.

Was so surprised when Cemetery Dance *picked this one up from the slush pile. The first of three I ran with them—consecutively, I think. Anyway, I wrote this initially because I was getting paranoid everybody was forgetting about G.L.O.W. (Gorgeous Ladies of Wrestling) And that was an important time of my life. Too, though, I'd been really studying on Tobias Wolff's "Bullet in the Brain," where that kid says "they" in that cool way. So I tried that on, with this blond kid in here saying "patting." That just completely and forever creeps me out. So, once I had that scene, and an excuse for that scene to get told—kids scaring each other—I then had to come up with a dramatic wrapper, with a somewhat graceful exit. Which I don't think I quite found. Or, I'm always suspicious of stories that end with the kind of stasis this one does. Stories that their ending could be a painting, I mean. This ending, to me, it feels like a cop-out. But, all the stories of mine I* don't *think are cop-outs? They're the ones that never get published. Could be my radar's busted. Could be it never even got plugged in.*

THE LONG TRIAL OF NOLAN DUGATTI

(excerpt)

3.

When I come back to the homicide detective, he's talking to somebody else, his phone hooked over his shoulder.

I can still hear him though.

Something about "he doesn't know about Mollock."

But I do.

And then I close my eyes in pain: the homicide detective wasn't even calling about my father. I'm like that kid in second grade, who gets called out by the teacher. "*Jimmy*," she says in her stern voice. Or, in my case, which this is, "*Nolan*."

Me, what I do, what I've done here with this homicide detective, or feel like I'm doing anyway, is look up and immediately fall into some traipsing-over-myself apology for the gum in my mouth. When all she wanted me to do was lean my chair forward, please, young man.

But he doesn't know anything. Can't. Not after this long.

And Mollock, Andrew Rice Mollock, "ARM" for short, but nobody talked to him much anyway, I don't think.

For however long Nitrox was here, which is about my whole life, I'd guess, twenty-two years, Mollock was the building's janitor and general fix-it man. He's probably the one who took down the glass from around my workstation, even, and did a thousand other things that nobody'll ever know about.

Whenever Simon would come up here to harass me, him and Mollock would always get into it in one way or the other, just playing around, jawing.

However.

The night of the big send-off party, where everybody but me was walking out the building's doors for the last time, Mollock got food poisoning bad enough from the shrimp at the bar that he wrecked his car on the way to the emergency room the next morning. It didn't kill him, the wreck. But maybe he wished it did.

Instead, it gave him a few cuts here and there, which somehow let his shrimp poisoning into his body where it didn't have to deal with the digestive enzymes. Which is to say it had its own party. The end result, just five days later, was Mollock in a wheelchair, the shrimp bacteria in his brain, swimming behind his eyes, rotting his flesh away.

What's worse—or what's the cap anyway—is that, because it was his last day, his health benefits with Nitrox had just expired. After twenty-two years of faithful service, and then attending a party he didn't want to attend anyway, and eating a single cocktail shrimp just to be polite, when he really didn't like seafood at all.

So he got screwed, yeah.

What Nitrox didn't know when they refused to extend his health plan, though, was that he had a son, just out of county lockup, for having done things that were now classified.

My guess, just looking at him, is that he was a teenage assassin for the CIA. A real wetworks kind of kid, I mean. About my height, build, all of that—like I'm un-average—but when you get close to him, and accidentally catch his eyes, then you can see why Mollock never brought him around.

The only reason I know any of this, too (it's not like it was in the weekly bulletin), is that Little Mollock cornered me in the parking garage one day after the shrimp party, his eyes darting around like minnows in shallow water.

He told me the story of his dad, and how he was going to get vengeance on Nitrox, and then asked me what I did for them.

"Lackey," I told him. "Customer Relations."

He hissed a laugh through his teeth, massaged my shoulder too hard with one of his gloved hands (gloved for the "mission," I guess), and then we talked the only thing I knew: video games. A conversation which finally bottomed out, of course, with *Camopede*. He'd gotten it free, from his dad. I didn't laugh about this, but that was just because I'd heard about it: eight years ago, when *Camopede* officially started tanking, Nitrox paid everybody their Christmas bonus in *Camopede* units.

Oh, those golden days.

Little Mollock had actually played the game though. Not all the way through, evidently—I could tell because he wasn't the right kind of bitter—but enough to stall out in some of the blind ninja rooms anyway, which everybody gets stuck in. The best way out, really, is just a cheat code.

Except Little Mollock kind of liked the being stuck, I think. He dug the blind ninjas, took them as role models or something, as better parents than his janitor dad anyway, and even showed me the scar under his right eye where, years ago, he'd made a half-assed attempt to blind himself, in order to quicken his lightning kick.

"So, your dad," I told him then, not wanting to ever see that scar on his eye again, for as long as anybody lived.

"You know any good ways in?" he said back, leaning close to me and casing the building. Like I was supposed to follow where he was looking.

I opened my mouth to tell him something, I don't know what—the code?—but then reconsidered, just shrugged.

He nodded like I'd answered anyway, and never looked away from the building, and then his eyes quit the darting they'd been doing, which was pretty random, and could be controlled with medication, I was pretty sure, though I was planning to just control it the old-fashioned way, with distance, and what his eyes started doing then was kind of like bouncing back and forth from wing to wing, from window to window.

It was like he was watching a tennis game only he could see.

Except his lips were kind of moving too, in this hopeful way.

And, it wasn't tennis, but table tennis, maybe, ping-pong.

Or, even shorter than that: *Pong*.

"What did he do?" I say to the homicide detective about Mollock, about Little Mollock, when what I really should have been asking was *Where is he?*

Because I wrote this in seventy-two hours, I didn't have to time to put on any of the usual masks. It's crazy seeing one of the non-suicide-letter parts getting excerpted too. For readings, I always default to the dad's letters to Nolan, which my wife says are crazy for her to read, because it's like I'm sitting right there talking to her. Anyway, cool seeing "Mollock" in there (I'm watching Sleepy Hollow *now, and he's a cool, horn-headed, blurry demon in there). And, reason I wrote this book, it's because I'd bought my son an NES, just so this strange world of video games wouldn't be as strange to him as it is to me. Like, he needed to understand what a controller was, what a game was. I thought. But then he liked it. It wasn't just a curiosity, something to get tired of in five minutes, what with the whole outdoors waiting (we lived in a cotton field then). Like, he wanted to play all the time. Which I had the most trouble trying to make sense of. Just, you mean, sit there and push a button? But people do it. This novel, it's me trying to figure out the why of that.*

THE DECOMPOSITION OF A CONVERSATION

MY FATHER WOULD jump into the pool with a new cigarette dangling from his lips. He had an ashtray on the diving board. Like he wanted to be responsible with his smoking until the last possible moment, until he couldn't be responsible anymore. After his dive he would stay under for minutes it seemed, the grey-scum water smoothing out over him, the backyard absorbing his splash, and then he would crash through the surface, cling to the side. Cough another cigarette into action.

This isn't a cancer story. It's about religion.

The one truth my father gave me to order my life by was that we lack the proper enzymes to digest ourselves. Saying good-bye at the airport once he gave me a complicated gift, and I held it in my hand and called out to him as he was walking away, asking him if it would last.

"It's a Polaroid," he called back, as if I was looking too deep, "your mother," and fourteen years and two wives later his plane is still roaring off.

In the picture she's wearing mirrored sunglasses. And she wasn't going to die that next day or month or year and she's still alive now, a grandmother. The picture was taken at a parade, in the sun. I don't blame her for being there. My father did die of cancer, too, but that doesn't prove anything. My mother smuggled cigarettes into his room for him even. My girlfriend says that's romantic, but the world's a romantic place to her.

I sit on the edge of the bed and try to tell her how it really was: the morning of the Polaroid I was the first to wake, to look over the tops of everybody sleeping in the sun-room. The Fourth of July, it was always the Fourth of July, all summer long. My father was the next to wake, and half-asleep he told me about his own father, their big fishing trip, his main childhood memory: the two of them out on the lake, his father fumbling a beer into the water, diving in after it, pulling his old trick of pretending to drown, my father at twelve years old knowing it was a joke but all the same picturing his dead father under the boat with the bass jigs, floating beside them, his eyes glassy black like theirs, all their heads turned to the fireworks blossoming in the sky miles away.

My mother shushed him when she woke, and so my girlfriend will understand what I'm trying to tell her, I bend my arm like my mother did that morning, to show where the spider had laid its egg: in the crook of her elbow. We watched it all morning, following the red streaks up her arm. It was blood poisoning. The story was that when the red fingers reached your heart, they would make a fist, and that was it. Even the nurse on the phone said so.

But my mother.

She watched the fingers reaching for her, and in a casual voice asked how long the parade usually went?

My father smiled. "Two o'clock," he said, drawing hash lines on her arm with a felt tip pen he had to wet with his tongue.

It was still nine in the morning.

At the parade I was the one who took the Polaroid of her. In it she's looking up, establishing the pattern of my life, her eyes hidden, her purse arm swelling in the sun, too stiff to bend. A spider growing in there.

My girlfriend doesn't know what to say when I'm done so she covers herself like girls do in the movies when they realize they've made a mistake, and I turn away politely, say that my father was right, we don't have the proper enzymes to digest ourselves. But our parents can give them to us when no one's paying attention. Stepping into the shower to think or to not think—to be in a different environment than the bedroom—I cup my hand around a cigarette, know it won't last, but just for the rush of life I hold the smoke in as long as I can against the water, close my eyes.

So many of these short pieces I run, they're all just stuff that happened when I was kid. Like this. My mom, she drew that circle on her arm, and we went to the parade, I mean. And I used to know somebody who would take cigarettes into water. Anyway, if this is from anywhere, it's from Robert Boswell's "The Darkness of Love." I've read that story over and over. It's maybe the first time I ever actually got invested as a reader in the relationship dynamics between a couple. Before, that had always been just chaff, just the stupid stuff you have to do in order to get a proper monster out on the lawn to fight. But Boswell's story, it resensitized me. Or, sensitized me in the first place maybe. This story is me, trying to do something with that. And then defaulting the way I usually do: to my own life. Because I don't know anybody else's.

ROCKET MAN

THE DEAD AREN'T exactly known for their baseball skills, but still, if you're a player short some afternoon, just need a body to prop up out in left field—it all comes down to how bad you want to play, really. Or, in our case—where you can understand that by "our" I mean "my," in that I promised off four of my dad's cigarettes, one of my big brother's magazines, and one sleepover lie—how bad you want to impress Amber Watson, on the walk back from the community pool, her lifeguard eyes already focused on everything at once.

Last week, I'd actually smacked the ball so hard that Rory at shortstop called time, to show how the cover'd rolled half back, the red stitching popped.

"You scalped it," he said, kind of curling his lip in awe. I should mention I'm Indian, except everybody's always doing that for me.

The plan that day we pulled a zombie in (it had used to be Michael T from over on Oak Circle, but you're not supposed to call zombies by their people names), my plan was to hit that same ball—I'd been saving it—even harder, so that there'd just be a cork center twirling up over our diamond, trailing leather and thread. Amber Watson would track back from that cracking sound to me, still holding my follow-through like I was posing for a trophy. And then of course I'd look through the chain link, kind of nod to her that this was me, yeah, this was who I really am, she's just never seen it, and she'd smile and look away, and things in the halls at school would be different between us then. More awkward. She might even start timing her walks to coincide with some guess at my spot in the batting order.

Anyway, it wasn't like there was anything else I could ever possibly do that might have a chance of impressing her.

But first, of course, we needed that body to prop up out in left field. Which, I know you're thinking "right, right field," these are sixth graders, they never wait, they always step out, slap the ball early, and, I mean, maybe the kids from Chesterton or Memphis City do, I don't know. But around here, we've been taught to wait, to time it out, to let that ball kind of hover in the pocket before we launch it into orbit. Kids from Chesterton? None of them are ever going pro. Not like us.

It's why we fail the spelling test each Friday, why we blow the math quiz if we're not sitting by somebody smart. You don't need to know how to spell "home run" to hit one. You don't have to add up runners in your head, so long as you knock them all in. Easy as that.

As for Michael T, none of us had had much to do with him since he got bit, started playing for the other team. There were the lunges from behind the fence on the way to school, there was that shape kind of scuffling around when you took the trash out some nights, but that could have been any zombie. It didn't have to be Michael T. And, pulling him in that day to just stand there, let the flies buzz in and out of his mouth—it's not like that's not what he did before he was dead. You only picked Michael T if he was the only one to pick, I'm saying. You wouldn't think that either, him being a year older than us and all, but he'd always just been our size too. Most kids like that, a grade up but not taller, they'd at least be fast, or be able to fling the ball home all the way from the center fence. Not Michael T. Michael T—the best way to explain him, I guess, it's that his big brother used to pin him down to the ground at recess, drop a line of spit down almost to his face, the rest of us looking but not looking. Glad just not to be him.

That day, though, with Amber Watson approaching on my radar, barefoot the way she usually was, her shoes hooked over her shoulder like a rich lady's purse, that day, it was either Michael T or nobody. Or, at first it was nobody, but then, just joking around, Theodore said he'd seen Michael T shuffling around down by the rocket park anyway.

"Michael T?" I asked.

"He still can't catch," Theodore said.

"That was all the way before lunch, though, yeah?" Rory said, socking the ball into his glove for punctuation.

It was nearly three now.

"Can you track him?" Les said, falling in as we rounded the backstop.

"Your nose not work?" I asked him back.

Just another perfect summer afternoon.

We kicked a lopsided rock nearly all the way to where Michael T was supposed to have been, and then we turned to Theodore. He shrugged, was ready to fight any of us, even tried some of the words he'd learned from spying on his uncles in the garage. He wasn't lying though. Splatted all over the bench were the crab apples him and Jefferson Banks had been zinging Michael T with.

"Jefferson," I said, "what about him?"

"Said he had to go home," Theodore shrugged, half-embarrassed for Jefferson. "His mom."

Figured. The one time I can impress Amber Watson and Jefferson's cleaning out all the ashtrays in the house then reading romance novels to his mom while she tans in the backyard.

"Who then?" Les asked, shading his eyes from the sun, squinting across all the glinty metal of the old playground.

None of us came to this one anymore. It was for kids.

"He's got to be around," Theodore said. "My dad said they like beef jerky."

I seconded this, had heard it as well.

You could lure a zombie anywhere if you had a twist of dried meat on a long string. It was supposed to be getting bad enough with the high schoolers that the stores in town had put a limit on beef jerky, two per customer.

I kicked at another rock that was there by the bench. It wasn't our lopsided one, was probably one Jefferson and Theodore had tried on Michael T. There was still a little bit of blood on it. All the ants were loving the crab apple leftovers, but, for them, there was a force field around where that rock had been. Until the next rain anyway.

"She's never going to see me," I said, just out loud.

"Who?" Theodore asked, studying the park like Amber Watson could possibly be walking through it.

I shook my head no, never mind, and, turning away, half-planning to set a mirror up in right field, let Gerald just stand kind of by it, so it would seem like we had a full team, I caught a flash of cloth all the way in the top of the rocket.

"It's not over yet," I said, pointing up there with my chin.

Somebody was up there, right at the top where the astronauts would sit if it were a real rocket. The capsule part. And they were moving.

"Jefferson?" Theodore asked, looking to us for support.

Like monkeys, Les and Rory crawled up the outside of the rocket, high enough that their moms had to be having heart attacks in their kitchens.

When they get there, Rory had to turn to the side to throw up. It took that loogey of puke forever to make it to the ground. We laughed because it was throw-up, then tracked back up to the top of the rocket.

"It's Michael T!" Les called down, waving his hand like there was anywhere else in the whole world we might be looking.

"What's he doing?" I asked, not really loud enough, my eyes kind of pre-squinted, because this might be going to mess our game up.

"It's Jefferson," Theodore filled in, standing right beside me, and he was right.

Instead of going home like his mom wanted, Jefferson had spiraled up into the top of the rocket, probably to check if his name was still there, and never guessed Michael T might still be lurking around. Even a first grader can outrun or outsmart a zombie, but, in a tight place like that, and especially if you're in a panic, are freaking out, then it's a different kind of game altogether.

"Shouldn't have thrown those horse apples at him," Gerald said, shaking his head.

"Shouldn't have been stupid, more like," I said, and slapped my glove into Gerald's chest, for him to hold.

Ten minutes later, Les and Rory using cigarettes from the outside of the rocket to herd him away from his meal, Michael T lumbered down onto the playground, stood in that crooked, hurt way zombies do.

"Hunh," Theodore said.

He was right.

In the year since Michael T had been bitten, he hadn't grown any. He was shorter than all us now. Rotted away, Jefferson's gore all drooled down his front side, some bones showing through the back of his hand, but still, that we'd outgrown him this past year. It felt like we'd cheated.

It was exhilarating.

One of us laughed and the rest fell in, and, using a piece of a sandwich Les finally volunteered to open his elbow scab on—we didn't have any beef jerky—we were able to lure Michael T back to the baseball diamond.

After everybody'd crossed the road, I studied up and down it, to be sure Amber Watson hadn't passed yet.

I didn't think so.

Not on an afternoon this perfect.

So then it was the big vote: whose glove was Michael T going to wear, probably try to gnaw on? When I got tired of it all, I just threw mine into his chest, glared all around.

"Warpath, chief," Les said, picking the glove up gingerly, watching Michael T the whole time.

"Scalp your dumb ass," I said, and turned around, didn't watch the complicated maneuver of getting the glove on Michael T's left hand, and only casually kept track of the stupid way he kept breaking position. Finally Timmy found a dead squirrel in the weeds, stuffed it into the school backpack that had kind of become part of Michael T's back. The smell kept him in place better than a spike through his foot. He kept kind of spinning around in his zombie way, tasting the air, but he wasn't going anywhere.

And then—this because my whole body was tuned into it, because the whole summer had been pointing at it—the adult swim whistle went off down at the community pool. Or maybe what I was tuned into was the groan from all the swimmers. Either way, this was always when the lifeguards would change chairs, was always when, if somebody was going off shift, they would go.

"Amber," I said to myself, tossing my ragged, lucky ball to Les then tapping my bat across home plate, waiting for him to wind up.

"Am-*what*?" Theodore asked from behind the catcher's mask his mom insisted on.

I shook my head no, nothing, and, because I was looking down the street, down that tunnel of trees, Les slipped the first pitch by me.

"That one's free," I called out to him, tapping my bat again. Licking my lips.

Les wound up, leaned back, and I stepped up like I was already going to swing. He cued into it, that I was ahead of him here, and it threw him off enough that he flung the ball over Theodore's mitt, rattled the backstop with it.

"That one's free too," he called out to me, and I smiled, took it.

Just wait, I was saying inside, sneaking a look up the road again, and, just like in the movies, the whole afternoon slowed almost to a stop right there.

It was her. I smiled, nodded, my own breath loud in my ears, and slit my eyes back to Les.

He drove one right into the pocket, and if I'd wanted I could have shoveled it over all of their heads, dropped it out past the fence, into no man's land.

Except it was too early.

After it slapped home, I spun out of the box, spit into the dirt, hammered my bat into the fence two times.

And it was definitely her. Shoes over her shoulder, gum going in her mouth, nose still zinced, jean shorts over her one-piece, the whole deal.

I timed it perfect, getting back to the box, was wound up to launch this ball just at the point when she'd be closest to me.

So of course Les threw it high.

I could see it coming a mile away, how he'd tried to knuckle it, had lost it on the downsling like he always did, so there was maybe even a little arc to the ball's path. Not that it mattered, it was too high to swing at, but still—now or never, right? This is what all my planning had come down to.

I stepped back, crowding Theodore, who was already leaned forward to catch the ball when it dropped, and I swung at a ball that was higher than my shoulders, a ball my dad would have already been turning away from in disgust, and knew the instant my bat cracked into it that there wasn't going to be any lift, that it was a line drive, an arrow I was shooting out, blind. One I was going to have to run faster than somehow.

Still, even though I didn't scoop under it like I would have liked, and even though I was making contact with it earlier than I would have wanted, I gave it every last thing I had, gave it everything I'd learned, everything I had to gamble.

And it worked. The cover flapping behind it just like a comet tail, it was a thing of beauty.

Les being Les, of course he bit the dirt to get out of the way, and Gerald and Rory—second and short—nearly hit each other, diving for what they knew was a two-run hit. A ball that wasn't even going to skip grass until—

Until left field, yeah.

Until Michael T.

And, if you're thinking he raised his glove here, that some long-forgotten reflex surfaced in his zombie brain for an instant, then guess again.

Dead or alive, he would have done the same thing: just stood there like the dunce he was.

Only, now, his face was kind of spongy, I guess.

The ball splatted into his left eye socket, sucked into place, stayed there, some kind of dark juice burping from his ears, trickling down along his jaw, the cover of the ball pasted to his cheek.

For a long moment we were all quiet, all holding our breaths—this was like hitting a pigeon with a pop-fly—and then, of everybody, I was the only one to hear Amber Watson stop on the sidewalk, look from the ball back to me, exactly like I'd planned.

I smiled, kind of shrugged, and then Gerald called it in his best umpire voice: "Out!"

I turned to him, my face going cold, and everybody in the infield was kind of shrugging that, yeah, the ball definitely hadn't hit the ground. No need to burn up the baseline.

"But, but," I said, pointing out to Michael T with my bat, to show how obvious it was that that wasn't a catch, that it didn't really count, and then Rory and Theodore and Les all started nodding that Gerald was right. Worse, now the outfield was chanting: "Mi-chael, Mi-chael, Mi-chael." And then my own dugout fell in, clapping some Indian whoops from their mouth to memorialize what had happened here, today. How I was the only one who could have done it.

But I wasn't out.

Michael T wasn't even a real player, was just a body we'd propped up out there.

I looked back to Amber Watson and could tell she was just waiting to see what I was going to do here, waiting to see what was going to happen.

So I showed her.

I charged the mound, and, when Les sidestepped, holding his hands up and out like a bullfighter, I kept going, bat in hand, held low behind me, Rory and Gerald each giving me room as well, so that by the time I got out to left field I was running.

"You didn't catch it!" I yelled to Michael T, singlehandedly trying to ruin my whole summer, wreck my love life, trash my reputation—"Even a zombie can get him out"—and I swung for the ball a second time.

Instead of driving it off the T his head was supposed to be, I thunked it deeper, into his brain, I think, so that the rest of him kind of spasmed in a brainstemmy way, the bat shivering out of my hands so I had to let it go. And, because I hadn't planned ahead—charging out of the box isn't exactly about thinking everything through, even my dad would cop to this—the follow-through of my swing, it wrapped me up into Michael T's dead arms, and we fell together, me first.

And, like everything else since Les's failed knuckle ball, it took forever to happen. Long enough for me to hear that little lopsided plastic ball rattling in Amber Watson's whistle right before she set her feet and blew it. Long enough for me to see the legs of a single fly, following us down. Long enough for me to hear my chanted name stop in the middle.

This wasn't just a freak thing happening anymore.

We were stepping over into legend now.

Because the town was always on alert these days, Amber Watson's whistle was going to line the fence with people in under five minutes, and now everybody on the field and in the dugout, they were going to be witness to this, were each going to have their own better vantage point to tell the story from.

Meaning, instead of me being the star, everybody else would be.

And Amber Watson.

It hurt to even think about.

We were going to have a special bond, now, sure, but not the kind where I was ever going to get to buy her a spirit ribbon. Not the kind where she'd ever tell me to quit smoking, because it was bad for me.

If I even got to live that far, I mean. If the yearbook staff wasn't already working my class photo onto the casualties page.

I wasn't there yet though.

This wasn't the top of a rocket, I mean.

Sure, I was on my back in left field, and Michael T was over me, pinning me down by accident, the slobber and blood and brain juice stringing down from his lips, swinging right in front of my face so that I wanted to scream, but I could still kick him away, right? Lock my arms against his chest, keep my mouth closed so nothing dripped in it.

All of which would have happened too.

Except for Les.

He'd picked up the bat that I guess I'd dragged through the chalk between second and third, so that, when he slapped it into the side of Michael T's head, a puff of white kind of breathed up. At first I thought it was bone, powdered skull—the whole top of Michael T's rotted-out head was coming off—but then there was sunlight above me again, and Les was hauling me up, and, on the sidewalk, Amber Watson was just staring at me, her whistle still in her mouth, her hair still wet enough to have left a dark patch on the canvas of the sneakers looped over her shoulder.

I put two of my fingers to my eyebrow like I'd seen my dad do, launched them off in salute to her, and in return she shook her head in disappointment. At the kid I still obviously was. So, yeah, if you want to know what it's like living with zombies, this is it, pretty much: they mess everything up. And if you want to know why I never went pro, it's because I got in the habit of charging the mound too much, like I had all this momentum from that day, all this unfairness built up inside. And if you want to know about Amber Watson, ask Les Moore—that's his real, stupid name, yeah. After that day he saved my life, became the real Indian because he'd been the one to scalp Michael T, he stopped coming to the diamond so much, started spending more time at the pool, his hair bleaching in the sun, his reflexes gone, always thirty-five cents in his trunks to buy a lifeguard a lemonade if she wanted.

And she did, she does.

And me? Some nights I still go to the old park, spiral up to the top of the rocket with a "Bury the Tomahawk" or "Circle the Wagons" spirit ribbon, and I let it flutter a bit through the grimy bars before letting it go, down through space, down to the planet I used to know, miles and miles from here.

Stymie *magazine called me up, said what if I wrote a sports story for them, for money? It was the "money" part I heard when I said yes, I'm pretty sure. The "sports" part, though, that's when it got rough. So I wrote back after a bit, asked if I could maybe slip a zombie or two in?* Stymie *said sure, they trusted me. Which, that's what your grandma always tells you when you're taking her car, right? The worst kind of responsibility. Anyway, I had no clue what to do, but I have, as a kid, watched a lifeguard walk up a sidewalk, her shoes hooked over her shoulder, and I figured as long as I made that moment real enough, the rest would fall into place. And, that rocket at the playground? Secretly, that's in all of my stories, all of my novels. I grew up in that rocket, in Stanton, Texas. And, for the baseball stuff, here, all the left-field/right-field stuff, I had to lean on friends again. Because I know less than nothing about all that. Don't get me wrong, I like batting. Or swinging and dreaming anyway. The rest of it, though, I could do without. So, yeah, this guy in here, he's me, swinging and dreaming. That's pretty much who I still am, too, I guess.*

NEITHER HEADS NOR TAILS

MY FATHER LOST his left nipple in a hunting-related accident. He said it didn't make him any less of a father—it made him more of a man, really. What happened was it was still hot two weeks before bow season opened, and he was in the garage in his undershirt, limbering up his favorite bow. After a couple of half draws to get the limbs warm he pulled the string back all the way, no arrow, and held it for a steady ten count. On eleven, though, his shaky fingers let the bowstring slip. It sliced forward like razor wire. His nipple spun through the air, slapped the wall of the garage, and stuck. The way he tells it he kind of grunted a smile then—the nerves in his new cavity were still too shocked to relay anything up to his head—and walked directly inside, cupping his hand over his chest to keep the air out. By the time he got a towel and made it back to the garage, which he'd had open, Telly, our golden retriever, was sitting there, sweeping the concrete with his matted palm frond of a tail. My father could see that what Telly was trying to do was what he always did when he was guilty: gulping down his smile. There was still a wet smear on the wall where he'd licked the nipple off. It didn't make him any less of a dog, my father says. Really, it made him more of a dog, probably. And it's not like they could have sewn it back on anyway, right? And risked getting it back on but rotated half-around now, like a dial? No, and anyway, my father and his nipple stump—does it make me any less of a son for staring at it when we're at the beach? "Oh, that," my mom says when she sees the fascination in my face, and then tells my father to be sure and get the sun block down into that, dear. That's the kind of place a cancer will just pool, if you let it. Because it's easier to play along, my father dollops the sunblock in, around, and after it's slick then, and we're all just lying there in the sun waiting to get dry enough for the drive home, I'll sometimes cue into my father's right hand, slapped across his chest like there's a flag in the area. But there's not. And he's asleep anyway, his right finger just skating around the oily rim of his caldera of scar tissue, that divot in his life.

What it does—and this is the part I mostly hate—is make me sneak touches up onto my own chest. Sneak touches and maybe even a light pinch, just to be sure, at least until my mom slaps the back of my hand and hisses, "Not in public" to me.

It doesn't make me any less of a man, I don't think. But it doesn't help either.

I wrote this after building my own bow. Well, story: when I was fourteen, my favorite bow maker was Dan Quillian. I saved his contact info for nearly twenty years, until I had three hundred bucks for a bow stock from him. At which point I called the number on the pamphlet I'd mailed off for once upon a time, and his daughter answered, because he was long dead. But I got her to go out to his garage, to sell me whatever was on his bench. Which I finished out, and sanded long enough that I even stupidly erased his writing off it. But it's still a Dan Quillian. It's a fast, slick bow, and I love it. But it'll eat all the skin off the inside of my left arm too. And, from shooting in the rags I call shirts, I found it'll scrape my chest up too, when I'm tired and my form gets bad. That's where this story comes from. Well, that and growing up with an air force dad. I've stood in so many stands with him when "The Star-Spangled Banner" or anthem or whatever is playing, where everybody takes their hat off. It's always a weird moment for me. I never have any idea what I'm really supposed to be doing. So I wrote this story to try to explain that weirdness, that thing everybody does when the music's playing. That look they get in their eyes. I don't think I'll ever understand.

ALL THE BEAUTIFUL SINNERS

(excerpt)

19 MAY 1982, NAZARETH, TEXAS

He was moving along the edge of town. The boots were too big for him, the jacket bulky, heavier than he would have guessed, and the helmet kept tipping over his eyes. His heart was slapping the inside of his chest. He wasn't even sure he was going to do it, yet. Maybe he would just look at them, at one of them. Or maybe they'd be already dead. Everywhere there was rain, and water, the sky spent. Power lines waved overhead like tree branches, and trees lay on their sides like fallen people, still reaching up for something. The root pans were gnarled and black and terrible. He held the back of his hand over his mouth, to not have to smell them.

The fireman he'd taken the jacket and boots and helmet from had been stuck in a barbed-wire fence. He'd looked up at the rock coming down for him, then just taken it, as he had to. The human skull was like a dried gourd. He'd half-expected flies to mass up out of it, each one with a fraction of intelligence, emotion. Scattering. He would have chased them and eaten them and saved them inside.

But it was just the usual grey, the usual red.

He put the boots on, and the jacket, and the gloves, over the cotton ones he was already wearing. His fingers were thick and protected now. He flexed them as he moved from tilted cornice to tilted cornice, telephone pole to telephone pole. Nazareth was gone. Things were still falling from the sky, even. The first dead people he'd found had been three women in an upside-down car.

They still had their seat belts on, were staring straight ahead, their ponytails hanging down, brushing the roof liner.

He'd wanted to take a picture, but the gloves were so thick, and the flash: somebody would see it.

He was supposed to be helping.

He laughed, ran.

He wasn't going to do it. He knew now. Because it could never work. How would he get them back to his car? No. The thing to do was walk back to that fireman in the fence, dress him, maybe leaving the jacket inside out or something, just because it would get blamed on the tornado. Everything would get blamed on the tornado, even him, maybe, if he got caught.

He ran, and laughed, and the cotton in his ear made the laughter sound foreign.

The fireproof jacket billowed around him, the air still charged blue.

People weren't even emerging from their homes yet, or their fallout shelters, or the mattresses they'd pulled over their bathtubs, the down jackets they'd wrapped themselves in, in the cedar closet, their grandmother's scent all around them.

After a few hundred feet, he just stood, listening, and finally a female cat broke from a tumbled wall, raced across what was left of the street. He knew she was female because they were all female. He'd heard it like that in a joke once. He looked behind an untouched car, for the idea of a dog, because dogs and cats went together. He had an axe in his hand, though, while he was looking. Which made it different. He looked down at the axe head as if just realizing it was there. Yes. He looked to the cat, nodded, smiling, and said it: "Here, kitty kitty kitty."

The cat just watched him, its ears slicked back.

They stared at each other like that until the woman stood from under her couch. She was bleeding. She stumbled through her open-air living room, leaned in the doorframe. It was the only thing left.

The fireman with the axe waved at her.

Her head wobbled to the side, like maybe a neck ligament had had some trauma.

"You okay?" he called out, cupping his mouth with his thick glove.

She looked around, her chest shuddering.

He walked to her at right angles.

"Are you hurt, ma'am?" he asked.

His face mask was down now, already, but it didn't matter. She was looking at his axe.

He looked at it too.

There were still pieces of the other fireman on it.

"It's not what you think," he told her.

"What do I think?" she said.

Her pupils were blown wide. There was blood trailing down from her right ear. He traced it with a gloved finger and she shivered, hugged herself.

"Are you going to save me?" she said.

He smiled, let his palm rest on her shoulder.

"Not all of you," he said.

This was like the old days, God.

But no. Not anymore. Just this once.

After her, he found a dog, maybe the dog the cat had been remembering to make it run, even, and he let it go with a broken pelvis, and then, for long, boring minutes, nothing. He was shrugging out of the yellow jacket—this was stupid stupid stupid—when the girl stood from the broken boards and gritty shingles. The children, yes. He'd nearly forgotten about them somehow. And she was so dark.

"Where's your brother?" the nice fireman asked.

A boy stood up beside her then, as dark as her and almost as tall.

Yes.

The fireman put the middle finger of his glove into his mouth, bit the empty part at the tip, pulled his hand away, then did it again with the cotton underneath, until it was just bare skin.

He held his hand out to the girl.

Later he would learn that it was always the girl who reached up first. Because he was the perfect father—the hero, saving her.

"Hello," he said to her.

She had wet Sheetrock dust over one side of her face.

She told him her name. He told her yes, he knew, it was a beautiful name too, and then she took her brother's hand and they picked their way out through the rubble, and he had no idea then where he was going to take them, what he was going to do. Just that they were holding his hand, that they were alive, warm, and that they would be enough.

This is my favorite part of this novel, by far. In the rewrite, I mean, I try to show it off by moving it up to the very first thing. That dialogue there, the "Are you going to save me?" she said / "Not all of you," he said, that's as good as I've ever done, I think. Well, aside from a line or two Con has in Demon Theory. *Dialogue is by far my weak, um, shoe, or suit, or whatever it is that's idiomatically weak. When I came to grad school, I wasn't even doing dialogue. Like, at all. The professors and workshops had to argue and argue with me to just get a character to say even one thing anywhere in a whole story. I didn't like dialogue. Or, I told myself I didn't like it. Truth told, it was more like I sucked at it, and knew it. And I still mostly suck at it, I think, always have to fake it. It's not natural, talking with mouth words. It's so much more natural to talk with eyes and chins and lips and hands and silences. It's probably from having gone without my tongue for a few months when I was a kid. It made me more aware, made me watch closer. It made talking feel unnecessary, like shouting.*

LUNCH

THE GIRL I trade jokes with at the cafeteria I eat at on Mondays has a new one for me this time: her son is going to live with his grandmother for a while. I ask her why—we're laughing, in our way: her filling tea glasses (tea first, halfway up, then the ice, which I guess is something you learn), me sliding two pieces of pie onto one saucer, like they let me do—and she says she's sending him to her mother's because this morning when she went in to wake him for school his breath was white, because she doesn't have a heater in her house. But her mother does, one of those big ones that shoots heat up through a vent in the living room. And then she nods for me to take my pie, that it's okay.

At one point a few minutes later, eating whatever I'm eating, I see a guy about twenty-five stand up from his table, then pull his dad—I think it's his dad, anyway, but it could be a boss, I guess—but what the guy does is pull him up from his plate and arrange him into the very specific shape he needs him to be in, to properly show this complicated karate move he saw on a show last night, or just thought of maybe.

Either way, his face when he slow motions through the move is deadly serious, and he does the sound effects too, or holds his lips like he's making the sounds, and I look away, want to fall in love with something, the first thing I see, but close my eyes instead, know that next week, and the week after, I'll be eating in a different place.

This is just me, eating at Furr's Cafeteria in Lubbock, Texas. Which I went back to recently, after eight years gone. And they still remembered me. I love that place. So many of my good memories, they're in Furr'ses all across Texas. Thanksgivings and Christmases and after-the-funerals. It's the best place in the world. Anyway, sometimes you just write down what you see happening in front of you, I guess? What I don't think I managed to get in here, though, it's that, at the stoplight that day, leaving Furr's, there were these two dudes on bikes. They were . . . whatever you are where when you're young but not a kid, you put on a tie and slacks and ride bikes around town and knock on people's doors and try to convert them to something. They were them. And they were riding in line on the sidewalk, past the mall. And the one in front, he was just pedaling, just getting to the next place. But the guy behind him—this is one of the best things I've ever, ever seen—he had a pale-red tire on the front of his bike, and the whole way past the mall, he was trying so hard to pull the front of that bike up into a wheelie. Just over and over, jerking at it, almost wrecking, then trying again. Know what? That guy with the red tire, he converted me that day. I've never been the same since.

RENDEZVOUS WITH SULA PRIME

MY WIFE DOESN'T want me to write any of this down. But that's probably just because of where it starts: with the wife before her, Muriel, who was herself pretty much just a replacement of my first wife and true love, Candace.

Since Candace was from my junior year of high school, she wasn't a stand-in for anybody. If she was anything, she was a girl I'd shaped from my dreams, equal parts movie and magazine, but somehow pure.

My current wife is Janie.

Where she found me was in the parking lot of a truck stop in Arizona. I was standing in the endless sea of pumps, just one rig out there, its running lights dull they were so far away.

Janie touched me on the elbow.

What she wanted was the coffee cup I'd carried out the door with me.

"Lose your balloon?" she said, nodding up to the sky. It was where I was looking.

I smiled, didn't lower my face.

"You know that guy?" I asked, lifting my cup to finish my coffee.

When Janie didn't answer I wiped my mouth and turned to her, to see if she'd heard.

"Ted," I told her, nodding inside.

She looked to all the plate glass then back to me, and the reason I asked her to marry me two years later, I think, was that not asking her would feel like a betrayal. She'd got it in her mind that I was coming back every weekend for her, I mean.

We're good together though, too, don't get me wrong.

Her waitress skills are more than enough to keep the books for what little veterinary work I do anymore, and in the mornings I make the coffee and bring it out to the porch for us and we watch the horses together and I count them in my head.

Who knows. We might make it all the way, me and Janie.

Maybe that's the secret—you start out on the wrong foot, with a misunderstanding, and then you hold onto each other just to keep from falling down, and pretty soon, a few years later, you're in stride together, holding hands, pulling each other across the rough ground. Not alone anymore.

Except, some mornings when I'm the porch before her, I look across the ancient landscape of Arizona, the sun painting reds and pinks on all the rocks, and I know that it could have been another way too.

All those times, going back to the truck stop weekend after weekend, it wasn't for Janie. Some nights she wasn't even there.

It was for Ted.

That's what I call him anyway.

The only time I ever saw him was two weeks after Muriel had left me. To say I was in a hole I'd dug myself was to put it mildly. I'll try not to bore you with the details either, as I'm sure you've sat through a soap opera at one time or another.

It's enough to say that she wasn't Candace, and so had always had one strike against her.

The bad thing was I'd figured that out, too, after three years of her saying it to me in every way she knew. How I wasn't just messing up my life, but somebody else's as well.

The first week of thinking about it I went to work every day and sleepwalked through the office visits, the dogs and cats and lizards in the consultation rooms, the horses in their trailers, the cattle I had to drive out to myself, at eight cents a mile.

The second week I started falling away though. When I placed my hand on a dog's neck to pinch up some skin to inject, the skin felt more like clay than anything living. But it wasn't the animals. It was me—like I was wearing gloves all the time, but on my eyes too, and my thoughts. By Wednesday I had a sign on the front door directing people to my friend Mick, who probably didn't need the business but got it anyway.

By Friday I was in my truck. Just driving.

I told myself things like *This is what you went to school twelve years for* and *You should have just gone and gotten the cigarettes yourself.* The world would be a lot happier then. If the milk truck had slammed into me instead of Candace.

But it hadn't, of course, and now I was floating away from one thing, probably about to fall into another. It didn't matter if my eyes were closed or open, really.

And, though Janie claims to remember the first time she saw me, the brass bell of the truck stop clanging against the door over my head, I don't remember her until the parking lot. Even though she'd brought me eggs and bacon and, all told, three cups of coffee.

It's because of Ted that I don't remember, yeah.

When he sat into the booth opposite me, everything changed.

Or, it almost did.

But that's the story of my life.

He waited until I looked up to him to speak. It was a good thirty seconds. I've been in enough truck stops to know that anybody who approaches you, it's probably not to just give you something. Not unless you have money, of course. Or a spare seat.

But Ted was different.

First—and I saw this right off, in spite of how unobservant Janie likes to tell everybody I am—was his shirt, and his hat. They were mine. Just like them.

To be sure, I leaned over, to see my jeans on his legs. My boots. It was like someone had slid a mirror across from me instead of a man.

I came back up. The only thing different was the face.

"What are the chances, right?" he said.

I chewed my eggs, swallowed them.

"Guess I'm waiting for somebody here," I finally told him.

"I've been waiting too," he said, like he was thrilled that I'd given him the chance to say that. "You," he added, and, as if suspicious, "Is that breakfast?"

I held up a forkful of eggs to inspect, said, "Their estimation of it, I suppose."

"But it's not morning . . ." he whispered, in a voice you use for secrets when you're ten years old. "I thought meals here were, um . . . regimented."

I chewed my eggs, raised my cup for more coffee.

"Hun?" the waitress I didn't know was Janie said to me, and the visitor held his hand up, palm out, his fingers tight against each other, almost military.

He's imitating something he saw, I told myself, then studied my plate instead.

Just like he'd wanted, the waitress had stopped talking.

"You're a cat doctor," he said then, once we were alone.

"Listen," I told him, dropping my crumpled napkin into my plate and pushing the whole affair away, "I don't know who you think I am here—"

He interrupted with my full name, and birth date, his voice eager.

"So you know I'm a vet," I said, hooking my head out to the parking lot. "It says so on my truck."

"And you're between right now," he said, like this too was a secret.

"Between?" I repeated. "This is—we're halfway to Scottsdale, yeah."

The visitor smiled, set both of his hands on the surface of the table.

"Right now," he said, "and you know this, I wouldn't be here if you didn't, right now you could disappear from this diner and from everything else, and never come back, and nothing would change."

"It's a truck stop," I corrected. "Not a diner."

"A revolver," he leaned forward to say. "Not a pistol."

It was a distinction my father had always insisted upon when I was young and learning guns.

I'd been thinking of it on the road because there was a loaded revolver in the glove compartment of my truck.

The watchdogs being what they were, I couldn't use it on injured horses myself, but I could loan it to friends or clients or whomever, to save them the cost of an injection. Just because it was faster, and, I thought, just as humane. More important, it closed the circles better, I'd always thought. Put the life back in the owner's hands.

I was just staring at the visitor now.

Not a muscle moved on his face.

The reason I was out here, though, where there was nobody else, was specifically because I'd been thinking of that revolver, and about circles, drawing themselves closed after forty-two years.

It was just luck that I'd decided to stop for a cup of coffee, I suppose.

But I think he'd have found me anyway.

I pushed away from the table, went to the bathroom, washed my face and dried it. I'd left my hat on the table to let the waitress know I wasn't gone.

I came back a few minutes later, sat down in my place.

"But you know cats," he said.

"Why?" I asked. "You got a sick one?"

He just stared at me. "If one were dying, I mean, you could probably save it."

"Depends if we're talking injury or disease."

"It's sick."

"How much you willing to spend?"

He smiled, his first real expression, but kept his hands in plain sight.

"I wouldn't have come to you if you weren't between," he said then, holding my eyes with his.

"Between what?"

"Worlds, Mr. Sam."

It was a name an Asian launderer might call me if we were in a Western.

"I don't follow," I finally said.

"You haven't decided to do it yet," he said. "And you haven't decided not to either."

"Do what?"

He held his pistol finger dead center to his forehead. Instead of his temple.

It would have been stupid, except that's where I told everybody I loaned my gun to aim.

I stared at this guy, this visitor, my hands on the table now as well.

"You don't know anything about me," I said.

"You fix cats," he said back.

"And I'm 'between.'"

He nodded. Like this was a real conversation we were having here.

"Perhaps you need more information to decide," he said, after neither of us had said anything for a bit.

"Decide what?"

"Whether to help or not."

I blew a laugh through my nose, looked away, into the parking lot.

"Yeah," I said, "perhaps."

I don't think he heard the joke in my voice.

"It's not a question of payment," he started, "or of transportation. That's all perfectly easy and already in place. Maybe we should just start with the cat."

"Or who you are, say."

"I'm what you would call a gamekeeper, Mr. Sam."

"It's just 'Sam.' Then—I take it we're not talking a house cat here, right?"

He acknowledged that with a nod.

"And," I went on, "what you're going to tell me is that it's after hours, you need somebody right away, not tomorrow morning."

"Well—"

"And you've already said money isn't an issue. Which I heard, don't get me wrong. But I wonder if it's enough? I mean, if you don't even have a name. What this tells me is that your cat doesn't have papers, is probably an exotic, and can get my license pulled."

"You weren't worried about your license when you walked in here."

"I'm just talking what-if here."

He nodded. "Cat fixers don't go between very often, Mr. Sam. You don't know how long I've been waiting for this exact moment."

"When I tell you no?"

"When I ask you if you've ever seen an atrox."

I rubbed a spot on my forehead, closed my eyes because this conversation was starting to hurt.

"Don't think they're really 'between' anymore," I said, smiling a little. "They're kind of dead and gone."

He grinned, his fingers spreading slightly on the table.

"Then you haven't seen one."

"Just the same way everybody else has," I told him. "In the books. From the tar pits."

"But your people—I'm sorry. You haven't bred any back, I mean?"

"Me personally?"

"Anybody."

I shook my head no.

Panthera atrox is Latin for "terrible panther," where "panther" really means "lion." It's just that, when you go back far enough, lions and tigers aren't so easy to tease apart. So "panther" covers them both.

I'd seen *P. atrox* in the books, though, yeah.

The sketches based on recovered skeletons suggested a cat that could offer an African lion shade. And, unlike its European self, the cave lion, the American didn't have any rock paintings to indicate whether it had been maned and tufted or striped, or both.

What always got *P. atrox* noted in the textbooks wasn't its size, though, but its braincase.

Going strictly by skull volume set against total body mass, *P. atrox* was maybe the most intelligent cat that had ever lived.

And nobody called it *atrox* either. Not unless you had a spread of, say, *Smilodon* and *P. atrox* bones on the table, and were trying to separate them into two piles: sabertooth and American lion. Which wouldn't be that hard a process, really—not as hard as teasing *P. atrox* from *P. leo spelaea*: the American lion, enough its own species that it doesn't carry the *leo* anymore, and the European cave lion. The problem there would be that *P. atrox* was *P. leo spelaea* more or less, a cave lion that had followed game across Beringia and then, for some reason—climate? terrain? prey? predation?—developed a slightly bigger brain.

At least the ones stupid enough to step into the tar pits had had a bigger brain.

What this guy sitting across from me was suggesting, though, was that there'd been ones smart enough to stay away from the pits too. To slip "between" and just keep on living, invisible.

And, not only that, but he had one. Alive enough to be sick.

I laid a ten by my plate, stood to leave.

Before I could walk all the way off, the guy, the visitor—Ted—had my wrist in his hand.

I jerked away, told myself to breathe once before doing anything, but then, because we were making contact, I think, and maybe because I wasn't looking at him so much, but to the side, so that his reflection in the plate glass was in my field of view, I saw him as he really maybe was.

He wasn't wearing clothes like mine.

And he was half again as tall.

And not human. The scales, the pupils, the ridges. The mouth.

I turned from the reflection to him and he nodded once, his lips thin like he hadn't wanted this to happen.

"Who are you?" I said, with less push than before.

He pulled me close and spit it out, whatever he was. Or maybe his name. I don't know.

It started with a *T* sound anyway, I was pretty sure.

I lowered myself back into the booth.

After that he just stared at me. What we were waiting for was my heart to stop punishing the back side of my chest. For a moment I was sure I was going to throw up.

My best explanation for what I'd seen in the glass, and what I'd heard him say, was that I'd already found my side road out in the desert, and placed my father's revolver to the bridge of my nose, angled it up so the exit wound would be the whole top of my head.

Maybe this truck stop was "between," like he kept saying. Halfway between suicide and hell.

Except I didn't feel dead.

"You're not," Ted said, across from me.

I rolled my eyes up to him.

He was just a man again. In clothes exactly like mine. I'd been his model for what would fit in, after all. What wouldn't draw attention.

He said it again: "We wouldn't be here if you were . . . what you say."

"Dead."

"If that's the term you prefer."

"But—but I could disappear right now and nothing would change . . ." I said, quoting him.

"Or you could go back too."

"Then—"

"I just want to borrow you," he said, the impatience in his voice rising a bit now. "Buy your services, is that how you say it?"

I stared at him a long time, trying to find shelves in my mind to arrange all this on. Finally I said it, the most obvious thing: "*Panthera atrox* died out with the megafauna."

Ted smiled, leaned forward, his hands under his chin now, his grin not as pleasant as I wanted. More like tolerant, I suppose.

"What would it take, Mr. Sam?"

"To what?"

"To come with me."

I took a long drink on my cold coffee, tried to study the situation from every angle.

"How far away are we talking?"

"How far . . . ?"

"Where is this place you want to take me?" I clarified.

He nodded that he understood now, then leaned back from the table. "Closer than you think," he said.

252

"So it's got a name then?"

His eyes settled on me but didn't focus. Like he was concentrating.

"Sula," he said, hitting each letter. "Sula Prime."

I looked away from him, out at all the pump islands.

At the counter Janie was folding napkins around forks and waiting for that brass bell above the door to ring, and, according to her, falling in love with me from first sight.

The way she paints it, it was romantic, me just sitting there alone, looking out at the Arizona night like it held something for me.

My hands were shaking though.

"Okay," I said to Ted at last. "But show me first."

I don't know what I was expecting, really. Was *P. atrox* supposed to materialize, sick, in the next booth? Was Ted supposed to have some kind of viewer I could look into? A picture postcard, his arm looped over the atrox's neck?

"Well?" I said, and he tilted his head outside, as if in defeat.

Backed up to the sidewalk just past our window, like it had been there the whole time, was a rusted-out two-horse trailer with a hog-wire roof.

Because I'd tacked that hog wire on myself, I didn't have to peer around the side of the trailer to know that the wheels didn't match. One was chrome spoke, from a kid's wrecked car, and one was just white.

I also didn't have to look to know what was pulling it—a 1968 three-quarter-ton Ford—but did anyway. The instant I saw that ragged wheel flare though, I came back to the booth, shook my head no.

For a long time I didn't say anything and Ted didn't say anything.

Every time I blinked, I was seeing that wheel flare again.

Finally I stirred my coffee, licked my lips, tried testing my voice to make sure it wasn't going to crack but then just went on anyway.

"You shouldn't have used that truck," I said.

Ted's face crinkled up a bit in question.

"You're using stuff from—from my head, I know," I told him, "can't show me anything new unless you have to, something like that. But that's the truck my wife . . ." I closed my eyes, said the rest in the dark: "It was destroyed in the wreck. That's what I'm saying."

"There are—" Ted started, then stopped himself, as if searching for just the right word. "You're right. There are rules you don't know about, but are going to have to accept as binding nevertheless. Like what you refer to as gravity. It constrains you whether you know about it or not. Or, just—let me say it like this. There are ways that things are done, and they've been done that way for so long that that's the only way they can be done anymore. I can say that much. I'm sorry for the . . . the association, but there's no other way."

"I'm just saying I know that truck isn't around anymore."

"The same way you know atrox isn't around anymore."

I smiled. "What I mean," I said, "is that anything that truck's pulling can't be real either. And anything inside that trailer."

Ted nodded about this, shrugged, and then, starting in the seats but spreading to the table and the floor and the plate glass so thin beside us, the whole truck stop started to tremble. Slow, like some massive door opening up for the first time in years, with a bit too much space between each creak. Like an alive thing, just drawing it out on purpose. The sound you can make with your throat, gargling air.

And it was coming from the horse trailer.

P. atrox had roared, and was still roaring. In pain, and in anger, and in loneliness—it was more than I could take.

My mouth opened and closed, and I think maybe my ears popped.

The waitresses at the counter ten feet away were still polishing and folding and stacking, oblivious to how everything was shaking around them.

"They don't know what an atrox is," Ted said.

The surface of my coffee was rippling from the sound.

I stared at it and smiled and then started laughing, inside at first but it spilled over more and more. Janie doesn't remember it but I know I was just sitting there, chuckling with my lips shut, tears in my eyes.

Ted cocked his head over, waited it out.

"This is an emotional response," he said.

I looked at the trailer some more. The farm tags on it were twenty years out of date.

I kept waiting for it to shimmer in the wind, maybe fade a bit so I could see the pumps through it, but it never did.

Ted was still staring at me.

"I've waited a long time for this," he said.

It was the beginning of his closing pitch, I could tell.

I drank some more of my coffee, held it in my mouth because it was so cold now. I thought it might wake me up. It didn't.

"Listen," I told him finally. "I think maybe you've got the wrong guy here. I'm a horse guy, really. I just do pets to pay the bills. I've seen exactly one lion in my life. It was on a table at a zoo, knocked out."

"But you have the training to make a diagnosis," he said, leaning forward for emphasis. "And you're—you're in the right place."

"'Between.'"

He nodded once. I shook my head no.

"Suppose this is all real then," I said. "How do you go about getting a *Panthera atrox* in this day and age?"

"You don't need to know that to fix it," he hissed, catching my tone better than I would have given him credit for.

"To make this happen, I need to know," I said, shrugging a weak apology.

He curled his top lip a little, looked out at the trailer himself.

"There are rules about this too," he said. "You don't even know what you're asking."

"I don't really have to be anywhere."

Ted covered his mouth like he was hiding a smile. "The rest of your life wouldn't be enough for even the beginning of the first part of it," he said.

"So, what?" I said. "It's a thirty-minute story?" I held my cup up to show it to him. "I only meant to stop for one, right? Unless I'm mistaken, that's what—what makes my services available."

With his eyebrows and lips, Ted acknowledged this. It was a very human gesture.

"It's not foregone yet though," he said, nodding all the same. "What you were considering. Otherwise I couldn't be here. It's a delicate situation, Mr. Sam. More delicate than you can possibly know."

I rubbed a spot on my forehead then studied my fingertip, like I'd expected a bug to be there on my skin, squashed.

"And it's just getting sicker, right?" I said, flicking my eyes up to him then out to the horse trailer.

Ted lowered his face and closed his eyes, clamped his temples with the thumb and forefinger of his right hand.

"Listen, if you don't want to tell me—" I started. It was the beginning of a fake good-bye; a tactic. Anybody would know that. Ted didn't call my bluff though. Instead, moving slow, he lowered his hand from his face, regarded me.

"Would that the choice were mine," he said, then dragged his eyes away from my face, as if he were feeling sorry for me.

After a long spell in the bathroom, Ted came back to the booth. While he'd been gone, Janie had collected my plate, asked where I was heading.

I don't know what I told her, and she doesn't remember either. Because of Ted, I think.

He did something to her, I'm pretty sure. Maybe just by being there, I mean.

The reason I think this is that, while he was there, she acknowledged his presence, sort of. Like he was really in that booth across me. But then as soon as he walked out, he was gone from her memory as well, like he'd never been.

This is what we do with impossible things, I think. Forget them.

Except that's precisely why I remember. Precisely why I'm still here.

But I'm getting ahead of myself.

Though Ted never spelled it out for me, I think that like everything else that night, the way he told me what he told me had to do with the revolver in my glove compartment. Instead of just saying it straight, he had to mash up a lot of different versions, just to be sure that nothing he told me was going to nudge me one way or the other, to my glove compartment or away. It wasn't because he cared for me either, I don't think. If he'd nudged me one way or the other, I wouldn't be what he called "between" anymore, and couldn't help his cat.

He blinked once, long, and then started, his voice like a growl, every word measured and weighed beforehand. In the bathroom most likely.

The first way he told it was that Felidae—felines, cats—they were a rare and beautiful thing, so rare that, to keep this area safe from daily intrusions, a few representative specimens had been spirited away, relocated to an area where breaches wouldn't matter.

"And no, they're not restrained, Mr. Sam," he added, in response to what I was thinking. "Who could restrain an atrox?"

"But you care for them, feed them."

"Atrox are sufficient unto themselves. I only manage."

"So they're not domestic—they hunt to eat."

"And are in turn hunted themselves, to mark certain events."

This stopped me. I studied his (my) shirt, said, "Then this is how it's injured."

He laughed, looked past me as if confirming what I'd just said with some-one else.

"A royal hunt is a form of communion, as I'm sure you understand. The most sincere form of worship, a one-becoming with another mind."

"A what?"

He smiled, leaned forward. "Or maybe it just looks like communion. Perhaps, over the millennia, atrox has developed the ability to project an avatar, me, to procure medical assistance in times of need."

"Then you're not really here."

"More like I'm not what you think I am."

I sat back, watched the restroom door, then the pay phone.

"What makes them so special?" I said, finally, trying to backpedal some. "Felidae?"

"It's not their bodies that make them cats," Ted said, in the voice you might save for a child. "It's their—it's how they exist."

"'Between'?"

It was his turn to look away now. Raise his lip again.

"So Sula Prime, this area they're in now," I said. "It must be between as well."

"Your Earth," he said, coming back to me, his eyes hot. "It's Sula Prime, Mr. Sam."

"Then you don't have to take me anywhere."

"Correct. You just need to come with me."

"Where?"

He was just staring at me again.

"Imagine a . . . a place, if you have to call it that," he said, "a place remote from where you are now but also congruent with it. A place where a pride of atrox developed and sustained that most rare of genetic mutations, sentience, but then starved to death when their prey died out. Can you imagine what it must have been like for them, to be burdened with the knowledge of what they were, and to know that they were about to be over?"

I digested this for maybe fifteen seconds.

"You're talking about the horses dying out," I said. In *P. atrox*'s day, the American horse had been its choice prey. "But they didn't have to starve. I mean, you manage them, you know what they can do. There were Giant Bison, and deer, and—"

"None of which had a pituitary gland quite like your primitive horse. Not that it knew what to do with it." He smiled. "Or what it tasted like to them."

I stared at him, waiting for a rogue cheek muscle, an eye tic.

"This pride," he said then. "Wouldn't you save them, if you could? Let them—let them develop as they were meant to?"

My heart was pounding again.

"Or," he went on, "what if there were a . . . what if that pride of atrox had been isolated for their own good but then left alone too long, so that they became a legitimate threat to many areas up and down the—?" He clipped his question short, started over. "Wouldn't it make sense to go back, see where they were in their infancy, before their eyes were truly opened?"

I was watching my hands on the table now. The spaces between my fingers.

"Only it might not want to go with you," I said. "It might get injured."

"Or sick from the journey."

I looked to the trailer again. Through the metal slats of the back gate I could sense it watching me, could tell when it had spun around to pace back to the rounded nose of the trailer.

Maybe I had killed myself already, I thought.

Maybe the heaven of animal doctors was a series of extinct animals, each in need of veterinary assistance.

Ted was shaking his head no though. Smiling behind his hand about this.

"I can think whatever I want," I told him.

"No," he said. "You can't."

I exhaled through my nose, as close as I could come to a laugh right then, and realized that hell for animal doctors would be the same thing, pretty much. Except, there, I wouldn't be able to save any of the beautiful creatures. There, every cut I made, no matter how precise, still the animals would bleed out, and they would each be the very last one of their kind. And look at me like they knew it.

"What if I can't save it?" I said.

Ted just stared at me.

If he'd have said "Then the great experiment is over" in his regal voice, I would have stood then, I think, gone with him. The same as if he'd said it was just one lion of many, then I could have shrugged, ordered an omelet.

There was no way to say them both though.

"It has to be your decision," he said.

I nodded, swallowed, then reached down to the seat for my hat, to step outside with him, lean into this thing, whatever it was.

Except—

This is why I remember this night, and Janie doesn't.

What happened next was at least as impossible as a *P. atrox*.

As I was standing, I looked up to the horse trailer again, just to see if there was any fur between the slats, but I had a different angle now, could see further down the side of the trailer, along the passenger side of the truck, to the tall rectangle of a mirror I'd mounted myself.

Framed in it at the wheel, looking back at me like she'd been caught, was Candace.

She opened her mouth to say something but Ted's large reptilian hand slammed onto the glass hard enough that Janie even remembers looking over.

What she thought was that I'd fallen asleep in my booth, slumped into the window after thirty-six hours on the road.

All I was doing was standing there though, still half in the booth, the crown of my hat in my fingers, the hat partway to my head.

Slowly, I lowered it back to the table, then sat down hard behind it.

Across from me Ted sighed, lowered his hand from the glass.

"Is that really her?" I whispered to him. If I talked too loud I would break the spell, I was sure. I didn't want to wake up anymore.

Ted nodded, didn't look up.

"She was—to find you in time . . . The window was small, and she was the only way. There are still . . . what you would call lines, I think, between the two of you. I can't explain it any better than that."

"But she's . . . she's not dead."

Ted looked at his hand where it had touched the glass then turned it out for me to see. The palm was his real skin now, kind of. The human was gone anyway.

"What's happening?" I said, but before Ted could say anything, Janie, suddenly beside us with a coffeepot, yelped a little, splashed coffee down onto the table. She'd seen something in the glass, I knew. Just for an instant.

Ted closed his hand into a fist, looked hard to me. Like I was supposed to save him here.

I understood, tilted my hat over so the felt brim could touch the spilled coffee.

Janie was on it in a flash, keeping it safe. Using her apron to pat the coffee away.

I waved away her apologies, even managed to float my coffee cup around as she filled it, in play. Just to keep her eyes there instead of on Ted, or the horse trailer.

As to what we said, if anything, I don't recall.

If Janie wants to remember it as flirting, though, then that's what it was. But in my head, pulsing, my heartbeat, was *Can-dace, Can-dace*.

"Thank you," Ted said a few moments later.

"She can see you," I said back, tilting my head to Janie.

"I have to be careful now." To show what he meant he held his balled hand up. When he looked at it he winced like it had been burned.

I nodded, kept my head down but couldn't help leaning back, to look down along the side of the trailer again.

The mirror was angled in now though.

Unless I was standing right at the bed of the truck, I couldn't use it to see behind the wheel anymore.

Ted was waiting when I came to back to him.

"It's her," I said. "I saw."

He conceded this.

I started to stand again, to rush out there, but Ted had my wrist in his burned hand.

"What?" I said, trying to shake loose.

"Not yet," he said.

I laughed about this, pulled harder, but it was useless.

I have no idea what this looked like to Janie either. That was Candace out there though. My wife, the first girl I'd ever loved, that I'd never even got to say good-bye to. The reason I was where I was.

"This is my fault," Ted said, and hooked his chin outside, to the idea of Candace. "I overstepped. But any system moves toward equilibrium. You know this. You push, and the world pushes back."

I stopped pulling against him, sat back down.

He thanked me with a curt nod.

"Seeing her is a . . . a correction," he said, shrugging like this was as close as he could come to telling me without being corrected again.

"I know," I said, "she was never supposed to die."

Ted closed his eyes in something like amusement, opened them again to study the trailer. Or whatever it looked like to him.

"The atrox," he said. "Have you decided?"

"I'll breathe for it if I have to," I said back, my hand still on my hat, my heels not touching the ground.

Ted laughed a breath out.

"And how do you know I'm not just this animal's feeder? That—that the hormones making you . . . that the chemistry leading you to your revolver, that it doesn't flush through your own limbic system in a way that makes you for the moment similar to the primitive horse atrox once knew? Perhaps you're a delicacy, Mr. Sam. Perhaps I'm there before every suicide."

"You're asking do I care if you're just leading me out for that thing to eat me, right?"

He nodded.

"No," I told him. "Let it."

He held my eyes for about ten seconds then, and, looking back, I think I understand what he was doing, asking me that. He was correcting the correction. To make up for him telling me too much, I'd been allowed to see Candace before I was supposed to. But that pushed me one way, not the other—away from that glove compartment. What that meant for him, and for the *P. atrox*, was that I was moving away from being between. So he had to nudge me back. Just, like everything else, he had to do it indirectly. Like there was no push at all really, but a steady, inexorable pull.

Either that or seeing Candace got my pituitary gland all bitter with hope, and he had to get that tamped down before letting me near the trailer.

I really and truly did not care though.

Whether it was a gun turning my lights out once and for all or a lion, it was going to be dark.

Ted was just looking at me now.

"Well?" I said, my fingertips on the table, ready to push off.

"If you—if you do this," he said, his burned hand suddenly an iron cuff around my wrist again, his tone reverential almost, "to have an atrox in your debt is to have anything, Mr. Sam. The way they exist, I mean. It allows them certain unique opportunities."

I looked to the trailer again, unable not to, desperate for that mirror to be angled out just the right amount again. It wasn't, but I took that as a positive sign anyway. It being turned in meant Candace was real enough to touch things, to push and pull them.

"A wish," I said, almost whispering again. "Right? And I've already made it?"

"If you say so. But not the way you think. If she steps out of that truck, into this area—"

"What?"

"I think you know that too. In this area, where we are now, she's . . . different."

"Dead."

"It would be like the night of the wreck, yes. The world would correct itself."

I looked to the mirror again, in disbelief. Except it hurt worse.

"Then what?" I said, my voice hardly making it across the table, I knew.

"You can choose to be paid in years."

I studied the pay phone again, and the two stools at the end of the counter. Janie polishing something down there, her hand in the rag going in tight, unconcerned circles. It reminded me of my mother somehow.

A napkin dispenser. She was polishing a chrome napkin dispenser. And then she sat it back down.

"Years?" I finally said, settling back on Ted.

"Twenty," he said back. "How it would work is this. You would get into the truck with her and drive away, into nineteen seventy-six, and never know any of this."

"Before the wreck."

Ted nodded, watching me close.

"But I have to fix the—the lion first, right?"

"Of course."

"And what if I can't?"

"I wouldn't be here if you couldn't."

His voice was so even, so serene.

"Breathe," he said, when I wasn't.

I did, deep, and then the truck outside started, the right taillight of the trailer glowing red, the left one dark, still wired bad.

"We're running out of time," he said.

I opened my mouth to say something, I don't know what, but cried a little, I think. Like, just from my throat. It's the only way I knew how anymore.

"I've got to—" I said, and pulled myself up, pointed with my chin to the bathroom.

Ted looked up to me and saw the bathroom window I was trying not to think about, I'm pretty sure. How I could just sneak around front, unhook the trailer, and ease the truck away, drive off into some perfect future.

He shook his head no, nodded for me to sit back down.

I swallowed the coffee I'd almost thrown up, laughed at myself a little.

Typical Sam, Muriel would have said about what I'd wanted to do, I knew.

If I have anyone to blame for what I did next, too, it's her.

And I owe her the world for it.

The last I'd seen her had been in the tight hall of the house I'd lived in for two years before moving her in. She was throwing hair brushes and ashtrays and pictures from the wall, and she wasn't a violent person. Or, she hadn't been before me anyway.

But I said I wasn't going to give you the whole soap opera, I know.

To unpack it just partway, though, it wasn't that I had girls on the side—vet's offices aren't exactly crawling with those kind of situations—and I didn't hit her, and it wasn't even the thousand little cuts thing, or the straws and the camel. And I don't think I was malicious either.

Still, though, six years into it, she was throwing things.

And some of them were even hitting me.

According to her, what was wrong with me was that I never treated people as people. And she wasn't going to listen to any more of that, about it being a milk truck that had left me just sleepwalking through life. I wasn't her second marriage, see; I was her third. She'd been through the mill enough to know a thing or two about what she called my kind—guys who are great out of the gates, when they're having to fight for each step forward, but once the course levels out and it's not so crowded anymore, they fall into a pace or something. One that's not about trying anymore, but coasting. All that matters is one foot after another, and saving their breath, and letting the people who stumble a little go ahead and fall. It's an attitude that she said leads to a feeling of already having won, almost. Of entitlement. But really it's just a rationalization for cheating, should the opportunity present itself. For taking a shortcut should a shortcut present itself.

And that was supposed to be the definition of our marriage: me, trying to save my breath for the long ugly haul it was going to be, and taking every shortcut I could find, just to make the years go faster.

It only proved her point when I refused to throw anything back at her, or slam her up against the wall, or yell at her that she was wrong, that it was her fault. I didn't have to, she told me, because none of it really mattered, right?

And yeah, I'm not stupid. Her argument, her accusations, they were shaped out of everything she didn't consider herself to be. Her good traits were missing in me, and the stuff she would never stoop to, that's what I was made of.

She was right though. That's the thing.

I didn't care enough to tell her any of this.

Which is why I started tapping my shirt pockets for a pack of cigarettes.

Until a few years ago, that's where I'd always carried them.

"Are you hurt?" Ted said, inspecting my chest it seemed, his eyes worried.

"A cigarette," I said back, more desperate sounding than I'd intended.

He threaded one up from his own shirt pocket, lit it somehow as he passed it across to me.

I pulled deep on it, coughed long and hard.

When I looked over to Janie she narrowed her eyes then turned importantly to the kitchen window.

What she was saying was that she wasn't the one who cared about smoking.

I nodded, cupped my body around the cigarette as best I could. Tried not to exhale too much.

"What are you doing, Mr. Sam?" Ted asked.

"It's just 'Sam,'" I spat back at him with a grey cough, my eyes watery from the smoke.

"Sam," Ted said, leaning forward.

I backed away from him, couldn't help looking out to the horse trailer one more time, its single taillight beckoning.

I closed my eyes against it, opened them on just the plate glass. I could see through Ted's reflection now, a little. I turned to make sure he was still there.

"You—" he started, feeling it too, I think, like I was: my future. That I even, suddenly had one, I mean.

And it was all Muriel's fault, for knowing me so well.

Holding that revolver to my head out on some lonely road, it would be the same as trying to slip out the bathroom window—it would be cheating. Which is far different from deserving to live, I know. Believe me, I know. But, sitting in that booth with Ted that night, I saw how, if I really wanted to punish myself, if I really hated myself as much as I thought I did, then I couldn't just sneak out of another life.

I nodded an apology to Ted about what we both knew. That I was going to live at least one more night.

"You can still go with her," he tried, tilting his head towards Candace.

I shook my head no though.

"If—if I went back," I started. "You've got to understand. What will happen. What I know will happen. It'll be the same as with Muriel after a while. I won't mean to do it, but I'll kill whatever's best in her. In Candace."

Ted touched the corners of his lips with the thumb and forefinger of his right hand. It was like he was stroking the memory of a mustache.

"And I won't do that to her," I added. "I don't know if you can understand this, but she's everything. I loved her like nothing else. Too much to even think about hurting her."

"You don't know it would go like that."

"I know who I am. How I am."

"Or could be."

"Will be."

"Even if you love her?"

"Maybe especially because of that. I don't know."

Ted nodded, reached out to ping my coffee cup with his fingernail, like, here at what felt like the end, he was savoring the hardness of things.

"I can still help your cat though," I said.

He shook his head no, I couldn't.

I stared at the trailer one last time.

"It's too late," he said, his voice different now. Less forceful, I guess.

"Is he the last one?" I asked, able at last to see the dirty gold hair pressed up against the slat.

Ted laughed through his nose in that way he'd learned, or picked up, and I smiled too, noticed how I could see all the way through his reflection now. Like it wasn't even there.

When I turned back to the other side of the booth, he was gone.

The next thing was the one taillight, flaring against the plate glass beside me as the truck lowered into gear.

I closed my eyes as hard as I could, and hid my face in my hands, and told Candace one last time that I was sorry, and that I loved her, and to never grow old.

I hope she never did.

Going on what she knows—Ted disappearing like he did, something about a sick horse and a trailer I recognized from when I was having to pull crazy hours and make calls in four counties at once—Janie thinks an angel came to see me that night, to talk me out of killing myself. The proof is that I'm here, now, with her. It's hard to argue with. Sometimes I even want to believe it, that I'm that important.

But Ted wasn't there that night for me, I know. He was there for his lion.

And it hasn't been as bad as I'd planned either, living.

I've heard a *Panthera atrox* roar across time, I mean, and down through the base of existence, and, when Janie walks out onto the porch in the mornings, I pass her coffee up to her and she pretends she can't still smell my smoke in the air. It's not perfect, what we have, and I'm not pretending it is, but when the sun's just up and the desert is crisp and our horses are looking to the sound of our voices on the porch, it's pretty close.

That doesn't explain why Janie doesn't want me writing all this down though.

The reason for that is that everybody in town already thinks I'm crazy. Something like this, well. It would confirm what I know they've been saying— that somewhere along the way I started doping myself with livestock tranquilizers or worse. As far as they're concerned, it's the only way to explain my last few business decisions.

What I've done is sell my practice nine years ago and invest all that money and then some in a breeding pair of tarpan ponies. But I haven't kept their bloodline pure. It's an outrage. Of all the types of horse in North America, the tarpan is perhaps the most rare, the most delicately balanced, genetically.

Another name for it is the Polish primitive horse.

It's a breed that was painstakingly bred back from wild horses out on the steppes of Russia. They're short and thick and towheaded like a donkey, but agile too, and—all the horse people say this, and the books too—"exceptionally intelligent."

It was that last part that got me interested.

As for what I breed my tarpan with, it's less about bloodline and more about stature, and wit. Being a vet, I know all the old Welsh ponies and the like in the area, and can usually collect them in trade for services, provided all the kids are too old to ride them anymore.

Too, though, I've poured a couple of zebras into the mix as well, just for the hell of it, and some burro as well, from deep in Brazil, and all kinds of scrub horses out of Mongolia, and even a dingy little grey spotted horse that the guy on the phone insisted was a cross between a Sorraia and, three generations back, an Exmoor, the only two breeds maybe as primitive as a tarpan.

The result is that the only two horses of my herd that resemble each other anymore are the original breeding pair.

But that's only half the outrage.

Aside from mixing the bloodlines, I also don't keep my horses in the pens up by the house, where they'll be safe from coyotes and dogs and thieves.

It's like throwing money away, yeah.

But it's my money too.

So here's what I think: with all his different stories—Earth was Sula Prime, *P. atrox* was "between," in need of help of some kind, help only I, the lapsed horse doctor, could give—Ted had been telling me something, preparing me specifically for this day.

I wasn't ever supposed to go out to the parking lot with him, I don't think. I was just supposed to come back to the truck stop over and over, until I got familiar with Janie, who counts the horses with me each morning and thinks an angel came down to talk to me.

I love her, yeah. Even when—maybe especially when—one of the horses is missing.

"What do you think got it?" she'll ask in a fake scared tone, holding the side of my hand, leaning forward out of her chair to be sure one's gone.

These last few weeks, it's become a game with us.

"Lions," I whisper to her like a secret, squeezing her hand back, and she'll look over to me, her eyes wide, and then smile with her whole face, so that for a few moments life is roaring past me, and through me, and into me, and I know all at once that ten thousand years wasn't that long ago. That it might even be tomorrow.

I wrote this one because I cannot, no matter what I do, seem to understand coffee. I mean, I don't get beer or cigarettes either, or football or poker. But it seems like coffee would be a mystery I could crack, right? Like, why people drink it when it tastes like it does? Finally I decided that maybe it's the ritual of it. That that's somehow good and necessary, like a center for the day, an anchor, a pivot.

So I wrote this story about invisible lions and suicide and time travel and all that, just so I could stage a coffee ritual at the end. And I think I felt it, for a moment—or, it made me wish I drank coffee, that even smelling it didn't make me want to gag. If I did, I mean, then I could someday carry a cup of it to my wife, when we're old. And it would be perfect. As is, I guess I'll just have to bring her a Dr Pepper. But maybe it'll be really hot that day. And there'll be like slivers and chunks of ice on the side of the can, sliding down. There are rituals everywhere, I suppose. There's a different center for each day. I'm always looking for them.

DEER

RUDOLPH HATED CHRISTMAS. It was the name, all the other kids singing it after him in the hall. He didn't want to play in any of their damn games. He didn't want anything from them, just to rocket out of the sixth grade into junior high, where his mom had told him he could just be *R* if he wanted. He did.

He hated her too, of course, for letting his father name him that.

And Miss Jeanie, for always looking up over her attendance book at him and saying of *course* Rudolph was here. It wouldn't be Christmas without Rudolph, now would it?

Rudolph's face would glow red with the attention, which didn't help.

All of them. He hated all of them.

After school sometimes he would walk the woods with his father the forest ranger, collecting the brandy bottles the out-of-town people brought with them to help steal their Christmas trees. His father's name was Gerald. He told Rudolph things like "Be sure to tie your shorts on tight *before* you jump off the diving board" and "Don't get other people's magazines out of the dumpster." Because his father was a ranger, he carried a gun. When they would stand looking at the splintered stumps of trees, Rudolph would stand on the side of his father with the gun.

Two weeks before Christmas break—when Rudolph's mom was still flipping the place mats over from Thanksgiving to Santa Claus—the new girl showed up, shy, big-eyed. Her name was Bambi.

Rudolph looked at her from the end of the hall.

That afternoon in the dentist's chair his mother said she'd heard the new girl was cute—"and it was too bad about her *mother*"—and Rudolph spit his words out into the bean-shaped aluminum basin. The rest of the afternoon was a numb fog that hazed up all the windows of the house. The next morning it was clinging to the ground, coming out of the forecaster's mouth. He called it a cold mist, impenetrable. He lowered his head on the screen, leaning forward for the kids, and said he was worried about Christmas.

At school they were all waiting for him, had seen the weather too. By lunchtime Rudolph was sitting as close as he could to the EXIT door, gnawing on a crust, and then Bambi was there.

"I know," she said, then: "At least for you it's just seasonal."

Rudolph stopped chewing, looked up at her.

The whole cafeteria was holding its breath.

"Let's get out of here," Rudolph said, and he stood and she followed. In the grass before the parking lot a rabbit perked its ears up at them, but they stared it down. Fiercely. The cold drew the blood to Rudolph's cheeks and he led them through the complicated playground and into the next week, where they were inseparable, even holding hands in the hall.

To Miss Jeannie they gave an apple, because she was so white. To the cheerleading squad they gave broken bottles, hidden under the pads of their shoes. The apple had aspirin powdered up in it, but that was just because neither of their parents took sleeping pills or cyanide. The cheerleaders' slippers were blood red ten minutes into the pep rally. It was over early. Miss Jeannie didn't give them any homework.

Bambi was already calling Rudolph *R* by then; Bambi was *B*. Miss Jankowitz in English explained to them when she confiscated one of their notes that *R* and *B* were just different conjugations of the same verb—*are* and *be*—then giggled off to the main office. Rudolph and Bambi looked at each other after Jankowitz was gone, and made plans to drop a house on the whole English class next Tuesday.

On the sidewalk on the way to the buses some high schoolers had built a proper snowman. It snickered at Rudolph; he pulled his pistol finger out, shot it between its black-button eyes, then Bambi lowered his hand for him, kept them walking.

On the bus, though, Rudolph couldn't unstraighten his finger, had to hide it in his jacket. They hit a rabbit two stops before Bambi's, but the thump of its small body didn't even make it up the frame to their seat. Everyone else looked back at it but them.

Two stops later Rudolph got off with Bambi, and the bus driver left the door open long enough for everyone to crowd over to the curb side of the bus, watch these two deer bounce away.

"I hate all of them," Rudolph said, turning his back.

"Christmas," Bambi said.

Rudolph nodded: Christmas.

Because over the weekend they couldn't get it right—how to drop a house on Jankowitz—they went to the mall instead. With Rudolph's father's gun. And stood in the picture line for SantaLand.

"We don't have to do this, y'know," Bambi said, holding Rudolph's arm in two places now, and Rudolph nodded. But they did. All the way to the front of the line, where the yellow brick road ended and the snow and elves began. They were the oldest two there, misfits, and Mrs. Claus had to help to get them both in Santa's lap (this is two days before the spree in the cafeteria), and if the picture were X-rayed, you could see Rudolph's hand already on the gun, the barrel nosing into red velvet.

Santa's breath smelled like brandy. He smiled and tousled their hair and helped them onto the EXIT ramp.

They were as tall as the elves, were giants stepping through the glittery snow.

Mrs. Claus lettered Rudolph's name onto the bottom of their photograph with careful ink. "You must love this time of year," she whispered, passing the plastic frame over, and Rudolph's hand clenched around Bambi's and in the calmest voice he had he told her that his father's name was Gerald, that he was the king of the forest, and then the two of them blended back into the down-filled mall, two twelve-year-olds trying out places to leave their photograph, so they could find their way back someday, should they ever need to.

This one was just supposed to be a three-paragrapher, a one-page job. It was just a joke, I mean, about being named "Rudolph." But then, soon as I put that kid in his desk, I realized it was me who'd been named Rudolph all my life. So I had to run the story down, see what was what, let him meet a girl anyway. My source for this, what I was reacting to, just coming off, it was David Sedaris's "The

SantaLand Diaries." That was my first real brush with nonfiction. But, instead of porting the structure or the style out, the tone or the voice, I just brought the "SantaLand" part. Because who knows how to do nonfiction? I was into one-word titles for this span of months, too. I was coming off a span of months of big, fancy titles, "The Minotaur at the End of Love," "The Complete Absence of Cats is Another Definition for Silence," stuff like that. But I thought maybe I was indulging myself a bit, with those. That I was maybe allowing the title to carry weight that should have been shouldered by the story. So I shifted it back. "Deer" is the shortest of any of my titles, I'm pretty sure.

LITTLE LAMBS

WE'RE NOT SUPPOSED to walk through the structure, but for eight years we've been watching it from sixty-two feet away. Watching it on so many monitors and at so many wavelengths that sometimes you just want to step outside the bunker, see it with your eyes. Just to be sure it's real, that it's still there.

For reasons of security, our watch only rotates among us four.

The crew cuts we had when first assigned to monitor the structure, they're grown out long and shaggy like our beards. Our BDUs are folded in our lockers. The last inspection was thirteen months ago. We look Wyoming now. Like we know the winter, like the sound of frozen grass breaking under our boots, we don't hear it with our ears anymore, but feel it instead, in the base of our jaws.

Our eyes have gone hollow with longing, but we don't blame Wyoming for that. It's more like people with that kind of vacant, yearning stare, they're always drifting to Wyoming. The way the open lands undulate, writhe almost, it's a cadence that feels right to us. After a while, you feel the swells of grass in your chest, I mean. And the sudden drops. And your face doesn't change expression because of it.

The structure seems to fit out here too, like it's always been here.

There are no fences or warning signs around it.

The four acres it occupies is Bureau of Land Management land. In the distance we've seen antelope and sheep and, once, two bull elk, walking with their chins in the air, as if their swept-back racks were unbearably heavy. Two winters ago one of the sheep wandered in from the snow. It was wearing a diaper because a rancher had pulled it into his trailer with him, to keep it alive.

I opened the first door of the bunker for it, but then Hendrikson took my forearm in his hand, shook his head no, maybe saved us all.

We don't know what's a trick, what's not.

The sheep finally walked away from the door, became a heat signature on our thermal monitor, a yellow-tinged splotch wending into the structure. But standing in the structure is no protection from winter.

What the structure is is rebar and iron girders and I-beams and chain link.

It looks like an unfinished project, like the funding fell through and now it's been abandoned, left to rust back into the earth.

This is why nobody stops.

How long we've been here is ninety-six months.

My daughter, Sheila, she's about that old now. When my wife called to report her first steps, there were approximately fourteen relays between her voice and my ear.

I walked out into the night after that, no jacket.

The structure was a skeletal silhouette against the bright sky.

Since we started monitoring it, it's moved north-northeast exactly six and one-eighth inches.

It doesn't displace the soil as it goes. In its track, the grass stands as if it's always been there.

On every spectrum we know to look at it with, it appears to be just what it is: iron and steel, the metal guts of a prison built in West Virginia in 1918.

The reason we're here is that, eight and a half years ago, that prison collapsed and killed all seventy-eight prisoners and guards sleeping inside it. The concrete walls just crumbled down on them, as if there was nothing supporting them anymore. Because there wasn't. It had been dreamed away.

Three months later, four Casper men were brought up on charges of killing their friend.

When they were arrested, they were in a bar. Only one of them was drinking. The other three were just sitting there, holding drinks as if they knew they were supposed to be drinking them, but the ice or the glass or the alcohol, it all had all just become too heavy.

Their testimony was that they were collecting scrap metal from some old place on BLM land, and their friend, an ex-lumberjack named Manny, he kept walking down all the halls trying to get an echo or something, and then he just suddenly wasn't there anymore.

Without a body to support foul play, or any kind of motive, or history of malice, the four men were never convicted. Instead, four different men were assigned to watch a structure that nobody remembered, that wasn't registered at the county courthouse, and didn't show up on satellite photos as recently as four months before. The structure that would turn out to have the same floor plan as that West Virginia prison.

What Hendrikson thinks is that what the lumberjack did was turn just the right series of corners, like cracking a code, and that the next time he looked up, it was to a chunk of concrete falling down onto him. A whole ceiling of concrete.

Maybe.

The first time I placed my naked palm to one of the I-beams of the structure, I was crying.

Later I would watch a recording of myself in infrared, touching the I-beam.

On the recording, of course, there's no sound.

What I was saying, though, was *please*.

Some nights Ben forgets he's sleeping, and sits at the controls, his fingers running over the board.

Used to be, we'd wake him, try to make him understand, but now we know he just recalibrates a lens or two then goes back to bed. And it's usually a lens that needs recalibrating.

For a while, Hendrikson had me believing I was doing that too, but then I tied my feet together with knotted-together socks one night, proved him wrong. Unless of course I retied them in my sleep as well.

Our commanding officer, Russell, he's tried to kill himself forty-two times now. We know all the ways to bring him back.

Because of Sheila, I've never tried to kill myself.

I think of that sheep in a diaper more than I should though.

We don't know if it ever left the structure or not. Maybe, just on dumb animal luck, it stumbled onto that series of halls that the lumberjack did, and went to someplace warmer.

The next morning, anyway, the structure was unchanged.

And it's a lie that I've never tried to kill myself, of course. I just did all that before coming here. It's out of my system now.

The joke we still say is what we were originally told: that this would be a temporary assignment. That relief's being trained as we speak.

My wife's name is Joella, and Maryann, and Wanda. Her face mixes with all the other girls I've known.

She's living with a guy off-base now.

She says she's sorry.

The one time I tried to run away, Hendrikson tracked me on satellite until I collapsed, and then he walked out with a sled and pulled me back, took my shift.

When I asked him why, he said it was because I was the life of the party, man, and then slapped me on the upper arm, cupped my shoulder in his large hand.

The northern lights with the naked eye are a curtain of light.

Your lips can turn blue, watching them, so that if you smiled, it would hurt. But smiling wouldn't be enough either.

One of the ways Russell tried to kill himself was by climbing as high as he could up the structure, and jumping off.

We nursed him back to health. Ben even gave him two pints of his own blood.

The structure moves so slowly you can only see its progress on paper.

It neither speeds up nor slows down.

If you get Hendrikson drunk enough, he'll explain it to you, the structure. How what happened was, one night some prisoner, probably a new one, he laid in bed all day just thinking about getting out. That that occupied his whole and complete mind. But he wasn't thinking rocket packs and helicopters or any of that. What that prisoner wanted to do was walk out. And, for that to happen, the prison would have to fall down around him.

Meaning, after he fell asleep, he somehow wished the prison gone.

Only he wasn't strong enough, or wasn't particular enough in his wish, or didn't word it right, or—and this is what I think—only metal of a certain age can be physically transported in a dream like that.

Of course this prisoner, what he really did that night was kill himself.

When Hendrikson tells this story, Russell leans forward on his cot and stares at him with his face turned half away.

Of the four of us, I'm the only one with a child.

The reason for this is Sheila was born after I was assigned here, to a woman who was only my girlfriend of two weeks then. She's my wife now, yeah—we were married on the telephone, and by mail, because the government wouldn't pay for her health care any other way—but I don't know that she's ever used my name.

The pictures of Sheila though.

I can tell which is which by how they feel.

The time Ben tried to run away, he was sleeping, so it doesn't count, I don't think, though he insists it does.

We got in a fight over this. It broke my nose.

Afterwards, we didn't talk for weeks, until, finally, just to prove himself right, he ran off into a blizzard.

Where I found him was curled up behind a shrub that was a sieve for the wind.

I held him to me until he was warm.

The northern lights on infrared are nothing. According to Russell, who saw them from the top of the structure, they're not what they seem to be, the lights, but he won't tell us anymore than that, even with vodka in him.

It doesn't matter though. For the lights not to be what they seem to be they would have to be seeming to be something in the first place.

Ben knows I walk through the structure for twenty minutes each night, but if I pretend to be asleep then he doesn't say anything to me about it.

Whether he tells the others or documents it in the log, I don't know.

The only thing we know for sure about the structure is that if you bolt a lightning rod to it, if you bolt two hundred lightning rods all over it, so it bristles, still, when the lightning finally comes months later, it'll strike our antenna instead, which is four meters lower.

This gives us faith that our watch is worthwhile.

Snow coats the structure like it coats everything in Wyoming though. And—we're not supposed to know this either—you can cut it with a torch, just like regular steel. The gas and smoke that rose from it as we were cutting, we saved it in an upside-down jar, and were going to keep it forever until Russell tried to kill himself one night by breathing it in all at once.

It didn't do anything to him.

It's embarrassing to try to kill yourself and have it not work out, I think. But it's good to not be dead too.

Whatever part of our rations we don't finish, Russell always eats.

Whether he came from a large family or grew up poor or both, or whether this is another, longer suicide attempt, we don't know, and don't ask.

If you could somehow live off light, cut it up on your plate and fork it in, that's what I would want to do, I think. Not because it would taste good or be filling, but because a little girl, watching her father do that, she wouldn't say anything, would just watch, her eyes wide with wonder, and she would never forget it for however long she'd live. Which would maybe be forever.

What I don't tell Hendrikson, even though it's regulation to, and we've made promises besides, is that a few nights ago, walking through the structure during my shift, I saw a shape walking ahead of me. Not if I looked straight on, but he was there.

It was the lumberjack.

When I stopped walking, he looked back.

The way I knew he was real was that he wasn't holding a double-edged axe, like all the lumberjacks from my childhood did.

He wasn't lost either.

"Tad," he called back to me.

That's my name.

I looked away and he was gone.

He's not on any of the recordings either. I checked.

What Ben thought I was doing, stopping like that in the hall, I don't know.

I did cry that night though, for some reason. Finally Hendrikson came over to my bunk and laid down beside me and touched my shoulder like he does, and then that made me cry more and harder.

It's nothing unusual in the bunker, though, crying like that.

You just have to ride it out.

That night I didn't dream of the sheep in the diaper, but I wanted to. I don't know if that counts or not.

If you look at the structure long enough, you lose a kind of perspective and it just becomes a tangle of rust-colored lines. They don't move or anything, and it's all in your head anyway, but—it's like if you say a word enough times, it starts to lose meaning. And then, the next time somebody says it just in normal conversation, you'll get a dull jolt, like you've got a funny story associated with that word, but then you won't be able to remember it and people will just think you've maybe had enough to drink already.

That's how it is with the structure. You get drunk on it. And then you laugh a little, because, for the four of you, it still is what it always was: a prison.

But then you think maybe it's more too.

And you don't tell anybody, even your best friend.

And it's winter of course, but this is Wyoming too. Even when it's not winter, it's winter.

Whatever you're planning though—you're afraid to even say it in your head, because somebody might steal it—Russell messes it up by making everybody get their gear on and do the drill he made up. All it is is walking up and down the halls of the path of rocks we've laid out to the north of the structure. They perfectly mirror, down to the inch, the floor plan of the structure. To the east, in more rocks, is the slightly smaller floor plan of the second floor. To the south, the single room of the third floor—the watchtower, Russell calls it. He's the only one who can stand there.

We didn't use the land west of the structure because Russell's superstitious.

And, though the rocks are tall, still, we have to dig them out until our mittens are crusted with ice.

What Russell thinks is the same thing he always thinks: that he's cracked the code, figured it out.

So what we do is tie strings between two of us, while the third watches the structure and Russell directs.

The idea is that when we unlock whatever's here, there'll be some glimmer or something in the real structure.

Russell's theory is that whatever happened, it wasn't because of the structure, but because of whatever pattern that one inmate walked the day before the prison fell down on him.

By the time we're done, our eyelashes are frozen stalks, our beards slush.

In the kitchen, Russell tries to stab his wrist with a dull fork, but his blood is sluggish, his skin over it calloused, tired.

Hendrikson says if we don't make him clean it up himself, he'll never learn.

We don't write any of this down in the log.

My daughter is almost nine. I say this out loud to Ben one night, but he's sleepwalking, sleepmonitoring, so I don't think it really registers. But then he says her name back to me in his toneless voice.

I stand, watching him adjust a dial, and, because it's either hit him in the back of the head or walk away, I walk away.

If you make your hand into a fist and blow into the tunnel of your palm, you can calm down from almost anything. It doesn't matter what your other hand's doing. It could be playing piano or cooking bacon or any of a hundred other things.

What I finally decide is that Ben saying my daughter's name like that, it means something. There are no accidents in the bunker. Not after nearly nine years.

Instead of just leaving Hendrikson without saying anything, I walk by his bunk to tell him bye while he's sleeping, but see that he's pulled the covers up from his feet. What's under them, tucked up against his wall, are powdery-white bricks, like the kind you build a fireplace from.

I stare at them and stare at them.

In the pictures we have of the old prison, before it crumbled, it's made of these exact same bricks.

What this means, God.

Is the structure growing back?

Are all the men going to still be inside, sleeping, or will they be dead?

But—Hendrikson.

What I think is that whatever bricks the structure's been able to call across the void to itself, he's been sneaking them back to his bunk.

Because he doesn't want our watch to be over?

Because he's afraid of the structure ever getting complete?

I lean against the wall by his bunk. I'm sweating.

In the bathroom, I towel it all off, keep nodding to myself, about what I'm not sure.

Ben tells me nighty-night as I shuffle past his chair. Like every other night, I don't say anything, just keep moving, a moth with no wings.

In the snow and the wind I just stand for a long time, my fingertips shoved up into my armpits, my breath swirling away to wrap around the planet.

The night I saw the lumberjack, I remember all the turns I made. It's something you learn to do, something you learn to do without really meaning to.

And I know that Ben's watching me, and know that he knows I know he's watching me, so I try to just stare straight ahead, not shake my head no or anything.

And then I duck into the wind, walk ahead to the structure, and step through the east-facing cell I started in that one night, and, and the trick is, I think, the way I remember it anyway, is that I'm mopping, and that I keep looking back to see my trail of wetness, and that's how I remember.

Two hours later, he's standing there at his end of the hall, the lumberjack. Manny.

My jaw is trembling, my heart in my throat.

Where I don't belong, I know, is Wyoming.

All he's doing is staring at me too. To see each other, we have to look sideways, not straight on, like we're each suspicious.

For him, I think, it's still the night he came to salvage metal.

What I am, then, is an authority, the owner of the structure maybe, who saw flashlights bobbing through all this scrap metal.

I don't know where the prisoners are, or the guards. Or West Virginia.

What I do know is that I've left my coat by Hendrikson's bunk. Or in the bathroom.

The way I know this is that Manny approaches, keeping close to one side of the hall, which is as open to the wind as any other part, that he approaches and offers me the second of the two flannel shirts he's wearing.

I take it, wrap it around my shoulders without pushing my hands through the sleeves, and Manny nods to me, smiles with one side of his face.

According to our training, the shirt I'm wearing isn't a shirt, but an artifact to be catalogued, processed, dissected.

But it's warm, from him.

I close my eyes to him in thanks, and then, when he's shuffling away, looking for his echo, waiting for his voice to come back to him, I get him to turn around somehow. Not with my voice, I don't think, though my mouth's open. But it doesn't matter. What does is that he waits for me to make my way closer, still pushing the idea of the mop, and then takes what I give him, holding it tight by the corner, against the wind: a picture of Sheila.

For a long time he studies it, then looks up to me, and then, behind him, there's a brick along the edge of the hall where there's never been a brick before.

I only notice this because I've been trained to.

"Yours?" he says, holding the picture up, and I nod, say that she looks like her mother, that her mother's a real beauty, and then I look behind me to the idea of the trail of wetness, just so I don't get lost in here like he has.

When I come back around, he's gone.

What this looks like to Ben, I have no idea, and don't care either. We don't make eye contact as I pass his station anyway. At the kitchen table, Russell has all of our pills, antibiotics and vitamins and mood regulators, lined up in the floor plan of the structure. What he's doing is taking them one by one, as if he's walking through. Since the last two times, though, they're filled with confectioner's sugar. He'll get a cavity maybe.

I don't make eye contact with him either, just feel my way to my bunk, lean over Hendrikson to put this next brick with all his.

"Yours," I whisper, almost smiling, and he stirs, feeling me over him, but doesn't wake, and, truly, I don't know how long we can go on like this. But I don't know what else we could be doing either.

I wrote this story because I'd seen a guy with a beard. And beards have always freaked me out a little. I can't grow one, I mean. But I always wonder what it must be like to have all that hair on my face like that. Would it be good? It must be, right? I mean, lots of people do it. So, I figured I wanted this beard to make sense, which meant "Wyoming" to me, in the winter. After that, the rest just kind of fell into place. I've always suspected things move around when we're not looking, I mean. That was the easy part. The hard part was the beards. I mean, not talking about them every line.

IT CAME FROM DEL RIO (PART I OF THE BUNNYHEAD CHRONICLES)

(excerpt)

I PULLED MY top lip in, tried to focus on her, relisten to what she was saying. When I'd called half an hour ago, a guy, a white guy with an Austin area code, had answered, given me the specifics.

"It was a girl, then," I said.

"She knew my name."

"What?"

There was no more, though. Just that. And it wasn't so much a threat as a negotiating tactic. I knew because I'd used it myself in bars, hustling pool. What you do is, while lining up your shot, say to whoever you're playing that you like their truck—*what, is that a '72 clip up under the front, yeah?*

What they'll say back is no, it's not theirs. They're driving that Monte Carlo with the wire wheels and the twenty-two layers of clear coat. At which point you nod, snap your ball against some unlikely series of rails to win the game, and say, *Yeah, that Monte Carlo. Sharp ride. What's a paint job like that go for anyway?*

The message they get is that now you know what they drive.

This is what these clients were telling me: that if, upon delivery, I made up some story about having to grease the border guys or buy a car off a lot or whatever, then, hey, they knew I had a daughter, yeah? Cute little girl named Laurie, about three hundred miles away?

It also meant I couldn't turn down this job.

Whether they were moving stuff in ziplock bags or a pallet of anvils, I was going to have to strap it onto my back, mule it up by starlight. Maybe I really would get a regular job after this, I told myself. One that didn't ransom my kid to get me to show up.

First, though, one more crossing.

But before that, like every time, a walk down to the pharmacist.

That trick with playing pool? It's from my brother. In high school, I quit my senior year to hang out at the pool hall (and work), and I got pretty good, could usually climb to the finals in a tournament. But my brother—you know how little brothers are. He had to go farther, do more. He became a much better pool player than I ever was. There's some more tricks he taught me, but this is the most useful one, I think. And, except for The Last Final Girl—*okay, and* Growing Up Dead in Texas, *which has that same little brother on it—this book has my favorite cover. Writing the sequel, I felt I had to live up to it. I mean, writing the first book, it was without the pressure of a great cover. And I had no idea where the book was going, anyway, was completely surprised when Laurie wrote herself in halfway through. But the sequel,* Once Upon a Time in Texas— *not published yet—man, it's got a wolf driving a Ferrari, I think, to chase a rabbit through the South by Southwested streets of Austin. It's got somebody with a spider for an eye. It's got monsters climbing buildings Kong-style. I so love that book. And I can see how the third one ends now too. Thinking about calling it* Night of the Rabbit *maybe. Or* They Call me Dodd. *Or* A Bunny So Vile. *Not sure. Need to write it to see.*

WELCOME TO THE REPTILE HOUSE

IT DIDN'T START the way you might think.

This is where I kind of pause, look off, bite my lip into my mouth so I can come up with the next big lie. With what my dad, talking loud for my little sister, would call Jamie Boy's next big excuse.

Let me try it again: it started pretty much exactly the way you'd think a thing like this would get going.

I was twenty-two, still flashing my high-school diploma at job interviews. Still doing stuff like stealing an extra bag of ice from the cooler if the clerk's not eyeballing me. Hiding a litter of mismatched puppies for the weekend for my friend Dell, and not asking any questions. Bumming smokes outside the bars, but sometimes having my own pack.

I was just getting into tattoos too. Not on me—my arms had been choked blue not four months after I moved into my own place—but *from* me. That was the idea anyway. I wasn't officially apprenticing anywhere, and nobody'd offered their skin to me yet, but I'd always been drawing. My notebooks from junior high are like a running autobiography in doodles, and I'd worked one summer applying decals and pinstriping at my uncle's body shop, and finally graduated to window tint before he trusted me with the front-door keys.

He should have known better.

But, tats, they were kind of the same as those junior-high notebooks. They were the one thing I could concentrate on. Just for hours. Planning, sketching, tracing. For now I was practicing on the back of my right calf, and the side of my left I could reach. Snakes and geckos mostly, though I could feel a dragon curled up inside me, waiting for the right swatch of skin. I've talked to the grizzly old-timers, the real gunslingers of the wild west of body art, and they say you go through phases. You get stuck on something, and talk all your clients into it. What you're trying to do is get it right, what's in your head. You want to get it right and make it permanent, and then watch it walk away.

Like I say, though, tattooing was strictly a sideline, and, as I couldn't afford supplies, it probably wouldn't have been just super-hygenic for me to draw on anybody either. It was just me so far, so I guess that didn't matter too much. But I could already see myself ten years down the road. My own shop, a girlfriend with my ink reaching north out of her bra, circling her shoulder, everybody but me having to imagine what the full image was.

Anyway, where it started: one night, to pay me back for the thing with the puppies, Dell's on my phone, has a shiny new job.

"Seriously, *morgue* attendant?" I said, turning away from my living room of three people with names I hadn't all-the-way caught.

"Different," he said.

I told him maybe, sure, but was there two hours after midnight all the same, a cigarette pinched between my thumb and index finger.

"Leave it," Dell said, opening the door on me and looking past in his important way. Into the parking lot.

Saddleview Funeral Chapel and Crematorium.

I rubbed my cherry out on the tall ashtray, followed him in.

On the way through the maze of viewing rooms to get to the back, Dell told me how his uncle got him this gravy gig. His uncle had worked here forever and a day ago, sitting up with dead soldiers mailed back from war. Or, not sitting up, but sleeping in the same room with, like a guard. It was because there had been some political vandalism or something. Anyway, the boss man now had been the boss man then, and remembered Dell's uncle, so here Dell was. His job was to buzz the alley door open for deliveries, and not touch anything.

He was Dell, though, right?

We toured through the cold room. It was slab city, naked dead people everywhere, their usually covered parts not nearly so interesting as I'd kind of been hoping. We put those paper mouth masks on and felt like mad scientists drifting through the frost, deciding who to bring back, who to let rot.

"Hell yeah," I said through my mask, and, ahead of me, Dell nodded that he knew, he knew.

I told him about who all'd been at my place earlier, maybe lying a little, and in return, like I owed him here, he asked me for the thousandth time for my little sister's number. Not permission, he'd always assumed he had permission to do what- and whoever he wanted. But he wanted me to middle-man it.

"Off-limits," I told him, about her, trying to make my voice sound all no-joke. Because it was.

"Fruit on the limb," Dell said, reaching up to pluck her. Except more graphically somehow. With distinct pornographic intent.

"She's not like us," I said, but before we could get into our usual dance where my sister was involved, the lights dimmed. A second later, a painful buzz filled the place, coming in from all sides, like the walls were speakers.

"Delivery," Dell said. "Hide."

Alone in the room with the dead moments later, I looked around, breathing harder than I was meaning to. All fun and games until one of those bright-white sheets slithers off, right? Until somebody sits up.

Finally I held my breath and crawled in under one of the tables, onto that clangy little shelf, some guy's naked ass not two feet over my face, his body bloated with all kinds of vileness.

After ten minutes in which I got terminally sober, the double doors slammed back. They were the same kind restaurants have, that are made for crashing open, that don't even have handles.

A gurney or whatever was rolling through, no legs pushing it. Just exactly what I needed, yeah. Finally it bumped into a cabinet, stopped. I breathed out but then its wheels started creaking again. It lurched its way over to right beside me, parked its haunted self inches from my face. Just far enough away for a hand to flop down in front of my face. It was pale, dead, the beds of the fingernails dark blue.

I flinched back, fell off my shelf, and Dell laughed, stepped off the belly of the new dead dude he'd been using like a knee board.

I flipped him off, pushed him away and lit up a cigarette. Not like anybody in there was going to mind. Dell took one too and we leaned back against stainless-steel edges, reflected on our lives.

Another lie.

What he did was haul a laser-tag kit up from his locker.

It was the best war ever, at least until, trying to duck my killshot, he crashed a cart over, a dead lady spilling out, sliding to a stop at a cabinet.

I read her toe tag, looked up to her face.

On her inner thigh was a chameleon.

Everything starts somewhere, Dad.

Before you get worried, no, this isn't some necro thing about to happen. I never asked Dell what those puppies were for, but I'm pretty sure he'd nabbed them from about twelve different backyards—people in the classifieds give their addresses over so willingly—and would guess he sold them from a box in the mall parking lot. Meaning they all have good lives now. He wasn't sacrificing them out on some lonely road or anything. He wasn't trying to conjure up a buddy to rape dead women with.

However, if what he was looking for was somebody to trade him rides and cigarettes and ex-girlfriends' numbers for some quality time alone in his cold room with a tat gun, well: there I was.

When you're looking to hire onto a parlor, to rent a booth—hell, even just to lure a mentor in—one thing you've always got to have, it's an art book. A portfolio. What you can do, your greatest hits, the story of your craft.

Problem is, every two-bit dropout can pull something like that together.

But. What if, say, you'd moved to the city only a couple of months ago. And had always just done ink for friends, but were looking to go legit now. And, what? Did I snap pics of any of those mythically good tats?

Yeah, yes, I did.

Here.

Play with the hue a bit on your buddy's computer, and a gecko crawling up a dead guy's shoulder, his skin will look so alive. And there won't even be any rash, any blood. Like you've got that light of a touch.

At first Dell would only let me practice on the bodies that were queued up for the oven, as that would erase evidence of our non-crime, but one night he left me alone to make a burger run—it's cliché that morgue attendants are always eating sloppy food, but I guess it's cliché for a reason—and I unplugged my gun, plugged it back in under the table of this woman I was pretty sure had been a yoga instructor. And recently.

Her skin was tight, springy. Most of the dead, I was having to really stretch their flesh out, then get Dell to hold it tight while I snapped the pic, so that night's lizard wouldn't look like it was melting off.

With her though. I was just halfway through the iguana's tail by the time Dell got back.

He had to let me finish, because who conks with only 10 percent of a tattoo done, right?

It was a beauty too. Just like in my head, I made the tongue curl the opposite direction the tail was, for symmetry. And where it was reaching, only her boyfriend would ever know.

Pretty as it was, though, I didn't get any burgers—this was Dell's punishment (like I would want to eat something his hands had been touching on)—and, to make him laugh, I inked Xs over the eyes of the guy at the front of the line for the oven. He was skinny, pale with death, still cold from the freezer, his two gunshot wounds puckered up like lips. He looked like a punk reject from 1977.

Dell shook his head, walked away smiling. I could see his reflection in all the stainless steel, and, as it turned out, Dell's uncle's reference didn't mean much when the boss man's just-dead, honor-student, choir-singing, yoga-bunny niece he'd been saving for the morning to embalm personally turned up with an evil bug-eyed lizard of some kind trying to crawl up her side, its tongue reaching up to circle her nipple in the most lecherous fashion.

Some people got no sense of art, I mean.

Dell in particular.

Like he had to, he came over, did what he needed to do to my face, to my television and my lamp. The television wasn't mine, but I wasn't saying anything. And then, so I would remember, he dug my tattoo gun up from my backseat, came back in and pulled me off the couch by the shirt I wasn't wearing, sat on my arms with his knees so he could drill some bathroom-wall version of a penis into my chest. Or maybe it was a novelty sprinkler, or a leaky cowboy hat, I don't know.

Chances are I could have bucked him off, but I kind of deserved it too, I guessed. Though if he'd been a real friend, he would have lit a cigarette for me. And maybe done a better job.

When he was done he threw my rig into the corner, slammed through my screen door, told me to forget his number if I knew what was good for me.

I spent the next two days turning his punishment tattoo into a Texas bluebonnet, because that's where I'd been born. At least that was the new story I was going to have ready.

How a flower was going to fit with the iguana theme I'd been studying on lately, I had no idea, but maybe it didn't matter so much either. Soon I wasn't going to have any skin left.

A week passed, then another, and, standing outside a bar one night with my shirt already gone, I saw the last girl Dell had been shacking up with. I'd taken her to prom once upon a time, when prom still existed. She was riding by on the back of another guy's motorcycle. Really pressing herself into him. Glaring us all down.

"She thinks we care?" I said to whoever was beside me.

"Probably thinks we did it," whoever it was said back, taking a deep drag and holding it, holding it.

I narrowed my eyes, looked over through her smoke: Sheila. From when I was a community-college student for three weeks.

"Story?" I said, offering her one from my pack.

She held it sideways, ran her fingers along the white paper and sneered about it like she always did, like she hated cigarettes, like she was just smoking them to kill them. But she threaded it behind her ear all the same. Your monkey's always whispering to you, I guess.

She shrugged, told me about Dell.

He'd been found not just normal dead, like OD'd or stabbed or drowned in vomit in a bed across town. No, he'd been like *exploded* behind a club. A dental-records-only kind of thing. Smeared on the brick, important footsteps leading away, the whole trip.

I eeked my mouth out, stood on the stoop for more smokes than I'd meant.

The bluebonnet on my chest was waving with each inhale.

I went home, watched it in the mirror. Added red buds in the blue, in memorium. I think that's the word.

When I searched Dell up on the newspaper site, two hits came up.

One was his obituary, the funeral I'd missed, and the other hit was about impropriety with the dead.

The blotter had nothing at all about the late-night, involuntary tattoo on the owner's car-wrecked niece—I guess I could have been famous, started a career right there—but it did mention how Saddleview was getting the funeral-home version of an audit. Evidently, one month it had taken in more bodies than it had buried.

I shook my head, clicked away. Dell.

He'd probably got the orders wrong. Pushed one too many into the oven one night, then tried to fix the manifest, had to burn a to-be-buried stiff as well.

It didn't have anything to do with me anyway.

That part of my life was over.

Lie number ten thousand there, I guess. But who's keeping count.

As for why Dell had turned inside out behind the club, I had no clue. He'd always been high-strung. In junior high, he'd always been the first one to put his lips to the Freon tube, the first one to spray thinner into the rag, press it against his mouth, so I figured it was some accumulated chemical reaction. Something the military would probably pay big bucks to the get the formula for. They should have been monitoring us the whole time. Every night, we were out there, experimenting.

And, just because Dell was gone, that didn't mean the lab was closed.

One night maybe three weeks after the funeral where I probably should have been a pallbearer, there we all were, miles out of the city, in a field with a bonfire, like the bonfire had always been there, waiting. There were sparks and, when the wood started to run out, everybody had to donate one article of clothing. And then two.

It was interesting in a decline-of-the-world kind of way. I was kicked back in a lawn chair, zoned out, just mellow, my shirt burning, keeping us all warm. I was watching this one girl named Kelly, already down to her pink clamshell bra, and thinking I might have to wait this situation out when another car pulled up and we all kind of sighed.

Too many cars meant the cops wouldn't be far behind.

Then, too, depending on who was in that car, it could all be worth it.

I shrugged to myself, leaned back to see who the new victims were going to be: first was a guy who could have been a surf bum in a movie ten years ago, second was his clone, and third was a redheaded girl I thought I knew from somewhere.

When the fourth stepped out, I knew where I knew Red from: my sister's friend from down the street at the old house.

Gigi was here.

"Hey!" my non-buddy Seth called out, dancing behind her, pointing down to her with both hands.

I settled deeper into my chair, looked back to the fire like maybe I could blind myself by staring.

Soon enough she found me, stood there with a silver can in her hand and said, "Dad's been trying to reach you."

"Dell?" I said.

"You were his best friend."

"He was a punk. A wastoid."

"And what are you?"

"You should leave," I told her.

"I'm the one who should be doing things, yeah," she said, and that was it.

For a while some guys were running at the fire and jumping over it, but that was short-lived. It was mostly quiet and surly, at least for me. Just music and muttering, and too many snapshot flashes of my sister with surfer boy two, his arm draped over her in a way that was making me swallow hard.

Before the night was over, there were going to be words. And probably more. But first I'd need to make sure he was eighteen—too old to press charges, according to Dell, who would have learned the hard way.

I was nodding to myself about how it was all going to play out, how I was about to step across to the cable spool they were using like a love seat, and was even halfway counting down in my head when a chainsaw pulled up to our little gathering in the sticks.

It was Dell's ex. On her new guy's motorcycle. She stepped off—dismounted, more like—and he just sat there still holding the grips, inspecting us all, the fire dancing in the black glass of his helmet.

I swallowed, looked away like I'd never seen them, tried not to track Gigi even though I did register the T-shirt she'd had on at one point. It was in the fire. The first chance I got I went to pee in the tall grass, never came back, just stopped at a convenience store, called the party in.

You do what you can to save your little sister, I guess. Even cash your friends in.

In my living room the next morning, still awake—I hadn't planned on coming home this early—I ran my hand over the elaborate, dragon-scaled salamander on the right side of my left calf.

I tried to keep the hair there shaved down, to really show it off, but, running my hand over it, it was crackly. And smelled worse than bad.

I sleuthed through my head, made the necessary connection: this was the leg I'd had kicked up on the cooler, close to the fire. On purpose, to show off my work, show what I could do. I'd even been wetting down the scales with beer when nobody was looking, just waiting for anybody to say anything.

Nobody had.

Instead I'd just curled all the hair on my leg, and singed the heel of my favorite shoe.

Everybody had to have seen though. It was beautiful, it was crawling, it was alive.

I smoothed it down, passed out on the couch with that lizard warm under my hand, its eyes open for me, wheeling in their orbits, the pupils just slits, like rips you could climb through, into another world.

I should have tried.

I woke at dusk and flinched back hard, deeper into the couch.

There was a black motorcycle helmet on my coffee table. Watching me.

"Recognized your work," a guy said from the kitchen, and punctuated it by closing my refrigerator hard enough to rattle the ketchup.

Dell's ex's new boyfriend.

"Be still my heart," I said, clutching it, sitting up.

"Don't be stupid," he told me, and stepped in, my tub of butter in his left hand, his right index finger smeared glossy yellow.

He ran it into his mouth, pulled his finger out like he was sneaking frosting off somebody's saved-back cupcake.

"Dairy," he said, running his finger along the edge of the tub again, then shaking his head to get his oily bangs out of his face.

I nearly screamed.

His eyes.

There were two crude Xs tattooed over them. Two Xs I'd done. When he was cold and dead on a rolling cart, two bullets punched through his chest.

"Been looking for someone with your particular . . . talents," he said, downing another fingerful.

I shook my head no, no, saw Dell smeared on a brick wall and stood to crash my way to the screen door, escape out into the night, into some other life.

The boyfriend's helmet caught me in the back like a bowling ball, threw me into the wall by the door, the whole house shaking when I hit.

He turned me over with the toe of his boot, stared down at my chest. Eating butter the whole while.

"Thought you were into reptiles," he said, about my bluebonnet, his accent tuned to the UK station, and just dialed over all the way to it.

I coughed, turned to the side, threw up.

He stepped his boot out of the way.

When I was done he kneeled down, jammed his butter finger into my mouth, smearing yellow all around inside. It was cold, wet, tasteless.

His face so close to mine.

"I'm sorry?" I said.

He laughed, pushed my head down, bouncing it off the carpet.

"You know cow milk is ninety-eight percent the same as cow blood?" he said, dipping his finger into the tub again.

I was just trying to breathe.

He shrugged, said, "Close enough," and set the butter down on a speaker.

From my angle on the floor, he was forever tall, and still pale like a junkie. But he did carry himself something like a British Invasion reject, definitely. Something self-consciously waifish and bad attitude about the way he caved his shoulders in around his chest. The hollow where his stomach should be. His low-slung jeans, like he was just daring you to trace his belt line.

There weren't supposed to be any of his kind anymore though. Them and the dragons, they were on the extinct list, right? All that were even close anymore were all the goths, I guess, the Sandman dreamers, the Bauhaus diehards, the velvet-vest crowd who'd read too much Anne Rice, were probably going to grow up into good little steampunk rejects one day.

This boyfriend, though, I had a sense he was their original. That Neil Gaiman had seen him at a party in the UK, that Anne Rice had followed him through the streets of New Orleans one night, that Sid Vicious had taken a cue or two from him.

"This," he said, giving me some jazz-hands action over his face, his eyes, those Xs, "this isn't just permanent, you know? With me it's kind of forever now, yeah? Get what I'm saying? What do you think of that, Jamie Boy?"

I pushed myself up against the wall, let some butter dribble from my mouth, down onto the bluebonnet.

"Jamie Boy?" I managed to say.

My dad was the only one who did that.

He just stared at me about that.

"She was nice," he said, falling back onto the couch like it was a throne, licking his lips in the most exaggerated way. "But little sisters are always nice, aren't they?"

"Who told you?"

"You did, telescope eyes."

Meaning he'd followed her home. Thinking that's where I was going to be. And then he'd made do with who *was* there.

I stood, but it was just to fall across the coffee table, into the hall. Not for any window but for the bathroom, for the toilet. To throw the rest of the world I used to know up.

In the shower, exploded, smeared all over the tile, was Dell's ex.

She had a bar of soap stuffed in what was left of her mouth.

"Sorry for the mess," the boyfriend said from the door, his leather pants somehow vulgar. "Got to clean up after you eat though. If you don't, they come back, all that. I'm sure you've heard."

He was bored with it, trailed off, looking down the hall like at something important.

I knew where he was looking though.

Four miles over, into the Crane Meadow subdivision. Into what could no longer really be considered a living room, I was pretty sure.

So, monsters are real. Surprise.

For some reason I'd never considered this.

Or—I'm lying again: *one* monster's real anyway.

And I get the sense that's just how he likes it.

When I was done emptying myself into the toilet, I zombied my way back to the living room, my peripheral vision just a smoky haze.

Instead of killing me like I expected, like I wanted, like I deserved, he slapped a pair of blue nitrile gloves down on the coffee table, told me to rubber up, whirred my gun in his other hand.

I looked down at myself to see what room was left for him to do his damage on.

I had it backwards.

Until thirty minutes before dawn, his left hand cupped around my balls the whole time—he'd crunched a metal thermos into tinfoil, to show what he could do—I worked on his face.

Every tattoo artist has to be able to repair somebody else's work. To cover up a name, fix a misspelling, fudge a date. Put a bikini top on that girl, make a pistol into a submarine, a submarine into a flying saucer, a flying saucer into a shadow, all that.

What I was supposed to do was make those dashed-on Xs over his eyes into something presentable enough for the coming eternity. Something he wouldn't have to hide behind a helmet, a helmet he could only explain if he had a motorcycle, and he hated motorcycles. Everything went by too fast.

While I did my thing, holding his dead, cold skin tight—I'd had practice—he told me about 1976. How glorious it had been. No cell-phone cameras, no bullshit DNA, no credit cards in the system, to track people with. Back then he never woke up in morgues, had to sneak out. Back then he was keeping the morgues *stocked*.

In his raspy singsong voice he told me about concerts and brushes with fame, and about a milkmaid he'd known with blond hair that curled on the side like she was an orthodox Jew, and how that framed her face so perfect, even though, where and when she'd lived, she probably hadn't even known Jews existed. How he never knew her name, only her insides. How she tasted.

Because I didn't have the barber patter down yet, and because this was my first time inking a *face*, I just worked, and kept light on my toes. It wasn't on purpose, but his hand on my balls—going up on your toes is kind of a natural response.

Still, even working fast enough to sweat, I was only able to get one eye done.

I was being careful, I mean.

I handed him the mirror, let him look, my balls still in his hand.

He looked side to side at himself and squeezed gently, rolling me like marbles, my spine straightening from it, and then he looked me straight on.

It wasn't bad.

That mime makeup trick, with a tapered, upside-down cross kind of coming through the eyebrow, leaking down onto the cheek? I'd taken some of that and mixed it with the diamond eyes harlequins in comic books have, and filled it all in solid, so that his right eyeball, looking out from all that black, it was seriously wicked. I'd gotten the idea . . . well, first from what I needed to cover that stupid X, but second from a face-paint band I'd seen one night—not KISS, please, and this wasn't a Juggalo night, and I've never seen Marilyn Manson live. Reading the show's write-up the next day, though, the show-off reviewer was saying how the lead singer's black-bagged eyes had been an insult to everything the Misfits had ever not stood for.

I didn't know Glenn Danzig's makeup well enough to make the link like the reviewer did—I was always more of a Sex Pistols kind of punk, I guess—but the guy with my balls in his hands seemed to recognize something. "Sick like a *dog*," he said, and held the mirror over to get a proper angle on his face. Run his other hand over the stubble he would probably never grow.

He liked it.

I breathed out for what felt like the first time in hours and he stood up into that one moment of relief I had, his lips right against mine, my balls tighter in his hand now, so that I was practically floating, my eyes watering whether I was telling them to or not.

I turned to the side to let him do what he was going to do and caught the sun, just starting to warm the very top of my gauzy ancient hand-me-down drapes.

"Hey," I said about it.

He hissed, brought his mouth down to my neck, his teeth grazing my skin there, and said, "We finish it tonight," tapping his naked eye, and then him and his black helmet and his perfumed stench were gone, stalking out the back, leaving my kitchen door open behind him, his bike tearing the morning open.

At first I just zoned out there after he was gone, staring at the pattern of the skirt tacked onto the bottom of my couch, pretending it was the curtain of a show I was waiting for. Pretending a tiny actor was about to prance out, ask how I'd liked the show, how I was liking this joke.

I made my way to the bedroom, rang my dad's phone.

No answer.

I shut my eyes, threw the phone into the wall.

Gigi. Gretchen, really, but really Gigi, since she was little.

I'd always felt like I was out here throwing my life away so she could go the other way. Like I was sacrificing myself so she wouldn't have to. Like this was the only way to save her, the only way to be a decent big brother.

It's stupid, I know. But I'm not smart.

My dad could have told you that.

Still, sometimes.

What I've done now, all day, it's scrawl a rough X over each eye. And then over every free inch of space I've got left on my body, I've traced out scales, like I'm going to shade them in with color later. On my left side, kind of where I always imagined my heart to be, four of those scales have names on them. Like tombstones.

Mom, Dad, Gigi. Me.

This is the kind of art that would get me space at any parlor in town. The kind of imagery bleeding into meaning that makes real tattoo artists wince.

But that's all over now, I guess.

It's almost dark again.

Soon the chainsaw sound will be dying in the air, the helmet on my couch. A monster kicked back in my easy chair, his right hand between my legs, keeping me honest.

One last job, right?

But it's also my first.

To prepare, and also because I can't help it anymore, I feel my way down to the bathroom, lick what I can off the tile walls of the shower, scraping the rest in with my fingers. Pushing it deep inside.

What's left of Dell's ex is black and dried, but that taste underneath, it's to die for. To kill for. Milk could never be like this, not in a thousand years. Cows got nothing on people.

I wore gloves when I was working on him, yeah, so I wouldn't catch anything that was catching.

But then I used the same needle on myself, and I went deeper than I had to for just the ink to set.

His blood spiked up and down me. All through me, hungry.

For two hours, between one and three, the sun right above the house instead of slashing in through the window, I'm pretty sure I was clinically dead.

And I kind of still am.

Will he be able to smell it on me right away, through the flannel shirt I've put on to cover my new ink, to cover the bluebonnet on my chest that's now my chest cracking open to reveal the real me, crawling out tooth and claw, or will we wait to do this thing until I've driven the needles through his naked eye into what the centuries have left of his brain?

It doesn't matter.

Either way I win.

There always was a dragon curled up inside me, Dad.

Tonight it's going to stand up.

I was really thinking about getting a tattoo at last when I wrote this one. But I wanted to practice first. So I wrote about a tattoo artist. Who's really this student I had in 1996, I think it was, whose left leg was all inked up, because he was practicing, and he was right-handed. He offered to practice on me if I bumped his grade, but, well, I'm still without a tattoo, and I think he failed. But the way he was failing on his leg, how all those tattoos had the wrong perspective, and smudges, it led me fifteen years later to this story. Which really comes from . . . that's a Jim Shepard book, right? Almost, I mean? I bought it after I'd shelved all my other books, and it wouldn't fit so I just laid it longwise on the shelf, but that meant that every single day when I went to my desk, this book was staring me down. Imprinting itself on me, yes. And, vampires, yep. I think this is my second vampire story, after "Monsters"? They're fun. Maybe I'll try a novel of them someday. Except it'd just be a Near Dark *rip-off. Oh, too: this story comes right after I politely declined an invitation to view an embalming on a Friday night, way after-hours. A scene I'm still very, very happy to have avoided. I can't even watch* AFV *(America's Funniest Home Videos) while eating Honeycombs, I mean, because some kid on there might have nose issues (I'm gagging right now, writing this), and then I'll be throwing up. No way could I handle an embalming. I remember things far, far too well to encounter that. Also, Zack Wentz helped me a lot with the story. Dude knows fiction, and is great with line-level, like, hammerings, I guess: he makes lines better. And, all the music references in here, they're his. Leave the music up to me and it'll either be Bob Seger or Waylon Jennings, pretty much.*

ADULTERY

A Failing Sestina

in the absence of grace

Dad brings the angel home from the horse trap. He lets her sit up front, and tells her that the window on her side won't roll down, so don't try it. And she isn't so much pretty as she is fragile. He leaves her in the cab of the truck through dinner, and the dome light that hasn't worked for years extends a halogen filament like a finger across some vacuum, pointing at her as we pretend to eat.

"Another one," Mom says.

Dad nods, looks at her through the window as if for the first time. Chews his grilled cheese and tells us the story of her capture, how he found her dehydrated at the salt lick, nearly transparent. All he had to do was bind her wrists together with baling wire, then lead her to the truck. But still, when she heard the engine idling it took all of his two hundred and twenty pounds to keep her on the ground.

"This is getting out of hand," Mom says.

"I did leave the radio on for her," Dad says back.

"And her . . . the wire?"

"It doesn't hurt them."

"Of course it doesn't."

"Like I said."

"And she believed that about the window?"

"She's an angel."

"What station, then?"

"Church," Dad tell hers, laughing when he says it, and Mom throws back her bourbon in anger.

"That's not what she came for," she says. "You don't know anything, do you?"

"She's different," Dad says back, winking at us, "special," but he said that about the last one too.

After dinner and dishes and shows the dome light is still a faint reminder in the yard. Dad returns to it again and again, stands at the window, his back to the table, the living room, mumbling about the goddamn battery he's not going to let her run down.

Through the bottom of her glass Mom watches him fill the front door for a moment, then walk away.

"Go to bed," she tells us, her voice flat and hard, and we pretend to do that too.

In the living room the television set blackens, and Mom sits on her end of the couch and doesn't pull the heavy amber drapes, which would mute Dad's leaf springs and cab bushings, the dry, awkward sounds of his desire. The dome light is a sheen in his back as he leans over the angel, straining.

He returns breathing hard, with the rearview mirror in hand. It slides across the kitchen counter, nestles against the cutting board.

"Superglue?" he asks Mom.

"It won't work."

"It has before."

"Well then there you are," she says, and his footsteps slouch to the television set, his chin lowers to his chest, and he's asleep for the night. His labored breathing fills the house, and his skin in the glow of the late-night nature shows is pale blue, the color of heaven.

"Go to bed," Mom says to us again, and her hands plunder needle-nose pliers from the pocket of Dad's discarded jacket. The kind with the wire cutters built into them. She flexes them like a jaw, an inarticulate mouth, and then fills the door herself for a moment in passing.

As she crosses the driveway, moving from the light of alternating current to direct, her layers of nightgown make it hard to tell where she begins and where she doesn't. She gets in the driver's side of Dad's truck and the dome light flickers, unsure, the angel rising from the floorboard. One of them nearly transparent, one of them too much there.

The angel offers her wrists because angels by nature are trusting, and Mom bites the wire with the pliers, again and again, and won't begin apologizing for hours yet.

interlude with hyenas

The thing about hyenas is they want to exist at the fringe of the savanna. Ask a talking hyena why all the night footage, the spotlights, the furtive, reflected eyes, and she'll slip off into the darkness without answering. It's not all about shame, though, as the British narrator speculates, mister tongue-in-cheek, his restrained chuckle spooling out over the hushed and expectant grassland, the concave darkness, volplaning down over the hyena, her retreat already footage: long, mismatched forelimbs collect the ground before her in an almost simian manner, pulling enough distance between her and the question that she can locate her own dead by scent, hunch over the carcass, lower her nose into the rough coat. The meat underneath will be dark, bitter, familiar. This is the answer: she eats her own not out of anything so mean as hunger, but a compelling need to leave no evidence for the crepuscular light of morning to reveal. A syllogism: 1) material existence entails displacing mass; 2) displacing mass entails consumption of matter foreign to you; 3) to consume unforeign matter is to deny material existence. The African corollary: through cannibalism, the hyena as a species is accepting an immaterial existence at the night edge of the savanna—seeking such an existence.

But it's not all about logic either.

Ask a talking hyena why all the night footage, the spotlights, the furtive, reflected eyes, and she'll slip off into the darkness only to wait just past the headlights, grinning with need, her painted black lips curling in to no easy reduction point.

the legend of the moth man

Dad brings the candy home from the convenience store and fills our mouths with it. Dinner is ruined. Dinner is always ruined. He's already made three runs to the convenience store since work—one for cigarettes, one for baking soda, and the last to fill the tank back up with gas. Our teeth hurt from sugar. He's still got a candy bracelet on his wrist from the gas run, the elastic between the powdery hearts straining.

"That all you have to show?" Mom asks.

Dad smiles at her, a question almost, but then follows her eyes down to his wrist, swallows as if just seeing the bracelet himself. Dinner passes in fits and starts, Dad chewing, chewing, studying the candy hearts. Two swallows later he looks back up and tells us the story of it, how the new cashier at the convenience store has been on shift for forty-two hours now, is giving the bracelets away just so she won't have to stock them. This draws a smile on Mom's face.

"What else might she be giving away?"

"She has a whole box of them."

"Poor dear."

"Are you wanting one—?"

"Because if I do," Mom says for him, "you can go back . . ."

"It's just down the street."

"Convenient, right?"

"I'm saying I don't mind."

"Of course you don't."

"I did get the baking soda, didn't I?"

"The baking soda, yes. What would we do?"

"Not play twenty questions at dinner maybe."

"Here's one. Why don't you just bring her home?"

"The cashier?" Dad asks, winking for us, "it's just candy, Mom, geez," but the bracelet when he tosses it over is heavy enough to slide off the table. We feign digestion, and Dad does the opposite, claims indigestion, the sudden need for antacid.

He reaches for his coat and Mom's already cleaning up. "One more for the road," she says to herself.

"The children are listening, y'know," Dad says back.

"Is that what it takes? Then they're going with you this time."

And we do, seat belts and all. To the convenience store. The cashier leans far over the counter in anticipation and there on her finger is a candy wedding ring, her mouth red from it. And she isn't so much pretty as she is pale from working nights. Almost fluorescent. We stand in front of the magazines while they talk on napkins, and instead of antacids Dad buys a kit to glue a rearview mirror on.

"Guess what it is," he says to Mom.

"You don't want me to."

"It's for the car. Always be prepared, y'know."

"My boy scout."

They stand in the hall, facing each other. Mom already has the vacuum cleaner assembled. She directs us upstairs and we don't need to be told twice. Below us the house gets severely clean. Dad counters mops and spray bottles with late-night TV, and the animals, when they die, die at full volume. Just as the bleach and ammonia and laundry detergent reach our room, our nostrils, two separate doors close—the utility (Mom) and the front (Dad). He doesn't turn the headlights on as he backs out.

It only takes him thirty minutes.

By the time he coasts back in, his skin stained pale like the cashier's, we're already packed, or, still packed from four nights ago.

"The clothes are running," Mom says as we pass him in the yard, file into the car, leave him standing under the bug light, token milk in hand. We drive around and around the loop. Mom looks at us once in the rearview mirror, says she's sorry, and soon enough the spin cycle is over and we're at the convenience-store pumps with her one more time, pumping gas she isn't going to pay for, and she's staring across the asphalt at the front of the store, the cashier, one of them almost asleep, the other unblinking.

interlude with hyenas, pt. 2

The other thing about hyenas is that when they have to kill for themselves, they select the weakest from the herd. And they can detect the subtlest of infirmities in a passing glance, infirmities even the lioness is blind to, as if such an advantage would take the art out of all the footage devoted to her— the impossibly patient stalk through tall grass, the trademark pounce, the prey suffocating beneath her, the hyena there at the edge of the kill, the outer limit of the spotlight, yawning in anticipation, already in lurk mode. Miss counterpoint for the narrator, his opportunist of the savanna, her radically sloped back speaking to him of generations of skulking away, of lingering, of *mal*-lingering, an inexact usage, he confesses, the cocksure smile audible, but a revealing one nevertheless, an accurate one. To malinger in the proper sense is to avoid duty, work, etc., from the French *malingre*, itself a combi- nation of the Latin *malus*—bad, evil—and the north Middle Eastern *lenger*, used chiefly in relation to immaterial things: to have a hunger or craving; to move about in a secret manner; to hang about a place beyond the proper time; to remain furtively or unobserved in one spot, waiting. In savanna terms, to be a hyena.

But there's more to it than etymology.

The thing about hyenas is that when the lioness chases them off her kill, she does so not with the inexpressive facial features you'd expect her to use outside her own pride, but with the bared teeth and guttural vocalizations typical of intraspecific strife. Features that suggest it's personal. That the hyena is laughing as she runs goes without saying; that she's leading the lioness deeper into the night doesn't.

dr. thomson and his lucretta

Dad brings the painting home from the hospital, leans it casually on the hearth, studies it over salad. Twice he draws our attention to it by almost commenting, his fork raised in thought, but each time withdraws. And it is well executed, give her that: a night study of fecal matter in short grass, days of it, rendered in white so as to evoke the counterintuitive reversals involved with photographic negatives. The effect is one of incompleteness, of continuation. At the table, Mom already has her back to it.

"So are we officially her patron now?" she asks.

"Tax write-off," Dad says, winking to us, but then when we're too old for his humor, too young yet to pity him, he launches into the painting, how it's from her Latrine series—"Ca3(PO4)2A1.5 Ca(OH2)," the chemical composition of digested bone. The spoor is the spoor of nocturnal scavengers, is the obverse of the long night they inhabit; the painter is Mom's old art student, in the hospital now with an ulna that cracked too easily for her fifty-one years.

"Scavengers?" Mom asks, her voice incredulous.

"For obvious reasons," Dad says, "she's interested in bones."

"Of course she is."

"It'll be worth something, someday . . ."

". . . to someone."

"She was admitted, M—. I was on call. There's nothing I can do about that."

"I should ring her up, I suppose."

"Yes. She'd like that."

"After all these years."

"That was a long time ago."

"Yes. It was."

"She talks about you, y'know."

"Yes. I noticed you were late."

"It's a good painting," Dad says, studying it again.

Mom smiles, for us, together at the table once more, and says that "as far as feces goes," but then trails off into the obvious. We stab the salad in unison, with resolve, avoiding eye contact. It could be fifteen years ago, and for a few moments it is—it really is—but Dad's beeper pulls us violently forward.

"She has your pager number," Mom says. It's not a question.

Dad excuses himself, opts for the phone in the kitchen over the remote behind him.

In his absence Mom studies the painting with narrow eyes. Like the rest, it's a finger painting. In the lower corner, too, instead of a signature, is the imprint of an arm band from the hospital, an ID, a name rolled in backwards. Mom laughs.

Dad returns with a medical journal in hand, one of the ones he subscribes to in order to keep up with "popular" medicine. On the cover is an over-the-shoulder shot of a recently retired gentleman, the road opening up before his RV. Looming in the rearview mirror, though, are a host of maladies—arthritis, osteoporosis, Parkinson's, etc.

"So is she better now?" Mom asks.

Dad holds up the magazine in disgust. "She thinks her bones are becoming lighter, for Chrissake."

"She's a fragile woman."

"M—."

"She needs special attention, I mean. I understand."

"Well, you know her," Dad says.

"Yes," Mom says, "I do."

Not long afterwards they fall into their apologetic routine about having to go to bed, and in the silence they leave, all the television has to offer in the way of distraction is the Serengeti. We mute it without forethought, can just make out Dad fumbling the straps of Mom's nightgown off her shoulder.

"Who am I?" Mom asks in the darkness of their bedroom.

The bed springs are motionless, suspended. "I'm home," Dad says, "isn't that enough? M—?"

Mom pulls him into her, her forearm surely pressing against the back of his head, and when the beeper screams on the dining room table we simply turn our heads on it, wait for it to cease.

Hours later Mom descends, thinking we're asleep, and pads into her studio, emerges minutes later with the pint can of halogen-white paint from the top shelf, the one with lead deposits in it. The one we were never supposed to touch. Mom is humming to herself as she passes, oblivious of us, the fecal matter on her hearth. She turns the television off out of habit, stands in its afterglow, and then becomes the shape of our mother silhouetted against the dining room window, placing two things next to the beeper for Dad to take to work, as gifts from a former teacher: the paint with the lead in it, and her own calcium supplement pills. Because of the latter, the former won't be questioned.

We feign sleep and feign it well.

all the beautiful sinners
In the morning the smell from the horse trap drives us from our beds, and we make our way through the front door, across the drive, to Dad's truck, his angel, her wrists turned inside out from Mom removing the baling wire again and again. And she's not so much dead as she is beautiful, draped across the bench seat, her eyes still open. Trusting. We don't talk about her though; we don't talk about anything. In the long hours before lunch we'll hang Dad's floor mats on the line to dry, we'll bring Mom water to drink, but now, before they wake, before they can remember, we take the angel to the barn, remove her bones—already dry, brittle—and with the refashioned meat grinder with the battery-driven mortar and pestle with the apparatus

with desire

we reduce her bones to chalk, and to the chalk we add salt, weak glue, geometry: in this manner it slowly becomes another cube, a lick to be placed in the bed of Dad's truck for delivery, and the horses in the trap when they apply their tongues will apply their tongues with care, because they need it too.

I wrote this story for two weeks, which was my record then. It might still be, I guess. Two afternoons is usually about where I max out. That's as long as I can put up with a story not coming together. After that, it's the axe, now on to the next one. But, the structure of this one, it was so, so enticing. Really, it's the

308

structure for so many of my novels, right? It's the real way of things, as far as I'm concerned. It's the truth. Still, that doesn't mean I nailed the end. I've always felt I overwrote this one. That, in trying out every possible way it could work out, I kind of erased the way it should have been. I like the way this one gets where it's going, definitely. But I'm not quite happy with where it finally gets to. Feels like another cop-out, I mean. And, I wrote this while writing The Fast Red Road, *which, at the time, was called* Golius: A Failing Sestina. *So, the whole time writing this, it felt like just an exercise, since no way could I subtitle* two *things the same, right? But titles change. The title for that book, it changed just about weekly. So I mailed this story out, and got lucky.*

SCREENTIME

WE HAD ALL seen the yellow-and-black vans line into town, sit outside the
drugstore for about ten minutes, then drive bee straight out to the old drive-in,
but it was Cheryl who found the ad in the paper, misplaced under Legal
Notices.

"Wanted," she read, laid across the hood of my truck, "a kissing boy."

I smiled and she talked me into it.

Lynn at the drugstore said the van people were from the movies, that
they'd rented the old drive-in for seven hundred and fifty dollars a day, and
still needed directions.

"Does he look like a kissing boy?" Cheryl asked Lynn, framing my face
with her hands, and Lynn said I sure looked like something. I stole a pack of
dusty rubbers off the wall while Lynn looked away politely, and then the cow-
bell was a brass ringing thing and we were gone, weaving in my truck off into
our last summer, trying to redo everything one last time before whatever was
coming came. We were just out of high school and hadn't learned yet about
how hard you had to watch, not to let ten years get behind you.

That next morning I was one of four who showed up at the drive-in, to be
a kissing boy, and the only one who'd had a Cheryl to pick my button-up shirt,
tuck it in right, and wash under my fingernails with a toothbrush and bleach.
Of the three others, two were Tim and Jim, twin linebackers from six years
back, when I'd been playing touch football during sixth-grade recess, my helmet overbalancing me, making me faster than I was. They were still drunk
from the night before, leaning on each other and blinking their eyes too fast.

One night my freshman year they'd stuffed me in a plastic trash can and sat on the lid smoking dope and waving at people who drove by. The other of the three was Old Chester from the gas station, who didn't even make it under the tarp before he ran his finger down the hollow line of the clipboard girl's back and was asked to leave.

I felt like John Schneider for some reason.

When I looked back the last time before stepping in, Cheryl was posing like a poster, her legs crossed at the shins, her lace-up boots skylined out the driver's side window of my truck. She was posing on purpose, to make me keep all my promises. We'd practiced for my audition deep into the night.

Still though, when I walked under the tarp I wasn't ready for Charley, with her hair too black and dull to be natural, her eyes green like she was from another world altogether. She was sitting to the right of the little man who turned out to be her uncle, who was introduced as Herr Director; she was smoking a cigarette fast and angry and balanced the ashes straight up, flirting with gravity. Later that year I would find in a catalogue all the bit parts she'd played, and have the tapes shipped to me COD. In one of the music videos she would dance around for a few seconds in a black bra and flared-out skirt. For discipline, I would only let myself watch that part after watching all of the other four videos, including the one we shot that week at the old drive-in, a place my dad always said held special significance for me and my beginnings, if I knew what he meant.

I watched them without sound, because somehow that made it all last longer.

That first day under the tarp we didn't test-run kiss, either, me and Charley. I did get in a fight though, with Tim and Jim, after Tim kneeled in front of Charley, took her hand, and held it to his unshaved cheek. He started singing some slow, fake song to her and she just smiled with her mouth and ashed behind the table. Herr Director rested his chin on the back of his laced fingers, hands bent at the wrists, elbows held close to his ribs, and watched. He had laryngitis or something and I never heard his voice, just followed his white-tipped baton all week.

Meaning I did get the job.

But that was in a few minutes. Right then, what was happening was Jim covered his hand with his mouth and elbowed me soft in the side, so I'd notice the fool his brother was making of himself, for her. When he touched me the second time I came back with a shoulder pushing him away, and when his big hand caressed the back of my neck like he was my father or something I was already punching and we were on the ground together in the sharp-stalked white weeds, rolling, Tim kicking both of us and finally diving in too. By the time the clipboard girl separated us her bikini top was most of the way pulled off and Tim and Jim were laughing, elbowing me in the side again.

That fight with them was one of the last things I'd meant to redo anyways, even if nobody won, or if they said they did.

It didn't matter.

The first thing Charley asked me was was I local?

I nodded.

The second thing was did I think I was a knight in shining armor or something.

I shrugged, then signed on for seventy dollars a day, and was probably standing in the exact same spot where my dad had unhooked my mom's bra eighteen years ago and told her not to worry, everything was going to be all right, some blue-and-white love scene burning into the screen for all time.

That night I had a handful of cash too.

Cheryl asked were my lips tired. She used the flat side of her voice and I told her it was her idea after all, my new job.

"So then, what're you going to buy me?" she asked.

I told her anything, because it was eight o'clock and all the stores were closed and we were going to eat at the Texaco anyways, like every night when we didn't want to get tied up with her parents or mine. I did buy her a huge candy wedding ring though, which stained her mouth blue and made her look like a little girl, nothing like Charley.

Parked out at the end of the old airstrip with our friends and the beer I'd bought, we played Bob Seger in my tape deck and let our headlights feel out into the scrub. I didn't know what song the video was going to be yet, but I knew it was going to be Bob Seger. One of the van drivers had told me that much earlier when we were both packed into the old projection booth, rigging up the camera they'd brought. My job was to keep the spiders off him. We were both sweating and drinking lemonade from pointy-bottomed cups we couldn't set down.

"That Charley girl," he said, whistling in without noise, and I nodded and looked away from the spider-web bridge caught between his hair and the low ceiling.

Outside our booth the parking lot was filling with people, with old car-club cars that Herr Director positioned mutely between the speakers with his baton, then repositioned. The clipboard girl showed me the car I would be performing in, third row back. It was a long low Impala with rally rims, and me and Charley were going to be in the backseat, the second-base crowd, no lines to remember, only motions to follow.

"Just pretend she's your girlfriend," she said, and that night when the headlights were off and no planes were coming I closed my eyes to Cheryl's blue-candy mouth and drove us into San Angelo, where we rented a motel room for the first time in our five years together. Cheryl rang her sister's house once to let her know she was safe. We ate at a Chinese restaurant with chopsticks I sharpened under the table with my knife, skewering the chicken and pork and feeding each other like lovers.

I never meant to marry her.

It was all make-believe.

That next morning they cut my hair, because I didn't look like I was from '62. The hair guy asked me was I the token local, and I didn't answer him. Charley watched as he cut and finally just took over, holding the comb in her teeth, touching sometimes on a shoulder or a knee.

"Bob's coming tomorrow," she said, then followed with "Bob *Seger*, you know."

I smiled and told her I knew.

The haircut took longer than most, because I kept moving at every last second. Finally she had to get out the shears and give me a flattop. Punishment, she called it, and hit me lightly with the comb. My wet hair was all around us. She told me I looked like I should be an extra in a movie about malt shops, and then led me by the hand to our Impala. She opened the passenger door and bent over, looking in. Behind us one of the van drivers clapped and whistled.

She shook her head and lit a cigarette. "We can't smoke in the cars, you know. Leather seats. Rules."

I told her I didn't smoke much anyways, and then we stood there with nothing to say, my white-skin sideburns and back of the neck burning wonderfully in the sun. Later that night, another seventy dollars in hand, Cheryl rubbed lotion into my small burns as I drove, and said she missed my hair.

That night in San Angelo it was custom-ordered pizza at some dark place we'd been to for prom, and when the waiter wasn't around I looked away and told Cheryl I liked my hair better like this, it was easier. That night one more of the dusty rubbers broke in the motel room, and one more night I opened my eyes and said don't worry.

When my son Rick gets old enough I plan on drinking hard one night and then lying to him that he was conceived out at the old drive in, in a low-slung Impala, Bob Seger's mouth moving with no noise, his guitar deep like the sound of thunder.

He'll never ask his mom about it.

Two days later Cheryl was on the set with me, holding my arm with both her hands. I was already calling it the set, not the old drive-in. She made fun of me, asked what was I going to do when the video was over. I shrugged, stood by the Impala, talked to the bearded accountant leaning under his hood, who said I was lucky, this car was a home-run car if there ever was one. He offered us beer and we sat in the shade of a van and drank and talked about where the rest of our class had wound up after graduation, where we might be winding up ourselves. She was already saying *we*, too, we both were. I didn't notice.

Instead I was watching the helicopter with Bob Seger approach, a day late.

They had to set it down a half mile off, to keep the dust off the cars; a yellow VW van picked him up and buzzed back, and when he stepped out he was a star and Cheryl was squeezing bruises into my arm and I was even getting a lump in my throat. In the floorboard of my truck were all the old eight-tracks my uncle wanted him to sign, even though his eight-track player was long dead.

The rest of the day we spent doing dry runs, Bob Seger straddling the hood of some car, pool-table felt glued to the bottom of his boots, me and Charley sitting in the backseat stage-kissing, the clipboard girl telling me what to do with my right arm, since that's mostly what would be seen when the windows were fogged. A lot of the time I was alone in the car, too, since Charley was the backseat girl in four other cars in different rows. Once a blond girl poked her head into my backseat and said oops, wiped her mouth, and then was gone.

When we finally shot the video it would take two nights. Cheryl would be sitting out at the road in my truck, the parking lights on, waiting for life to begin. We'd spend the days between the nights at her sister's empty house, and her sister was nice enough to ring once before coming home from work.

I never got Bob Seger's autograph either. I did talk to him, though, the day after the shoot, when everybody was gone, when he came back on his own time with a small video camera, to stand in the old drive-in and look around and find me sitting in the third row.

I told him I was the kissing boy, and he smiled and said aren't we all.

The other day Rick asked me why I liked that old video so much. I told him it was a good song, but had the volume turned all the way down too. He shook his head and left on his bicycle, to wherever nine-year-olds go in the summer heat. Cheryl was in the kitchen on the phone, trying to organize the class reunion, trying to get everybody together one more time. I was pushing play, rewind, play, rewind, no discipline at all, remembering that second night of shooting, when the fire trucks were there to make the rain, when the camera crane hovered impossibly over our Impala and Charley climbed on top of me and made me kiss her hard and deep. She was out of breath from running from the first three cars, and her shirt was wet. In the front seat the battery-driven humidifier was turned up to 10 and the windows were impenetrable, and somewhere one of the yellow vans was playing Bob Seger at full tilt, and Bob Seger himself was leaning back into the fans, singing, his voice getting pulled behind him to lose itself on the drive-in screen, where there were spliced together love scenes in blue, all turning into each other.

In the video my right arm curves around Charley Waine's lower back, pulls her close, and her too-black hair is falling all over the both of us, her hands on my shoulder, both pushing away and not letting go.

Blink and you'll miss me.

I wrote this one in forty-five minutes, right after the Pop-Up Video episode where they do their thing to Bob Seger's "Night Moves." That completely opened up a whole new world for me. Seriously. There were footnotes popping up over everything? It was amazing. This is one of the places Demon Theory was born, definitely. So, me writing this one, it's just me and people I used to know, kind of as a sham, or an excuse, because what I was really after, it was *Bob Seger making this video*. I wanted to see it up close, I mean, not just through my television in Florida. I wanted to go back in time to then, to there. Which meant tunneling back to me in high school, like always. I don't like the prose in this one much, but I've gone back to it a few times too, to try to fix it, and everything in this story, man, it's already locked in place. This story's a shell. All I can do is polish it, knock on it. It's all too set for me to ever change it again. I've always meant to do a collection with this one and "State" and "Fairies" in it too. And a couple others. And some I haven't written yet. Those are the important ones, too, the ones why I haven't done this collection yet: because they don't exist. Not even in my head. My stories without demons and killers, I mean, they're getting farther and farther between.

DEMON THEORY 👽

A Work of Fiction

(excerpt)

ON THE COUCH again, Nona is shivering and sweating both, Con dabbing the nosebleed off her chin, the medicine drawer beside him, *PDR* open.

"She went outside, didn't she?" Nona asks, taking her chin back. "Seri?"

"I don't know whose idea it was," Con says, and Nona looks at him for more. He supplies: "Hers or his, I mean."

Nona grins through her fever.

"I guess she didn't believe me," she says, "about him."

Con pauses, looks to Nona in question, then follows her deadpan gaze

→outside, Seri in the calm spot but no longer calm: through the snow there's a large figure coalescing.

"No," she says, "this isn't possible," but then the figure dissolves. Seri spins, panics, and is facing the wrong way when a leathery black hand settles on her shoulder. Skopek, frost on his eyebrows.

Seri exhales, wraps her arms around his neck, Skopek unsure where to place his hands. Unsure enough that his POV just studies the ground, the powdered snow suspended some six inches off the ground.

The hug lasts long enough for the floating snow Skopek's watching to shift in subtle anticipation, get pressed down in the middle, curl back up at the edges. In the reaction shot, Skopek flares his animal eyes, turns his head just in time for a DEMON to enter the frame, diving hard and loud out of the storm, not anticipated by an aerial POV as it usually has been before.

It grabs him, carries him up at an angle, the massive wings cratering the snow around them, Skopek's jacket already tearing away, saving him.

In the wake of all this Seri's back down to her original black bra, the first thing we ever saw her in. Breathless too. And still in the eye of the blizzard, or whatever it is. She tries to step out but gets buffeted back.

"This isn't happening," she says, voice rising, "*Goddammit, Daddy*!" but then notices what's in her hand, left over from impact with Skopek: the neon key string.

For a flickering moment, the ambulance resolves in her POV.

She leans into the wind and stumbles toward it, swaying her back, swaying her back, falling, getting up, glancing off the Chevelle.

She slams up against the passenger-side door, forcing the close-up of the key through the ice.

X distance behind her, Skopek is lying facedown in the snow, his back bloody. Just when it seems he's dead for sure he resumes consciousness all at once, his massive frame shivering awake. He doesn't panic though, like a sane person, but keeps his head still, watching the snow for irregularities.

When there are none he stands, finds Stan's blade in one of his hands.

Smiles.

Watches the sky.

This time the demon isn't airborne, but standing a few yards out. Big enough that even Skopek has to look up. It steps awkwardly forward, everything about it unnatural,[1] unholy,[2] unnamable,[3] etc.

Skopek hides the blade down the back of his leg. Plays hurt. The demon approaches, stands over him. Looks down to him. Raises a clawed hand for the killing blow but when the hand falls Skopek severs it cleanly, right at the delicately thick wrist.

At first the demon doesn't respond at all, and then it shrieks, stands farther up on its toes, head thrown back, and Skopek takes advantage, opens up its midsection, wrong-wrong stuff spilling out, melting the snow, scorching the blade.

The demon tries to hold the close-up of its insides in.

When the shot backs off, Skopek's disappeared.

Back to Seri, in the driver's seat now, the ambulance not even bothering to turn over for her ignition key. She dials too fast through the static of the radio—still working somehow. "Please please oh God please," she screams as quietly as she can. Which is to say her panic is killing her. Her mouth is pressed hard to the mouthpiece when Skopek's backside crashes into the windshield, showering her with glass.

She screams, screams some more. Keeps screaming. Tries the doors but they're buckled shut. Finally she kicks and crawls away from Skopek, into the back, where a tray of pill bottles spills over her, dialing her panic up a few notches. We stay with the bottles as they scatter, zero in on the label of one— NONA PEARSON, rolled out from its hiding place evidently—stay with it as a voice replies through the static: "Skopek, Skopek, is that you? If you could just tell us where she's taken you, just let us know that no one's going to get hurt this time—" but then the voice goes dead, demon feet coming through the glass on either side of Skopek, answering the question.

On the hood of the ambulance the wounded demon leans down to Skopek, smelling him, studying him, and Skopek takes it, even takes the blood dripping onto his skin, burning craters. The close-up of his hand is still wrapped around the blade handle, waiting patiently. Soon enough Seri makes some noise in the ambulance and the demon backs off like an animal, trying to look in, and Skopek takes advantage, runs the blade up through the demon's chin, out the top of its head, then rips it to the side, opening the demon's face bone-deep, if bones are what that whiteness is. For a moment, from the side, the demon arches back in pain, its massive wings unfolding three-quarters of the way across the screen, sharp, bat-like and beautiful,[4] the ambulance rocking with pain.

In the poster version, the headlights are on, for the anthropomorphic touch, and Skopek's brushed out, so that the demon's attacking the ambulance. Meaning this scene completes the image for us.

The demon falls back, into the storm.

Skopek extracts himself calmly and deliberately from the windshield, leans back into the wind. To finish it is the idea.

In spite of his second-story POV, *something* going on through the storm, Hale's looking at the little-girl reflection in the window. Maybe's been looking at it the whole time.

"Jenny?" he says, turning away from the glass just as a huge wing floats across it, no sound.

The doorway the reflection was framed in is empty now.

Hale shakes his head as if he's losing it, sits on the edge of the bed. Holds his face in his hands and falls back, closes his eyes. Is starting to lean up when there's a girl's voice behind him: "*No.*"

Hale rolls over, looking in the doorway, and in that moment the modified garden-shear blade comes slicing up, through the close-up of a single pane of the window, shaving the air just above Hale's face, where he would have been. Which is to say that single word, that *No*, saved his life.

The blade buries itself in the opposite wall of the hall, smoking hot, trembling with history.

Hale turns to it, focuses hard on it.

"Father?" he says, the formal ring of it somehow unsettling.

On the couch Con is inexplicably oblivious to the crashing glass, etc. upstairs. Occupied instead comparing pill bottles to the *PDR*, a half-eaten can of corn within reach.

"Wherever his mother is," he says, adding another bottle to the pile, "she can't possibly be as happy as she was here. Jim Morrison wasn't even this happy."[5]

Nona stands unsteadily, gropes her way to the window. Parts the curtain.

"They're gone," Con tells her.

"One way or another," Nona creaks, her POV stopping at the frosted glass.

"You can't remember what they had you on?" Con asks. "Haldol, clozapine . . . even a family would help . . ."

"Or a diagnosis, right?" Nona asks, mentally on her feet, at least.

Con nods.

Nona shakes her head. "You won't find it in there," she says, about the drawer, her POV singling out the corroded candy on the coffee table.

She sits by it, gingerly tries to salvage a bar or two.

"They tell me it's psychosomatic," she explains, peeling, chewing. "All in my head."

"But fevers and nosebleeds aren't—"

"Manifestations of an imagined condition," Nona interrupts, "I know. Just don't worry about it, okay? It's happening to me, not you."[6]

Con shakes his head no.

Nona stares back, holds the blanket over her shoulders, dances a fake little jig of health. "Anyway," she says, "I—" but Con's already finishing for her, with an English accent: "'You got better.' Yeah. Got some battery acid on your candy there, Noan."

"Leave her alone," Hale says from halfway down the stairs and out of nowhere.

Con leans back, closes the *PDR* grandly. "I'm just saying it'll happen again," he says, relaxing with the corn, "not that I would know anything . . ."

Nona and Hale aren't listening though, are watching each other instead.

"What do you remember?" she asks. "About last time?"

Hale looks away, around, etc. "It's like a movie in my head," he says, swirling his finger first by his temple then just in front of his face, like an old-style projector, which is easy to miss the first time.

"You're a child of the twentieth century, Haley," Con says, bored. "You remember *everything* in cinematic terms. They're the only ones you have.[7] Your life is a movie."

"What kind though?"[8] Nona adds, to Hale.

"Limited engagement, low production values . . ." Con drones on, already annoying b.g. for Hale and Nona: "Us?" Hale finally says, hesitantly, and Nona looks away, eyes wet as if this could be a love story.[9] To emphasize that it's not, the door suddenly gets rammed hard, the whole house shaking with it.

Neither Hale nor Nona nor Con flinch though. Con appreciates this. "Right on schedule," he says, then looks to Nona as if waiting for her to ask Hale the question. She does: "What do you think?"

Hale looks back to her, down her, to the close-up of her lower legs and feet, both wet. "You went . . ." and then he looks back up to her face: "It was you." He nods outside to show her what he means, what he saw.

Nona looks at her feet as well, doesn't answer; can't. Looks at the floor all around, as if trying to figure it out too.

Before she can get anywhere, though, the door is rammed again.

Hale takes a long time deciding, then turns to Nona.

"Gun?" he asks.

Nona hands it over butt first. Hale runs his finger up where the clip should be. In answer—or in question too—Nona holds her empty hands up.

"Didn't you have it?" Hale asks, Nona apparently just as confused about it as he is.

"It was too dangerous," Con explains. "The one-armed man[10] might have shot everybody . . ."

Hale shakes his head with early regret, holds the gun with one hand and unlocks the door with the other, turning the close-up of the knob reluctantly, still playing FBI.

"One, two," he counts, and on what would have been three the door crashes in on him, and in a blinding rush of snow Seri falls through, in her black bra and crying eyes. Latches onto Hale, who sees Nona see this, a complicated little triangle.

Hale kicks the door closed, and, both hands behind Seri—in hug mode—manages to lock it.

NOTES

1. A 1952 movie, which, though twenty-one years after *Frankenstein*, thirty-five before *Cherry 2000*, and fifty before *Simone*, is nevertheless a mixture of the three.

2. A 1988 Ned Beatty outing, where a priest fights a demon that keeps killing sinners in the act of sinning. Has had a longer-than-average video-shelf life, perhaps because of the excellent cover.

3. Another 1988 movie, this one based on an H. P. Lovecraft story about a monster so ugly/evil that it can't really be named. The tagline: "There are things on God's earth that we can't explain and we can't describe. From the depths of Hell comes . . . The Unnameable." Has also had a longer-than-average shelf life.

4. A hallucination from *The Lost Weekend* (1945). Not to be confused with the "daydreams" in *The Secret Life of Walter Mitty* (1947).

5. I.e., the Jim Morrison of the later years of The Doors (1965–1971), when, if we're to believe Oliver Stone's screen version (1991), he was fairly oblivious, mostly mellow, more interested in completely opening William Blake's "doors of perception"[†] than tuning the real world back in.

> † From Blake's 1790 *Marriage of Heaven and Hell*: "If the doors of perception were cleansed everything would appear to man as it is, infinite"; Blake of course, for a while, was a member of the Swedenborgian Church, founded on the works of Emanuel Swedenborg, who *also* wrote a book called *Heaven and Hell*. More important, however, is a passage from his (Swedenborg's) *True Christian Religion*: "There are two worlds, a spiritual world where angels and spirits are,[A] and a natural world where men are." His *De Telluribus* would be important as well, influencing writers as far away as 1937 (Olaf Stapledon's 1937 novel *Star Maker*, which in turn [in scope] would have no small effect on Clarke's *Childhood's End*).

>> A. This being of course where Swedenborg and the equally cerebral Spock part ways, as Spock indicates in the "The Galileo Seven" (January 5, 1967) episode of the original series: "I, for one, do not believe in angels."

6. *The Exorcist*'s Regan (1973, Friedkin and Blatty). Pertinent: "Something beyond comprehension is happening to a little girl on this street, in this house." †

> † Sixteen years later, this would get updated to "Strange things are afoot at the Circle K" (*Bill & Ted's Excellent Adventure.*)

7. Novelist and Nobel Laureate Claude Simon (1913–2005): "I cannot write my novels other than by constantly defining the different positions that the narrator or narrators occupy in space (field of vision, distance, mobility in relation to the scene described—or, if you prefer, in another vocabulary: camera angle. Close-up, medium shot, motionless shot, etc.)."

8. The first time Billy Loomis† asks this in *Scream*, indirectly (the "edited for television" line), his girlfriend Sidney Prescott's suggestive answer is to ask back if he would "settle for a PG-13 relationship." Once the corn syrup‡ starts flying, however, they're not as sentimental: "But this is not a movie," Sidney tells him; his answer is "Yes it is, Sidney. It's all one big movie."

> † No direct relation either to the Sam Loomis of *Halloween* or to the Sam Loomis of *Psycho* or to the (teenage) Sam Loomis of 1989's *Night Visitor*, a.k.a. *Never Cry Devil*.
> ‡ About this "corn syrup," or whatever proprietary mix different directors and special-effects artists use to simulate human blood, legendary effects guru Tom Savini would say he has "way too much movie blood on [his] hands."[A]

>> A. From the foreword to 1992's *Still Dead*, a zombie anthology based in Romero's world of, as they're called in *Land of the Dead*, "stenches."

9. As is *The Story of Us* (1999): Rob Reiner's situational comedy/date movie starring Bruce Willis and Michelle Pfeiffer, which James Berardinelli calls "*When Harry Met Sally* 15 Years Later."†

> † From 1989, with Billy Crystal and Meg Ryan, the first of a string of romantic comedies for each, culminating, respectively, in *Forget Paris*[A] (1995) and *Sleepless in Seattle* (1993), each of which consciously riff on the ghosts of romantic comedies past (i.e., respectively, *An American in Paris*[B] [1951] and *An Affair to Remember* [1957]).

>> A. Rick's goal in *Casablanca* (1942).
>> B. Not to be confused with *An American Werewolf in Paris* (1997), the seemingly logical sequel to John Landis's *An American Werewolf in London*.

10. Bill Raisch, from the 1963–1967 series *The Fugitive* (wrapped up into a feature film for Harrison Ford in 1993).

That "Goddammit, Daddy!" in this excerpt, know where it's from? Think Meat Loaf. I was. Or, I always am. Anyway, I'm very proud of this whole novel. One of the few I can really say that about. Not all the footnotes necessarily—when I go back for another edition, some of that's going to change, is going to acquire new and better edges—but, aside from The Bird is Gone, this one comes closest on the page to how it was in my head. I didn't have to compromise, I mean. Any failures, they're just failures of talent, of technique, of indulgence. Which can be serious, don't get me wrong, and I'm no less susceptible to them than the next dude. But sometimes you get lucky too. With this novel, I think I got lucky. But, talking footnotes, and this excerpt in particular, I so love saying mouth-filling stuff like "logical sequel." I'll spin a whole chapter just to stage something like that, and then not be embarrassed by having done that at all. And, going into this scene, I really had no idea what was going to happen. Could Skopek take a demon? I kind of secretly hoped so. And, the Swedenborg stuff in here—first, it was so hard not to make a Borg joke. But I think I managed to resist; it wasn't futile, this time out. And, for some stupid reason I knew all about the dude. Even now, I still do. Like, I'm always looking at a thing and thinking, "What would Swedenborg think of that?" I can't imagine how or why he's in my head so constantly. The university I was at for Demon Theory, though, lo and be-something, they had this whole special Swedenborg library. I found it when I was working in book cataloging there one summer, between teaching, because I was always fabulously broke. So one lunch, I crept up there, like I was climbing the mountain to enlightenment. Only, the dude up there, this philosophy professor I'd had a few years back, getting my undergrad degree, he most definitely saw me, asked what I was up to. I told him I was just looking around. He said that was fine, I could do that; this was a library after all. Except, then, he stood right behind me everywhere I went, like making sure I didn't slide a book into my sleeve. Finally I nodded thanks, sulked back down to the third floor, to the place in the stacks I usually tried to sit to eat my can of pork and beans (PN1997, where all the BFI series were), and I didn't know anything more about Swedenborg than I did before, and I never went back. Still, though, he refuses to go away from my head. I'm probably going to need an exorcism soon, just to think my own thoughts for a few minutes. It would be particularly nice, I suspect.

BOYS WITH GUITARS

TRIX ARE FOR everybody, Lindy decides.

It's her fourth night stocking cereals.

It's meant to be punishment, either a temporary demotion from working the register or a toe-in-the-dark-waters-of-the-vampire shift—her decision.

The first couple of nights are bleary, and she can't wait to get back to the front of the store. To daylight. To people.

The third night, though, she does like all the other stockers, and plugs into her music. Pretty soon she's pretty sure she's discovered the next Olympic sport: running down aisle 14 with an armful of Cheerios and closing her eyes and just sliding on the slick floor.

Until Vic, the assistant manager, calls her in, shows her the video of what he calls her antics.

On the fourth night, then, and because she needs this job, she listens to music she doesn't really like, and imagines her shoelaces are tied together. And also that she's a robot in some bleak future—no, she's a human in that bleak future, but is having to pretend she's a robot.

Vic won't be able to see it on the recording, but she's making the machine noises in her throat. Without moving her lips.

And, because this particular future is so bleak, she's crying on the inside.

The next thing she gets in trouble for is alphabetizing the cereals, from Apple Jacks to Wheaties.

Vic tells her he doesn't want to be the bad guy here.

It's nighttime for Lindy when he's saying this. Two in the afternoon. Her eyes keep wanting to twitch into REM, take her to a better place.

On Vic's security monitor, she sees Adam, dragging his fingers through the frost in Dairy.

Lindy licks her lips for control. She looks away. Back to the reason she's working nights now: Adam coming through her register last week, trying to make a joke about how this is awkward.

What he was buying were condoms.

Lindy ran their barcode through her nest of red lasers, then, her arm almost moving without her, dragged them back through. And again. And once more.

By the time she was done, Adam owed her one hundred fourteen dollars and seventy-six cents.

It wasn't nearly enough.

"I'm sorry," Lindy says to Vic, and he just keeps staring at her, like he's waiting for his telepathy to tune her in.

Don't smile, she tells herself.

You need this job, girl.

For Lindy's one-week anniversary, Camille swipes her way through the trucker door in back, finds Lindy in the break room.

"Coming back to the land of the living anytime soon?" she asks, stretching a curl of her more-than-perfect hair out to study it for split ends that aren't going to be there.

Lindy and Camille started at Piggly Wiggly together the summer after graduation, but it was Camille who lucked onto the absolute right shampoo and conditioner. Lindy's tried them all too, working her way down the shelf just the same, but, like the bottles say, results have definitely varied.

Her hair this week is mostly blond, with leftover blue streaks from the breakup with Adam.

"Remember Link?" she says to Camille.

Camille tracks a shuffler past the break-room door.

"Fifth grade, babygirl," Camille says, shrugging, letting her strand of hair spring back into place.

Link was their shared crush, in elementary. He was perfect: valiant, brave, always willing. So wide-eyed. All they would have to do is keep some jars around for him to kick. From the couch in Lindy's basement, they could see into forever, with him. He even measured his life in hearts, just like Camille and Lindy.

"I think he poisoned us," Lindy says. "Me anyway."

"I didn't go to the concert," Camille says.

Adam's band. Because it's Saturday night.

She thinks not saying his name is not saying his name.

"You could have," Lindy says. "They're good."

"If you're into that sort of thing," Camille says, and she'd pop a bubble of gum for punctuation if she was chewing any.

"He was up here again the other day," Lindy says, studying the refrigerator now.

"I know," Camille says, kind of eeking her eyes away from contact.

Like that's ever actually worked.

"What?" Lindy asks.

"He might have left a note," Camille says, bringing her face back around, to gauge Lindy's reaction.

"Well?"

"I burned it. And then I fed it to a rat."

"What did it say?"

"The rat? It committed suicide. It had a little noose and everything. There was a big rat funeral back in Produce. Even Marilyn cried."

Lindy has to look away to smile. Marilyn's too biker to even brush her teeth.

"You deserve better," Camille says. "He's no Richard Gere. He's not an officer or a gentlemen. He's barely even human, got it?"

"I'm still Debra Winger here though," Lindy says, trying to lift her eyebrows whimsically enough to make it into a joke.

In the movie, Richard Gere waltzes into the assembly line, picks Debra Winger up and carries her out, into another life.

All her coworkers clap and throw their hats.

Camille says, "You've just got to, to—"

"Pick somebody better? In this town? Who's left now, Camie? Does Teegan have a twin brother I don't know about?"

Teegan, Camille's boyfriend since junior year.

"I'll ask," Camille says.

Lindy laughs, or tries to, and says, "I'm not coming back. To days. I like the vampire shift."

"Anybody cute at four in the morning?" Camille asks, faking a look around.

"Vampires and freshmen," Lindy says. "But, you know. Beggars can't be picky."

"You can be picky."

"I stock Honeycomb and Grape-Nuts."

"You just have to pick better. Like, the opposite of whatever—whatever criteria you've been using."

"Like, breathing, you mean? Someone who breathes, and maybe plays guitar?"

"What's your thing with guitars?"

"It's not guitars."

"Well it's not clarinets."

"I don't know."

"Lie."

"Okay. Adam—when you have a guitar, it's like . . . he wore it like a life jacket, right? No, like a jet pack. He always knew he was just starting in Henderson. But he was going somewhere else."

"And the guitar was going to take him?"

"It's stupid, I know."

"I get it. Really. But what you're missing is that you're falling for boys with guitars because you—you understand them, like."

"What?"

"What's your guitar, stocker girl?"

Lindy looks around, processing. Finally she says, "Boys?"

"And do you see anything wrong with that?"

"I just want one who—"

"Who isn't Adam," Camille completes. "I get that too. Believe me. I even got it before the fact. What you need to get is that he's out there somewhere, this guy. The one for you." She sits back to let it settle. "But what's the rush? You're twenty-one years old."

"And there's sixteen hundred people in this town. We graduated with twenty-five of them. Twelve of them are boys. I've dated ten of them."

"Eleven. Jeremy?"

"Oh, yeah. Did he have a guitar or a motorcycle?"

"He was a sleazeball. With a guitar."

"They all are. Except Teegan."

"Except Teegan."

At which point Camille looks up to the doorway, tightens her lips in a way imperceptible to anyone but Lindy.

"Fifteen minutes?" Vic says from the hall.

He's in a Kermit the Frog shirt and grey slacks. Just keeping the night shift honest.

"Back to the assembly line," Lindy says, wowing her eyes out, then pushes back from the table, gets her Golden Grahams face back on. Her Frosted Flakes face.

Robots don't care.

Because the music piping into her ears is less than insipid—it was the word on her mother's calendar at dinner, before her shift started—Lindy stocks and thinks, thinks and stocks.

Where it strands her is in the middle of the aisle, her arms full of Kix.

The camera. She's looking at the camera.

There's not enough hours in his shift for Vic to watch all the night-shift feeds. Not even with the screen split into quarters. Not taking into account all the customers and schedules and meat-department emergencies he always has to juggle and solve.

"You're watching me," Lindy says, and has to bite her lip to keep from smiling.

Vic's story is he was a senior when she and Camille were in tenth grade.

He got married straight out of high school, and that lasted maybe two years, because Melissa Banks was still Melissa Banks, even after the big name-change ordeal. Now he's married to the Piggly Wiggly, is sharing custody of his two little girls.

Because Lindy babysat them in high school some, one of her prior employers on her application had been Vic.

What had Camille said? Something about new criteria?

No: do the opposite.

Because the usual hasn't worked so far. The usual hasn't even come close to working.

Two years isn't that big a gap, Lindy tells herself. And he probably only wears those grey slacks because of store policy, not by choice. And so what if Melissa Banks had had her claws in him? If it was Adam who knocked up the homecoming queen, he would have been goner than gone, times two. Condoms were the only reason he still even lived in Henderson. Vic had tried with Melissa though. That had to speak well of him. Never mind the Tercel he parked back by Recycling. Tercels are sensible, and he has to be sensible now, with kids. And all these antics of Lindy's, they'll make a good story someday. If there is a someday. And that Kermit shirt was on the road to cute anyway.

This is how it always starts, right?

In a small town, you don't find new guys, you rediscover old ones.

When Lindy stacks the Kix onto their shelf, she pretends she's an ancient priestess, feeding these boxes into a huge mouth. That she's laying them on this giant, patient tongue, and they're just rolling back into the darkness. That if she doesn't do this, the floor will buckle, the ceiling crumble, the world collapse.

For the good of all, she feeds the monster, scuffles back to her pallet each time there's a grumble in the store. Everybody else thinks it's forklifts back on the dock. Everybody else is wrong.

The monster's full long before any respectable monster should be though.

Lindy stumbles on, into the dead hours of her shift, using the yardstick to get all her boxes lined up, just like she was taught. Double-checking the granola bars nobody buys, the chips the world can't live without, the sauces and dips that are all the same, just in different jars.

When a little brown mouse darts out for a crumb, gets stranded out in the aisle for all the world to see, Lindy steps between it and the camera, whispers to it, *hurry, hurry.*

In reward for that good deed, she clicks into some of her music, and the rhythm works its way into aisle 14. Like she's dancing with the cereal.

It ends with her reshelving all the boxes into layers.

Alphabets are at the back of the shelf, followed by Special K (the "K" is the surname), then it's Rice Krispies, and so on, about eight deep, with Raisin Bran facing out even though it's slightly out of order. But there's a reason. It's because if the old people have to reach to the back of the shelf, they're going to hurt themselves.

She's still awake at lunch when Vic calls her in.

For maybe thirty seconds he just creaks his chair back and forth, a pencil in his skinny fingers. He studies her over it.

"It's like you want to come in here," he finally says, tilting his head over at the end to indicate it's her turn now. He's ready for her big explanation. He's ready for the excuse she's got in her hip pocket.

"We should take the girls for ice cream," she says.

Vic's chair stops creaking.

"What are they, first grade, and kindergarten?" Lindy adds.

Her hair's Camille's color, now: Honeywood.

Just don't touch it, she reminds herself.

Unlike Camille's, hers is a helmet. A safe could fall on her head, bounce off. A colony of roaches could spend a nuclear winter under there. Their very own biodome. All she needs to complete the look is some cat-eye glasses. Some prim lipstick.

"They do ask about you," Vic finally says, not committing to this line of inquiry yet.

"It'll be fun."

He stares at her and stares at her, his assistant-manager eyes probing every angle of this.

"There's—the store has . . . policy."

"Tomorrow afternoon? We can pick them up from school."

Vic's pencil doesn't break like it would in a movie, but how can he say no here, really?

Camille straightarms Lindy back into a pallet about this. Hard.

"But it's the opposite," Lindy says, the back of her shirt sticking to the shrink-wrap. "Isn't that supposed to be good? If everything I do is stupid, then the other way's got to be smart, right?"

"You're not putting this on me," Camille says.

"I just want to see the girls."

"You're rebounding," Camille tells her. "This isn't a good bounce either. Your boss, Lindy? Seriously?"

"Our boss. And it's not even a date."

"Has this kind of relationship ever ended well in the history of anything?"

"Have any of my others?"

"Is it because he has kids? Is that your new criteria?"

"We used to write his name in our notebooks. Remember?"

"And he asked me to the dance freshman year. I was there, Lindy."

"Are you still . . . saving him? In case Teegan—?"

"I told him no then."

"Because he was two years older. Your dad made you. And you hated him for it. He was ruining your life."

"He was right, Lindy. I was fifteen years old."

"He was only right because you ended up going to the dance with Teegan."

Camille shakes her head, exasperated. "This isn't about me. You. And—and you want to skip straight from now to being a stepmom? Seriously?"

"It's just a date," Lindy says.

"That's not a date," Camille adds. "Listen, he's not looking for a month or two of fun, a romp in the hay. He's trying on mothers to his girls."

"I would have to deal with Melissa, wouldn't I?"

"Are you a mom, Lindy?"

Lindy can't answer. There isn't an answer.

"I can't—" Camille finally says, brushing the idea of this away like spider webs. "This isn't real. I need to wake up."

"You're afraid I'll pass you at last, aren't you?" Lindy says then. "You got the good boyfriend first, you're supposed to get married first. Have kids first."

"It's not like that."

"Then what? You think he's going to play favorites, give me the good shifts?"

"I don't care about shifts. I care about you. Can't you see that? What do you need? What can I do to keep you from—just tell me, I'm on it."

"Nothing," Lindy says. "You don't always have to be saving me."

"Somebody's got to."

"I can save myself, Camie."

"I know. Great track record."

Lindy reaches across, for a twist of Camille's hair. "We can't all be perfect," she says.

"So you cash it all in at twenty-freaking-one?" Camille says, guiding Lindy's hand away.

"Twenty-one in this town, that's like, thirty-six, at least."

Camille shakes her head. It's something like a laugh, just without the smile part. "I'll be here, okay?" she says. "After? Like always."

"Thanks for the confidence," Lindy says, and turns, cuts the shrink-wrap off all at once, and loud. "It nice up there on Fairy Tale Hill, with your Prince Charming? Do we all look like, what, ants—no, peasant ants to you and him?"

"It's pheasants, I think."

"Pheasants?"

"You don't look like a pheasant."

"Thank you?"

"And I'm not going to feel guilty for Teegan."

It's not their first fight since second grade, but it's their first one in a while, where they're not working registers side-by-side, can't make eyes about the sheep and cows coming through their lanes.

In the morning, the cereal aisle matches the diagram perfectly.

Lindy comes in at three. Because Vic always leaves at three-fifteen. School's out at three-thirty.

He sees her and his eyes are minnows in his head.

Good, Lindy tells herself, and shops, just like a normal customer.

Walking aisle 14 in the daytime, running her fingertips along the front of the cereal boxes, she feels like an interloper. Like everybody's going to see her, start pointing and shrieking.

She retreats through the perv-lands of Dairy to the grandma's house smell of Breads, then steps over to the endless hair bands of Beauty.

Teegan's there.

He's still got his kneepads on, from his uncle's sometimes carpet business. Maybe it's lunch for him. Or five o'clock. Or it doesn't matter.

What he's buying are scissors.

Not utility ones, like from aisle 4, but stylist ones, with the extra little finger rest on back, like a comma. Like a raised eyebrow. He holds them up and snips them as far as the packaging will allow.

Lindy gulps a mental gulp and two-steps neatly to the break in the aisle, turns her back and fades into Shampoos, already breathing hard, her eyes wide like a scream.

Anything but scissors.

Every pair she and Lindy scan for a guy shopper, they're always sure to catch each other's eyes about it. Because of Trina, the Dairy Queen.

After Trina flunked out of cosmetology school, she hired on making dip cones. But she's still a stylist at heart. All the high-school boys, and their dads besides, know that she'll cut hair for free in her kitchen after her shift. Just for practice.

Except, all the brushing, both of hair and of her against arms, across faces, on backs of necks, legend has it that it leads elsewhere every time.

And all she ever asks for is a new pair of scissors. Like notches in a bed-post, scratches on a lipstick case.

Worse, she can't cut bangs straight to save her life.

It's the famous dead giveaway.

At least twice, Lindy and Camille have seen seniors in the Piggly Wiggly parking lot, straightening each other's hair. So their girlfriends won't know.

"No no no," Lindy says to herself, trying to focus on a row of black scrunchies.

And then he's behind her. Teegan.

"Shouldn't you be asleep?" he says, cuffing her on the shoulder like he always does. Like she's his little brother.

"Girl emergency," Lindy says, not meeting his eyes, just tilting her head vaguely down-aisle.

It turns Teegan into a ninja. One poof of smoke and he's gone.

It's for the best.

Except—"She won't believe me," Lindy says, out loud. As if hearing it will convince her.

Isn't she fighting with Camille? Of course she would try to knock Teegan off his pedestal.

It would be salt on their slug of a friendship. The silver bullet in the werewolf of their long and complicated history together. The kryptonite—

"You're stalling," Lindy says, louder this time, in what she considers her mom voice.

She grabs the closest hair band and stalks out into the open, her eyes fierce, her boots so made for walking.

Teegan's at her old register, two in from the door.

He hasn't done it yet. She saw him for a reason. Maybe she can't save her own love life, but she can save Camille's anyway. Better one of them gets to live the fairy tale than neither, right? Hadn't they made some kind of promise like that in fifth grade, about what if they met Link, and there was only one of him?

If they didn't, they should have. But Lindy's pretty sure they did.

She wishes she had got a box of pads now. Just to scooch them up the belt, closer to Teegan's gross scissors.

Instead, she fumbles the hair band onto the ground in front of her, then steps on it.

Because of the check-out boy.

Her replacement.

Teegan's good looking, Lindy will give Camille that—your standard working-class quarterback, shaggy hair and tight jeans, those eyes—but this check-out boy is something else altogether. Like a mannequin come to life.

"You're not from around here," Lindy says.

Apparently out loud.

For a solid five count, the only sound is the store CD, shuffling down at them. The one Lindy had lobbied for, offered to burn.

"So how'd you break it?" Teegan finally says, palming the scissors into his far pocket. Lindy registers it distantly, as if in a dream. Like it's somebody else clocking his movements. Recording them for later.

The check-out boy shrugs, his crutches now apparent.

Of course.

Piggly Wiggly is old-school sexist: guys cut meat or work in the coolers, and girls work up front, to put a pretty face on the store.

Unless the guy is banged up. Unless he has a prettier face than any of the girls.

The women of Henderson are going to be coming in for single items this summer, Lindy knows. Spreading their shopping out over the week.

Zen.

That's actually the name on his name tag. Zen.

Lindy looks away, just to prove she can. At some level of reality she hears him telling Teegan he wouldn't believe it if he told him, how he messed his knee up, and then, years before she's ready and at least one lifetime too late, the UPC of Lindy's hair band is crossing the red lasers.

"Umm . . ." Zen says, looking from the cracked hair band to Lindy's hair, maybe trying to imagine the two of them together. See if they match.

We do, Lindy says, with her eyes.

"You're not supposed to comment on the content of shoppers' items," she hears herself recite. It's from the handbook.

Zen flashes his killer eyes up to her, holds them, holds them, then nods, keys his drawer open.

"This must be yours," he says.

It's the photo-booth snapshots she used to keep under the hundreds, stashed with the stamps when her shift was over. Her and Adam, goofing in black and white.

"Not anymore," she says, and Zen bites his lower lip in crookedly, deposits the strip into the trash at his knees.

"What did you do?" Lindy says, about the crutches.

"Kind of a long story," Zen says, and they both look up when his manager light glows on.

It's Vic, standing in the lane of aisle 1, reaching through.

The way he's looking past Zen, to Lindy, at Lindy, she knows she's working nights forever now. That her aisle 14 tryout is going to graduate to Dry Goods, to a whole swath of aisles. And her antics aren't going to be antics anymore, but infractions.

"You need manager approval for her to use her store discount," Vic says, clicking the button again, to turn the light off. "We went through this, didn't we?"

"It's broke," Zen says, holding the hair band up to show, doing his shoulders to put a question mark at the end of it.

Vic takes it, huffs past, to Beauty.

"He always like this?" Zen says to Lindy.

"Your knee?" she says.

"Yeah," Zen says, leaning back on his crutches, looking out the front windows to the parking lot. To Henderson. "I was supposed to be in Puerto Rico until July. My parents retired here last year. Guess I'm local now? I mean, for the summer."

"You're not telling me on purpose," Lindy says.

He smiles a shy smile. A caught smile.

"Where do people go around here to tell long, complicated, boring stories?" he says, his eyes coming up to her at exactly the right time in her life.

Because she doesn't trust her voice, Lindy reaches over into his space, to feed a few inches of receipt paper up. She rips it off, snags a pen from the coffee cup, and tells him the when, the where. And her name, her number.

"Tonight," he says, studying the paper, and they both look up when the belt hums on.

A new hair band is coming up.

Behind it, Vic, his lips firm, his eyes not so much betrayed as just bored with this scene, this inevitability.

When there's enough space behind the hair band that Zen won't confuse his purchase with Lindy's, Vic hauls a gallon bucket of generic vanilla ice cream up.

"I promised them," he says, right to Lindy, and reaches across, to key in his authorization, for the fourteen cents Lindy's getting off the headband.

It's exactly then that Adam's band's radio song leaks down from the speakers. From the CD Lindy burned, once upon a time.

Zen rings her up, shakes his head in amusement, and, giving her change, says a word under his breath about the track.

"Excuse me?" Lindy says.

He shakes his head no, nothing.

"No, what?" Lindy says.

"Insipid," he says, as if embarrassed to know the word, then scans Vic's ice cream across.

"Life's full of surprises," Lindy says, and for once she's not talking about cereal.

Lindy's waiting by the time clock when Camille slumps in for her five o'clock shift.

Her eyes go wary when she sees Lindy.

"This is an ambush, yes," Lindy says, and wheels Camille into the dead space behind Dairy. It always smells like pot. "Why didn't you tell me about him?" Lindy says.

It takes Camille a stare or two into the past to catch up with Lindy. It makes her shake her head, tongue her lower lip out.

"Zen," she says.

"Zap," Lindy says, finger shooting her.

"I was going to," Camille says. "But . . . he plays guitar, you know? I saw the case in the back of his car."

Lindy narrows her eyes, trying to track Camille's logic. "You really don't want me to be happy, do you?"

"He also—he, well—"

Lindy finishes it: "He asked you what you were doing after work."

"He meant *who*. He meant *him*."

"What do you expect?" Lindy says, fluffing Camille's hair out. "You said no, and now he's moving on. How is this different from every other one of my boyfriends?"

"So . . . does this mean you and Vic?"

"It means every guy asks you out first. And no on Vic. It kind of fell through. You were right. Happy now?"

"Let's just move to another town," Camille says. "Teegan'll come visit on weekends. You and me though. We can start all over. Fresh."

"And I can end up right where I already am."

"Lin."

Lindy shakes her head no. "Not so sure you'd want Teegan to come visit anyway," she says.

"What do you mean?"

"Nothing. Ask Trina."

Camille's eyes go from zero to boiling in a blink.

"Ask him," Lindy says, like a dare.

"I don't have to," Camille says.

"Then you're just as dumb as me."

Before Camille can come back with anything, Vic comes across the PA, using his usual code to get Marilyn back to Meats.

"Blood in the cheese again," Lindy says. Obviously.

"I don't know what you think you know," Camille says.

"I know I'm meeting Zen tonight," Lindy says. "Might even go to the Dairy Queen. I'll let you know if I see anybody I . . . recognize."

Camille shakes her head in disgust, brushes past Lindy to the time clock.

Her card's halfway in the slot when she stops, burns her eyes back to Lindy.

"I hate you sometimes," she says, and doesn't click her card, just racks it, storms out the trucker door.

"Line starts here," Lindy says, and, after putting Camille's card in the right place, she drifts around behind Produce, comes out in Meats.

Marilyn's sitting with her back to the cabinet, her arms bloody to the elbow, her hair double-netted since the complaints.

Her story is that she stabbed her last husband with a broken pool stick. It didn't kill him. By the time the police showed up, there were nine other stabs that weren't going to kill him either.

What she's hiding from is the meat situation. The cheese situation. The problem is they're in cases right beside each other, and share a gutter, a drain. It usually doesn't matter, is just for frost melting off. But sometimes a roast pops its wrap, bleeds out into that shared gutter, and nobody wants to reach across an open vein to buy a quarter-pound of Swiss.

At Marilyn's counter, somebody's ringing the bell so, so politely.

Marilyn chuckles, her great shoulders rising and falling.

"Heard you and Pretty Girl going at it," Marilyn says.

Lindy sits down beside her.

"My name's Lindy," she says.

"David Bowie," Marilyn corrects.

It's their usual routine.

"Do you believe in love at first sight?" Lindy asks, apropos very little.

"It's the only kind," Marilyn says, right in stride.

"What do you mean it's the only kind?"

"Get it while you can," Marilyn says, clapping Lindy on the thigh, leaving a bloody handprint. "It won't last. Never does."

"What about fairy tales?"

"Disney kind or the real ones?" Marilyn asks. "Real or fake?"

"You ever thought about working the suicide hotline?" Lindy asks. "I mean, as a form of population control."

"You didn't come here for advice," Marilyn says, leaning around to start the long process of standing.

"I don't know why I come here," Lindy says, and stands in time to help Marilyn the rest of the way up.

"You're the only one can do it," Marilyn says, and nods to the meat display.

"The only one who will," Lindy corrects, and rolls her sleeve to reach all the way up to the front of display, to wiggle the make-do divider back into place, keep the blood out of the cheese gutter.

"You ever been in love?" Lindy asks, taking the back off the case.

"Sure," Marilyn says. "Had an outhouse seat break on me once too, at a Doobie Brothers concert." She waits to deliver the punch line until Lindy looks around: "At least there was some good music, then."

Lindy tries to laugh, closes her eyes, and forces her arm past the hams, past the turkey loaf, imagines she's reaching for a magic key.

She is.

Three days later, she's digging the secret treasure from a box of Cocoa Puffs.

Because she's cuckoo, yes.

For Zen.

When he was a kid, he collected all the treasures, submitted box tops, won a trip to Disneyland for his family.

And now Lindy works in cereals.

It's kind of perfect.

The treasure is a magnifying glass with a red tint.

With it, she can find the secret path on the back of the box.

Her plan is to use it on Zen's knee, at lunch, before his shift. To finally get the true story.

One of the explanations he's told her so far he's is that when he was flying out to see his parents, somebody'd left an alligator in the luggage bin, and things got all action hero after that, and, because of some obscure FAA law, he was technically an air marshal now.

Next it was that a truck blew through a crosswalk, and he felt it coming more than saw it, was able to stop mid-stride, so the truck's bumper just knicked his knee, spun him back onto the sidewalk, and somehow his coffee didn't even spill. Lindy was hanging on every word.

After that—night two, parked out by the water tower, her favorite place— it was that he'd blown it out in high school, never got it fixed right, but it was finally time. Pretty soon he isn't going to be on his parents' health insurance.

Then there was the giant-robot version, told while looking into the distance, his voice as flat and regretful as the ground at the cemetery.

Then it was a mis-thrown boomerang at the park, then a spilled drink at the movies, then the mosh pit at a concert, him trying to help a pink-haired girl passed out at everybody's feet.

This can go on forever, Lindy knows. That's not a bad thing.

And he does play guitar, Camille was right about that, but he's good. Not as technical and fast as Adam. More like he's just finding the notes by sound, just picking them from memory, never sure if this chord is matching up exactly or not. Simon and Garfunkel. Eagles' greatest hits, volume one.

It's like Lindy fell asleep one night, designed him in a dream.

She wants to tell Camille that wasn't a guitar case in the back of his car, it was a wooden shield. Except they're still in the glare stage of things. Camille's eyes always leaking apology. Lindy always pretending to just be walking through.

Nights are better anyway. Days are stupid. She doesn't know why she ever worked days.

And Camille was lying anyway. About moving to some other town, starting over.

You don't just do that. If you're still you, then everybody else is going to fall into their roles as well.

By the time Lindy has all the magnifying glasses, eight boxes of Cocoa Puffs have been opened. But just from the bottom.

She makes like a ghost, sneaks up to Vic's office.

Because taking the roll of Scotch tape from his dispenser would be too obvious, she snakes the whole heavy thing.

On the other side of the pallet, where the camera can't see, she tapes the bottom of the boxes shut.

Good as new. And not even unhygienic. It's not like she's sneaking a handful from the bags of cereal. Just the toys.

Except then she thinks about some little second grader out there, eating an extra bowl just so she can get to the bottom of the box before Big Brother.

"Consciences suck," Lindy says, and steps over to the toy aisle.

This will be better.

She has to use the box cutter to cut the Scotch tape, and then layer more tape on, and the action figures don't fit just absolutely perfect, but it's pretty good.

Until Camille calls at ten in the morning.

"He wants to see you," she says, her voice giving nothing away.

"Vic? This about the ice cream?"

"You stock Dairy now?"

"You make his calls for him now?"

"I don't know—no."

"Then this isn't a real conversation."

"Neither's one o'clock."

"He's really messing with my beauty sleep."

"Listen, I've got customers."

"He there then? You know who?"

"That's not even his real name."

"Camille."

"I don't know. Yes."

And Lindy knows Zen isn't his real name. It's Zane. But his little brother couldn't say it, and that's how things happen in the real world.

Zen and Lindy. Lindy and Zen. Zendy and Lin.

People are going to be introducing them wrong forever.

Lindy smiles, pours a handful of cereal.

It's Shredded Wheat, one of the boxes the forklift tore.

Zen's favorite.

This week the forklift's already tore three boxes of it.

The door by the dock is supposed to be for truckers only, but Lindy might miss him, sneaking in like that.

Is this what love feels like? Parking farther away than you have to? Caring what your makeup looks like when you're just going in to get chewed out by your boss?

Maybe, Lindy tells herself. Probably.

Definitely.

He's not there though.

Lindy makes eyes to Camille about it, and Camille just stares at her, trying to do her Disappointment Eyes.

Lindy gives her back some Jealous Much? eyes.

"See me after," Camille says.

"So's his hair . . . ?" Lindy says, snipping her fingers up, about Teegan and Trina.

"You've got it all wrong," Camille tells her.

"Said the blind girl."

"To the blinder girl."

Lindy doesn't let this slow her down.

Thirty seconds later she's standing in the metal doorframe of Vic's office.

He crosses a *t*, dots an *i*, and finally looks up to her.

"What'd I do now?" Lindy says.

"Sit," Vic tells her.

"Listen," Lindy starts, winding up the big speech she's got planned, but Vic shakes his head no.

"This is about cereal," he says.

"You've come to the right place," Lindy says, shrugging.

Vic sets an action figure down by his nameplate.

It's a generic superhero. A brightly colored superhero from Toys, because those seemed better, but 'generic' so it wouldn't be stealing as much from the store.

Lindy tries to keep her face blank.

"Post is quite generous with their prizes, wouldn't you say?" Vic says. "But Karoline had other . . . expectations."

Karoline, his youngest daughter.

"I didn't know she—"

Vic interrupts her by just shaking his head. "And I take it the, the original merchandise, the intended merchandise, it's still on the premises?"

Lindy feels her heart beating down.

"Because otherwise, of course, their removal would constitute stealing from Piggly Wiggly."

"I was still going to go with, the other day," Lindy says. "You left before I could tell you."

"I left first when I was in line behind you?" Vic says.

"Want me to go get the magnifying glass thingies?" Lindy says, pushing up from the chair. "I was just trying to, you know. Improve. Make it more like a real treasure."

"I'm not sure what other department I can put you in," Vic says. "You like Marilyn, don't you? The store will pay for you to take the course for meat cutting. It's just an afternoon. It might be your calling."

Because she can't trust her voice anymore, Lindy just grins as pleasantly as possible, makes her exit.

She doesn't breathe until she's out on the floor.

"If," she says out loud, ignoring the shopper looking up to her for the next part: if Zen is back from lunch; if he still has those magnifying glasses in the cupholder of his dad's car; if Vic will still accept them, out of their plastic.

Lindy touches cans all the way up the vegetable aisle, for luck.

It doesn't work.

Camille's line is three deep. Meaning there's just one register open.

"Yes?" Camille says, swiping a six-pack of Jell-O cups.

"Where is he?" Lindy says.

"You don't want to know," Camille says.

"Camie."

Camille swipes a *People* magazine, a pack of batteries, then a pair of blister-packed Barbie walkie-talkies.

"Okay then," she says, keeping the walkie-talkies instead of bagging them. "You can cover?"

"What?" Lindy says, but steps in when Camille abandons her register.

You never forget.

345

Behind her, Camille is wrestling with the walkie-talkies' blister-pack, taking a two-pack of AAs from the rack above the gum.

Lindy thumbs her box cutter from her pocket—it's a part of her now—and Camille slices through the plastic, takes a broccoli rubber band from Lindy's old register, makes it so one of the walkie-talkies has its speaker right up against the microphone Lindy used to have to talk into for both of them, as Camille's has something crusty on it that looks like a dried loogey, and probably is.

With an industrial-strength hair clip from her own hair, she keys Lindy's old microphone open.

The music sucks back into the speakers, is replaced by the hiss of Camille not saying anything into her walkie-talkie.

"I don't—" Lindy says, totaling the shopper out.

Camille doesn't answer, just stalks back, down Coffee and Tea.

Ten seconds later, the double doors at back open, shut.

"Here," Lindy says, on autopilot with the shopper. The shopper takes the receipt, her eyes peeling down it for the walkie-talkies that shouldn't be there, that's she's definitely going to be talking to somebody about, and then the pink walkie-talkie one lane over crackles into the open microphone.

What comes down from the ceiling is guitar. Acoustic guitar.

Zen.

Lindy smiles, bites on corner of her lips.

He's back on the dock practicing. For her, for Lindy. Her favorite song, somehow.

She looks up to the ceiling to let it wash over her, and the song stops that kind of stop that means fingers on the strings, keeping them still.

"No, man, you've got to . . . here," a voice not Zen's says, around what Lindy knows is the stub of a Marlboro Red.

Adam.

"She really loves it if you—" Adam says, and the walkie-talkie clicks off.

Lindy shakes her head no, looks to the shopper in front of her.

"What, dear?" the shopper-lady says, but Lindy can't even have words. There aren't any words.

She coughs a laugh out, can feel her eyes heating up, her throat filling with tears.

Moving like a zombie, she feels her way around to the walkie-talkie, hits the button.

"I hate you," she says into it, then sets it down so gently, turns, walks out the doors.

That the door opens for her is the only confirmation she has anymore that she's human. That she's still in this world.

But she doesn't want to be.

Before her shift starts that night, Lindy sneaks back into the stainless-steel future of Meats.

And that's if she's lucky. If she offers to pay for eight boxes of Cocoa Puffs. If she can keep from spontaneously confessing to four boxes of Shredded Wheat.

The hairnet dispenser is by the door.

Shaking her head no the whole time, Lindy peels one out, tucks her hair up into it, sees herself reflected on every surface in the room.

"So?" she says back to them all.

So she's Marilyn, thirty years ago. Marilyn's her, plus half a lifetime.

Maybe this is how it happens, right?

Lindy reaches shoulder-deep into the display case, her fingers stabbing into the gutter, feeling to make sure the divider's in place. Police your area; it's right there in the handbook.

"Midnight snack?" Marilyn says, startling Lindy so hard she has to laugh.

"What are you doing up here?" Lindy says, standing, wiping off the front of her shirt.

"Where am I going to be?" Marilyn says.

In her hand, not quite hidden along her right leg in spite of her efforts, is a straightened-out coat hanger, with a little magnet-dart from Toys taped to the end of it.

Because her arm's too biker to fit all the way up to the gutter at the front of the display.

She's been the one messing the divider up. The whole time.

Lindy pretends not to be figuring this out.

"Bad design," she says. "Bet it'll mess up tomorrow."

"Probably," Marilyn says. "Quiet at night, isn't it?"

"Is the class gross?" Lindy asks. "To learn to cut?"

"You won't eat hamburgers anymore," Marilyn tells her.

Lindy shrugs, looks out over the floor as if studying this future without hamburgers.

"I like cereal anyway," she says.

"Good girl," Marilyn says, and Lindy nods, salutes Marilyn good-bye. Walking back through the dock to clock in and then down the long hall to the floor, she tries to imagine that the hydraulic hiss of the pallet jacks are lava. That she's a giant, that she's stepping through the dinosaur past. That she can go that far back.

But she's just her.

And she knows how Zen's knee got trashed now.

A girl did it to him. In every single one of the ways he made up: with a truck, with a boomerang, with a football, with an alligator—with a football made from an alligator, and tied to the front bumper of a truck, one with a stupid boomerang antenna on top.

And that's just the beginning.

Lindy smiles and hides it, moves like a knight (four tiles ahead, one over) past the break room, then freezes halfway through a step.

What?

She backs up, backs up.

The lights in the break room are off—policy when it's not being used—but the television mounted up in the corner, somebody's wired into it.

With Zelda.

Lindy sees the silhouette of Zen's crutches before she sees him. He's sitting on the floor, because the controller's cable won't reach the table.

"You're going to need help getting up," Lindy tells him.

"Shh," he says. "I love this part."

It's one of the dungeon rooms, with giant shadow hands reaching from the walls.

"You have to—" Lindy says, and just steps in, takes the controller, gets him through the door.

"You play," he says.

"As I'm sure Adam told you," Lindy says back, tossing the controller back down to him.

Zen shakes his head no though.

"I don't think he even knows," he says.

"Then . . . what? Camie told you? I'm not going to believe that."

"I just, like, put our names together," Zen says.

Lindy narrows her eyes, doing the letter math here.

It almost works.

Still.

"Lucky guess," she says. "We're the same age. We grew up with the same consoles."

"Sit?" Zen says, moving over on the floor.

"My shift—"

"I don't—" he starts, closing his eyes to do it better, it seems. "It's not what it looks like."

"What? Adam helping you into my pants? Giving you pointers?"

"I found him," Zen says. "Because I didn't want to mess this up. Okay? Maybe? What's that movie, the one where—"

"*Roxanne*," Lindy says, trying to make it into a hiss. "Cyrano de Bergerac. But it only applies here if Adam was using you to get back with me. Which is not going to happen."

"I don't want it to. That's what I'm saying. I just wanted to get it right. To not mess it up. Not mess us up."

Lindy just stares down at him.

"Steve Martin has this huge nose too," she says. "You don't."

He smiles his smile.

Lindy shakes her head no, sits back on the edge of the table. It dislodges his crutches, sends them clattering.

"Listen, I've got to—" she says, walking around the table to get them.

"I can get them," Zen says, standing, hobbling in place. "What I can't get is you."

Lindy tries to tell herself that the heat in her face, it's because she's bending over to get the crutches. That the blood is all rushing to the lowest place. That something.

She gulps it down, passes his crutches over.

"And, what?" she says. "When summer's gone, so are you, college boy."

It's what she's been calling him, the last few days.

"Maybe I won't be alone," Zen says.

Lindy stares at him, stares at him.

"I'm just supposed to move in with all your roommates?" she finally says. "Summer girls don't do that, don't you know?"

"You're not a summer girl, Lindy. You're a forever girl."

Lindy shakes her head again, to keep her lips from smiling. But she can see in his eyes that her dimples are showing.

"You know how to beat this level?" she says, about the game.

"Would I be anybody you're interested in if I didn't?" he says back.

Lindy doesn't shrug, can't nod, doesn't know what to do.

"The real story," Zen says. "I jumped off the balcony of our house, into the back of Tank's—into the back of a friend's truck. And he had one of those hitch things, like for trailers."

"Gooseneck ball," Lindy fills in, because she's a Henderson girl.

"They're not good for knees."

Lindy laughs without meaning to.

"And now you can't go to Brazil."

"I'm glad," Zen says.

Lindy still doesn't know what to do, what to say or how to say it.

So she leaves.

Out on the floor, she remembers what she was doing, that this was a big chessboard.

She's a bishop now, only going on the diagonal, tile to tile.

It's a stupid game, but it's better than thinking about Adam. About Zen. About all the boys between.

It's easy not to think of Adam.

Zen though.

Does *Lindy* plus him equal Zelda? Is that stupid, or is it the world whispering to her?

Because her shift starts going too fast—there's not that much cereal gone on a weekday, in Henderson—she becomes a king, just moving one tile at a time, stepping ahead with her right foot then dragging the left to meet it.

It's like dancing, though. Where you have to imagine a partner. A very specific one.

She feels herself start to cry, shakes her head no about that, and, going for a last infraction, builds a pyramid of cereal boxes in the middle of the aisle, then crawls inside it like the igloo it is.

She takes a box of Froot Loops from the doorway, sits down and shovels them in by the handful.

Vic's here, she knows. Probably watching in real time.

It doesn't matter.

There's no prize at the bottom of the Froot Loops. Big surprise.

Lindy closes the box, puts it back in place, another brick. Another dead soldier.

"At least I don't work dog food," she says out loud, and blows out a breath of rainbow dust.

It floats, drifts, hangs.

In black and white, on Vic's monitor, it must look like she's breathing death through the doorway.

She's wondering what it would like if she breathed back in, and if that would make her throw up (definitely), and then she hears it, so distant she has to be making it up, so unlikely she has to shake her head no, it's not possible: "Up Where We Belong."

From *An Officer and a Gentleman.*

She and Camille used to sing it back and forth, changing parts.

There are mountains in our way, but we climb the stairs every day.

Love lift us up—

Lindy shakes her head, has to smile.

From Household Goods at the front of the store, then, she hears some-body clapping.

It's standard procedure for when something breakable gets dropped, but there's been no crash.

Then another stocker starts clapping. Or somebody from the sweep-up crew.

Lindy's throat lumps up when she realizes the clapping is a swell, that it's heading for her.

How can Zen know this?

He can't.

Because it's Camille.

She's dressed in navy whites from who knows where, is just standing there, her eyes fierce like when she was a twirler, about to go into her routine for a whole football crowd.

She's got the white cap on, too, and her hair, God. It's gone, it's a pageboy. She's Richard Gere. That's what the scissors were for.

"You didn't," Lindy says, and steps into the main aisle to feel, to see.

"We're all packed," Camille says, ducking away, her eyes full now too, and, because people are light in dreams—no, because people are strong—she picks Lindy up and walks to the front of the store, all the other stockers at the end of their aisles, clapping, the girls wiping their eyes, the guys biting their lips in.

Lindy can't stop smiling.

"He's in the break room," Lindy says to Camille.

"And he's gone in August," Camille says right back, and Lindy nods, knew it all along.

What she didn't know, and never would have guessed, is Teegan's truck through the front window, his bed loaded down, Teegan leaning over the steering wheel, watching something across the street.

"Oh," Lindy says to Camille.

"He still owes his dad money," Camille says back. "Got to stay, work for his uncle."

"You're leaving him?"

"He'll still be here, Lindy."

"I'm a screw-up, Camie, I'm not worth it. You've got a chance—"

"Where was he in fifth grade? Did the two of us even know he existed?"

"But you can't just, just leave . . ."

"He'll come see me, if it's real," Camille says. "He helped me cut my hair. He even lied that he likes it like this."

"I hate you, you know that, right?"

"Well hate me in our apartment in Grady, okay?" Camille says, then does an audible gulp, sets Lindy down on the belt.

It jerks forward before Lindy can look around. She jumps off.

It's Vic. Standing at the register.

"This is my two—it's kind of like my two-minute notice, I guess . . ." Camille says, no chance of eye contact.

Vic nods, is looking only at Lindy.

"And you?" he says.

"And me," she says.

He nods like he knew this already and looks away, to the night crew watching him, waiting, and then he looks across the whole store, like checking counts. On everything.

"One new life," he says at last, in his customer's-always-right voice, and dings the drawer open with his manager code.

He stares into the drawer as if looking for something. Waiting for the right words.

There aren't any, though. Lindy knows.

"Cleanup, aisle fourteen," she says, instead, smiling a bit.

Cereals.

Vic shakes his head, still isn't looking up to her, but he finally has to nod, agree. "I think I'm going to miss that," he says.

"Me too," Lindy says, and walks past the bagging station, dragging her fingers across the countertop, her mind taking pictures of each moment now, each half a moment. Each quarter, each slice, each—

But no.

"What?" Camille says, when Lindy drifts to a stop. "It's just off because it's night."

She's talking about the electric eye of the front door.

That's not what's snagged in Lindy's head though.

She turns around, to Vic, policing the register, his hand on the mismatched cap of a blue pen, the pen in a coffee cup, the cup taped to the half wall.

"Wait," she says to Camille, and makes her way back to the second register.

Vic looks up to her, his eyes guarded.

Lindy reaches across the space between them. To the left shoulder of his faded Kermit the Frog shirt.

It's more faded there.

More worn through.

Lindy claps one hand over her mouth.

"You were going to let me go," she says, or hears herself saying, then peels her hand from her mouth, lets her fingertips walk across Vic's collarbone like a bridge. To the cheap, dull ball chain around his neck.

"Lucky charm?" she says.

She pulls it up.

A guitar pick.

"You—you were going to miss me," she says, looking up to Vic, and he folds his hand around hers, on his guitar pick. "But you wanted me to be happy. You wanted me to have a good life. Even if it meant me . . . me leaving forever."

Lindy looks to Camille, in the doorway with her short hair. To Teegan's truck, mounded with boxes. To the whole vampire crew in a half-moon at the front of the store, watching them. To the parking lot and Henderson and the rest of her life.

"I think I already am though," Lindy says, "happy," and swallows hard, meets Vic at the bagging station two steps down, like she's leading him onto a dance floor. "Ice cream?" she asks.

"With Froot Loops," Vic manages to say, rubbing a crumb from the corner of Lindy's mouth, then replacing it with his breath, his lips, hardly even long enough for Lindy to ring it up in her head.

"With this Fruit Loop," she says, and when she looks over the register, it's to Marilyn, standing at the end of Coffee and Tea.

She flips Lindy off and holds her finger there, but she's crying behind it.

Lindy nods *thank you* to her, and, at the door, Camille reaches over, peels Lindy's hairnet off and frisbees it up, up, and away. And then her own hat as well.

"Good luck," she whispers to Lindy.

"The only kind," Lindy says, her heart going snap, crackle, pop in her chest.

But no.

It's just beating, she tells herself.

It's ready.

I wrote this one because mixer *was letting me run all their categories, one issue. Science fiction and horror and noir and the rest were easy, that's always what I'm doing anyway. But this, "romance," that was a completely new thing. And I was scared. Which isn't to say I don't love romantic comedy. I really and seriously do, even the cheesy stuff. I don't know. No, I do. That old Charly McClain song, "Sentimental Ol' You"? Not long after I met my wife, when she was still my girlfriend, when she was first my girlfriend, I guess (she still is), when we were nineteen or twenty, this came on the radio and she said, "This is you, isn't it?" Guilty. The hard part at the end of stories for me, it's not quite stepping over that line, into the precious. Each and every time. But that's always my instinct. That may even be why I write a horror, a kind of paranoid way overcorrection. Anyway, this was a very difficult story to write. I knew it had to end with some version of a kiss, but I also knew I wouldn't let myself do that kiss if it wasn't earned. And, to earn it, I had to set up obstacles in front of it. Real obstacles, not just baffles. Writing romance, man, it's a real trick, as I found out. But it's completely worth it too. I'm way proud of this story. Really, I kind of want to write a collection of ones to go along with it—I've got them sketched out somewhere, I think. Or, I did, for my old agent, but she never bit on the idea. As for the grocery store setting, like usual, this is just me nabbing from my own employment history, giving it to my characters. I've always been the night stocker, never the one running the register. It lets me live in my own head. It lets me write.*

THE LAST FINAL GIRL

(excerpt)

ACT 1

A wide grimy blade cuts into a neck hard before we can look away, the blood welling up black around the meat, the sound wicked and intimate.

Before we can even process the rest of the scene—it's nighttime, it's that cabin in the woods we all know, it's a blond girl standing there shrieking—we back off this kill, come around behind this guy's body that's already twitching, is only held up now by the blade, we back off so we can see through the new wedge carved out of his neck. So we can see the blond girl framed by it, her bikini top spattered with blood and gore, her chin moving with her mouth, her mouth trying for a word but—

Nothing.

The screen doesn't fade to black, it slams there, takes us with it, takes us straight to

→a girl's voice, shaky like this is a second try: "I guess it probably started when that Halloween supply truck crashed off the road."

Beat, beat.

"I didn't even know there *were* Halloween trucks, right?"

Nervous laughter, the weepy kind, then close on this voicing-over girl's delicate white fingers twining her short blond hair, and we stay there for the next bit:

"I guess that's where he got the idea though. The mask anyway. And then, well, we were just out there for some free costumes, you know? It was just supposed to be a fun weekend, and I mean, they're not biodegradable, would

355

probably just kill fish—just kill the raccoons—" but her voice is already breaking up again, because of all this

→violence in the woods, that night.

We're still behind the action. It's exactly where we left it.

The jock who had his neck cut into, his head rolls too far over then folds back, is upside down, looking straight at us, his eyes still alive.

A boot chocks up on his thigh, pushes him down, away. Discarding him.

Then that blade—it's an actual *long*sword?—it points across at the girl, is Morpheus calling Neo in to spar, is Christopher Lambert being polite before the beheading, and we see what this girl's seeing: some complete freak in an unlicensed Michael Jackson mask.

The pale, grinning lips have had their redness scrubbed off but are locked into some latex grin, and the eyeholes are sagging, and there's more eyeliner clumped on, but it's him, right down to the red-and-gold letterman's jacket.

In case we don't get it, though, that "Thriller" bass line digs in.

It's chase music.

The girl's turned, is running hard through the trees, her labored breathing the main sound now.

This slasher watches her go, looks around at the carnage. The half-decapitated guy on the ground twitches and the slasher watches him die, is fascinated.

Once the guy's dead, the slasher steps past, after this girl, and we cut ahead, to

→her crashing through the trees blind. Scratching her arms on the branches, crying, her bikini top trying to come off but she's just managing to hold onto it.

"*Help!*" she screams, "it's—it's Billy Jean!"

Behind her, the slasher hears this. It stops him. He looks down to his jacket, all around, such that we can read his mind: *Billy Jean?*

Still, this is what it is.

He slices an innocent sapling out of his way, steps through with authority, and, now, because of what she's calling him, there's some legitimate anger too. Like, before it was just business for him.

Now it's personal.

Yards ahead of him, the girl bursts from the trees, almost goes falling off a sudden cliff.

A hundred feet below is a river, moving so fast we can even see the white water at night, and hear it all around.

"No no no no no," the girl's saying, casting around for a bridge, a hang glider, a parachute, a zip line, a magic door, anything.

Instead, behind her something huffs air, announcing itself.

Something *big*.

She steps back, so close to the edge that the sole of her left shoe is in open air, little flakes of shale crumbling off into space behind her.

Is this it?

Then she sees the eyes, and they're too tall, too wide.

She's just shaking her head now, mumbling a prayer, making a deal, and it must be a good deal because what steps out isn't the next monster in this nightmare, but a tall, regal horse, its skin jumping in the moonlight, steam coming from its nostrils.

"Wildfire?" she says, at which point the screen sucks down to black again, taking us back to

→her voice, coming from the blackness: "I hadn't ridden since the—since my dad, you know. I'm the one who found him in the stall that day. But—but he's the one who taught me to ride, right? But he's also the one who taught me to moonwalk. Or what he thought was a moonwalk."

She smiles, remembering.

We can hear it.

"Come here, boy," she says, holding her hand out. "It wasn't your fault, I know, he shouldn't have tried to ride you, he knew I was the only one who could—"

Wildfire stamps, blows. Isn't ready for any apologies yet, apparently.

But there's a reason: Billy Jean's standing there, just past the trees.

The girl backs perilously close to the edge again, even has to wave her arms, and's about to go over when—

The longsword thrusts out, cuts into her shoulder and out the back, holding her there, a drippy ribbon of blood draining down the blade to the cross guard, those drops plummeting down to the crashing river, the river pulling them instantly away.

Back to the cliff though.

The girl's *trying* to scream now, doesn't have the breath anymore.

"I thought I was dead," she says in voice-over. "I thought that's why Wildfire was there. That I was in heaven. But Billy Jean had followed me there too, so I knew it was . . . it was the other place."

Billy Jean dials the blade over as if in response to being called that again, opening the girl's chest for more blood to pour out, the sharp edge pushing on the bikini strap now, like a blood-slick breast is exactly the thing we all want to see.

Still, Billy Jean seems interested, is acutely aware he's about to cut through that delicate string, is so concentrated on it in fact that he doesn't feel the horse's head, suddenly long and alien beside his own, those massive jaws practically resting on his shoulder.

He shoulder-butts the horse but the horse just blows.

Billy Jean hauls the girl around to the side, over ground instead of a hundred feet of nothing, and fixes his boot in her chest, slides her off his sword. Then he turns to face this interfering horse, maybe the only thing big enough to finally take him down once and for all.

The horse rears, slashing with its hooves, and Billy Jean has no choice but to fall back.

"*Kill him, Wildfire!*" the girl screams from her place on the ground, one hand trying to hold her shoulder together, her face tear-streaked, her bikini top even more tenuous now.

When Wildfire finally comes down, Billy Jean steps forward, swinging his sword like a baseball bat into shoulder meat, stopping short at the bone.

Shaken, he steps back, remembers his fencing.

He feints at Wildfire's shoulders but cuts across the face instead, a little slow motion on that blade-through-eyeball number, the horse screaming in a way that hurts our heart.

"*Nooooo!*" the girl screams as well, reaching, having to *hold* her bikini top on now.

It's too late though.

Billy Jean's going to work, is slicing into Wildfire from wherever he wants, just flaying the horse open, getting the other eye as well.

Finally he brings the sword all the way back to swing for the bleachers, go for the horse decap we're all secretly waiting for now that it's gone this far, but something's got his blade.

He turns.

It's the girl.

She has her bikini top wrapped around the sword.

"You won't write this part, will you?" the voice-over says. "I wouldn't ever take my top—I just really, really wanted to live, I mean . . ."

The slasher, like he's scared of her breasts, takes a stumbling step back.

It leaves him just right at the edge of the cliff.

"And then I remembered my Sunday school," the voice-over says, and we're right there with her that night, her on her knees, topless but somehow not showing any skin, and what she's doing, it's some David and Goliath action: using her bikini top as a sling, a grapefruit of a rock going around and around.

"I guess I'm lucky I'm a C cup," the voice-over says just as the girl releases the rock.

It slams into Billy Jean's lower face, just *crushing* it

→but the voice-over interrupts: "That's how it was supposed to go, I mean."

The do-over is in painfully slow motion: that rock in her left cup, rolling out end over end over end.

For all her screaming, though, and even though she nails the follow-through, still, this rock, it hurtles past Billy Jean's face, and because he's a slasher, he doesn't even flinch.

His mask doesn't show it, but still, there's a smile in there.

At least until the bikini top reaches the end of its length, whips its string out like a dry tentacle, right into the eyehole of Billy Jean's mask.

Without meaning to, he flinches back, steps behind himself for a brace.

There's only open air.

"But sometimes you get lucky," the voice-over goes on, and Billy Jean reaches forward for balance, isn't going to find it.

He looks to the girl as if she's betraying him here.

"Moonwalk now, you fucker," she says to him, and he doesn't, can't. He just falls and falls, and, in case it looks too much like a sequel set-up, he catches a couple of shattering ledges on the way down, and, on the chance *that's* not enough, we go

→under that dark water with him, bubbles and blood roiling everywhere.

It's that slowed-down moment when he's touching the stony bottom of the river with his back, hard.

An instant later, the sword comes down, right through him.

Above, on the cliff, there's a kind of musical sigh, dawn even starting to break.

The girl's just getting her bikini back on, favoring her injured shoulder.

"Let's go home," she says to her now-blind horse, and lets him smell her hand then rubs her hand along his neck to his mane, grabs a handful of that to haul herself up. "I'll be your eyes," she says, about to fall over herself, and we pull off this sentimental image, a girl and her horse, go higher and higher, finally

→ come down upriver, *on* the river, where that Halloween supply truck crashed.

It's still leaking masks.

"So he's really and finally dead," a male voice says, intruding, and we open up onto

→ a hospital room. The voice-over girl's there, shaken up by her own story, dabbing at her eyes instead of rubbing them. Because of her makeup.

A young, good-looking guy is putting his equipment away, just jabbing down one last note, an imposing Sheriff's deputy parked across the room, his pythons crossed over his chest, his haircut pure jarhead, and proud of it.

The girl's shoulder is wrapped. Her hair's been professionally done, it looks like.

"It was terrible," she says. "I never—I never—but it's over, right?"

"They only come back in the movies . . ."

This piece is fun to read out loud, though I usually smooth over or just skip the hospital parts. They make sense on the page, that cutting back and forth visually, but just read out loud, it doesn't quite track, I don't think. But I cut it off at some different point too, it seems—oh, with the sword-through-the-chest, I think. Anyway, for a long time I've wondered why more women don't use their bikini tops as slings to throw rocks at slashers. I kind of felt compelled to write this, just as a survival manual. Also, this whole novel, it's right exactly where I'll always and forever live. Where I'll happily live. If there's anything more true than the slasher, then I haven't found it anyway. Storytelling, I mean, it starts, what, with

Gilgamesh? It finally reaches a zenith with Michael Myers, I'd say. And we're still on that plateau, just riding out wave after wave of blood. I hope it never ends. Also, I should say that this title, I had to be convinced into it. My title for this novel was Part II. I thought it was brilliant, that it was perfect, that it was bullet-proof. Which should be proof of something or another, I'm sure. Thanks to my then agent Kate Garrick, for saving me yet again.

HOW BILLY HANSON DESTROYED THE PLANET EARTH, AND EVERYONE ON IT

HE WOULDN'T SAY this later, because he'd be dead along with everyone else, blasted into a cloud of comparatively warm ash swirling around in what had been Earth's orbital plane, but it wasn't his fault. Really. Or, if there was any fault, it was that he was human in the first place, a species built specifically, it would seem, to push buttons clearly marked DON'T PUSH, a species that had only evolved in the first place because it kept reaching up to that next level of the beach instead of being satisfied with where it already was.

Given the chance, of course, Billy Hanson might have blamed the political situation of the lab he was with on a three-year grant, a political situation which was purely typical of any money-driven research setting, and beneath mentioning here except to say that there was the usual amount of pressure to collect some data, which could then be cribbed down into a prospectus for an article, dropped into whatever mailbox was marked for the latest pickup.

So, yes, had he had the luxury of time, Billy Hanson might have tried to shift the blame from himself, say it was the lab's fault, the same way he used to blame his older sister for grape juice he'd just spilled on the beige carpet, but, at the same time, had he not destroyed the Earth that fine June evening, then of course all the acclaim would have been his and his alone.

Because, almost on accident, he'd finally done it.

Not scheduled some prime observatory time—that had been scheduled for months, by some process Billy assumed involved darts—but decided, half on a whim, to let the computer cycle the telescope through one of its lighter diagnostic routines, which involved settling its cross hairs on some arbitrarily chosen but rigorously mapped set of coordinates, so it could fine-tune itself, compensate for continental drift, smog, and all the rest of the usual variables, then hum and mutter to itself in binary for a while, finally give Billy the green light to redirect.

Which, to his credit, Billy Hanson almost did, thereby saving Earth and everyone on it.

Except—and this is where the political situation of the lab he was working with comes into play—instead of automatically redirecting, Billy first did a manual check of the computer's date and time, as that was what was going to get stamped onto each image he was about to record. Last week, either as a joke or to maliciously corrupt everyone else's data (the latter, surely), some joker who'd pulled an early a.m. shift had set the date back enough years that the days and month numbers still matched up, meaning nobody caught it for about thirty-six hours.

Luckily, nothing Billy had recorded that night was going into an article.

But that was just luck.

So, to be thorough—in a hostile environment, paranoia was just survival—Billy tabbed down to the clock, and, in doing so, happened to glance at the coordinates the telescope had already focused on.

It wasn't one of the naked-eye clusters.

Billy thought it was a joke, at first. Another joke.

It had to be.

But his face, it was so hot. And his heart, there in his chest. And he was even crying a little.

He had been right.

To back up a little: eight years ago, Billy Hanson had been halfway through his first postdoc gig, and, following the advice of his dissertation director, was already sketching out a series of questions which he could then narrow down into a legitimate research proposal. The key of it, his director said, was that he had to come up with something revolutionary, or at least revolutionary sounding. Because all those boards of directors, they wanted to be discovering the next big thing. Failing that, however, at least give them the promise of a valiant, newsworthy effort, with a data set that could possibly be recycled, even, so long as their foundation's name was still attached to it.

So Billy gave it to them.

His idea was that, if gravitational lensing was a real thing, allowing starlight to bend around bodies of significant-enough mass—and it was real, thank you—then shouldn't it also be possible to somehow focus through a "web" or "network" or "crystalline arrangement" of stellar bodies, such that you were looking down the "corridor" of their combined gravity, a sweet spot maybe just a few centimeters wide but infinitely deep, where the combined, equalized "pull" would essentially be opening up a hole in space, maybe even time? What could you see then?

That was how he'd ended his proposal: What could we see then?

The headlines would be along the lines of "Mankind Looks for God," and have Billy's picture under it somewhere, smiling just mischievously enough to usher in another age, where the scientists could again be celebrities.

His project didn't even make the first cut, though, and no new age dawned, or took him for its darling, its media child. As his director said, Billy'd made the cardinal mistake: proposed a project which required no lab work, allowed no empirical results. Instead, all he needed was a pencil, some paper, and a brain. The right brain, granted, but still—the board didn't think their money would be best spent on a thought experiment, one that could only ever be proven over the course of a million years, so, the next season, Billy and a colleague had a new, only slightly revolutionary proposal to submit, and he filed his Spatial Tunneling Debacle (as his director called it) into the bottom drawer, waited for the math to come.

Instead of the math, though, what Billy got that balmy night in June was proof, the kind that can be written to a digital image file.

And, because he was still in diagnostic mode, what he was seeing was beyond question, was untampered with, and, even better, whatever magical conduit of stars had lined up around his coordinates, to focus his series of lenses some exponential amount farther away than humans had ever even dreamed, they were each being recorded as well. So this would be a repeatable thing. If not physically, then at least in simulation. Let other people do the math, now; Billy Hanson already had the pictures.

It was all so overpowering that he didn't even bother to wipe the tear from his right cheek. He wasn't aware of it, really. Like a child, he was just smiling with wonder, leaning in, as if to touch the screen.

On some as yet unnamed planet an untold numbers of light-years away, a form of life wholly alien to him was sitting at what was probably a table, in what might be just another backyard.

As near as Billy could tell, this "alien" was just staring straight ahead. For all Billy knew, though, this—this whatever-it-was, it was telepathically communing with its species, or gestating a litter of young, or turning to stone like it did every third year when the solar flares came, or using some of its complicated neck apparatus to filter the methane from its air, or whatever it breathed, if it even breathed.

It wasn't quite bipedal either, Billy didn't think, but did seem to be bilateral. From where Billy was looking anyway.

Which is the exact point, not counting that first fish flopping up into the dirty sunlight, when humanity started to wink out of existence.

Billy Hanson's fingers fell to the keyboard as they had a hundred other nights, to adjust the second lens, which needed regrinding, really, not just another gear pulling on it, and his gravity peephole focused down across the universe, tight enough that, for an instant, the skin or covering of his subject's forelimb blurred, then snapped back in fine detail.

Billy nodded, backed off a hair—had anybody ever done this, even? was he, in addition to testing the limits of physics, pioneering exobiology as well?—and when the image finally settled again he nodded to himself, content, and only stopped when the alien cocked its head over the slightest bit, in a way that made Billy feel suddenly hollow inside.

This was the way the deer on the golf course he'd grown up by would stop, when they became aware of him and his sister, trying to sneak up.

"No," he mouthed, as if even voicing the word would give his position away, but it was too late.

The alien was tilting his head around now, then focusing up, back along the gravity tunnel, using some sixth or forty-first sense that Billy Hanson couldn't even conceive . . . had it felt the pressure of his stare? was this a species so hunted across both time and galaxies that it had developed a sensitivity to observation acute enough that it even kicked in across light-years? Or—or could it even be knowledge-based, part of some maniacally epistemic religion, where knowing something about a fellow creature was tantamount to rape, or murder? It could even be that, sitting there, this alien was involved in the most dire offense known to its kind, so all its senses were already turned up, listening, feeling.

It didn't matter.

What did was that it had turned its head up to Billy Hanson in direct response to Billy leaning closer to his monitor. Never mind that Billy was holding his breath now, shaking his head no, insisting that this wasn't in his research, that this shouldn't even be possible, according to the laws of physics as he understood them.

But neither should looking across the universe.

"No," he said again, instead of all the famous and enduring things he could have said. By then the alien was standing, looking back down the tunnel of stars, into Billy Hanson's heart, and it was only when the alien smiled that Billy realized what he was thinking: that this was a bilateral species, yes.

The only reason he noticed this was that the smile spreading across the alien's main face, it was lopsided, not really meant to indicate pleasure. The kind of smile Billy Hanson associated with an older cousin standing perfectly still in an empty hall during a game of hide-and-seek. Standing perfectly still and listening to the linen closet.

In that closet, Billy closed his eyes, tried to pretend he wasn't really there, and so never saw the backlash of power boring now through the fabric of space for Earth, to implode it with such suddenness that the brief vacuum left by it would, for a few breaths, pull all the surface flame from the sun, allowing what had been his solar system a moment of darkness, followed by a cold millennium marked by a shroud of dust, that, because the implosion had been so thorough, no longer contained even the building blocks of life, much less any memory of man.

That was all still seconds away though.

A lifetime, an eternity.

In it, Billy Hanson opened his eyes, smiled the way you smile when you're caught, and, in the last and perhaps purest gesture humankind would be afforded, pulled the phone up to his ear and dialed the first six digits not of his girlfriend's number—he had no girlfriend—but of a girl from his department who always touched her right eyebrow when she laughed, as if there were a button there to make her stop embarrassing herself.

What Billy was going to tell her, maybe, was not to worry about it, you're beautiful and perfect and everything good, and I love you I love you I love you, please.

What he did instead was wait to call her for what turned out to be too long, and then, along with everybody else, wink out of existence with the phone to his ear, as if that mattered, what he meant to do.

My dream has always been to be a science-fiction writer. That's always seemed the most honest of all the shelves, to me. It's, I don't know, it's just pure. To give the reader that sense of awe? To let them be ten years old again for a few pages, just looking up at the sky? But I never feel I'm good enough yet. Or, I make science fiction so holy that I can't quite touch it. But I can get close anyway. With stories like these. And I'm not worried. Someday I'll figure it out, someday I'll get it right. Until then, I'll just be looking through whatever telescope I can rig up, out into the depths of space, and waiting for someone to look back. Fiction, stories, it's all about connection, isn't it? About connecting. Billy here, that's all he wants. Just to be a little less alone. It's what we all want. At least, I think, that's why I write.

CREDITS

Grateful acknowledgment is made to the following presses and journals in which these excerpts and stories (some in slightly different versions) first appeared:

Excerpt from *The Fast Red Road: A Plainsong*: copyright © 2000 by Stephen Graham Jones. This and other FC2 books are used with permission of the University of Alabama Press.

"Lonegan's Luck," "So Perfect," "Father, Son, Holy Rabbit," and "Raphael": reproduced from *The Ones That Got Away*; reprinted with the permission of Prime Books.

"The Wages: An Argument": *Spring Gun Press*.

"State": *Quarterly West*.

"Captivity Narrative 109," "Carbon," "To Run Without Falling," and "Discovering America": reproduced from *Bleed into Me: A Book of Stories* by Stephen Graham Jones, by permission of the University of Nebraska Press. Copyright © 2005 by Stephen Graham Jones.

"Exodus": *5_trope*.

Excerpt from *It Came from Del Rio (Part I of the Bunnyhead Chronicles)*: re-printed with the permission of Trapdoor Publisher.

"Welcome to the Reptile House": *Strange Aeons*.

"Adultery: A Failing Sestina": *Alaska Quarterly Review*.

"Screentime": *Sundog*.

Excerpt from *Demon Theory*: published by MacAdam/Cage; reprinted with the permission of Stephen Graham Jones.

"Boys with Guitars" and "Foreverafterword": *mixer*.

Excerpt from *The Last Final Girl*: reprinted with the permission of Lazy Fascist Press.